OFF MIDWAY
STATION

BOOKS BY MARC ALAN EDELHEIT

FANTASY

THE STIGER CHRONICLES

Book One: Stiger's Tigers

Book Two: The Tiger

Book Three: The Tiger's Fate

Book Four: The Tiger's Time

Book Five: The Tiger's Wrath

Book Six: The Tiger's Imperium

Book Seven: The Tiger's Fight

Book Eight: The Tiger's Rage

STIGER: TALES OF THE SEVENTH

Book One: Stiger

Book Two: Fort Covenant

Book Three: A Dark Foretoken

THE KARUS SAGA

Book One: Lost Legio IX

Book Two: Fortress of Radiance

Book Three: The First Compact

Book Four: Rapax Pax

THE ELI CHRONICLES

Book One: Eli

OFF MIDWAY STATION

MARC ALAN EDELHEIT

SECOND SKY

Published by Second Sky in 2024

An imprint of Storyfire Ltd.
Carmelite House
50 Victoria Embankment
London EC4Y 0DZ

www.secondskybooks.com

ISBN: 978-1-83525-986-3
eBook ISBN: 978-1-83525-985-6

To my incredible readers,

Your passion and support fuel my imagination. Thank you for embracing my worlds and characters with such enthusiasm. This journey would not be possible without you.

With heartfelt gratitude,

Marc Alan Edelheit

ONE

GARRETT

The gravity field oscillated in a series of rapid, jarring flickers, each pulse more erratic than the last, before finally achieving a tenuous equilibrium as the ship's automatic backup systems fought to take command. Garrett felt the disconcerting churn in his stomach, a visceral reaction to the unnatural shifts in gravity.

The eggs he'd consumed for breakfast lurched ominously within him, threatening a revolt. But that was not his main concern. He blinked rapidly, attempting to clear the unexpected haziness clouding his vision. He failed. Clarity remained elusive, replaced instead by a burgeoning pain that crept through his body, an insidious tide engulfing his senses.

He groaned, a low sound more felt than heard, as he tried to make sense of the disorientation swirling within him. Pain radiated from every fiber of his being, an all-encompassing ache that seemed to originate from deep within his bones.

It took him a moment to realize he was lying down. Beneath him, the deck plating of the starship added to his discomfort, emitting a low, continuous rumble. It was as if the very deck was trembling, resonating with the chaotic energy unleashed by the malfunctioning gravity field. The sensation was not just a vibration; it was akin to the tremors of a living entity, an ominous harbinger of the turmoil that had beset the vessel. Garrett, grappling with the physical and sensory onslaught, could only wonder what had gone so terribly wrong.

He shook his head, a futile attempt to dispel the fog that clouded his thoughts, and pushed himself off the decking. He struggled onto all fours, his movements sluggish and heavy, as if he were moving through a thick, unseen mire. Pain lanced through his right side, a sharp, unyielding torment that eclipsed the general ache pervading his body.

Still unable to see clearly, he gave his head another shake. As he labored to steady himself, fragments of memory began to coalesce in his mind, disjointed and hazy at first. He recalled a sensation of weightlessness, a sudden, forceful launch through the air, followed by a jarring impact as he collided with the unforgiving deck. A cursory self-assessment suggested nothing was broken, but every movement spoke to the ferocity of the fall; his body was a tapestry of pain.

Then, like a floodgate bursting open, memory surged back in a vivid, alarming rush. The mission to restore order and Confederation rule to Antares Station; the final beacon jump, the *Valiant*, the trap, so cunningly laid and expertly sprung; an ambush, an eruption of violence; a shocking exchange of fire, lasers, masers, and missiles streaking through the void.

Vision blurry, Garrett felt his breath catch in his throat as the full weight of the situation settled upon him. They had been baited, lured in, and savagely attacked. Fear, sharp and cold, began to seep into his veins, mingling with the adrenaline that still coursed through him.

"Report," came Captain Marlowe's voice through the speaker of Garrett's emergency helmet. The mere fact that his helmet had automatically deployed and sealed was a dire indicator in itself, silently proclaiming the compromise of the bridge's atmosphere.

"We have, ah, auxiliary power, Captain," responded a voice, strained with evident pain and disorientation.

It took a moment for Garrett to recognize it as belonging to Helm Technician First Class Darrust. Confusion mingled with concern as he processed her words. It was unusual for Darrust, a helm technician, to report on the ship's power systems, a task typically reserved for the engineering team assigned to the bridge.

"Main reactors are offline," Darrust continued, her voice laced with the strain of her own injuries or the gravity of the situation itself. "Emergency shutdown procedures have been implemented."

Garrett's mind whirred with the implications of her report. The shutdown of the main reactors was a significant blow, reducing their power capabilities drastically and limiting their options for maneuvering or escape. The auxiliary power reservoir would sustain life support and basic systems for a time, but their capabilities for defense or long-range travel were severely hampered.

"Engines?" the captain queried, before adding a groan that betrayed her own discomfort. "Maneuvering? What do we have left?"

"Main engines are offline, ma'am. We have maneuvering thrusters only, so basic movements, station-keeping—that sort of thing. We are currently moving at seven hundred klicks per second on the bearing we were headed prior to exchanging fire. I do not believe there is an immediate danger of hitting anything, but sensors are completely down..."

Garrett's head spun, a fresh wave of nausea threatening to overwhelm him. Shaking his head, he fought it back, refusing to upchuck in his suit and focusing on regaining his bearings. As the queasiness subsided, his vision gradually sharpened, bringing into focus the extent of the devastation around him.

With considerable effort, he hauled himself to his feet, each movement sending jolts of pain through his battered body. Inside his emergency helmet, his breathing echoed loudly, the recycled air tasting stale and metallic.

As he surveyed his surroundings, the reality of the situation struck him with brutal force. The bridge, the nerve center of the ship, lay in ruin. It was a scene of devastation. The space was twisted and mangled into an almost unrecognizable state. The decking and walls were a patchwork of damage, in some places warped and distorted, in others violently breached, leaving gaping holes that exposed the void beyond.

Debris littered the area, a chaotic spread of shattered composite materials and fragments of equipment. The ceiling on the starboard side had succumbed, collapsing inward and burying that portion of the bridge under a mass of twisted metal and cabling. Several duty stations, once orderly and efficient, had been violently uprooted, their screens flickering or dead, their interfaces torn asunder.

Garrett's heart skipped a beat as his eyes caught sight of something far more harrowing than the structural damage. Scattered amidst the wreckage were remnants of the crew who had been at their stations, an arm here, a leg there, fingers and gloved hands strewn grotesquely across the floor, chunks of unrecognizable and frozen flesh.

For a moment, Garrett stood still, his mind grappling with the horror before him. He knew he needed to push past the shock, to focus on survival, but the scene of carnage made it difficult to concentrate. Somewhere in the back of his mind, he understood that every second mattered, yet the devastation around him seemed to slow time to a crawl, each moment a struggle against despair and disbelief.

"Almighty god," Garrett breathed, his own voice unnaturally loud in his ears. "Almighty god."

The captain and Darrust, communicating over the comms, were the only other signs of life amidst the carnage. Tactical

Technician Second Class Silver's lifeless form was a haunting sight. Seated rigidly at her duty station, her body was a macabre tableau, headless, yet with hands eerily positioned above the control panel. It was as if in her final moments, her dedication to her duty had transcended the horror of the attack. The grisly nature of her death made it a scene straight from a nightmare, unsettling in its stillness and silence.

Nearby lay the body of the sensor technician, Kramer. Something had cleaved through his body with such force that it bisected him completely. This same violent force had obliterated his station, leaving it in ruins.

The first officer was conspicuously absent. Amidst the flickering emergency lights, Garrett's eyes searched for any sign of him. Then, in a chilling moment of realization, his gaze fell upon a solitary boot protruding awkwardly from beneath a heap of twisted metal and shattered panels, remnants of the ceiling that had succumbed to the ferocity of the battle. The distinctive design of the boot, unmistakably part of an officer's ship suit, sent a jolt through him that shocked Garrett to his core.

"Number Three," the captain's voice cut through the air, sharp and commanding.

By reflex, Garrett pivoted toward her.

"Ma'am." It was then that he saw the captain's injuries.

Despite her evident pain, the captain maintained a stoic facade. She was pressing her hand against the side of her ship suit, which was torn and burned in several places. An emergency patch and seal had been hastily applied. But it was a futile effort; the suit, though equipped with basic first aid nanite capabilities, was likely struggling to cope with the severity of the wounds, which were quite possibly mortal. Blood, a stark red against the dark fabric of her suit, oozed out from under her fingers, bubbling and boiling as it hit the vacuum before freezing solid against the glove of her hand.

"You're injured, ma'am," he stated, though it was obvious.

"Never mind me," Captain Marlowe insisted, her voice strained through gritted teeth. "We have to focus on the ship. Take over at tactical. See if you can pull up sensors as well while you're at it."

"Yes, ma'am," escaped his lips as he quickly moved toward the tactical station and the lifeless, headless body of Silver.

Forcing himself to focus, Garrett began the somber and grisly task of unhooking the restraints that held Silver's corpse in place. The image of her as she had been—a pretty, kind-eyed and brown-haired vivacious woman, now reduced to this tragic end—threatened to overwhelm him. He remembered her lively spirit, the way her laughter used to echo through the corridors of the ship. The stark contrast of her current state sent a chill down his spine.

He pushed such thoughts away, compartmentalizing his emotions.

"Hurry up." There was an unmistakable note of irritation laced with pain in the captain's tone. "The enemy is still out there."

Her words served as a sharp reminder of the imminent danger they were in, propelling Garrett to act with renewed urgency. Garrett stole a quick glance back at Captain Marlowe, only to find her deeply engrossed, her gaze fixed intently on a solitary functioning screen at her command station. Despite her obvious pain, she was determinedly working a backup mobile keyboard that rested on her lap, one-handed, her gloved fingers moving with precision, albeit with a slight tremble, a subtle indication of her struggle.

Most of the screens around her were either lifeless, their functions halted, or visibly damaged, with cracks and breaks from the impact of flying debris. The bridge, once a hub of meticulous activity and precise command, now looked like a scene from a nightmare, with its flickering lights.

"Hurry the fuck up, Lieutenant," the captain said, having

glanced up from her screen, "or do I need to issue you a written invitation to this party?"

Garrett hastily turned back to the daunting task at hand. He finished unfastening the restraints, his movements deliberate and respectful as he laid Silver's lifeless body onto the deck beside her former station.

As he moved to sit at the station, he couldn't help but notice the blood that had stained and frozen to the restraints, seat, and console before him.

The monitors presented a horrifying sight. They were splattered with a film of blood and gray matter, a stark and gruesome canvas. Fragments of white bone were scattered across the screens, and a piece of an earlobe hung grotesquely from one of the monitors. Garrett found himself struggling to suppress the urge to retch.

Determined to push past the horror, he activated his internal implants, reaching out to connect with the tactical station. His attempt was met with an unsettling silence; there was no response, no electronic handshake to acknowledge his connection and command codes. The station remained ominously dark, unresponsive to his efforts.

Undeterred, Garrett tried a different approach, attempting to access the central computer. Yet again, his efforts were met with nothing. The lack of response was troubling, indicating a deeper problem with the ship's systems. Garrett knew he needed to find a way to restore some semblance of control and functionality to their crippled vessel, and he needed to do it fast. As the captain had said, the enemy was still out there, and time was not on their side.

Garrett was not entirely unprepared. His rigorous training at the academy had included scenarios just like this, albeit in simulations far removed from the grim reality he now faced. Furthermore, Captain Marlowe's insistence on regular drills encompassing a range of catastrophic failures, including those of the ship's computers and implant links, now proved to be invaluable. These drills, once seen as tedious and overly repetitive, had equipped him with the necessary skills to navigate this crisis.

Garrett began the process of manually restarting the station. He retrieved a portable keyboard from a compartment under the console, a relic of an earlier era of starship technology—now a potential lifeline. His hands moved with practiced ease as he activated the keyboard, and a wave of relief washed over him when its keys lit up, showing signs of life. This was a positive development, a serious step in the right direction; it indicated that, despite the extensive damage, the station remained hardwired into the ship's power systems, perhaps even to the backup computer core.

Garrett methodically tabbed the buttons to bring each monitor back online. His heart sank slightly as only three out of the seven monitors flickered to life. The main holographic display, crucial for a comprehensive tactical overview of the field of space around the ship, remained frustratingly dark, its inactivity a stark symbol of their hampered capabilities.

One of the resurrected monitors immediately began scrolling a lengthy list of the ship's offensive and defensive systems, categorizing each as offline, functional, or of questionable status. Garrett's eyes darted across the screen, quickly assessing the information. He efficiently navigated through the data, dialing down to focus on the most critical systems. Time was of the essence; he needed to ascertain their remaining capabilities and assess how they could still fend off potential threats and strike back.

When he spoke, Garrett found his voice was surprisingly steady, yet underscored with a sense of urgency as he delivered the status report. "Captain, railguns are completely offline, and the laser batteries aren't responding either," he began, his eyes continuously scanning the limited data available on the monitors. He tapped at the keypad, bringing up new information. "Maser cannons six through ten are down. However, we have a bit of good news. Maser cannons one through four on the port-side are operational and have a full charge for shot."

Garrett paused, his attention shifting to the diagnostics of one of the weapon systems. His fingers flew over the keyboard as he worked.

"Number two cannon is damaged but might still be functional. The weapon system is fully charged for shot. The system's diagnostic is advising to stand it down due to the potential malfunction. Captain, it could fire, or it might exacerbate our situation."

"Meaning the turret could detonate."

"Yes, ma'am." His report grew more somber as he moved on. "All torpedo tubes are inoperable, except for tubes two through six. They're currently loaded with compression torpedoes and are ready to launch. But there's a significant issue: I'm not confident in our ability to reload once we've deployed them. The automatic reloading system is showing a number of serious faults. I think it is questionable at best. It's not a guarantee that we can maintain a sustained offensive action, ma'am."

"Sensors?" Captain Marlowe inquired, her gaze shifting toward Garrett with a mixture of hope and apprehension. Her eyes, though clouded with pain, still held the sharp intensity of a seasoned commander. "The *Valiant*—is that ship still out there? Those damned bastards hit us hard as we emerged from the beacon jump."

Everyone had thought the rebels incapable of manning and operating a ship of the line. They had been very wrong. The proof of that was around him.

Garrett's fingers moved swiftly over the keypad, working to reroute the sensor feeds to his station. The importance of regaining their sensory capabilities was paramount; without them, they were essentially blind in the vastness of space.

"Recycling now," Garrett announced, a trace of relief in his voice as the system began to respond to his commands. It was clear the backup computer core was functioning to a degree. The lights on his console flickered, signaling the start of the sensor system's reboot process. "It'll take another thirty seconds, and with a bit of luck, we'll have eyes again."

The tension was palpable, each second stretching out interminably. Garrett kept his eyes fixed on the console, willing the sensors to come back online more quickly. If the sensors were operational, they would at least have a chance to assess their surroundings, identify potential threats, and devise a strategy. If not, they would remain in a vulnerable state, blind and adrift in the unforgiving expanse of space, at the mercy of any lurking adversaries.

"What is the status of our defenses?" Captain Marlowe's voice cut through the tense atmosphere, her expression taut with concern. Despite her injury, she remained focused on the task of assessing their ship's capabilities. "Electronic warfare, point defense, defensive screens?"

Garrett quickly inputted the data request into the system, his fingers deftly navigating the keyboard. He pulled up the defense status on one of the few monitors that was still operational, all the while keeping a vigilant eye on the sensor display, which was inching closer to completion. "Point defense cannons are completely offline," he reported, his tone even. "Defensive screens are nonfunctional as well. EW is out too. Essentially, Captain, the only thing standing between us and any incoming enemy fire is the hull of the ship."

"That is not encouraging," Captain Marlowe responded. "But considering the damage we've sustained, it's only to be expected."

The sensor screen flickered to life. Garrett let go a breath of relief. The text display that had occupied the screen was suddenly replaced by a three-dimensional map of the immediate space surrounding their ship. The system had completed its recycling process, providing them with a much-needed view of their external environment, at least close-in.

Garrett's eyes quickly scanned the display, searching for any signs of the enemy ship or other potential threats. As Garrett's eyes adjusted to the intricate display of the sensor map, a chilling realization slowly dawned upon him. The icon that should have represented their sister ship, the *Reprise*, Commodore Maskin's command, was conspicuously absent. Instead, all that was left in its place was a stark navigational hazard warning.

The once-mighty *Reprise* had been reduced to nothing more than a rapidly expanding cloud of radioactive gas and debris, floating ominously just sixty klicks to their portside.

The gravity of this revelation hit Garrett with the force of a physical blow. The destruction of the *Reprise* was not just a tactical loss; it was a profound human tragedy. Over two hundred souls who had been aboard her were now lost, their lives snuffed out in the unforgiving vacuum of space. This catastrophic event was likely the cause of much of the damage his own ship had sustained. The thought made Garrett's stomach churn with a mix of grief and horror.

"The *Reprise*," he began, the words catching in his throat, "is gone, ma'am. There are no signs of any emergency pods, or lifeboats, let alone any beacons."

The captain did not immediately reply.

"Damn," Captain Marlowe muttered finally, her expression hardening as she processed the loss of the *Reprise*. She quickly refocused on their immediate concerns. "What about the enemy? Are they still out there?"

Garrett returned to his keyboard, typing rapidly as he attempted to gather the necessary data. Under normal circumstances, his neural implants would have allowed him to access this information almost instantaneously. However, with the internal systems compromised and the backup core engaged, he was forced to rely on the more cumbersome method of manual input.

"Long-range scanners and sensors are down," he reported, his voice laced with frustration. "The system is struggling to compile a comprehensive picture of our near-space environment."

Captain Marlowe reached out over the ship's intercom and keyed a manual button. "Engineering, this is the captain. Is there anyone down there?"

The bridge was met with an unsettling silence, no reply forthcoming. A sudden rumbling communicated through the deck plating sent a wave of apprehension through Garrett. The overhead lights dimmed momentarily in response to the disturbance. The rumbling subsided after a few tense moments, and the lights, after a brief flicker, returned to their normal intensity.

Garrett's mind raced with possibilities. The rumbling could have been a secondary explosion. Alternatively, it might have been a segment of the ship depressurizing, a catastrophic event that could lead to further structural damage or loss of vital resources, including lives.

"Engineering," the captain demanded, "answer me."

The bridge remained eerily silent, with no response from engineering, but Garrett's attention was riveted elsewhere. His focus was entirely on the tactical display, which was gradually providing a clearer image of the space surrounding their crippled ship. Each second brought more data, offering a better understanding of their precarious situation.

"Captain," Garrett announced. "I've located the *Valiant*—ah—the enemy ship. She's positioned two hundred thousand twenty-two klicks to our starboard side."

In the vast emptiness of space, this distance was alarmingly close, a fact not lost on Garrett. The proximity of the once-friendly-ship-turned-enemy raised a host of worrying possibilities. Were they planning a boarding action? Were they maneuvering to deliver a finishing blow? He anxiously awaited further sensor data to reveal their course and intentions.

As more information streamed in, Garrett's hand instinctively moved to check his Mk-72 pulse blaster, securely holstered at his side. The weight and familiarity of his personal sidearm provided a small but significant comfort in the face of uncertainty. Knowing it was there, ready if needed, was a reassurance amidst the chaos.

Finally, as the sensor data began to stabilize, Garrett allowed himself a moment of relief. The developing picture of their surroundings was becoming clearer. Garrett continued to analyze the enemy ship's status with growing astonishment.

"She's not maneuvering, but she's heavily damaged," he reported, his voice tinged with a mix of surprise and cautious optimism. "There's significant atmospheric leakage, a lot of it. Sensors indicate that one of her reactors is still functioning, but the other three are in standby mode, shut down. Looks like our earlier attack hit her hard, ma'am." He paused, his throat catching slightly as the magnitude of the enemy ship's damage became clear.

Turning toward Captain Marlowe, Garrett added, "Her energy shielding is down as well, Captain. I can't discern much more than that, but it seems she's in as bad a state as we are, possibly worse." He paused to suck in a breath. "She's a sitting duck."

"Lock weapons," the captain ordered without a moment's hesitation, her voice firm and resolute. "We're going to finish them, before they can recover and finish us. Throw everything we have at the bastards."

Garrett promptly entered the commands into the sluggish system, his fingers moving over the keys. The ship's backup computer core, hampered by damage and system failures, operated at a frustratingly slow pace. It felt like an eternity as he waited for the target solutions to be set and accepted. Finally, a green light on the display flashed, signaling readiness.

"Weapons locked, ma'am," Garrett announced, confirming their readiness to engage the enemy.

"Fire the masers and, on second thought, all but one of our torpedoes," Captain Marlowe commanded, her tone sharp and decisive. "Save the last torpedo. We might need it later."

"Aye, ma'am, firing," Garrett responded. He swiftly keyed in the commands. The torpedoes were the first to launch. Catapulted into space, their powerful engines ignited as they streaked away, bright comets tailing into the void as depicted on the display. A moment later, three of the four operational maser cannons responded, discharging their intense, deadly beams of energy toward the enemy as they shot.

However, the fourth maser turret remained silent, a glaring omission in their salvo. Garrett's heart sank as a deep rumbling vibrated through the deck beneath his feet, signaling that the cannon hadn't merely failed, but had done so in a catastrophic manner. He dreaded to think if any crewmembers had been in proximity to the turret when its miniature fusion reactor detonated. The loss of life, on top of what they had already endured, was a grim thought.

As if tired, the ship itself seemed to protest the strain of their actions. Communicated through his suit, it groaned as if in agony. The overhead lights flickered and dimmed, succumbing momentarily to the ship's taxed and damaged emergency power systems before eventually stabilizing and returning to full illumination.

"Confirmed hits from the masers," Garrett announced, his voice tense as he leaned in closer to the tactical display. The situation was critical, and every piece of information was vital. He attempted to clear away some of the frozen blood and gray matter that obscured the screen, hoping for a cleaner view of the data streaming forth. However, his efforts only smeared the

mess further across the display, complicating his task of inter-
preting the rapidly updating information.

His eyes remained fixed on the screen, tracking the trajectory of their torpedoes.

"There's no point-defensive fire from the enemy against our
torpedoes, or EW," he reported, noting the lack of countermeasures from the crippled enemy ship. The countdown was almost
palpable in the tense air of the bridge. "Impact in
four... three... two... one."

The moment of successive impacts was marked by a
dramatic change on the tactical display. The target indicator
representing the enemy ship flashed red multiple times, indicating direct hits. Garrett held his breath as time seemed to
stretch. Had they killed her, destroyed the enemy? Then, in a
decisive moment, the icon morphed into a navigational hazard
symbol, mirroring the one that now marked the remains of the
Reprise.

"Enemy target has been destroyed." Garrett couldn't help
but feel a sense of relief and fierce satisfaction. They had
avenged their fallen comrades and defended themselves against
an overwhelming threat. The successful strike represented a
significant, albeit costly, victory in their desperate and personal
battle for survival.

"Serves the bastards right for what they did," Darrust said.

"Good job, Number Three," Captain Marlowe's voice broke
through his reverie. "Very good job."

The captain's praise, though rare, carried a significant
weight for Garrett. He racked his brain, trying to recall the last
time she had offered him a compliment. The captain was
known for her stringent standards, always demanding excellence from her officers and crew. She was not one to hand out
commendations lightly; her acknowledgments were earned, not
freely given.

In the face of her typically critical nature, Garrett had

grown to deeply respect her. She was a formidable figure in the Fleet, a first-class officer whose reputation was well established, unassailable, and widely respected. Serving under her command was not just a challenge, but also a privilege. It was commonly known that officers who had the opportunity to serve on her ship often went on to achieve remarkable things, including captaining their own vessels. Her command was like a crucible, forging stronger, more capable officers through rigorous discipline and high expectations.

Garrett felt a surge of pride at her acknowledgment. "Thank you, ma'am."

"Now—" Marlowe coughed painfully "—we need only deal with the station and the traitors there. It is time to set an example. How far are we from Antares Station?"

Garrett immediately turned his attention back to the display, his fingers moving swiftly over the keyboard as he entered a series of commands to calculate their current position relative to Antares Station. The data was slow to come, hindered by the damaged systems, but Garrett was adept at working with what he had.

"We're approximately five hundred thousand klicks away, ma'am, and moving farther with every passing moment," he reported after a brief pause. His eyes continued to scan the readouts, seeking any signs of hostile intent from the station. "I'm detecting no target locks or offensive actions from the station itself. However, I should note that the sensors are still not fully operational, and our long-range detectors are down."

"Is the data clear enough to get a solid target lock?" Marlowe pressed. "Are they in any way trying to spoof our targeting solutions?"

Garrett reviewed the sensor data, cross-referencing it with the capabilities of their remaining weapon systems. Despite the limitations of their damaged sensors, he was confident in his ability to execute the task. "Yes, Captain, I can hit the station, and no, they don't appear to be attempting any electronic coun-termeasures. The lock is clean."

"Ma'am," Darrust interjected, her voice cutting through the tense atmosphere on the bridge. "I'm receiving a transmission from the station. They're broadcasting in the clear on all local frequencies and the emergency bands. They are hailing us."

"Put it on audio," the captain commanded. "I don't want them seeing the state of our bridge or getting any idea of our condition."

A moment later, the voice of a man emanated from the ship's audio system, filling the bridge with its urgent tone.

"This is Antares Mining Station," the voice said, betraying a hint of nervousness and underlying stress. "I am Station Admin-istrator Kellen and the Confederation governor. The mutineers have surrendered and been subdued. We are standing by to receive a boarding party and request a detail of marines for additional security. We also offer our medical services, should you have need of them. We have a level-one trauma center." There was a long pause. "I can't express enough how relieved we are that you've arrived."

Garrett let go a breath of relief and leaned back in the chair, relaxing slightly as he looked back over at his captain. There would be no more need for killing.

Captain Marlowe was slumped forward slightly, leaning heavily against the restraints of her command chair. Her expres-sion remained unreadable as she processed the information. Garrett could see her grimace from the pain she was clearly feeling. She issued a deep groan, causing Darrust to look back at her captain.

"You need medical attention, ma'am," Garrett said.

"I am fine." The captain straightened and then cleared her throat, spitting up blood onto the faceplate of her helmet. "I am fine. Now, put me on with them, audio only."

"You are live, Captain," Darrust said.

"Antares Mining Station, this is Captain Marlowe of the Confederation Navy Starship *Repulse*. You have rebelled against the rightful authority of the Confederation. Your people seized the CNS *Valiant* by force and publicly executed her crew before declaring independence. You then used that battle-cruiser to fire upon two Navy warships dispatched to restore order and put down your petty rebellion. As the senior officer on station tasked with resolving this matter, I am sentencing you all to death. The sentence is to be carried out immediately."

There was a long moment of silence. Garrett could not believe what he was hearing.

"I just told you," Kellen replied, in near panic. "Order has been restored. Captain, the Confederation is in control of this station. I am the appointed governor and was released from my holding cell less than five minutes ago."

"I don't believe you." Marlowe looked at Darrust. "Cut my feed."

"You are cut, ma'am," Darrust said. "They can't hear you, but we can still hear them."

"Very good." The captain turned painfully, grimacing as she did so, to look directly at Garrett. "Number Three, lock weapons on that station. We're going to blow them all to hell. Use our final torpedo and whatever masers are still capable of firing."

Garrett found himself hesitating. Was the captain seriously considering destroying the station?

"Mister Garrett, did you hear my order?"

"Aye, ma'am." Garrett locked the weapons as ordered, checking their power levels. Two of the masers would fire a full charge. The others were done and depleted. The torpedo alone, a shipkiller, would likely be overkill for Antares. He looked back on the captain. Surely she was bluffing—testing to see if this was some kind of trick on the station's part.

"My god," Kellen said. "Captain, I beg you. Do not fire. We

have women and children over here. The mutineers have surrendered. They will stand trial for their crimes and pay for what they have done. Come over and see for yourself. We have no weapons, no defenses. What more do you want from us?"

"Your deaths," the captain said, so quietly that it barely triggered her suit mic. It was little more than a whisper, but Garrett could sense the anger radiating forth. Her voice hardened and became stronger. "Number Three, are weapons locked?"

"They are, ma'am," Garrett reported, "two of the masers and last torpedo, everything we have left."

"Captain!" Kellen fairly screamed. "Do not fire upon us!"

"On my order, Mister Garrett, you will fire, is that understood?"

Garrett hesitated before answering. When he spoke, his tone was a near whisper. "Aye, ma'am. I understand."

The sharp pinging of the alarm from the tactical console blared within his helmet and jolted Garrett's attention back to his station. His heart rate spiked as he wondered what new crisis had emerged. His fingers danced rapidly over the keyboard, seeking the cause of the alert. Then, the situation became clear: their ship was unexpectedly maneuvering, pivoting in a way that was shifting their alignment.

As the ship swung around, Garrett realized with a sinking feeling that he was losing his target lock on Antares Station. The undamaged weapons, all located on the portside, were moving out of firing position.

"Helm, what are you doing?" Captain Marlowe's voice cut through the tension, her tone sharp and demanding. From her console, she could see the ship's unexpected change in course and was just as baffled by it.

"I will not allow you to fire on that station, ma'am," Darrust declared, her voice resolute. "I will not be a party to the murder and slaughter of helpless people, children. I did not sign up for that."

Garrett looked up from his station, his mind reeling with disbelief and horror. The situation had taken an unthinkable turn. He blinked, not quite believing what was happening.

"How dare you?" the captain hissed. She unbuckled her restraints and stood with some effort. Her limbs were trembling. For a moment she swayed unsteadily on her feet. "How dare you defy my orders, crewman? This is mutiny."

Darrust stood up from her station, turning to face Captain Marlowe with a resolute expression of her own. She placed her hands behind her back in a position of parade rest, a gesture of discipline, respect, and her defiance. It was at this moment that Garrett noticed her injuries. Both the arm and leg of her ship suit bore makeshift patches, evidence of the wounds she had sustained during the brief exchange of fire. Behind the face-plate, her skin was pale, a clear indication of blood loss, yet she maintained her composed demeanor.

"I have locked helm control, Captain," Darrust announced, her voice unwavering. "We will not murder those people. There's been enough killing this day."

The captain's face was a mask of fury as she stared back at the helm tech. The situation was unprecedented, a direct challenge to her authority. As Garrett absorbed the scene unfolding before him, a profound sense of disillusionment washed over him. He had joined the service with a clear and noble purpose, a pursuit: to combat the existential threat known as the Push, Surge, or whatever name people called their true enemy. Those aliens were the real threat, not some miners on an isolated penal mining station that had risen up and mutinied.

This was Garrett's first taste of actual combat. It had shattered any illusions of glory he had harbored. The ruined bridge, with its damaged panels, bloodstains, and bodies was a far cry from the sanitized, glorified versions of combat often portrayed in stories and media.

Now he understood the true nature of warfare: it was not

about heroism or honor, but about killing, death, and suffering—killing others first before they could do the same to you. His gaze drifted across the bridge, taking in the carnage and destruction that surrounded him. Until this moment, Garrett had not fully realized the truth.

"Please do not fire upon us," Kellen begged. "The mutineers are prisoners. We have families, not counting the prisoners, over ten thousand civilians. Don't do this... I beg you."

"They are trying to trick us," the captain spat, wavering slightly. She coughed, spitting up more blood. "Don't you see that? They murdered the *Valiant*'s crew, *Reprise*, the commodore too... our own brothers and sisters. And now, they're playing the same game they did with the *Valiant*, waiting for us to let our guard down."

"I don't think so, ma'am," Darrust said. "Captain, you are injured and you're not thinking clearly. You need medical attention."

"That's not the governor," the captain said.

"The backups say it is. I checked the voice pattern." Darrust looked to Garrett. "Lieutenant, I believe the captain is seriously injured and not thinking straight. She is clearly not herself, for the woman I served would not give such an order. As third in command of the ship, with the second officer dead, it is your duty to relieve her, at least until a qualified doctor can clear her for service."

"You mutinous dog," the captain hissed.

"I am doing what I think is—"

In a split second, the helm technician was violently thrown back over her console, a hole evident in the left side of her chest as the explosive round detonated after impact. Without atmosphere on the bridge, Garrett had never heard the shot.

For a brief moment, the technician's body shuddered in a final, involuntary spasm before going disturbingly still. The abruptness of her demise was shocking. Garrett, frozen in horror, could only stare at the grim scene that had just played out before him. His mind struggled to process the reality that Captain Marlowe, the leader he had respected and followed, sidearm in hand, had just taken the life of one of their own.

"Now," the captain said to Garrett, before glancing down at her station's monitors, as she lowered her pistol, "kindly fire that torpedo, Lieutenant. It can still track and hit the station, even if the masers can't. Kill the bastards dead before everything on this ship fails and we're left helpless, adrift, and at their bloody mercy."

Garrett's own sidearm bucked in his hand. He had not even been conscious of drawing the weapon, as if the response had been reflexive. The first explosive antipersonnel slug tore into the captain's shoulder, jerking her back around to face Garrett. There was a stunned look upon her face as they stared at one another for a protracted moment. Her eyes narrowed. Then the captain's hand holding her pistol began to rise.

The weapon in his hand bucked again, almost painfully. The next round hammered square into the captain's faceplate, drilling a neat hole straight through. It snapped the woman's helmeted head back violently. She collapsed, falling to the floor next to her station, finished, and like so many others this day— stone dead.

Hands shaking uncontrollably, Garrett returned the sidearm to his holster. It took two tries before he managed to secure it. He glanced around, at first unsure what to do. He was the only living soul left on the bridge... maybe even the entire ship, though he seriously doubted that. *Repulse* might be a wreck of a starship, but there were surely other survivors.

A sob escaped his lips, the emotion of the moment overcoming him. Then he straightened and clamped down on his feelings. He had more pressing concerns to deal with.

Duty—he had a duty to the ship and the crew. He needed to begin working to save those who were still alive, injured, and in need of help, even if in the end he was tried for murder and mutiny. He returned to the tactical station and keyed the communication channel, opening it up.

"This is Lieutenant Garrett. I am in command of *Repulse*. We will not fire upon your station. I repeat, we will not be firing upon Antares Mining Station." He paused, fighting another sob for those who had died and for himself. He was a killer now, especially after destroying the mutineers' ship, a murderer also —he glanced at the captain's body—and now a mutineer. He'd had such high hopes, but he knew the truth. By his own actions, his career in the Navy was now over. "If you have medical personnel and a shuttle, we could use the help. It's a bit of a mess over here."

"Thank you, Lieutenant," Kellen said, relief seeming to pour over the connection. "We have two shuttles. I will have them prepped and launched as soon as we can manage it."

"Thank you, Governor." Garrett wanted to sit down in the chair at the tactical station. He felt drained, exhausted, spent.

"God bless you, son," Kellen said.

"Standing by for your shuttles," Garrett replied. "*Repulse* out."

He cut the connection and stood there for a long moment, thinking on what he needed to do next. Garrett turned toward the bridge hatch, which was sealed. There was no sign of the marine sentry who had stood guard by it. That poor bastard was likely buried under debris or had been sucked out into space when the hull had been breached. He started for the hatch. With the main computer down, it would have to be opened manually. Regardless of his actions, and the consequences that would follow, he had work to do. There was not only a ship but a crew to save.

TWO

GARRETT

The room Garrett found himself in was the very embodiment of austerity, its walls painted a stark, clinical white that gave off an almost antiseptic aura. In this modest space, the only furnishings were a small table flanked by two unadorned metal chairs, creating an atmosphere that was sparse and functional.

Dominating the left wall, just above chest height, was an old, round mechanical clock, its presence both anachronistic and commanding. The clock's relentless ticking reverberated through the room, each second marked by a pronounced echo that seemed to amplify the solitude and anticipation in the air.

Garrett, clad in his immaculate dress whites, was the room's sole occupant. He sat with a disciplined posture, embodying the patience and composure befitting a man of his standing, an officer in the Confederation Navy.

In this electronically purged environment, where every gadget had been deliberately deactivated, Garrett was left with nothing but his own thoughts, the stark surroundings, and the relentless ticking of the clock as time slowly passed him by. The sound, which should have been mundane, took on a foreboding quality in the silence, each tick resonating like a subtle drum-beat counting down to an unknown climax.

His arrival here was no accident. Upon receiving the orders to report, Garrett had made his way to the base's headquarters with a sense of urgency, understanding the gravity of such summons, especially coming a week after he had testified to the Navy board.

The building was a fortress of sorts, guarded with the utmost security. Upon entering, he was immediately met by a marine sentry, a formidable figure who exuded authority and discipline. His escort to headquarters left him at the door. This new escort and guard was a woman of few words, her communication limited to the essential task of escorting him to this very room. Once inside, he was left alone, her silent presence on the other side of the door a reminder of the seriousness of his situation.

He had been intentionally kept away from others. When he'd been let out of the room assigned to him, not only had he been escorted everywhere by marines, but he had also been eyed warily by nearly everyone, as if they knew he was a dead man walking.

The isolation had left him with only his thoughts and worries about what lay in his immediate future. There had also been the survivor's guilt. It was a stupid thing, but he felt terribly guilty that he had made it through when so many others had not.

Late at night, the thought of it burned at him. He knew he had ultimately saved lives, but Garrett understood he should have died. It was a miracle he had not. On the bridge of the *Repulse* and throughout much of the ship, life and death had been a random thing, nothing more than chance.

As Garrett sat in silent contemplation, a light knock abruptly punctuated the quiet. He instinctively rose to his feet, his training kicking in, as the door swung open. Commander

Yenga, a figure commanding respect and authority, stepped into the room. He was dressed in his naval finery, his dress whites immaculate despite the inclement weather outside and his service cap neatly tucked under one arm.

The notable gold slash adorning his right shoulder was a distinguished mark, signifying his position as the commander of a starship, the *Argus*, a fast attack destroyer. Yet, in stark contrast to his polished appearance, he was conspicuously drenched, rainwater still clinging to his uniform, particularly his shoulders, back, and lower legs.

At that precise moment, the distant rumble of thunder resonated, seeming to shake the building, as if to underscore the dramatic entrance and what lay ahead in both of their futures. Outside the room, the marine sentry silently shut the door, leaving Garrett and Yenga in a private, albeit unconventional, meeting.

Commander Yenga, seemingly unfazed by his soaked condition, attempted to shake off the remnants of the storm from his uniform. He carried with him a sense of casual authority that seemed to fill the room.

"I love coming planetside," he began, breaking the silence with a tone that bordered on the conversational, "but have you ever noticed how Fleet always seems to select the worst places to build their dirtside facilities? Surely, on this rock of a world, there was a better place, like where the colonists settled, a nice temperate location, other than a humid rainforest at the equator, where it literally rains buckets on a daily basis." His words carried a hint of humor to the seriousness of the environment and the situation at hand.

The question, rhetorical as it might have been, seemed to momentarily bridge the gap between the formality of their roles and the absurdity of the moment, with Yenga standing there, a drenched commander in a room that felt far removed from the tempest outside. Garrett, still standing in his crisp dress whites, faced his superior, aware that the conversation was about to shift to matters far more consequential than the weather, matters that directly affected his future.

After a slight hesitation, Garrett acknowledged Commander Yenga's lighthearted comment with a respectful nod, maintaining the decorum befitting his and the other man's rank. He observed Yenga with a sense of quiet appraisal. The commander, a man roughly fifteen years his senior, bore the distinct features of Asian heritage, likely from a world that had been originally colonized by the Chinese or Koreans.

Despite his shorter stature, Yenga carried himself with an undeniable presence. His build was compact yet robust, indicative of a life dedicated to military discipline, with an eye toward physical fitness. His eyes were sharp and observant, missing nothing, yet there was an underlying kindness in his demeanor that softened the otherwise stern visage of a seasoned command-level naval officer.

"Lieutenant," Yenga addressed Garrett with a tone that seamlessly blended authority with a subtle hint of camaraderie. He gestured toward the chair, an unspoken invitation for Garrett to be at ease.

Garrett complied, resuming his seat with a composed grace. He watched as the commander carefully placed his leather briefcase on the floor, a movement that was deliberate and measured. Yenga then proceeded to pull out the chair from under the table, taking a seat directly across from Garrett. He put his drenched cover on the surface of the table. The simple act of sitting down seemed to subtly shift the atmosphere in the room, creating a space that was more conducive to serious conversation.

The room, once filled with the ticking of the clock and the weight of anticipation, now seemed to be bracing itself for the exchange that was about to take place.

"How are you holding up?" Yenga inquired, his tone

carrying a genuine interest in Garrett's well-being. "It has been a week since we last saw each other."

Garrett, maintaining his composed demeanor, replied candidly, "I am not sleeping, sir, if that is what you are asking."

Yenga nodded, his expression reflecting understanding. "I can imagine, especially after what you have been through."

"Yes, sir," Garrett concurred, internally recognizing the depth of understatement in his own words. The events leading up to his testimony before the Navy board had been tumultuous, leaving a mark on him that was not easily conveyed or, for that matter, understood by others. He was utterly exhausted and felt it in his bones. What had happened off Antares Station and after, like an old dishrag, had wrung him out.

"And the psych heads—have you talked to them?"

"I've talked to them." Garrett omitted that he had not told them how exactly he was feeling. In the military, that could be a dangerous thing.

Yenga's gaze briefly wandered around the room, taking in the stark surroundings, before he asked another question. "How long have you been here?"

"About an hour, sir." Garrett's response was factual, yet it carried the weight of the week that had elapsed since he'd last seen Yenga, when he had given testimony to the board. That had taken two entire days, for the board had peppered him with an endless array of questions.

"That is my fault, I am afraid. When I received the summons, I was aboard the *Argus* and needed to shuttle down to the surface. The storm that moved in had air traffic backed up. We circled for half an hour before the tower granted us permission to land." Yenga's concern deepened as he broached a more personal aspect. "Are they treating you okay, son?"

"Yes. I have been confined to quarters but allowed exercise. They've fed me. I have been under guard the entire time. But I have also been isolated and cut off from the wider world. I cannot even access the system net."

"That is only to be expected. You did kill your commanding officer." It was a blunt acknowledgment of the grim reality Garrett was entangled in.

Garrett's response was a mix of resignation and a quiet assertion of his moral standing. He looked down at the table, the gravity of his actions evident in his posture.

"I had no choice, sir," he said, his voice steady yet carrying an undercurrent of the turmoil he felt.

"You had a difficult decision to make. Honestly, at your age and of junior rank, I am not sure I could have done the same, were I in your shoes. In fact, I hope never to be put in that situation."

Garrett shifted in his chair, the conversation stirring a mix of emotions within him. He then posed a question that had clearly been on his mind since they had first met.

"Why did you choose, or really volunteer, to represent me, sir? No one in the JAG Corps wanted to take my case. In the end, they assigned me a junior-grade lieutenant fresh out of the academy. I was his first case, and he was far from eager. It was like I had the Promethium plague, and no one wanted to touch me."

The question seemed to resonate with Yenga, prompting a moment of introspection. He glanced down at the tabletop, falling silent as he gathered his thoughts. When he finally looked up, his eyes had taken on a steely resolve. "I guess you could say I didn't like the scuttlebutt I was hearing about your case, the direction it was moving in." Yenga rubbed his jaw before continuing. "Son, you are the talk of the system. There are all kinds of rumors going on about what went down on that bridge. I read the public after-action report in the *Fleet Gazette* and it was lacking on details, especially concerning you. I also made a few discreet calls and got the skinny on what really occurred."

Yenga hesitated a moment. As if thinking, he glanced at the ceiling and looked like he was about to say something, then shook his head ever so slightly.

"I have a certain sense of fairness and got the impression you were being railroaded, so I stepped in and volunteered my services. As a command-level officer, I have the authority to act as another officer's legal representative, especially if the Judge Advocate General's office on planet is far from motivated or willing to help." Yenga held up a hand as Garrett was about to speak. "Before you ask, yes, it ruffled some feathers, but I have powerful friends and am not terribly concerned about blow-back. I am doing what I believe to be right. More importantly, you made the right decision when you accepted my offer to represent you."

Garrett absorbed Yenga's words with a sense of gratitude and a deeper understanding of the commander's motivations. "I see," he said, his voice carrying a mix of appreciation and solemnity.

"Do you?"

"I believe so. Thank you, sir." The acknowledgment was simple, but it conveyed a profound sense of respect and grati-tude for Yenga's advocacy.

"Whatever happens in the next few minutes, Lieutenant," he said, his gaze fixed on Garrett with a sudden unwavering intensity, "know that I believe you made the correct—the only— decision open to you. The case we presented to the board demonstrated that. If they are halfway fair, they will recognize that reality."

"Do you think it will move them, sir?" Garrett asked, barely daring to hope.

"We will find out soon enough."

The sudden knock at the door broke the momentary stillness. It almost caused Garrett to jump.

"Come," Yenga responded promptly, looking around, for his back was to the door. As the door opened, the marine sentry appeared, her figure silhouetted against the corridor beyond. Noise flooded in as thunder rumbled once more, this time distantly.

"They are ready for you, gentlemen," she announced, her tone formal.

Yenga's reaction was immediate and decisive. Looking back around at Garrett, he slapped his palms lightly on the table, a physical manifestation of his readiness to face whatever lay ahead. As he pushed back his chair and stood, his demeanor was one of determined confidence. He turned to Garrett, offering both a question and an invitation. "Shall we find out what the board has to say on the matter concerning you?"

Garrett's internal state was a maelstrom of emotions as he rose to his feet. Despite the churn of anxiety and uncertainty within him, he managed to project a facade of calm determination. He nodded in silent and grim agreement as Yenga gathered his briefcase and cover, slipping it once more under an arm.

Garrett's thoughts became resolute, steeling himself for the worst. He recognized that whatever verdict the board delivered, it would be another chapter in a saga of challenges he had already endured. He clenched his jaw as his heart hardened with the resolve of a man who had faced terrible adversity, almost died, and survived. He was prepared even for the possibility of a court-martial. He would face it as a man who had looked death in the eye. This readiness was not born of indifference, but of a deep-seated resilience. In truth, the board could do little worse than he had already faced or done to himself mentally after he had killed Captain Marlowe and survived the experience.

"I am ready, sir," Garrett stated, his voice carrying an unexpected firmness and a hard edge.

"Good man," Yenga replied, acknowledging Garrett's resolve with a pleased look. He then led the way out of the room and into the bustling corridor of the headquarters. The corridor was a hive of activity, with ratings and officers busily navigating their way through their tasks, a typical scene in such a nerve center of military operations. He was on Yanno's World, where the sector headquarters for Fleet was located. After he had managed to coax the damaged *Repulse* back to the nearest shipyard, he'd immediately been relieved and transported here, where he had spent the last four weeks either being debriefed or testifying before the board.

Garrett and Yenga were just another pair moving through the halls, largely unnoticed amidst the daily hustle of those who worked at headquarters and strode these corridors of power. The marine who had been guarding Garrett followed closely behind, a silent sentinel ensuring protocol, security, and that Garrett did not wander.

As they approached a guarded door, flanked by two more armed marine sentries, the air of formality and importance surrounding their destination became apparent. He was returning to the room the board had used to hold their hearings. One of the sentries, recognizing Yenga and Garrett, promptly opened the door, granting them passage.

As Garrett stepped into the room, a sense of déjà vu washed over him, the familiar setting of his previous appearance before the board now layered with an added intensity. The room, with its imposing decor and the solemn air of military justice, was a stark reminder of the gravity of his situation, the seriousness. It hit him like a slap in the face, instantly driving away his exhaustion.

At the far end, sitting at a long polished wooden table, sat the three officers who would determine his fate, all of them one-

and two-star admirals, the pinnacle of naval authority. Admiral Killingsly, the only woman on the panel, was positioned on the left. Next to her were Admirals Berhorst and then Harris on the far right. Their stern expressions, as they noticed Garrett's entry, conveyed the seriousness with which they were approaching the proceedings. This was no mere formality; it was a moment of critical judgment, one which lay heavily upon him.

This time, however, the courtroom was not the isolated arena it had been during his last appearance. An audience was present in the rows of chairs facing the board, adding a new layer of scrutiny and significance to the proceedings. Four additional admirals were in attendance, positioned in chairs behind the table he and Yenga would shortly sit at.

Three of these admirals, all men, sat together, their expressions unreadable, their attention shifting to him as he moved farther into the room. A fourth figure, a woman, sat apart from the trio, her presence singular and notable. She was not looking at them but had turned away and was studying a tablet, seemingly deeply engrossed.

Garrett scanned the unfamiliar faces, curiosity and a hint of apprehension mingling within him. Who were these additional admirals, and what role would they play in the proceedings? Their presence was a variable he had not anticipated, adding a layer of complexity to an already tense situation.

As Garrett processed this new development, the weight of the moment settled upon him. The room, filled with some of the Navy's highest-ranking officials in this sector, spoke of the significance of the decision that lay ahead. His actions, his fate, were now under the scrutiny of a formidable assembly, making the stakes higher than ever.

As they made their way into the courtroom, approaching their table, Commander Yenga leaned in close to Garrett, providing a crucial piece of information in a discreet whisper.

"Off to our right is Fleet Admiral Omaga," he murmured, indicating the dark-skinned man among the additional admirals who had come to watch the proceedings.

Garrett's attention instantly shifted to the admiral, a three-star, recognizing the importance of this figure. Omaga was in charge of Fleet operations for the sector. He was a key player in the naval hierarchy and likely the most senior person on the planet. His presence in the courtroom, as an observer, underscored the extraordinary significance of the proceedings Garrett was about to face. The other two admirals with him were two-stars and therefore junior, likely the man's direct aides.

With this new awareness, Garrett moved with a sense of purpose and discipline. He approached the table designated for him and Yenga, noting the pitcher of water placed there, along with two small glass cups. He suddenly found his mouth terribly dry and desired a drink but dared not, for he could feel his hands shaking slightly.

Garrett then executed a move that was second nature to him, yet laden with profound meaning under the circumstances. He drew himself up to full attention and saluted the board. Behind the board was the Confederation's flag, a large central star on a black background with numerous smaller stars of various colors and luminosity, symbolizing the states that made up the government.

At the bottom of the flag was written UNITY, STRENGTH, PURPOSE, HUMANITY.

Garrett's salute was more than a mere military formality; it was a symbol of his respect for the naval institution and its processes, regardless of his personal predicament. It was a gesture that spoke of his commitment to duty and honor, qualities that had guided him throughout his career and had led him to the pivotal moment he now faced. A heartbeat later, Yenga did the same, snapping to and offering a crisp and rapid salute.

As the courtroom settled into a tense silence, all eyes on

Garrett and Yenga, the stage was set for the proceedings to begin. The weight of the moment was palpable, with the outcome of this meeting poised to have far-reaching implications for Garrett's career and life.

"Lieutenant," Admiral Berhorst said, his tone cold, "please have a seat."

Garrett's response to Berhorst's directive was prompt and respectful. He pulled out the chair and took his seat, his movements deliberate, reflecting his awareness of the gravity of the situation. Commander Yenga, a silent pillar of support, settled into the seat to Garrett's left. He set his briefcase on the ground and his cover on the tabletop. The sound of the door closing behind them with a resonant boom added finality to the moment, signifying that the proceedings were about to commence in earnest.

Berhorst, assuming the role of the presiding officer, picked up the gavel in front of him. With a single, authoritative rap upon a solid block of wood, he signaled the start of the session, then placed the polished wooden hammer back down.

"This board investigating the matters that occurred at Antares Station is back in session," he began formally. "Before we begin and announce our findings concerning Lieutenant Garrett's actions, do any of the board members have anything they wish to say or add to the official record?"

"No," replied Admiral Killingsly in a brief, definitive tone. If anything, her expression hardened as she gazed directly at Garrett. He could almost read the distaste in her eyes.

"I do not," added Admiral Harris, equally succinct. "I have said all I aim to on this matter."

With no further comments from the board members, Berhorst's gaze turned squarely toward Garrett. The air in the room seemed to tighten with anticipation.

"Lieutenant." Berhorst addressed Garrett directly, his voice carrying a weight that underscored the seriousness of the moment. "As the surviving senior officer for the *Repulse*, do you have anything you would care to add to your testimony or say at this time? This will be your last opportunity before the board rules and delivers its findings."

This was a critical juncture for Garrett. The invitation to speak was more than a procedural formality; it was a final and unlikely chance to influence the board's impending decision. The eyes of the admirals, along with those of the additional observers, were fixed on him, awaiting his response. At a time like this, Garrett had learned from Yenga that many threw themselves upon the board's mercy, begged or apologized. Garrett was not the begging sort.

"I do, sir," Garrett said, rising to his feet.

Yenga, caught off guard by Garrett's sudden decision to address the board, looked over at him with a mixture of curiosity and concern. They had agreed, when they had last met, to refrain from adding anything more, believing that everything necessary had been said during previous testimony. Yet Garrett, driven by a deeper sense of duty and introspection, chose to break from this agreed path. He felt the need to speak, and badly too.

"Then do so," Berhorst prompted, giving Garrett the floor.

Garrett's voice carried an unexpected strength as he began. "Sirs, I love the Navy and the Confederation. I desire to continue to serve and wish to defend humanity when the next Push arrives. I do not want to find myself sitting it out, watching from the sidelines. That said, over the last few weeks, I have thought long and hard on what occurred off Antares Station. Though I regret killing Captain Marlowe, I would not change my actions were I given the opportunity to do things differently. If that consigns me to losing my career or, worse, facing prison time, my conscience is clear and satisfied. I did what I had to do, nothing less, nothing more. As I said, I would do it again without a second's thought."

The reaction from the admirals on the board was immediate. They shifted in their chairs as his words landed. Harris and Berhorst shared a look. Behind him, Garrett could hear someone whispering from Omaga's group.

"Is that all?" Berhorst asked, turning his attention back to Garrett.

"Yes, sir. I have nothing more to say."

"Very well, your statement has been entered into the log." Berhorst tapped the tablet before him, formalizing Garrett's heartfelt declaration as part of the official record. Garrett then took his seat, his part played, his fate now in the hands of the board.

Yenga leaned in. "Nicely said."

"It is the truth," Garrett responded, his reply underscored by the sincerity that had driven his actions throughout the ordeal. "That is how I feel."

"I know," Yenga said softly.

"Lieutenant," Berhorst began, "we have compiled a detailed report, along with our findings, and delivered it a short time ago to the senior officers of this station."

Garrett suddenly realized that was why the other admirals were present.

"That report has been filed with Fleet Command, along with our recommendations to keep such things from occurring again. A copy has also been sent to your personal account for your review. To summarize, we found significant mistakes and lapses in judgment made by the commanding officer of the expedition sent to Antares, Commodore Maskin, that directly led to the destruction of the *Reprise* and crippling of *Repulse*. The fault for what occurred primarily rests in his lap and his alone."

Garrett felt a glimmer of hope spark deep within him. This revelation marked a significant turn in the proceedings, attributing primary responsibility to Commodore Maskin, a detail that could have considerable implications for Garrett's case.

Berhorst paused, his gaze dropping to the tablet before him, a moment of preparation before delivering the board's conclusions on Garrett's own actions. "Lieutenant, are you prepared to hear our findings on your actions?" The admiral's tone was neutral, yet laden with the weight of the impending judgment.

Even as his stomach did a flip-flop, Garrett, having spoken his truth and standing by his actions, braced himself to receive the board's decision. This moment was the culmination of all the events that had transpired since Antares Station, the point at which his future in the Navy would be decided.

"I am, sir."

"Then, along with counsel, please stand."

Garrett stood and prepared himself to receive his judgment. Yenga stood as well.

"Lieutenant," Berhorst began, his voice clear and authoritative, "this board has come to the conclusion that a court-martial proceeding against you is not warranted, let alone required. We have found your actions to be exemplary, and in the finest traditions of the service."

Garrett blinked in shock. He almost took an inadvertent step backward but resisted the temptation at the last moment.

"The fact that bridge and audio recordings of what occurred survived the battle showed us the difficult situation you found yourself in. Captain Marlowe was gravely injured and, we believe, not thinking clearly. Her wounds, studied postmortem, were determined to be mortal. She had less than an hour to live without advanced medical care. Moreover, your direct actions saved over ten thousand civilians on the station. The governor filed a brief on your behalf detailing his interactions with you after the battle and spoke of your courage, determination, and the effort you put in to save your ship. We judge that your subsequent actions in taking command of *Repulse* not only saved the ship but also sixty-two of her surviving crew. We have recommended you be commended for your actions and a letter added to your file absolving you of responsibility for what occurred not only to *Repulse* but also on the bridge in the aftermath of the battle."

Garrett was stunned by the board's ruling. He blinked rapidly, trying to process the reality that he was not only being absolved of any wrongdoing in the death of his captain but was also being praised for his actions. Not quite believing what he was hearing, he glanced over at Yenga, who appeared equally surprised by the board's favorable judgment. A small, tight smile began to draw itself out across his face.

"Do you have any questions for the board?" Berhorst inquired, offering Garrett a chance to address any lingering doubts or concerns.

Garrett, still grappling with the enormity of the board's decision, found his voice momentarily caught in his throat.

"No—sir," he managed to reply, his voice steadying as he spoke. "Thank you, sirs."

"Then these proceedings are concluded." With that, the admiral picked up the gavel, rapped it decisively, and then stood up, followed by the other members of the board. Admiral Killingsly, however, cast a hard look toward Garrett, her gaze bordering on hostility, a silent indication that, despite the board's ruling, not everyone might agree with the outcome. Then, along with the rest of the admirals of the board, she exited through a side door. Berhorst was last. He stopped and glanced back, not at Garrett, but at the woman to his left, the admiral who was sitting alone.

"Congratulations, son." Yenga offered his hand, drawing Garrett's attention. "It's over."

The heartfelt sentiment from Commander Yenga brought a semblance of warmth to the otherwise cold and formal proceedings. Garrett's handshake with him was firm, a symbol of mutual respect and gratitude.

"I can't thank you enough, sir," Garrett expressed sincerely, deeply aware of Yenga's instrumental role in his defense. The man had saved his career and likely more, for during the hearings he had fought tooth and nail for Garrett.

"There is no need to thank," Yenga said. "You did your duty, as I did mine."

"What now, sir?" Despite the board's decision, the path forward was unclear. He had braced himself for a very different outcome and was now navigating uncharted waters.

"I suppose, now you wait for orders," Yenga said. "Then, the next step is up to you, son."

"You will never serve aboard a commissioned starship again, Lieutenant. On that I promise."

Surprised, Garrett and Yenga turned to find Fleet Admiral Omaga behind them.

"You may still wear that uniform, but it will not be under my command. Better yet, I am going to find a hellhole to stick you in, from which there will be no return." The man's face was flushed with the heat of anger. The admiral's gaze, as it bored into him, left no room for doubt or discussion.

The admiral spared a disgusted look at Yenga, then whirled around and started for the door. As Omaga departed with his entourage, Garrett was left to grapple with the stark reality of his situation. The commendation from the board, while vindicating him legally and morally, did not erase the practical consequences of his actions. His lifelong dream of commanding a starship, a goal that had been within his grasp, now seemed firmly out of reach, a casualty of the complex and unforgiving nature of military hierarchy and politics. This revelation marked a bittersweet moment for him.

Yenga clapped him reassuringly on the shoulder. "You look like you could use a stiff drink, and I know just the place, though we are going to have to walk in the rain to get to it." Despite his seniority and age, his tone was friendly, almost brotherly, offering not just a respite from the tension, but also an unspoken promise of friendship and support.

"You are right," Garrett said. "I can use a drink."

"Captain Marlowe was Omaga's protégée," another voice said. "She was his pet project and he her mentor."

Garrett swiveled around, only to come face to face with a commanding presence. Standing before him was an older four-star admiral, her uniform crisp and adorned with medals and service ribbons that spoke of a long and storied career. She had been the admiral sitting apart from the others, the one Berhorst had looked back at. Her eyes sized him up, then she extended a firm hand toward him.

"I am Admiral Gray," she introduced herself with an authoritative yet measured tone. "It is my distinct pleasure to meet you, Lieutenant Garrett."

As Garrett clasped her hand, a wave of realization washed over him. He was not just shaking hands with any high-ranking officer; he was in the presence of the woman who'd spearheaded Construction Command for the entire Fleet. Before that, she had been in charge of Fleet's research and development division. Admiral Gray was a figure of immense power and influence, directly reporting to the chief of naval operations, her authority even surpassing that of Omaga.

What was she doing here?

"Ma'am," Garrett managed, but the word felt underwhelming, almost lost amidst the gravity of the moment. He stood there, caught in the admiral's steely, brown-eyed gaze, which seemed to measure him in an instant.

Admiral Gray's expression softened slightly as she continued. "I was on a tour of Rimward facilities when Commander Yenga brought your case to my attention. He keeps his eyes open for exceptional people, and when he finds one—well, here I am."

Garrett's gaze shifted toward Commander Yenga, searching for a hint of explanation. Yenga, however, remained impassive, giving nothing away.

"I am pleased I took the time to stop by and watch this process come to its natural conclusion," she remarked, her gaze flicking to the table where the board had presided. "Not many junior officers have the fortitude to hold their ground against a Navy board, especially one that wouldn't hesitate to send you to the gallows were it not for proper representation."

Garrett, still grappling with the surreal turn of events, chose to remain silent. He felt a growing sense of awe and apprehension at the admiral's direct and forthright manner. Had she intervened on his behalf? If so, why?

"If Omaga doesn't see the quality in you, I certainly do." She paused for a moment, her eyes locking with Garrett's. "Want a job?"

THREE

TABBY

Twelve Years Later

As she woke from her slumber, the Typhoon class assault boat, a similar concept to the motor torpedo boats from Old Earth and the Second World War, vibrated with a sense of barely contained energy, the twin coiled gravitic drives emitting a deep, pulsating thrum as they ramped up in tandem. The boat's heartbeat reverberated through Captain Tabby's seat, a tangible reminder of the immense power at her fingertips and command.

Encircled by a constellation of screens, her station buzzed with life—beeps, scrolling lines of intricate data, and readouts—all in response to the awakening of the boat.

The pilot's chair, in which she sat, was strategically positioned just behind the boat's two other stations, weapons, and electronic warfare. Raised slightly above the other two seats, which were set side by side, her position offered her an unobstructed view of both her crew. Here, she was more than a pilot; she was the boat's commander, a conductor of an orchestra of advanced technology.

Her weapons and electronic warfare techs, experts in their

respective fields, worked in harmonious synchrony. Their fingers danced over control panels and touchscreen displays with practiced ease, performing rigorous preflight checks on their systems. Each readout, each confirmation, brought them a step closer to the moment of launch.

The atmosphere in the cockpit was electric with anticipation of what was to come. Just the thought of piloting the aggressive little boat got Tabby's heart beating faster. The comm channel crackled to life, slicing through the tension-laden air with the crisp voice of the carrier's catapult officer.

"Oscar Flight Lead, *Neptune Shooter*," the voice announced, its clarity cutting through the background hum of the boat, "roughly eight minutes till transition through Midway jump point. Prepare final procedures for launch."

Tabby knew the rest of her squadron were receiving similar notifications. She felt an urge to check in with them, but she had trained her people well and they would do their jobs. She had to trust in that, so she resisted the temptation. Right now, she had to be concerned solely with her own boat and prepping for launch.

"Control, Oscar Flight Lead confirms," she transmitted back with confident brevity, then brought up a preflight checklist on one of her displays. Flipping off the mic, she turned her attention to her crew, her voice carrying the weight of imminent action. "Ready for preflight?"

"Ready, ma'am," Petty Officer Second Class Kiera Sanchez affirmed, her tone a mix of focus and clear anticipation. Sanchez was an integral part of the team, her expertise in weaponry a cornerstone of the boat's combat readiness.

With a practiced movement, Tabby reached forward and engaged the fusion reactors in a standard test. The boat responded instantly, the reactors ramping up to maximum power output for a vital ten seconds. It was a display of raw power, a controlled burst of energy.

Even positioned twenty meters away at the rear of the craft where the power plants were located, the hum of the reactors was unmistakable. It was a deep, resonant sound that spoke of incredible energy and capability, the boat's desire to go. As the test concluded, the reactors cycled down to standby mode. The hum died off.

"Reactors one and two functioning nominally," she announced, confirming the primary power sources were operating within expected parameters. Tabby's voice carried a calm, methodical tone as she systematically worked through the preflight checks. Her fingers moved with practiced precision, tapping out another command to bring up the backup power supply readout on her screen. "Backup power bank fully charged," she relayed.

In response, Sanchez diligently made a corresponding entry on her tablet, which was securely strapped to her right thigh. Their actions were a coordinated dance of efficiency, attention to detail, and thorough preparation.

"Auxiliary power unit fully charged," Tabby noted, her eyes scanning the readouts on the screen. With a few more deft strokes, she activated the unit. "APU is now primed and armed."

Sanchez, in sync with the captain's rhythm, made another precise notation on her tablet.

Turning her attention to the life support systems, Tabby tapped on the screen before her. She studied the results for a long moment.

"Functionality of oxygen generation, scrubbers, and storage nominal. Full tanks. Cabin pressure nominal, no leaks detected. Temperature control nominal as well. Life support is green."

She swiveled toward another monitor, her fingers dancing across its control surface with a sense of purpose.

"Navigation systems and charts updated and calibrated for Midway Central," she reported, her voice steady and assured.

"Planetary data, navigational hazards, gravity pools, and anomalies loaded."

This statement affirmed that the boat was equipped with the most current and comprehensive navigational information, essential for safely traversing the intricate pathways of open space, especially in a system as busy and as heavily trafficked as Midway, one of Fleet's forward bases.

Without missing a beat, she turned her attention to a screen positioned to her left. Here, she began a meticulous examination of the boat's communication capabilities. Tabby tested both the internal and external communication channels, ensuring that they were in perfect working order. She also scrutinized the signal and receiving antennas and arrays.

The quantum encryption systems, vital for secure communications across the vast distances of space, were the next focus. With a few inputs, she confirmed their operational status.

"Communication systems, nominal operation," Tabby declared, indicating that the boat's communication infrastructure was fully functional and secure. Her gaze fixed on the sensor and electronic warfare station, where Petty Officer First Class Liam Chen was strapped in. "Heat sink?"

"Heat sink nominal," Chen replied promptly, his voice steady and reassuring. "The adaptive camouflage system checks out as nominal as well, ma'am."

As Chen relayed this vital information, Sanchez made another meticulous note on her tablet.

"Emergency cloaking?" Tabby continued, delving further into the boat's array of defensive systems. "Rapid cooldown of systems?"

"Functioning, powered, and ready," Chen confirmed.

"Inertial dampening system?" Tabby queried. "How does it look?"

"Armed, functioning, and powered. It *looks* like we won't be squashed like bugs today, ma'am," Chen replied, a hint of dry humor in his voice. Tabby had heard it all before, but his comment underlined the importance of the inertial dampening system, crucial for mitigating the intense forces experienced during high-speed maneuvers, especially in combat.

"Sanchez, weapons preflight."

"Aye, ma'am."

Their helmet visors were still open so they could speak. Prior to launch they would seal. The atmosphere within the cabin would be removed as a safety measure, creating a vacuum to protect the crew in the event of an explosive hull breach.

"Maser and laser turrets calibrating," Sanchez announced, initiating the procedure to ensure that the boat's primary offensive systems were precisely aligned and ready for operation.

Within the robust frame of the assault boat, the forward and smaller turrets, strategically positioned along the hull for optimal coverage, responded to her commands for a diagnostic test. The sound of their servos whirring as they deployed from the hull and moved resonated through the boat, a mechanical chorus signifying their readiness.

"Turrets are aligned and calibrated. Targeting system is online and nominal. System is charged and ready to track and fire." Sanchez made another notation on her tablet. She leaned forward, her hands tapping away at one of her screens, and paused. "Missile system check. All tubes online and functioning. Testing missile bay doors." Her fingers moved swiftly over her screen to engage the necessary protocols.

Tabby could discern the distinct sounds of the missile bay doors opening and then closing again, the heavy, muffled thuds a reassuring confirmation of their functionality.

"Missile bay doors functional," Sanchez confirmed, following the successful test.

"Confirm missile loadout and readiness," Captain Tabby instructed.

"We have five type six specter shipkillers, fourteen sparrow hunter killers, and two anti-radiation growlers, ma'am," she detailed. "Good and solid links to all missile control systems." Her report painted a picture of a well-armed vessel, capable of handling a variety of combat scenarios with its diverse and powerful weaponry.

Satisfied with the weapons check, Tabby moved on to the next critical system. "Electronic warfare systems check."

"Jamming equipment functional," Chen reported. "Electronic countermeasure systems powered, armed, and responsive. Spoofing charges and proximity fusion flares loaded and armed."

As each report rolled in, Tabby diligently cross-checked the data provided by her crew, ensuring that every report was accurate and all systems were indeed operational. Her approach was not just a matter of protocol; it was a commitment to safety, one she took very seriously, for spaceflight was unforgiving.

"Sensor suite?" she asked.

"Online and powered, ma'am," came the prompt response from Chen. "All systems are showing as green." The boat's sensor arrays were ready to gather critical data from their surrounding environment.

"Validate radar, LIDAR, optical," Tabby instructed, seeking confirmation on the boat's various means of spatial and object detection.

"Validated, ma'am," came the affirmation from Chen.

"Thermal imaging array?" Tabby continued, covering every aspect of the boat's sensory capabilities. Once they were away from the carrier, there was no coming back for repairs, patches, or fixes. It was better to make certain that everything was in proper working order now.

"Online and functioning nominally," Chen said.

"Gravimetric detection systems?" she queried next, checking on the system designed to detect and analyze gravitational fields and their corresponding fluctuations, which could and frequently did indicate the presence of other ships or worse threats.

"Online and functioning nominally," Chen said.

Tabby turned her attention to the holographic tactical display (HTD). She ran a test on the sophisticated system, which was crucial for situational awareness, navigation, and the boat's normal operations. It would show them what was directly around the boat, allowing her to effectively fly the Typhoon.

Tabby was satisfied with its performance. "HTD functioning nominally."

Finally, she switched to the flight control systems. It was imperative to ensure that both the automated and manual backups were fully operational, as they were essential for the safe navigation and control of the boat.

"Control surfaces functioning," she reported, confirming that the craft's physical mechanisms for maneuvering and attitude control were in perfect working order for both in space and inside a planetary body's atmosphere. "Maneuvering thrusters powered and ready. Gravitic drives online and ready," she continued, verifying the boat's primary propulsion systems. The maneuvering thrusters, essential for fine-tuned movements and docking procedures, and the powerful gravitic drives, the heart of the boat's long-distance travel capabilities, were both fully operational and responsive. After the extensive maintenance the carrier's crew had done, she expected nothing less.

She then paused, her attention shifting to one of the boat's most advanced and crucial systems. Tabby performed a rapid self-diagnostic and then studied the result carefully. There could be no mistakes with this one.

"Warp bubble ready," she announced.

A brief silence fell over the cockpit as Tabby glanced over her screens, each one a portal to a different aspect of the boat's countless systems, all of them in their own way critical to operations. On the HTD, the countdown had commenced, a digital ticker steadily counting down. They were at four minutes and twenty-eight seconds to jump transition.

As the pre-launch atmosphere intensified with the ticking countdown, Tabby orchestrated the final checks with a calm demeanor.

"Cockpit check," she called out, her eyes methodically scanning the array of displays before her, as well as the manual controls ensuring everything was in order. "Pilot green," she confirmed after a heartbeat, indicating that all systems under her direct control were fully operational and ready.

"Weapons green," Sanchez reported back, signifying that the boat's arsenal was primed and ready for any contingency.

"EW and sensors green," Chen added, confirming the readiness of the electronic warfare systems and the sophisticated array of sensors critical for navigation and threat detection.

"Egress flight path is logged, and auto-clearance for launch is forthcoming," Tabby announced. "Emergency procedure review."

"Escape pods and ejection system armed," Chen reported promptly, indicating their readiness for a worst-case scenario.

"Fire suppression systems?" Tabby asked.

"Armed and ready," Chen stated.

"Verify medical kits and accessibility." Tabby leaned forward against her restraints to check her own kit, located strategically behind her feet. The restraints moved with her. "Verified."

"Verified," Sanchez echoed, having checked her own station.

"Verified," Chen added a moment later.

These final checks encapsulated the thoroughness necessary for space travel. Tabby had trained her crew well with an eye toward proficiency and professionalism. The rapid answers demonstrated not just their technical proficiency, but also their preparedness for the host of challenges they may face beyond the confines of the launch bay and in deep space.

Tabby sent a text message to the *Neptune* that her bird was ready for flight. She tapped the comm, activating the squadron channel, a conduit to her pilots and crew, all members in the 712th Nighthawks. It was her squadron, an experimental unit with a mix of spacecraft, and this was her first deployment with them. With the exception of herself and her executive officer, it was the first time her people had ever been on a space carrier.

Her squadron was only a few months old and was designated to transfer to a light carrier, the *Furious*, that had just finished her trials and would soon be arriving at Midway Station. Tabby was excited, for months of work were finally coming together.

"All Oscars report in readiness," she commanded.

"Oscar Two is green," came the first response, followed by, "Oscar Three is green," and so on. The reports streamed in methodically, a chorus of readiness from the squadron. All twelve craft—six Typhoon class assault boats, four Raptor class single-seat fighters, and two Hawk class three-seated torpedo bombers—echoed their prepared state. With her squadron, fleet was testing a new concept of combining different craft in a single squadron. The idea was to allow a single squadron multiple attack packages and operational profiles from space to atmospheric operations.

"Listen up, boys and girls," she transmitted, her voice steady over the comm. She checked the HTD countdown. They were now down to slightly more than four minutes till launch from the carrier. "We've got a little over two minutes till the *Neptune* transits into Midway, then a hot launch and slow cruise all the way to Midway Station. Get comfortable because it's a fifty-plus-hour journey. After that, we will have some downtime, a week or so until *Furious* arrives and we ship out for the far Rim. This will be your last chance at some quality rest and relaxation. Make sure it counts." They already knew this from the mission brief, but she'd learned it did not hurt to repeat things.

"Roger that, Tabby Cat," Lieutenant Cooper, her executive officer with the call sign Husky, responded in kind, like most pilots, his tone both relaxed and confident. "Ma'am, after all that training you ran us through on the way out, I plan on catching up on some sleep once we're away from this rust bucket and the autopilot's engaged. I hear that the civie side of Midway is something to be experienced before one dies, and I intend on fully experiencing all she has to offer, so I'm going to rest now. Once released you won't be seeing me till that week is up."

Knowing Husky as she did, Tabby had expected nothing less. She grinned at the thought of what most of her pilots and crew would do once they got stationside and had a week of freedom.

Heck, at twenty-eight, she wasn't much older than most of her pilots, who averaged around twenty-four years of age. Once, she'd likely have done the same, but now, as squadron comman-der, Fleet expected a certain decorum out of her. She would find her own entertainment, but it would be more restrained and, more importantly, private. She had worked too hard to get to where she was to ruin it with excess and indiscretion.

"If any of you knuckleheads get picked up by shore patrol or station security," Tabby warned, forcing sternness into her tone, "know that I won't be coming to spring your asses until my own leave is over. You will see the side of Midway most don't. Get me?"

There was a chorus of acknowledgments, along with some laughs.

An alarm began to beep, giving her a two-minute warning on the carrier jumping.

"I'm looking forward to seeing that Mothership they're building," Lieutenant Danton, call sign Buster, chimed in.

"That ship is supposed to revolutionize warfare. She doesn't even need jump points. Can you imagine that? I've seen pics and some of the specs Fleet released, but I want to see her with my own eyes." Even through the comm channel, his excitement was palpable.

"She's gonna change the war as we know it," Lieutenant Punkari, call sign Punkster, said. "No more fighting over control of jump points, but hit the enemy when and where you want. For a change we will be able to take the war to them."

"Imagine what it would be like to be stationed on her instead of a light carrier," Buster sent back.

"I think we're all looking forward to seeing that beast," Husky responded, "but me, first, my priority is finding a nice bar and some company of the female persuasion. It's been a long transit to Midway, too long, not to mention Mom worked us hard all the way here."

"Comms clear until after launch," Tabby instructed firmly as she watched the countdown. Her directive was a reminder of the need to minimize distractions. She knew that without intervention, the channel could quickly become cluttered with enthusiastic banter, which, while good for morale, could detract from the focus required in these crucial moments, especially when it came to launch.

At the same time, she resisted a grin. None of her pilots ever called her Skipper. It was either Cat, Tabby Cat, or Mom. The latter she really liked. It was a little informal, but then so too were nearly all squadron pilots. She preferred it that way, for that was how she'd come up.

"Once in flight, pilots come up with a shift rotation for watch. Stand by for launch. I will see you in the black."

Almost every craft in the squadron, designed for efficiency and functionality, was also equipped with a single bunk for long flights, offering a sparse but crucial respite for the crew. This feature was particularly important given the lengthy duration of some missions, where the opportunity to rest could mean the difference between sharp, effective decision-making and potentially hazardous fatigue.

Despite the availability of bunks, the chance to stretch out, and the convenience of a head—a toilet—as a bonus, much of the crew's time during the journey would be spent at their stations, especially the pilots. The single-seat fighters were the only craft that did not have a bunk, but their seats did recline some.

The nature of space travel required prolonged periods of seated vigilance. However, the burden was somewhat eased. The autopilot system would handle a significant portion of the navigational duties, allowing the pilots some degree of relaxation without compromising the mission's safety.

Tabby's gaze shifted to the countdown clock again. In these final moments before launch, she accessed the external cameras, her eyes drawn to the live feed displaying the exterior of her boat.

The view on her screen showed the launch tube extending in front of her Typhoon, a narrow corridor about a quarter of a kilometer long, leading to the vastness of open space. The magnetic launch coils, an integral part of the carrier's catapult mechanism, were visible, glowing with heat and energy that was ready for release.

Some thought the Typhoons ugly, but Tabby did not think so. Its sleek, angular hull, coupled with a dark matte finish, was not just visually striking, but also contributed significantly to the boat's stealth capabilities. The missile launch tubes, a key component of the boat's offensive arsenal, were integrated subtly into the body of the vessel, maintaining its streamlined profile. The maser turret, with its distinct and menacing appearance, was a clear statement of the boat's offensive firepower.

Additionally, the smaller quad laser turrets, strategically placed around the craft, offered maximum point defense coverage. These turrets were specifically designed to destroy incoming missiles. All of them but the maser cannon were currently retracted into the hull. The eyes and mouth painted on the nose made her boat look like a fearsome predator and completed the overall effect.

For Tabby, the boat was more than just a sophisticated machine; she was a source of pride and affection. Tabby's connection to the boat was palpable, a bond forged through countless hours of training, trusting in the hull and systems to keep her and her crew safe in the unforgiving realm of space. Heck, they'd even named the boat *Max*, which was short for maximum effort. Even though she wasn't sentient, for sentient AI was banned by Confederation law, *Max* was still a member of her crew.

As she cycled through the camera feeds, Tabby meticulously confirmed that the space around the Typhoon, both within and ahead of the launch tube, was clear of personnel. This final check was crucial to ensure a safe and unobstructed launch. The boat and her crew were as ready as they could be for the mission that lay ahead.

Suddenly, a claxon sounded in her ears, a piercing alert signaling the carrier's imminent transit through the jump point.

"Visors down. Seal yourselves in," Tabby ordered, setting into motion the final step in the pre-launch sequence. With practiced ease, she closed her own visor, initiating the automatic sealing and pressurization of her flight suit. The hiss of the mechanisms was a familiar sound, a harbinger of what was to come. As the suit pressurized, she felt the familiar sensation of her ears popping, a physical reminder of the transition to a self-contained environment.

Her gaze swept across the cockpit, visually confirming that Sanchez and Chen had followed suit. They had.

With a deliberate tabbing of the control to her right, Tabby initiated the depressurization of the cockpit atmosphere. The air was methodically siphoned away to holding tanks within the hull, creating a vacuum inside the cockpit. This procedure was a vital safety measure, ensuring that in the event of a hull breach during launch, the risk of explosive decompression was mitigated. The precaution of removing the cockpit's atmosphere, while temporarily uncomfortable, was a necessary adaptation to the realities of the dangerous environment in which they regularly operated.

Once clear of the carrier and safely on their way, the atmosphere would be restored. This would allow them to remove their helmets and gloves, providing a degree of comfort. However, for the moment, as they braced for launch, safety was paramount.

As the massive space carrier initiated the transit from the Nikura Star System to Midway, the moment of transition through the jump point was always a disconcerting experience, even for seasoned spacefarers like Tabby and her crew. In an instant, the gravity oscillated with a sickening intensity. This abrupt fluctuation in gravitational forces was an unavoidable aspect of faster-than-light travel, a brief but intense experience that often left even the most experienced feeling unsettled.

For Tabby, the sensation was all too familiar. Her stomach responded with its usual uncomfortable flip-flop, a visceral reaction that no amount of training or experience seemed to alleviate. It was why she had skipped breakfast, as had likely most of her squadron. Despite her extensive history of transits through jump points, the feeling of nausea and disorientation never became easier. It was a reminder of the unnaturalness of such rapid spatial displacement.

Amidst this brief physical turmoil, the power systems and displays in the cockpit flickered rapidly, a transient but expected disturbance caused by the jump. Then, just as quickly as they had faltered, they returned to normal. This rapid recovery was the signal that the jump had been successful.

Tabby let go a relieved breath, and as expected, the nausea rapidly fell away. The enigma of the jump points remained one of the great mysteries of human space exploration. They were essentially unnatural folds in the fabric of local space-time, massive gravity anomalies, apparently constructed by an unknown civilization or entity, their origins shrouded in mystery and speculation.

However, the significance of these jump points to humanity was unequivocal, revolutionizing space travel, providing a means of cheap, easy, and instantaneous access to the stars. The groundbreaking discovery on how to use them had effectively rendered the concept of generational ships, spacecraft designed for journeys spanning multiple generations, obsolete.

Human beings could now travel vast interstellar distances in a fraction of the time, making the exploration and colonization of distant star systems a feasible endeavor. That said, there were limitations. Each star system typically had at least two of these jump points, functioning as gateways to other locations farther out in the galaxy. Some systems, like Midway, endowed with three or more jump points, were known as junction systems. These were particularly valuable, serving as critical hubs in the network of interstellar travel.

These jump points facilitated point-to-point transport, each a portal to a specific destination, forming chains of star systems through which humanity had rapidly expanded. This characteristic made the jump points incredibly efficient but also limited, in the sense that they only ever led to one predetermined place. Still, it had opened up new frontiers, not to mention possibilities for humanity.

However, Tabby had often wondered if the jump point network was really a curse, for it had also introduced humanity to its greatest threat. They had bumped into another starfaring race, one that was bent on utter domination and conquest, one without mercy.

"Oscar Flight, prepare to launch," echoed through the comm, a clear signal that the time for departure had arrived. At the sound of these words, an all-too-familiar surge of adrenaline coursed through Tabby, causing her heart to race in anticipation. The restraints automatically tightened.

The exhilaration of a catapult launch, a blend of fear and excitement, was an experience that never dulled, no matter how many times she had been through it. The only thing that ever topped it was a hot landing on a carrier deck.

"Oscar Flight ready." Tabby's voice was steady despite the quickening of her pulse. She maintained her focus, keeping the exterior cameras trained forward. The lights in the launch tube, initially flashing red as a warning, suddenly switched to green. In that instant, with a shocking jolt, *Max* was propelled forward with incredible force, magnetically rocketing down the tube.

Despite the inertial dampeners, a system designed to mitigate the effects of such rapid acceleration, Tabby felt the unmistakable pressure and weight against her body as she was shoved almost violently back into her seat as the boat accelerated to launch speed.

Staring at the forward camera, she never tired of the view as the boat hurtled down the launch tube, the lights flashing by, one after another. This moment of intense acceleration was both thrilling and daunting, for if something went wrong, it was catastrophic.

With the magnetics involved, few survived a failed catapult launch.

Then, just as abruptly as it had begun, the boat burst into the blackness of space and out of the *Neptune*'s gravity field. Almost instantly, the inertial dampeners adjusted. The weight pressing her back into her seat fell off and once more she could breathe easily. The holographic display in front of her came to life, filling with data and visual icons, populating space around *Max* with contacts, dozens of them.

"We are free and clear to navigate, ma'am," Chen reported.

Tabby hesitated a moment, letting her boat get farther away from the *Neptune*'s gravity field, then her fingers deftly navigated the display, engaging the boat's powerful drives at twenty percent power. At the same time, she brought up the warp bubble, taking a segment of space-time with them. The propulsion system rumbled to life with a deep, resonant thrum that permeated the entire boat. As the drive coils spooled and came online, *Max* experienced a dramatic increase in acceleration, seamlessly transitioning from ten gravities to fifty.

As *Max* surged forward, Tabby's attention was keenly focused on the space ahead, ensuring a clear path. Through her displays she observed, as they were launched, one after another, the rest of her squadron maneuvering to follow. She counted the icons and then let go a breath. All had launched successfully. There had been no last-minute holds or problems.

"Mamma's little ducks," she said under her breath.

Meanwhile, the massive carrier that had launched them, now clear of the jump point and the gravitational wake it bled, had activated her own gravity drive, a glowing beacon of power on the holographic scope that flared brilliantly, along with the ship's icon and name. *Neptune* was beginning to accelerate and maneuver away, setting a course toward the next jump point located on the far side of the system.

Tabby manipulated the boat's external camera system for a closer look at the carrier, adjusting the focus and zooming in. Despite the rapidly increasing distance between them, the camera's powerful magnification brought details of *Neptune* into sharp relief, emphasizing her massive scale and intricate cigar-shape design as the system's yellow sunlight played against her white hull.

Neptune was the embodiment of human engineering prowess, and even from several hundred kilometers away, her formidable presence was undeniable. For a carrier, *Neptune* was older and on the smaller side, but still, Tabby found herself deeply impressed that something so large could have been built by humans.

Though she and her squadron were headed to Midway Station, *Neptune* had a different trajectory, destined to join the Third Fleet on the Outer Rim. In stark contrast to the carrier's size, the two Denver class destroyers, accompanying her as escorts, seemed almost tiny by comparison. These destroyers, following astern of *Neptune*, were formidable platforms on their own, but their scale was overshadowed by the carrier's sheer magnitude.

At long last, the Confederation had begun deploying its assets, preparing for the moment when the enemy resumed their push into human space. Like clockwork, every fifty years they came, advanced, gobbling up entire star systems, and then, after a year or two—sometimes more—they simply and inexplicably stopped. It had been a little more than forty-five years since the last Great Push had ended. Soon, the fight would be on again, and Tabby was resolved to be ready.

Shifting the camera once more, she directed her attention to the jump point's defense network, which consisted of five fixed asteroid fortress stations. They were strategically positioned around the jump point itself, just outside the gravitic wake.

These fortifications were massive hardened defensive structures, designed to protect the critical gateway from any potential threats attempting to force their way through. By comparison, they made even *Neptune* seem small.

When the enemy finally came again, if they reached Midway, fortresses like those on the Rimward jump points would be part of the frontline defense. Despite their significant size, the full magnification of the camera rendered them small against the backdrop of space.

"All Oscars," Tabby transmitted, returning her attention to the HTD. "Fall in on my wing, delta formation."

Tabby shifted her gaze back to the HTD and watched her squadron, each craft accelerating and maneuvering with practiced precision, falling into their designated positions with seamless coordination. Over the last few months, she had worked them hard, almost too hard, and it showed. She felt a stirring of pride within her chest.

Tabby opened a comm channel to the carrier.

"*Neptune*, Oscar Flight Lead," she said, her voice carrying a tone of gratitude. "Thanks for the ride."

"Our pleasure. Safe journeys, Oscar Flight. *Neptune* out," came the response, a final farewell as the carrier continued on her own path.

Tabby noted another squadron, a few dozen klicks behind them. Their formation was not as tight as hers, their pilots clearly not as proficient or disciplined. That squadron was escorting a pair of large shuttles, Condors, likely involved in transporting personnel to Midway Station and to the Twenty-First Fleet, which was based in this system.

The movement of these shuttles underscored the constant flow of personnel and resources essential to maintaining the operational capabilities of the Fleet. Like her squadron, they had simply hitched a ride on the carrier.

"We are tied into the system comm chain," Chen reported. "IFF handshake confirmed. We are noted and logged."

"Very good," Tabby acknowledged. "Download traffic patterns along our planned route. Feed them into navigation and the HTD."

"Yes, ma'am."

"Jump beacon in twelve hours and twenty-eight minutes," she stated, setting a clear timeline for the next phase of their mission, which would take them clear across the system to Midway Station, a sprawling Fleet facility Tabby had always wanted to see. More than two million people called the place home. The station was huge, with not only repair and maintenance but also construction yards for major Fleet assets like the new class Mothership. And yes, she too was more than interested in that ship.

Tabby keyed in the command to reintroduce the atmosphere into the cabin. As the cabin atmosphere normalized, the crew began to remove their helmets and gloves, Tabby included. It was the first step of settling into a long journey ahead.

Looking over the displays before her, Tabby leaned back into her seat, her heart still beating from the catapult launch. She had to resist grinning. The Navy paid her to fly, to do this and lead the Nighthawks. If they'd asked, she'd have done it for free.

FOUR

GARRETT

"Sir, what are you doing?"

Garrett had been on the brink of releasing a sigh of relief. Instead, it came out as one of frustration at yet another inevitable interruption. He lay sprawled under the access panel of the captain's station, his body contorted in the cramped space. He glanced back and saw a pair of ship boots standing just outside.

For over an hour, he had been working in this confined area, with his battered toolbox positioned strategically to his right. He had a variety of tools scattered next to the box. Alongside it was a portable light, its beam cutting through the dimness and illuminating his workspace.

"Sir, what are you doing?" the voice asked again.

"I'm almost done. I'll be out in just a moment," Garrett responded as he made the final connection, the last bit of work that would see this station go from an inoperable state to fully operable, or so he hoped. He paused to scrutinize his work, looking over each connection he'd made, tugging on more than one to make certain it was secure. He glanced at the small tablet he had propped up against the toolbox. It contained technical schematics and plans for the workstation. Using it, he double-checked his work. After a moment, he decided everything looked good.

Activating the station was the next step. He reached out with his mind, tapping into the neural implants embedded within his skull. These implants were his interface, his control over accessing the ship's more advanced systems. With a mental command, he initiated the station's activation sequence, his heart rate spiking in anticipation. As long as there were no faulty parts, or he'd not made a mistake during the final power assembly, it should work. The crucial word there was *should*.

There was a long moment of nothing...

A deep, resonant hum began to vibrate through the crawl space as the workstation over him powered to life for the first time. It was a sound that signified success. Garrett's held breath escaped him in a whoosh, morphing into a triumphant grin.

Under the harsh light of his lamp, he surveyed his work with a critical eye, meticulously examining each connection once more. His attention to detail was unwavering, leaving no stone unturned in his quest for perfection. As he visually scanned the neatly bundled array of wires and connectors, he reached for a tube of non-conducting bonding paste, pulling it from his toolkit.

There was a moment of hesitation before he applied the paste. He felt sorry for the poor bastard that one day, in the future, would have to undo the paste—that was, if the station was ever overhauled or upgraded. Garrett shrugged and then skillfully applied a measured amount of the paste around the last connection he had made, the power coupling. Although it was already firmly screwed into place, Garrett believed in taking every precaution. In his mind, the possibility of it coming loose, however remote, warranted this extra step. The paste, once set, would act as an additional safeguard, fortifying and hardening the connection.

Garrett's approach to his work, really any job, was methodical and deliberate. He took pride in his workmanship, the effort he put into things, adhering to a personal standard that went beyond what was generally expected.

To him, doing a job right wasn't just about meeting the basic requirements; it was about exceeding them, ensuring reliability and durability in the harsh environment of space and combat.

Garrett smoothly rolled onto his side, beginning the process of tidying up. One by one, he carefully picked up his tools, each finding its designated place in his kit. His movements were methodical, a practiced routine that spoke of countless hours spent working in maintenance and repair. The bonding paste was next. After that followed the tablet, which he powered down first. He then secured a small box of A26 screws, double-checking the lid to ensure none of the tiny, yet vital, components would escape.

As he stowed away the screws in his toolkit, a thought struck him, one that had wandered into his mind amidst his work. Humanity had made colossal strides in technology, expanding beyond her home solar system and venturing into the vast, uncharted realms of space, yet some things remained surprisingly unchanged.

The humble screw, a simple and ancient invention, still held its ground as an indispensable component in even the most advanced of spacefaring crafts. This blend of the old and the new spoke to the enduring nature of some of humanity's earliest and most important innovations.

With his tools and lamp secured, Garrett maneuvered and wriggled himself out from under the station. As he emerged, still lying on his back, his eyes met the towering figure of Lieutenant Commander Shaw. The officer's presence was marked by a distinct disapproving scowl as he gazed down upon Garrett.

"If you had wanted to become a grease monkey, you should

have followed the engineering and maintenance track, not command."

Garrett gave an amused grunt.

Standing just over six feet tall, Shaw cut an imposing figure, his presence commanding attention. His eyes were notably piercing, hinting at the keen mind underneath. Complementing this, his brown hair was kept close-cropped, adding a touch of neatness and discipline to his appearance.

Shaw's physique was a balance of fitness and leanness, almost verging on being lanky. His attire was the standard ship suit, functional and unadorned, save for his rank insignia prominently displayed on his shoulders and his last name neatly embroidered on the right breast. A patch on his right shoulder told all he was part of Construction Command.

Garrett wore a similar patch.

"Shaw," Garrett greeted, extending his hand upward. Shaw leaned forward and grasped the hand firmly. With a steady pull, he helped Garrett rise from the deck to his feet.

"Thank you."

"I am not sure I should say you're welcome." Shaw glanced at his hand, his expression morphing into one of visible distaste. He held the hand up for Garrett to see. The traces of grease, cooling gel, and bonding paste from Garrett's hand had transferred onto his.

"Here." Garrett reached for his utility belt, retrieving a clean rag. He tossed it over to Shaw, who caught it.

"This Mothership will not be built in a day. We have engineers and civilian techs that can do that kind of work," he said, nodding toward the captain's station while meticulously cleaning his hand with the rag. Shaw's remark carried a hint of rebuke, emphasizing the abundance of skilled personnel available for tasks like the one Garrett had just undertaken.

"We do?" Garrett asked in an overly innocent tone. "I had not noticed."

"There are over five thousand of them aboard at any one time, all hard at work. You can hardly walk down a corridor without bumping into one or a tech checking over newly installed systems."

Garrett absorbed Shaw's words. It wasn't the first time he and his acting first officer had had this conversation. It was an old argument. It had become more playful than anything else.

"The keywords in your sentence, I believe, are 'hard at work'," Garrett said. "I was free and so I did the work."

"Oh really?" Shaw's tone was laced with mild skepticism as he continued to wipe his hand with the rag. "And you think they wouldn't have addressed this issue if you had made it a priority, pushed a little harder?"

"They would have, but I got tired of waiting for them to get around to it," Garrett admitted frankly, his gaze sweeping across the bridge.

Circular in shape, the bridge was impressive in its size, far larger than any he had seen on other starships, even dreadnaughts, which he had not only worked on but helped finish.

Save for a few missing wall panels and some components still in the process of being installed, this Job's bridge was almost fully complete. The fact that the captain's station had remained partially assembled had offended his sense of orderliness.

The bridge of the ship, designed to be the nerve center of operations, housed a total of twelve stations strategically positioned around the captain's station, each serving a specific function critical to the vessel's performance. Along the walls were additional screens and standing-only stations that could be manned at need. At this juncture, only two of the stations were occupied: communications and engineering.

Communications was vital for maintaining contact with the shipyard, coordinating with the various teams involved in work around the ship, and ensuring that all necessary information flowed seamlessly to where it needed to go. Lieutenant

Liza Keeli was the comm officer currently assigned to the bridge.

Engineering, meanwhile, was a hub of activity, closely monitoring the ship's vital systems as they were brought online and repeatedly tested. The engineering tech, Lieutenant Allister McKay, who currently manned the station, was really the liaison between main engineering and the captain or the officer on watch.

The fact that the other stations remained unstaffed was not unusual given the ship's current status. Since she hadn't yet been officially commissioned, the full complement of crew required to properly operate the ship was not yet present, though with every passing day, more and more arrived.

This lean staffing was sufficient for the ship's present needs, which primarily revolved around finalizing construction, systems testing, and preparation for trials and eventual commissioning.

"Besides," Garrett added, "there are other things that are more important and really need to be wrapped up first, like finishing up the CIC. I would rather have them work on those items. I also got tired of staring at a screen and reading reports, so a little hands-on was needed."

"Admit it, you just like getting your hands dirty. Don't even think about denying that."

"Guilty as charged." In Garrett's mind, the completion of work on the captain's station was a significant milestone in the ship's journey toward full operational status. It was more a symbol than anything else, that this Job was finally, after so many long months, nearing completion.

With the ship's reactors and drives powered up and her hull securely sealed and pressurized, three weeks ago, the vessel had been carefully towed and maneuvered away from the dock, a major leap forward in her readiness and operational deployment. Almost every system on board was either fully functional or on the cusp of being so. Everything was being rigorously tested and certified for use.

The massive shipyard at Midway Station had not paused to celebrate this achievement of the first-ever Mothership going from the yard to the finishing slip. The yard hands and their Navy bosses had wasted no time in commencing their next ambitious project.

Almost as fast as Garrett's ship had been nudged and towed away from the construction dock, the keel of a new vessel, a sister ship to the one he was currently assigned, was being laid down. This rapid cycle of construction and deployment was a direct reflection of humanity's effort at readying themselves for the next Push and the fight to come.

"Don't you think the captain of a starship has better things to do than manual labor?" Shaw queried.

As Garrett took back the towel and started to wipe his own hands clean, he held Shaw's gaze for a prolonged moment. Garrett was acutely aware that his role as the captain of this starship was a temporary assignment, set to change immediately prior to her commissioning.

The permanent command would be passed to another, someone whose career hadn't been marred by the complexities of a troubled past. This reality, one he had reluctantly come to accept, ignited a pang of regret and a sense of loss within him. Shaw knew it as well, for he too had his own past and, like Garrett, had found an unlikely home in Construction Command. They both owed Admiral Gray a great deal.

Turning his attention back to the captain's station, now alive with the glow of functional screens, Garrett found a small measure of solace. When there was time later, he would run a full diagnostic on each and every system to ensure everything was working properly. He wanted to sit down and try it now, but he was filthy from the assembly process and did not wish to mar the pristine state of the workstation.

"I wanted to see this station fully operational and HTD active, and look, now it is, along with everything else," Garrett said, his voice carrying a mix of pride and wistfulness. "One less item cluttering up the punch list."

Garrett's hands-on approach, while generally unorthodox for someone of his rank, was driven by a deep-seated commitment to the ship and his mission in helping to prepare the Confederation for the Push. He had committed to that wholeheartedly. It was more than just a task for him; it was a personal goal to see the ship reach her full potential, even if he wouldn't be her commander for long.

"A job well done." Shaw clapped his hands together. "We're not scheduled for trials for another few weeks and Fleet is considering delaying them so Admiral Isabel can be on hand. Honestly, this could have waited."

"Why are you pestering me?" Garrett asked. His tone was teasing rather than annoyed. The absence of a first officer on the ship added to the unique dynamics of their interactions, with Shaw temporarily filling a gap in the command structure. "To what do I owe this honor, or should I say interruption?"

"You weren't answering your personal comm. I figured I would just find you. Sometimes that's easier than sending a rating to hunt you down."

"I turned it off. Fewer distractions that way. Fewer people, like you, pestering me. Besides, if something important had popped up, Keeli would have let me know."

"That I can understand." Shaw glanced at the comm officer, who was engrossed in a call with someone. They could hear her talking about a supply delivery of some sort that was inbound.

"So, you have your own headaches to manage. Why come all the way to the bridge? Weren't you in engineering working with Tam running tests on the Gripper drive and the main battery?"

Commander Sing La Tam was the ship's chief engineer. He

had actually been assigned to the project long before Garrett and knew more about the Mothership's unique drive and power systems than anyone else alive.

"I was," Shaw admitted. "We went through everything. The drive is in perfect working order, at least Tam says so. The main battery should fire as well. All we need to do is test the damn thing. That should be something to see."

Garrett agreed. Along with the ship's drive, the main battery was a new type of weapon, a game changer, one that research and development had come up with.

"So, I take it you have nothing to do other than bothering your captain? Want me to find you something?"

"I believe you have a dinner appointment." Shaw grinned at him. "Or did you forget?"

Garrett activated his implants and checked the time. He winced. Realization dawned on him as he faced Shaw once more. The underlying reason for his presence on the bridge was clear. The protocols of starship operation dictated a crucial requirement: Now that Job 22-01A had her reactors and drives fully operational, it was mandatory for a senior, command-level officer to be present on the bridge at all times. Currently, there were only five officers who fit that billing, Tam included.

This rule was a fundamental aspect of naval regulations, a measure put in place to ensure that there was always an experienced leader on hand to make critical decisions, oversee operations, and manage any emergent situations. With the ship's key systems now active, she had transitioned from being a mere construction project to a near fully functioning vessel, albeit one yet to complete her shakedown trials.

"I figured as much," Shaw said. "By my estimation, you have about an hour to clean up and still make it to Little Hill in time. Those reservations are hard to get. I'd hate for you to miss your reunion."

Garrett did not reply.

"I've taken the liberty of calling a launch. She's already docked and waiting at the admiral's port."

That meant the boat was only a few steps away, near the admiral's bridge, an area which wasn't anywhere near completion. It also reminded Garrett of another task on his long punch list, one which was a priority: to follow up with the yard hands. When it came time for trials, there were bound to be several admirals and dignitaries in attendance, and they'd want to be on the flag bridge, observing in relative comfort.

As Garrett's gaze returned to Shaw, a sense of appreciation washed over him. Since they had been thrown together, their professional relationship had evolved over the past year and a half, the intensive phase of finalizing the ship. The time had allowed them to collaborate closely, fostering a bond of friendship and teamwork between them. Garrett could not have accomplished as much as he had without Shaw.

"Good thinking." Garrett acknowledged Shaw's initiative with a brief nod before his attention drifted back to the captain's station. He gazed over his work, feeling a sense of accomplishment. His eyes lingered on the HTD display, now active and diligently tracking the space surrounding the ship, which was currently moored to a finishing slip. The HTD screen revealed a dynamic ballet of hundreds of contacts, automated supply drones, tugs, shuttles, and various construction craft of all types, all buzzing around the ship in a meticulously orchestrated dance of spacefaring logistics.

"Pleased with yourself, I take it?" Shaw inquired, a hint of amusement in his tone. The question was more than a casual remark; it was an acknowledgment and understanding of Garrett's tendency and need to involve himself in hands-on tasks throughout the ship.

Indeed, Garrett had made it a habit to engage in manual jobs several times a week. This was not just a break from the monotony of routine, but a necessary escape from the deluge of meetings, calls, problems, and reports that dominated much of his time as captain of this Job. These moments of physical work offered him a sense of grounding, a connection to the ship he had come to love that went beyond administrative duties.

With a sense of finality, Garrett bent down to close the access hatch, securing it firmly in place. He then gathered his toolkit and lamp, the latter of which he switched off with a quick tap.

"Might I suggest you get a move on?" Shaw prodded. "The clock is ticking."

"Very well."

As Garrett's eyes swept once more across the bridge, a complex mixture of emotions stirred within him. With its array of stations, the bridge was more than just a physical space; it was the brain of the starship, a place where, one day soon, critical decisions would be made and destinies shaped.

His gaze came to rest and lingered on the captain's station, a symbol of authority and responsibility sitting square in the center of it all. The longing in his heart was palpable, a deep-seated desire to command a starship. He allowed his hand to rest on the arm of the captain's couch. The touch was almost reverent, a physical connection to the dream that, even with Admiral Gray's support, was forever beyond his reach.

This moment of reflection was bittersweet. Garrett understood that, despite his qualifications and the dedication he had shown to his work, the command of this starship was not his to claim, not now, not ever. What had happened on *Repulse* had put the final nail in the coffin. It had been a bitter pill to swallow, but he had mostly come to accept it.

Yet, even in the face of this realization, Garrett's commitment to the ship and his work never wavered. He had poured his all into this job, making sure he left his mark on the vessel along with those that had come before it, all smaller ships. The bridge, with its humming screens and general background noise of soft notification pings from the various stations, the life it represented, stood as a reminder of what he had helped to create and the legacy he would leave behind, even if he would not be the one to guide her through the stars and the fight to come.

"You have the bridge while I am gone. The ship is yours," Garrett said, formally transferring command.

"Some ship," Shaw said, glancing around himself. "She's not even moved under her own power yet."

"She will, and soon." Garrett's brief comment was filled with confidence and, he had to admit, anticipation. After all the work they had put into her, he wanted to see that happen. He needed to see this ship move. He was certain it would affect him profoundly.

With these words lingering in the air, he made his way toward the captain's office and cabin, situated conveniently just off to the left side of the bridge. The location of the cabin was strategic, allowing for quick access to the command center in moments of need.

"Jim?" Shaw called after him.

Garrett stopped and turned to look back at Shaw.

"It's been several weeks since you took leave and left the ship. Make sure you enjoy yourself."

Garrett gave a nod and continued on.

As he approached, he noted the presence of an armed marine sentry standing guard by the cabin hatch. Another marine was stationed at the main bridge access hatch. Security was a paramount concern, especially given the advanced state of the ship. The presence of marines was a standard precaution, ensuring the safety and integrity of the ship's key areas.

This sentry guarding his office and cabin snapped to attention as Garrett neared, a sign of respect and protocol toward a senior officer. Garrett acknowledged the marine with a nod as he passed.

The hatch to his cabin, having recognized his implants, slid seamlessly open at his approach. Stepping through, he entered a space that served as a personal office and a sanctuary from the bustling activity of the bridge. As the hatch hissed closed behind him, it created a sudden and profound quiet, effectively sealing off the sounds of the bridge. He set the toolbox on the floor next to the hatch, where it would be easily retrieved for when he wanted it later. The only thing that could be heard were the air handlers hissing softly in the background.

Garrett's office, with its spartan furnishings, spoke to his no-nonsense approach to life, leadership, and work, his dedication to the job. The desk, accompanied by two chairs positioned before it, was for work and important discussions, rather than comfort or ostentation.

Prominently displayed on the walls were two plaques, each bearing significant personal and professional milestones. One was his Naval Academy graduation diploma, a verification of his academic and theoretical knowledge in his field. It was also a sign he had survived the crucible of the academy.

The other, even more precious to him, was his Master Certificate, officially certifying him for starship command. This plaque represented not just his expertise and skill, but also the trust and responsibility bestowed upon him to lead and make critical decisions.

One of the walls in the cabin, directly opposite the desk, featured a screen displaying a live camera view of Midway Station. The station, a sprawling hub of spacefaring activity, stretched off into the distance. Dozens of slips, each housing a ship, were in view. The closest was a dreadnaught.

Garrett knew that there were more than two dozen capital ships under construction at the station at any one time, with another dozen that had put in for varying degrees of maintenance and repair. Midway was the major Fleet base for the sector supporting the Confederation's efforts on the Rim.

The screen also showed hundreds of smaller craft and drones, buzzing around in a choreographed dance of logistics and maintenance. Despite the captivating view, Garrett paid it little attention.

His cabin, though a retreat from the immediate demands of the bridge, was not an escape from the responsibilities that came with the position he held. The desk bearing his personal tablet waited. As usual, there would be a multitude of reports, mail, and other business that needed tending.

At times, it seemed never-ending. The reports alone covered a wide range of topics, from staffing to operational updates, construction timelines and estimates, to strategic planning for the weeks ahead and much, much more. Nearly each required his attention and a response.

Even with personal time scheduled stationside, Garrett was acutely aware that a backlog of work would be waiting upon his return, several hours' worth, especially since he'd taken time out of his day to finish the assembly of the captain's station. He would pay for that with a late night filled with work.

There was a stack of mail piled neatly upon his desk. His orderly had placed it there. On top rested a secure bag, red in color, which meant the information within was classified and for his eyes only. There was only one person who sent him secure mail and that was Admiral Gray. It came all the way from Fleet HQ in the Core, a journey of several weeks by fast packet courier.

He considered opening the secure mail, then changed his mind. He did not have time for that. Besides, she likely wanted a detailed update and had specific questions that were for him alone. Her keen interest in his current assignment made this communication a priority. After he returned this evening, Garrett would tackle this task first. He well understood the importance of keeping the admiral, his mentor, informed, involved, and happy.

Beyond the immediate demands of his current posting, Garrett's contributions to the wider naval community were also calling for a measure of his attention. His current Job was the most difficult of his career and possibly the most important asset the Confederation would shortly have at its disposal. Ships like her might even change the course of the war. In fact, given time, he believed they would. In a matter of mere weeks, his would be the first that would deploy, with a second and third of the class following within a couple of years. Those two ships were being constructed in the Core.

Not only was he directly supervising the final construction effort for the Navy, but he had also been intimately involved in developing new tactics and utilization theories for employing such a revolutionary design as this Mothership.

Admiral Gray had insisted upon his involvement, along with Shaw's and Tam's, when it came to tactics. No one knew this ship and her operational capability better, for it was their sole focus. Over the last two years, while he'd worked finishing her, he had given the subject serious thought and corresponded with other strategists throughout the Confederation, including those at the War College, where staff officers and future admirals trained.

His latest paper on tactics, a deep dive on how to employ this ship as a raider on enemy fleet assets, had sparked significant interest, along with serious debate within the college, for it had challenged assumptions. Receiving correspondence from dozens of senior officers, including admirals who were involved in the project, was a clear indicator of the impact and value of his work.

Responding to these inquiries was more than a matter of professional courtesy; it was crucial for maintaining healthy relationships within the naval hierarchy, something Garrett had difficulty doing given his history. Some of the queries and responses to his paper had even been hostile. He would reply to those too, diplomatically, of course.

Garrett found himself in a situation familiar to many in high-demand roles: needing more time than was readily available. Balancing the immediate demands of his current position with the broader responsibilities of his career was a continuous challenge, one that required meticulous time management and prioritization. In short, it was a lot of work.

As he opened the next hatch, located behind his desk, with a hand, he entered an area that offered a stark contrast to the functional austerity of his office. The captain's cabin, his cabin, adorned with simulated wood-paneled walls, exuded a sense of spaciousness and comfort, a haven designed for relaxation and privacy. The only room on the ship that exceeded what he had were the admiral's quarters, and those were currently unoccupied. Once the ship passed her trials, that would change.

The cabin was thoughtfully laid out, with a single bed, which was neatly made and positioned against the right wall. The presence of a couch, an easy chair, and a small table added elements of hominess. The lighting was also a softer yellow hue.

A picture of a destroyer, the CNS *Valhalla*, majestically in orbit around a gas giant adorned one wall. She had been the first Job that he had captained and completed. Compared to what he was doing now, the *Valhalla* had been a simple project. At the time, she had been a real challenge. It had been a test, one which he had passed with flying colors. The painting had been a gift from Admiral Gray.

The table served a dual purpose, offering a space for meals or a place for work, despite the proximity of his desk. This flexibility in his living quarters allowed Garrett to manage his workload in a more relaxed setting when desired.

A notable luxury in Garrett's cabin was his private head, complete with a shower. This personal bathroom, a rarity on a ship where space was at a premium, highlighted the privileges accorded to his rank. He also had a small fridge that was stocked with drinks and snacks. Compared to the general crew accommodations, his quarters were almost decadent, providing a level of comfort and privacy unavailable to everyone else on board.

On the table sat a half-empty bottle of bourbon, accompanied by a single mug. The sight momentarily tempted Garrett, for it had been a long and hard day. A picture of his mother, father, and little sister also rested on the table. As he eyed them, he almost reached for the bottle—almost.

However, after a brief consideration, he decided against indulging in drink. There would be time later, at dinner. He had to get moving, for as Shaw had said, the clock was ticking. With that thought, Garrett turned away from the bottle and headed toward the shower to clean up.

FIVE

STROUD

Lieutenant Colonel Robert Taylor Stroud leaned back in his chair, eyes intently scanning the training and duty schedule on the screen before him, searching for any glaring mistakes or conflicts. The chair creaked loudly under his weight, a persistent annoyance that reminded him of the need for oiling its hinges.

He shifted in the chair, the joints creaking again. He fought off a scowl. The chair needed attending to, and soon. Otherwise, it had the capacity to drive him insane.

Stroud knew he could always submit a request to obtain a new chair, but that wasn't his way. He'd eventually get around to personally fixing it himself. In the Corps, you overcame obstacles and problems by improvising and adapting. Besides, fixing it would give him a sense of accomplishment. Just because something was old did not mean it was useless.

Putting the annoyance from his mind, he pondered over the details of the schedule and roster he'd just spent the last two hours developing, trying to think of anything he'd overlooked. His hand instinctively moved to rub his clean-shaven jaw as he reviewed it another time.

After a moment's more study, he allowed himself a satisfied nod of approval. "That should work nicely."

In the background, the soothing strains of classical jazz wafted through the air from hidden speakers set into the walls, creating a serene atmosphere in his otherwise stark office. The jazz calmed his aggressive nature.

Stroud's office was notably spartan, devoid of any real personal touches except for a solitary framed photograph that sat on a small round meeting table to the left of his desk. Two chairs flanked the table.

He traveled light and always had. As a marine in service to the Confederation, you learned not to pack more than was necessary, for there generally was not much room on deployment vessels. If you did, it inevitably became a problem, and as an officer in the Corps, there were plenty of problems to occupy your time as it was. Why add to the list?

His office was good-sized. It contained a desk and the table for meetings. At most, it could accommodate three people comfortably. Everything but the chair was new. There was a secure bag resting on the left side of his desk, along with a series of hard data chits and crystals that contained Corps business Command did not want transmitted over open connections. So some communications went the old-fashioned way, by courier or mail service.

An empty coffee mug rested on the desk as well. Stroud knew he drank too much coffee. It was one of his few vices. He liked to think the coffee was the reason he rarely ever got a full night's sleep. Deep down he knew the truth, the horrors he'd seen, the things he'd done in the name of service. They haunted his nights.

The picture on the table depicted a young girl standing on a beach in the middle of winter. Snow was on the ground and the wind was blowing, tugging at her long brown hair. She was looking at the camera with an infectious smile, clearly enjoying the moment. It was his daughter, Samantha, now seventeen, who lived with his ex-wife. They were both safe in the Core and far away from the enemy and what Stroud knew was about to happen in the next few years: the resumption of the war.

The photograph served as a silent reminder of a part of his life that remained distant yet deeply cherished. Though he and his ex-wife were no longer on speaking terms, his daughter was someone worth fighting for. It was one of the reasons he drove himself so hard. He took time to write and message at least once a week. Receiving a reply brightened his day.

Glancing at the photo, he felt a pang in his heart. He missed her. She was the one last connection to the civilian world. Even his parents and siblings were gone. All he had now, beyond her, was the Corps.

He'd captured that image on his last visit, during leave, before his unit had shipped out for Midway. That had been over twelve months ago, and now he was halfway across the galaxy, preparing to go to war against the worst enemy humanity had ever faced, one that was utterly merciless.

Three weeks ago, after he had made a long and hard transit all the way from the Core, Stroud had arrived at Midway Station and soon after boarded the Mothership with his battalion of marines. Since then, the frenetic pace of his duties had left him little time to settle in properly or even, for that matter, to catch his breath. Heck, he'd not even fully unpacked his bag in his quarters.

His battalion's arrival was a strategic move, one of many the Confederation was making in preparation for the resumption of fighting. Stroud had relieved the two marine companies that had been tasked with the security of the gargantuan vessel. As the project neared completion, the job had grown beyond them, and the major leading the two companies had only been too happy to hand over the responsibility.

This changeover marked the beginning of a new phase in

the ship's operational timeline, something he was fiercely proud to be part of. The Navy was staffing up the Mothership, and soon, through her, the Confederation would finally take the war to the enemy, something they had been unable to do. And Stroud would be there for that.

Another battalion was scheduled to arrive within the next month. With it would come their new general. Upon his arrival, the general would assume command of the ship's entire marine detachment, effectively superseding Stroud's current authority, which was fine with him. He would rather focus exclusively on his own battalion and, like the major, would gladly pass off the responsibility for the security of the ship.

The impending change in command was not just a mere transfer of responsibilities; it heralded the approach of the Mothership's commissioning and deployment, the culmination of years of work by hundreds of thousands. Stroud couldn't help but speculate about the challenges that awaited them once the ship was fully operational and deployed.

"Interesting times ahead," he mused, his thoughts tinged with a blend of excitement and, truth be told, apprehension for what was to come. No one in their right mind looked forward to combat, but Stroud was a pragmatist. He was focused on fighting for the survival of humanity, and that included his daughter. If they managed to stop and halt the Push, she and her descendants would live. If not, it was ultimately lights out for the human race, something Stroud would give his life to prevent.

Until the general arrived, he remained the acting commander of the security detachment and the marine contingent on the ship. That included the pilots and crew of the marine aviation wing, at least while they were on the ship. This role was not something he took lightly. His journey to this point in his career had been arduous and filled with challenges. Against all odds, he had climbed the ranks through sheer determination, hard work, and unwavering commitment to service.

Stroud had entered the Corps as an enlisted ranker, a basic rifleman. After twelve years of service and a promotion to gunnery sergeant, he found himself wanting more, a command of his own. So he took and passed the officer candidate test. Since then, he'd not looked back, and it had been one wild ride from second lieutenant to lieutenant colonel.

Aware of the weight of responsibility resting on his shoulders, he was determined not to falter. Complacency was an enemy he refused to entertain, let alone permit to creep up on him. He knew that maintaining discipline was imperative, not just for the success of the mission, but for the safety and well-being of everyone on board.

For Stroud, this was more than a duty; it was a personal mission to uphold the standards not only expected of him, but those he had set for himself throughout his military career. Some thought those standards unrealistic. Stroud did not.

The sharp rap at the hatch caused him to sit up and the chair to creak once more. The interruption was not unexpected. In fact, he had been anticipating it for the last half-hour.

"Come in," he responded, his voice resonating with authority. "The hatch's open."

Unlike the chair, the hatch hissed open quietly, and Major Carlos Ramirez stepped inside. His executive officer's stature was not imposing in terms of height, but his well-built physique spoke of strength, discipline, hardness, and a life dedicated to the Corps—very much like Stroud's.

Dressed in the standard gray shipboard fatigues, Ramirez presented a figure of professional military efficiency. His skin, a rich, warm tone, contrasted slightly with Stroud's lighter complexion. The major's hair, black and trimmed to a near razor shortness, added to his no-nonsense and hard-looking appearance. With a square jaw and hard brown eyes, there was a sense of seriousness about him that conveyed resoluteness and unyielding determination. That said, the man had a lighter side with a sharp sense of humor that Stroud had come to appreciate. He also wore a coveted academy graduation ring, something Stroud did not have.

"You called for me, sir?" Ramirez's voice was clear and direct. He had a slight Latin accent, a gift from his home world, New Madrid. In Stroud's experience, a lot of good marines came from that world, Ramirez included.

With a thought sent via his implants, Stroud deactivated the display on his desk, its light rapidly fading away. As he stood up, he felt stiff from sitting so long. He also killed the music with a thought. There was a certain gravitas in his demeanor as he stepped around the desk, indicating that the conversation to follow was of a more informal nature, or at least he intended it to begin that way.

"Carlos, let's go for a walk," Stroud proposed. Ramirez had been his second in command for the last year and a half. In that time, they had developed a close working relationship that went beyond the professional. They had become solid friends, partners, in making their battalion the best in the Corps. When alone and out of earshot of the ranks, they referred to one another by their first names.

The other marine officer stepped out of the way, backing up into the corridor. Stroud emerged from his office and glanced around. They were in the headquarters wing for his battalion, and the corridor, which was empty, was part of marine country. The hiss of the hatch sealing shut behind him punctuated the transition from the seclusion of his office to the broader domain he commanded, his real-world responsibilities.

The walls of the corridor directly outside his office bore the painting of an old-style cannon, his battalion's emblem. Emblazoned in large, stenciled white letters under the cannon was the unit's motto: PER IGNEM ET FERRUM, a Latin phrase translating to "Through Fire and Iron."

This motto was more than just words; it encapsulated the spirit and resilience of his command. Directly above the motto, the designation 213TH RECON BATTALION, FORTY-FIFTH MARINE ASSAULT DIVISION was prominently displayed in bold white letters.

The Fire and Iron Battalion, as it was known, boasted a rich and storied history going back more than two centuries to Old Earth. Having recently been reactivated, it carried the weight of its legacy into a new era, something Stroud was keen to uphold and honor.

The corridor was a long, straight stretch, flanked by hatches at intervals of about ten meters. It exuded a sense of order and cleanliness, characteristic of a military establishment. It was so early in the morning, the absence of personnel in the immediate vicinity lent a temporary calm to the area.

Along the corridor's length, more than twenty offices lined the walls, each serving as the workspace for his battalion's officers and senior non-commissioned officers. These offices were the administrative backbone of the battalion, where strategies were crafted, orders issued, and the day-to-day affairs of the unit managed.

"I finished my morning PT with E Company, had cleaned up, and was just about to grab some chow when I saw your message pop up," Ramirez said. "Wanna go grab some grub?"

Stroud was tempted but shook his head. "No. I'll eat later."

"What's up then, Bob?"

"Aside from the fact that I've spent entirely too much time at my desk this morning?" Stroud asked as he turned left and began walking down the corridor.

Ramirez fell into step beside him, the sound of their boots echoing hollowly off the walls and decking. "That's it?" he asked, a note of amusement in his voice. "You wanted some company for a walk, a stroll about the ship? I'm sure Sergeant Major Burns would have been happy to oblige. He's got such a sunny disposition, especially early in the morning. If you ask, I bet he'd even hold hands with you. I bet our people would love seeing that..."

Stroud grinned at his executive officer as they reached the end of the corridor, coming to a large, reinforced hatch. HANGAR BAY SIX was stenciled next to the hatch.

Using his implants, Stroud triggered the hatch, activating its opening sequence. With a soft hiss, the thick hatch slid slowly open, moving aside and revealing a hangar bay beyond. The bay was rectangular in shape, immense, a cavernous expanse stretching a hundred meters high and over four hundred in length, not to mention two hundred meters from side to side. The scale of it was awe-inspiring. Stroud had been seriously impressed when he'd first seen it, and this was just one of ten. It was the largest ship space he had ever seen, dwarfing even that of the largest space carriers and assault transports.

A wave of noise washed over them as Stroud led the way out into the bay. The large doors at either end stood closed. These led directly to launch tubes along the portside of the ship.

Along the walls, smaller hatches of various sizes peppered the structure, each one leading to vital spaces of the ship: storage facilities, maintenance areas, and offices, along with barracks and mess areas for additional marine battalions and crew. There were also extensive training centers designed specifically for marines, a luxury that even the largest assault transports did not have.

Throughout the bay and along the floor were painted warnings, markers, and lines for ships and crew to follow. Stroud paused for a moment, taking in the scene. This hangar was dedicated solely to marine operations and would soon house multiple squadrons of dropships, not to mention other craft that would help support ground and space operations that involved his people.

Despite the current assignment of only his battalion to the Mothership, the colossal dimensions of the ship were designed to accommodate a far larger force. There was enough space to house more than two full divisions, including support elements.

This bay was one of two specially engineered to support marine flight operations. In the coming weeks, Stroud knew the bay would witness a significant increase in activity as more and more crew were assigned to the ship. Even though the hallways and corridors seemed nearly empty now, Stroud could envision a time when things became quite crowded and tight. Then space and privacy would be at a premium and precious.

Shipping containers and crates were positioned throughout the space, alongside various pieces of construction and maintenance equipment. Several of the walls still had large sections of paneling missing as the yard dogs worked on the finishing touches.

The air around them was filled with the sound of machinery and the coordinated shouts of the crew who worked the deck. Two dropships off to the left commanded immediate attention. They were huge craft, hulking, each capable of holding an entire company or several vehicles, not to mention supplies.

Both dropships were in the process of being assembled. Crated up, they had arrived a week ago, shortly after Stroud and his men had come aboard. Under the watchful eye of a chief, deck crews swarmed around them both. He had been told the first would be completed and ready for a test flight within a week.

A platoon of marines jogged past in a tight formation, the rhythm of their boots echoing in unison against the bay's deck. Their gunnery sergeant, Davis Jefferson, ran alongside them, maintaining the pace and order.

"Fine morning for a run, sir." Jefferson saluted him on the run, an acknowledgment of respect and protocol in the military hierarchy.

"It is, Gunny," Stroud called back.

Then the platoon was by. Stroud watched them for a moment before turning his attention in the opposite direction. Farther along the bay, heading aft, a platoon was engaged in physical training. About a hundred meters away, under the eye of another gunnery sergeant, they were methodically performing sit-ups.

"Are you going to tell me why you called?" Ramirez asked. "Or are you going to make me guess?"

"I've revised the schedule for patrolling the ship. I want to step our patrols up," Stroud said with decisiveness. "You'll find the updated plans in your mailbox. Look them over and let me know if you see any problems. I've sent a copy to the sergeant major. I will speak with him on it later."

"I thought we were going to increase range and simulator time."

"Things change."

"We've been conducting regular patrols already," Ramirez pointed out. "What's prompting the increase in tempo?"

"It's mostly about familiarity, Carlos. Our people need to know this ship intimately, every centimeter of her. This is more than routine; it's about readiness. I had a frank discussion with the captain yesterday evening, discussing the latest intelligence briefings. He emphasized the urgency of getting everyone up to speed, especially with the brigadier's imminent arrival."

"The ship's captain?" Ramirez echoed, a hint of surprise in his voice.

Stroud affirmed with a nod and started making his way across the bay. Ramirez stayed with him.

"But he's just a Job captain. Why is he interfering with our business? His focus should be on riding the civilian yard dogs to get off their asses—finishing the ship up so she can be commissioned."

"That doesn't diminish his authority," Stroud replied firmly. "He's the one in charge now, effectively our commanding officer, and that means his directives are to be followed."

Ramirez's expression shifted to one of resignation. "For now, I guess. But as soon as she's commissioned and we get a permanent captain, he'll be replaced, just like all the other finishers. Everyone knows those like him are ones who can't make the grade for command. They're placeholders, nothing more."

Stroud paused, stopping, his stance reflecting a blend of discipline and patience. Turning, he met Ramirez's gaze squarely, a subtle but clear assertion of the chain of command. It was time to crack down on this sort of talk and thinking, to nip it in the bud before it spread. There was nothing worse and more insidious, in Stroud's opinion, than undermining the chain of command, no matter how little one respected their ultimate superior.

Stroud hardened his tone. "Major, until he is replaced, his orders stand. More importantly, we will both treat him with the utmost respect and deference. He's the skipper of the ship, the one making the calls. Construction Command would not have given him such an important assignment were he not competent. Trust me on this. I've been dealing with Captain Garrett since we arrived, and he knows what he's doing. We follow his commands, without question. Is that clear?"

"It is, sir," Ramirez acknowledged, signaling his readiness to comply and clearly understanding the shift in conversation from informal to formal.

Stroud did not mention that he had looked into the captain's eyes. He'd seen something he had only ever seen in a combat veteran's gaze. That had been the thousand-meter stare. There was steel in the man's backbone that had been born out of combat. It was something Stroud knew only too well himself.

"He's still a Job captain..."

"I don't want to hear any more of this kind of talk, especially from you or any of the other officers of the battalion," Stroud said firmly. "You pick up on it downstream and you quash it. Got that?"

"I do and I will," Ramirez said.

"Good. I don't need any unnecessary complications. And when the brigadier arrives, the last thing we want are issues or complaints about not only our behavior but our readiness. The captain suggested we up the tempo of our training and that's just what we're going to do."

"Yes, sir," Ramirez responded.

"There was also an attack last night in the civilian section of the station," Stroud added, "a bombing."

"Another terrorist attack? Who's claiming responsibility this time?"

"The Red Section," Stroud said.

"Those people are the worst. They think they can deal with the enemy by surrendering, that they will let humanity simply survive. Fucking idiots, the lot of them."

"Yeah." Stroud shifted his stance, putting his weight on his left foot. "Even though Construction Command does a fairly good job of screening everyone and everything coming aboard, we need to up our game as well, come up with a plan in the event someone gets it in their heads to mess with this ship. They might miss something. We can't afford that to happen, especially given the critical nature of this ship to the coming fight."

"She is a big target."

"She is," Stroud said, "and she's gotten a lot of attention in the press faxes."

Unlike the paper-based fax transmissions of the past, news faxes were digital, interactive reports that were transmitted directly to users' personal devices, public display screens, and even to augmented reality interfaces, via neural implants. They were also custom-tailored to the recipient's preferences, location, and even their schedule, ensuring that the news was not only relevant but also accessible when and where they preferred. At the same time, much of the news served as Confederation propaganda.

Ramirez gave a nod. Curiosity then clearly piqued his interest. "Do we have any word on who the brigadier will be?"

Stroud nodded as he continued walking, the rhythm of his steps steady and purposeful. "I was briefed yesterday evening by Midway's marine commandant. It's going to be Collins. He's on his way out on a transport from the Core with the Eightieth Heavy Battalion. Until they arrive, we are the ship's marine detachment and security."

Ramirez looked sharply at Stroud. "Collins, huh? He's known for being tough, a real hard-ass."

"That he is," Stroud confirmed, his voice carrying a note of respect for the brigadier's well-earned reputation as he began walking again. Though he had never met the man, Stroud was looking forward to working with him. Collins was widely respected in the Corps as not only a marine's marine but also a leader. "And that's precisely why our people need to be thoroughly familiar with every nook and cranny of this ship. When Collins arrives, I want him to see we've not been idle and our people have been kept busy, our edge sharpened."

"I understand, sir."

As they approached the heavy-duty hatch on the other side of the bay, Stroud mentally triggered it. The hatch slid open, revealing another chapter of the ship's bustling life. The broad corridor before them was teeming with marines. This was where his people were quartered. Their barracks, training centers, supply depots, and mess hall were all centralized.

Some marines were clad in powered armor, an embodiment

of automated strength, speed, and resilience, not to mention fire-power, while others were armed with lighter weapons and unpowered armor. Gear was strewn all over as nearly five hundred marines readied themselves for the day's training exercises and time at the range. The air was filled with noise and a sense of purpose and determination.

"A Company—on me. I say again, A Company on me!" A sergeant's voice farther down the corridor cut through the ambient noise and chatter, his commands sharp and clear. "A Company to range five."

He was directing and pointing a group of marines, who were preparing to head to the firing range, a routine yet crucial part of their regular training regimen. The scene was a microcosm of the disciplined life in the Corps, each marine a vital cog in the vast machinery of their collective mission.

Turning to face Ramirez, Stroud's expression was one of solemn resolve.

"Listen," he began, keeping his tone low, so only the two of them could hear, "I have a gut feeling about this deployment and what's to come. It isn't going to be a cake walk. We'll be the forefront of the next Push, the point of the spear, maybe sooner than we think. Our battalion was chosen for this mission because we're the best. The captain is right and that's why our training needs to be more rigorous than ever, especially when it comes to the ship. When Collins arrives, he won't find a single issue with what we've been doing. We're going to push our people harder than they've ever been pushed before and then some. That starts today."

The major nodded in understanding. The message was clear: they were not just preparing for their new commanding officer; they were readying themselves for the challenges that lay ahead in uncharted territories of space and war.

"This ship will be our home for the next five years, maybe longer, especially with the Push looming over the Confederation like an executioner," Stroud stated, underscoring the extended nature of their deployment.

Ramirez's response was a simple yet firm acknowledgment. "Yes, sir."

"We're already collaborating closely with the engineering team on damage control, firefighting, repair, rescue, and recovery." This aspect of their duty highlighted the marines' versatility and the importance of their integration with other departments while aboard ship. "Our patrol duties will be stepped up, particularly covering the ship's secure areas. Beyond our regular training, starting today, we're initiating enemy boarding drills."

"Repelling boarders?" Ramirez asked, surprise lacing his tone. "There have only ever been a handful of cases of that being attempted. With the amount of firepower this ship carries, will that even be possible?"

"I don't know. But I can tell you that when the enemy discovers her potential, they will want to capture the technology that makes this ship work. That means a boarding action. The captain thinks so too, and he wants us to guard against that. So, possible or not, we're going to train for it."

"Yes, sir." His reply was more than mere compliance; it was an understanding and acceptance of the necessity of such preparations. Stroud had decided what the battalion would do and that was the end of it. There was no arguing, for Ramirez was a professional.

"Companies A and B already have their orders," he informed Ramirez. "Starting at 1400, they'll be running drills focused on securing vital areas like the bridge and engineering from potential boarders. I need you to oversee these drills, assess their effectiveness, and identify areas for improvement. We will want staging positions near each critical system and area to post a standing ready reaction force. We also need to come up with different scenarios to train against."

"I will get right on that, sir," Ramirez responded.

"Oh, and make sure the training includes scenarios with both biological threats and technicals."

Ramirez's surprise was evident, for his eyebrows rose. "Technicals? You mean robots, war machines?"

"According to the latest intelligence from Command, there's a possibility the enemy might deploy technicals in the next engagement. An alert was sent with the latest intelligence dispatches. It's sitting on my desk if you want to read it."

"That's certainly interesting and I do want to read it. Where did Fleet get that intel from?"

"I don't know the specifics of their source and they don't say, but regardless, we need to be prepared to face such a threat."

Stroud cast a discerning eye over the marines in the corridor ahead. He loved the Corps. It was his life. He suddenly felt a powerful need to engage in a physical activity to help kick-start his day and shake off the rust, especially after he'd spent so much time at his desk.

"She's a moving station," Ramirez observed, his tone a mix of respect and awe for the massive vessel they were aboard as he too looked out on their marines readying themselves.

Stroud offered a nod of agreement but did not speak.

"Learning every centimeter of her will not be easy."

"That's why we're going to get a head start on it." Stroud looked over at the major. "Let's meet tonight after dinner. I'd like to get your perspective on the boarding drills, how they went, and how we can improve them. I will invite the sergeant major as well."

"Yes, sir. And where will you be, should I need you today?"

"I'll be at the firing range for the next couple of hours. After that, I think I will take a run, chow, and then find my office. There are several reports that I need to reply to and write."

"That's why you fill the big shoes," Ramirez said.

"I will see you tonight."

"Yes, sir."

With a sense of purpose, Stroud left Ramirez and strode toward the armory to procure a weapon and the necessary ammunition from the armorer. As he made his way down the corridor, his men respectfully moved aside and out of the way for him.

Stroud's mind was already on the range, visualizing the targets and the satisfying recoil of the rifle as it bucked his shoulder. It was more than just practice, a routine; this was a ritual that grounded him, a moment of focus and attention to detail, work toward perfection amidst the continual demands of command.

"In the Corps, everyone's a rifleman first," Stroud said to himself.

SIX

GARRETT

"I will be back in a few minutes to take your order," the waiter said and then retreated, moving to another table.

Leaning back into the luxurious embrace of the vintage-style, high-backed chair, crafted from genuine leather, Garrett set the menu down without looking at it and allowed himself a moment of indulgence. He took a leisurely sip of his straight-up bourbon, a rare treat from one of the Core worlds.

The rich, authentic flavor, made with real ingredients, was a stark contrast to the synthetic substitutes that were readily available on Midway Station. Closing his eyes, he enjoyed the feeling as the liquid danced on his tongue and ran down his throat, burning slightly as it went down.

In the opulent ambiance of this upscale restaurant, extravagance was the norm. Garrett's thoughts briefly wandered to the astronomical cost of such a simple pleasure. Every item on the menu boasted an origin from the Core worlds, guaranteeing authenticity but also ensuring a hefty price tag.

His choice was a luxury that had cost him dearly—more than a week's worth of energy ration allowance, or ERA, the Confederation's currency. This small act of rebellion against the mundane, synthetic routine was both a source of enjoyment and a silent protest, albeit an expensive one.

As he relished his drink, he couldn't help but reflect on the wider implications of such indulgences. The Core worlds, with their abundant resources and advanced technologies, produced goods of unparalleled quality, but out on Midway, cost made them unattainable for most who called the station home.

Around the small, elegantly set table, Garrett's friends from his academy days were gathered, each one an integral part of a reunion that felt almost serendipitous. After years of navigating their separate paths across the vast expanse of Confederation space, a twist of fate and the enigmatic workings of Fleet orders had reunited the old team, if only for a few hours.

His friends had not only been in Garrett's academy class but had also since carved their own distinguished paths within the Fleet, climbing the ranks to starship command. In Garrett's opinion, they were all exceptional.

Tonight, like Garrett, they wore their dress uniforms. To his left was Commander Julia Müller. She was as beautiful as she was smart, a dark-haired and sharp-eyed woman. She had scored in the top of their class at the academy.

Next to her sat Commander Eric Arrens. Pale with a thin nose and hawk-like eyes, originating from an orbital habitat in the Sol System, he held himself erect in his seat. There seemed to be a haunted look in his gaze that Garrett had not noticed the last time he'd seen the man. It was as if he were not quite enjoying himself.

Shifting his gaze around the table, Garrett's eyes fell on Lieutenant Commander Tina Martin. She was shorter than the rest of them, standing just over a hundred fifty-seven centimeters, but she was a firecracker and tough as they came. Her body was hardened from intense exercise. She had always been into physical fitness. After the academy, he and she had had an affair. It had been an intense and passionate thing and then it was not. Garrett still found himself somewhat confused about how and why it had ended, other than Fleet had soon issued orders taking them to near opposite ends of the Confederation.

Sitting to Garrett's immediate right was Captain Jason Grimes, affectionately nicknamed "Grim" by their group due to his perpetual stern expression. Jason's exterior hid a thoughtful side, along with a giving nature. Garrett wondered if the man's subordinates knew or suspected the real man behind the facade.

Garrett found the atmosphere charged with a blend of nostalgia and excitement as they found themselves sharing the same space once more. Their careers, dictated by the capricious will of Fleet Command, had taken them to distant corners of the Confederation, weaving through a tapestry of experiences that was as diverse as the stars themselves. Yet here they were, their journeys intersecting once again, as if guided by some unseen hand.

This gathering was more than just a dinner; it was a celebration, a commemoration of their unexpected reunion. The setting for this occasion was chosen with care—a fine-dining establishment known for its exquisite and, admittedly, exorbitantly priced cuisine. The cost was secondary to the opportunity of reliving old times and making new memories.

The exclusive establishment where this reunion was unfolding was known as Little Hill, a name that carried a certain prestige and symbolism within its walls. Perched prominently on the bulkhead wall outside the entry port, a sign declared with unapologetic boldness: FOR COMMAND STAFF ONLY. This was a clear statement to the restaurant's exclusivity, a place reserved for the elite echelons of the Fleet.

An attendant stood vigilantly to the right of the entry port, a symbol of the establishment's commitment to maintaining its exclusive clientele. This attendant was not merely a gatekeeper to check reservations, but a guardian of tradition, ensuring that only those of proper rank, or those fortunate enough to be in the company of a command-ranked officer, were permitted entry.

Little Hill was the brainchild of the legendary and now-deceased Admiral Hendricks, a figure revered and respected in Fleet history. The choice of the restaurant's name was intentional and deeply symbolic. It served as an aide-memoire, a gentle reminder to all who had achieved the prestigious rank of an active starship or station command position. This name spoke of a journey, a climb to the heights of leadership and responsibility within the Fleet. It was a nod to the hard-earned success of its patrons, an homage to their journey up the proverbial hill to reach the pinnacle of their careers. In this way, Little Hill was not just a place to dine; it was a testament to achievement and a celebration of the journey that led there.

At the dedication of Little Hill, Admiral Hendricks imparted words that would resonate through time and become the cornerstone of the restaurant's ethos. He said, "Command is a 'little hill' upon which we aspire, come to rest—however, it is best to remember the tumble to the bottom is not so very far."

To immortalize this wisdom, the admiral commissioned a bronze plaque and had it hung on the bulkhead wall just before the entrance. Over time, the plaque had acquired the dignified patina of age, its surface bearing witness to the years that had passed since its installation. It greeted every visitor with a silent reminder of the admiral's counsel.

Little Hill presented a striking contrast to the typical ambiance one would expect in a space station environment. Crossing its threshold was like journeying back through time, immersing oneself in a bygone era. The restaurant was meticulously stylized as an exact replica of an upscale English gentleman's society club from the 1880s, a period steeped in elegance and the sophistication of London's higher-end history.

Every aspect of Little Hill was curated to evoke the rich, refined atmosphere of that distinguished era. The walls of the restaurant were adorned with genuine oak paneling, imparting a warmth and grandeur reminiscent of those historic clubs. Lining these walls, shelves were filled with thousands of books.

The original Persian rugs that once graced the floor had long since worn out, but their replacements were skillfully simulated, maintaining the aesthetic integrity of the space. Wooden tables and leather chairs dotted the dining area, their classic design and quality craftsmanship harking back to the nineteenth century. The tables were set with silver cutlery and fine china, each piece carefully selected to complement the historical theme.

To step into Little Hill was to enter a carefully constructed scene of the past. It was evident to any patron that attention had been lavished on even the smallest detail, creating an immersive experience that transcended time and space. The restaurant was not merely a place to dine; it was a portal to a different age, an homage to a style and elegance that stood in contrast to the utilitarian nature of life on a space station. This meticulous recreation of a nineteenth-century English gentleman's club served as a unique escape, a brief respite from the realities of life in the vastness of space.

Little Hill, in its meticulous recreation of an era long past, offered more than just a dining experience for those accustomed to the confines of starship or station environments. It provided a poignant taste or, rather, a tangible reminder of the world they had left behind. For many officers this establishment repre-sented a connection to the Earthly origins and traditions that underpinned their service in space. It was a reminder of the heritage and values they were upholding, a tether to the past that gave context and meaning to their present endeavors in the vast expanse of the universe.

The restaurant's capacity was notably modest, especially when compared to the average restaurant on Midway Station, which could seat over a thousand patrons. With its limitation to no more than fifteen tables, Little Hill offered an experience that was rare and sought-after: a sense of intimacy and privacy. In a world where space was a commodity and the hustle of station life was ever-present, the small, secluded environment was a cherished oasis.

"Tina, this is your first stop at Midway, right?" Jason asked as he glanced up from the menu, looking over at her. "You've held command of your ship for what, six months?

"It is," she replied. "And yes, it's been about that long."

"Have you donated your book yet?" Jason asked.

Over the years, Little Hill had evolved to become more than just a replication of historical luxury; it had started to foster its own unique traditions. One such tradition, steeped in symbolism and honor, involved the "authentic" books that adorned the bookcases in the establishment's "smoking room"— a space designed to replicate the leisurely, contemplative atmosphere of its terrestrial counterpart.

She grinned infectiously. "Just this morning. I had breakfast here with my first officer. It was quite good."

"Big spender," Julia teased as she took a sip from her coffee. Garrett eyed her choice of drink. It informed him she would soon be on duty. Jason too.

"Since this is my first stop at Midway, I figured I'd make it count. I got my holo picture taken with the maître d' and it's already up in my office." Tina's grin only grew. "She told me the book would be in the station's library before day's end. Unfortunately, they no longer have room within the restaurant itself. Do you know that they've taken over an entire warehouse in Section Two for the library? There are that many books."

"I suppose nearly two hundred years of donations by commanding officers would do that," Jason said. "It's become a rite of passage. Still, it is the act that means something."

"It does," Tina said, "especially if you make a name for yourself. Everyone wants to check out your book, to get an insight into the person."

"Speaking of which, what was your choice of book?" Eric asked curiously as he took another sip from his own coffee. "What did you donate to Midway's library?"

"*The March Up*, by Xenophon."

Jason gave a slow nod. "If I recall, that was required reading at the academy. It was written by a Greek general, wasn't it?"

"It was," Tina confirmed.

"The book was about that army that marched to a Persian civil war," Jason said with a far-off look, as if recalling the details. "When they got there, they found their side had lost and they were surrounded by enemies."

"Good memory," Tina said.

"Why that one?" Eric asked. "Why choose such an obscure book?"

"I always thought it a fascinating story," Tina admitted with a slight shrug of her shoulders. "Xenophon leading a retreat back to Greece, being hounded every step of the way by an enemy army—everything they saw along the way, which he chronicled. I guess you could say his small world was broadened. Mine was too—once I joined Fleet and took to the stars. It seemed appropriate."

"Interesting," Jason said.

The practice of donating and signing books, and the resulting assembly of literature at the station's library, fostered a sense of continuity and community among the officers of the Fleet. It was a tradition that went beyond the mere act of reading, becoming a symbolic bridge between generations, a way for officers to leave a part of themselves behind, a small legacy, as they journeyed through the vast expanse of space.

As Garrett's gaze swept around the table, taking in the familiar faces of his academy mates grown older, wiser, and harder by the demands of command, a bittersweet realization dawned upon him. The unpredictable nature of their lives in the Fleet, with its myriad assignments and distant postings, meant that gatherings like this were rare treasures. He understood, with a tinge of melancholy, that it might be a long time before such an opportunity arose again, if it ever did.

Garrett felt a profound sense of gratitude for this rare assembly of old friends. Each person at the table represented a unique thread in the tapestry of his life, and their collective journey through the rigors of the academy and beyond had forged bonds that were as strong as they were rare, especially for him.

Julia's light touch on his forearm gently pulled Garrett back from his thoughts, reconnecting him with the here and now. Her words, delivered with a faint, knowing smile, acknowledged his momentary drift into memories. "Jim... so distant and yet we're so close."

Garrett's response was instinctive and heartfelt. Lifting his glass in a symbolic gesture, he acknowledged his friends with genuine appreciation.

"Just enjoying the moment," he replied, his voice tinged with a mix of nostalgia and contentment before taking a sip of his drink. "It's been far too long since we've done this, since we've come together."

"Always the sappy one," Jason commented wryly while sipping his coffee.

The black coffee, served in a "real" glass, complete with a handle, was yet another touch of authenticity that Little Hill prided itself on, a small but significant reminder of the world they had left behind.

Tina, with her characteristic enthusiasm, raised her coffee in a toast.

"To Jim!" she declared. "The tough one. Jim was the glue that held us together during those difficult years at the academy, especially during the crucible. Without him, I don't know if I would have survived, let alone made it."

"Our final year was a bitch," Jason said. "Tina's right. To Jim!"

"To Jim," echoed the others, their voices blending in a unified tribute.

Garrett felt a mix of pride and embarrassment at being the center of attention. A few of the other officers at the nearest tables looked around curiously at the commotion. Garrett acknowledged the toast with a modest nod.

"Jim, the toughest miscreant of our bunch," Tina called. "That the Navy threw us together so long ago was a rare treasure, one at the time we didn't appreciate until the ordeal was over." Her eyes seemed to sparkle as she gazed upon him.

Was there something still there, a hint of interest? An invitation?

"To Jim," Tina said.

"To Jim!" they echoed once more.

Tearing his gaze from Tina, he glanced around the table and then drank a sip. Garrett found himself reflecting on the irony of their perception. To him, each of his friends had been a pillar of strength during their academy years, offering support and camaraderie that had helped him navigate challenging times. That they saw him as the cohesive force that held them together, their leader, was proof of the subjective nature of perception and memory. At least, he thought so.

"You must get yourself a ship, Jim, beyond a Job." Jest laced Tina's words. "Command and some time in deep space might do the opposite and soften that hardened exterior you've built up around yourself."

Garrett's internal reaction to Tina's playful jab was a mix of understanding and concealed discomfort. He had long mastered the art of taking such comments in stride, recognizing the fine line between friendly banter and deeper, often unspoken sentiments. His experience had taught him the importance of maintaining composure, of not allowing offhand remarks, whether from friends or adversaries, to affect him too deeply.

Despite the lighthearted nature of the exchange, the comment touched on a sensitive aspect of his career trajectory. In the informal hierarchy of the Fleet, a "Job captain," despite holding the rank and privileges that came with it, didn't carry the same prestige as a captain or commander at the helm of a commissioned starship. This distinction, though unofficial, was keenly felt within their professional circles.

The irony of his situation was not lost on Garrett. Among his friends at the table, he was the first to have been promoted to the rank of captain and therefore was technically the senior ranked officer among them. Yet, despite this achievement, his status as a Job captain seemed to overshadow the actual authority his rank conferred. This perception among his peers, that his rank was somehow less consequential, was a source of silent frustration.

"I hear that you will be getting a command after your current assignment," Jason said, speaking up. "At least, that is the word in circles around the station, a reward for the work you've done on your latest Job."

Garrett nodded. Given Jason's track record with scuttlebutt, which often proved to be unreliable, Garrett wasn't quick to embrace this rumor. His friend's attempt at encouragement, though well intentioned, did little to dispel his realistic, clear-eyed assessment of his career prospects.

Commanding his own starship was a dream that, over time, had become more distant, overshadowed by the trajectory his career had taken. He suspected that most of his friends at the table, with the exception of Tina, were acutely aware of this likelihood too, their understanding of Fleet dynamics making them all too familiar with the challenges he faced.

His gaze drifted to Tina and he felt a hunger for her, something he'd thought he'd long gotten over. After she had broken off their relationship, they had not talked much over the years, only exchanging the occasional note, little more.

Heck, it had been thirteen years since he'd last seen her, and she was terribly beautiful to his eyes. Sure, there were a few more lines around her eyes, but he felt a stirring within him, a longing he'd not known he'd been missing. After all these years... Garrett shoved such thinking aside. What had happened was done and gone. His thoughts shifted back to his career.

The truth was, he had found a different kind of recognition within Construction Command than he ever did in Fleet Command. Over the years, he had carved a niche for himself, where his skills, hard work, and dedication were highly valued, prized even. His performance had not gone unnoticed, and it was clear to him that Construction Command was reluctant to part with his services, especially Admiral Gray. In many ways, his success in this domain had become both a blessing and a curse.

Garrett's long tenure as a Job captain had allowed him to develop a unique skill set, making him indispensable in his current role but paradoxically hindering his advancement to a traditional command position. This irony was not lost on him; his diligence and hard work had inadvertently become barriers to the very goal he once aspired to achieve. Coupled with the long shadow cast by the incident off Antares Station, Garrett found himself in a complex professional limbo, one of his own making.

After the Navy board, Fleet, or more precisely Admiral Omaga, had swept that matter mostly under the rug. There were plenty of rumors concerning what had occurred, but few knew the truth.

"Julia," Garrett said, hoping his friends would take the subtle hint. "You're pushing back in, what, four hours?"

"Believe it or not, *Cerberus* is headed to the Outer Rim and the front line," she revealed with an energy that was almost contagious, "ultimately the Dows System, to join up with Third Fleet."

Those around the table shifted.

"Admiral Joseph Bryer, 'Fighting Joe'," Garrett remarked, referencing the commander of Third Fleet. His words carried a tone of respect and a hint of pride for his friend's achievement. He offered her a nod of congratulation. "Well done. Only the best of the best are sent to serve under the admiral. A successful tour with the Third, coupled with a recommendation from the good admiral, could easily make your career."

Garrett did not mention that Julia would be on the front line when the fighting resumed and the enemy came at them once more. When that happened, it would be brutal and unforgiving. There was a strong chance the Third would be badly mauled within the first hours of engaging with the enemy.

"Don't I know it," Julia said. "In transit, we're to escort a convoy bound for the Outer Rim. We're going to meet up with them in Ryollo, then take them to Mysana Station. Escort duty will take us a few weeks out of the way, but you don't see me complaining, especially considering where I'm headed."

"To Julia!" Garrett raised his bourbon in toast.

"Julia!" they replied.

"Congratulations." Eric leaned over and thumped her shoulder heartily. Garrett detected what he thought was a touch of envy in Eric's tone. Wrapped up in her own excitement, Julia apparently failed to notice. "I would love to have an opportunity to head for the Outer Rim. Instead, I've been stuck on permanent convoy duty, following and shepherding slow-assed 'merchies' across the space lanes from the edge of the Core all the way to Midway and then back again. Rinse and repeat has been the story of my life for the last thirteen months. I can only imagine what you will see and find out on the Rim. It's called the Wild West for a reason, you know."

"At least you've fired your weapons in anger," Julia replied, suddenly turning it around on him. "*Cerberus* has not yet been blooded."

Eric shifted in his seat. He forced a smile. "Not much effort dealing with the occasional pirate."

The mood around the table subtly shifted with Eric's response, marked by a noticeable change in his demeanor. The earlier traces of envy and excitement had vanished, replaced by a quiet, almost introspective tone. Garrett couldn't help but notice how Eric's expression had turned guarded, his body language hinting at a slight withdrawal into himself.

"I was wondering why *Chimera* was in for repairs," Jason remarked, his words sounding more like a statement than a question as he took another sip from his coffee. "What happened?"

"It was nothing really—just a bit of nothing. A scrap with pirates, is all."

"As I hear it, Rear Admiral Bart and Admiral Isabel put you up for a commendation," Julia stated.

Garrett's surprise upon learning about the *Chimera*'s recent encounter was a reflection of how engrossed he had been in his own duties. His inability to keep up with the *Fleet Gazette*, a practice almost sacrosanct among naval officers, was a consequence of the demanding nature of his current job.

The *Fleet Gazette* served as a vital source of information, connecting officers with the broader happenings within the Fleet, and keeping abreast of such news was considered essential for staying informed about peers and the dynamics of Fleet operations.

"This morning's edition of the *Gazette*," Julia said, "has it *Chimera*'s jump drive was damaged during the engagement. Estimates put your ship in the class two structural damage range."

This revelation brought into sharp focus the severity of the situation Eric had downplayed. Those around the table sat up, with Tina leaning forward. Class two damage was significant, indicating that the ship had endured intense enemy fire, sufficient to penetrate her energy shields, breach the armor, and expose parts of the inner hull to the vacuum of space. Garrett knew only too well what that was like, for *Repulse* had been a wreck after the battle.

Jason eyed his friend closely. "Sounds like you were a bit more involved than 'nothing really'."

Eric remained silent. Garrett thought he looked a bit ashamed and embarrassed at the attention.

"Come on, man," Julia urged. "Tell your friends how you not only engaged but took on not one, but two Marauder class raiders in a bid to save an isolated freighter who had been tackled and was in the process of being boarded."

"I lost seventeen of my crew," Eric managed quietly, "with another forty-five injured, most of whom will not return to service. They will be discharged as permanently disabled."

The table fell silent for a moment before Julia leaned forward. "He saved the freighter, which was carrying passengers as well as freight, and rescued more than one hundred souls who would have likely been killed or, worse, ultimately sold as slaves on the black market." Julia glanced around the table, a proud and fierce look in her gaze. "Courtesy of a friend, I got my hands on the preliminary after-action report. In a gutsy move, *Chimera* caught both raiders by surprise, disabled them, and in the process, Eric here"—she jerked a thumb in his direction—"took over two hundred and forty prisoners, along with both hulls of the pirate ships. One of the raiders was later identified by Fleet intel as having participated in over twelve separate attacks, responsible for the deaths and disappearance of more than nine hundred civilians." She turned to Eric with fire in her eyes. "I would say that more than balances things out, not to mention how many were saved from future attacks."

"Sounds like a good day," Tina put in, placing a comforting hand upon Eric's arm.

"It was the first time I lost people under my command," Eric admitted with a weary sigh as he leaned back into his chair, almost collapsing into it. He took a long pull on his drink. It was clear he had been beating himself up over what had happened and if he could have done things differently. Garrett supposed he wasn't getting much sleep either. "I did not find it to be a pleasant experience."

"You did good," Garrett told Eric. "Real good. A win is a win, no matter how painful."

Looking far from convinced, Eric nodded in reply and took another pull on his drink, which, like Garrett's, was alcoholic.

"He's been ordered to take his ship to the Outer Core for repairs," Julia added.

"When do you put back to space?" Garrett asked.

"Tomorrow, actually," Eric reported. "Fleet has done a quick patch job on the jump drive and main propulsion. We can pull eighty percent power and have been ordered to join an evacuation convoy that's coming in from the Outer Rim and is headed toward the Core systems for resettlement."

As the Confederation prepared for the Push and what was to come, with every passing day more worlds were being evacuated. Millions of people were being displaced. It was heartbreaking, but it was either that or leave them to the tender mercies of the enemy. As far as Garrett knew, the enemy were bent on extermination of the human race.

"We will be breaking off at New Berlin," Eric continued, "where *Chimera* will undergo not only extensive repairs but also a complete refit and upgrade. She's an old ship, but a good one, solid. She brought me home." Eric looked down at his drink as if he wanted to dive into it.

Garrett could understand why. The refit and upgrade would take time, meaning that his friend would likely be reassigned to a new ship, especially since he had combat experience. A captain who had been under fire, distinguished himself, and taken two hulls as prizes was someone who was unlikely to sit on the sidelines for long.

"Well..." Tina stepped in, breaking the uneasy moment, "all I can say is life on a light frigate is much less exciting."

"And how is the *Valkyrie* these days?" Garrett asked, looking to steer the conversation in a new direction, as it was clear to all at the table Eric was decidedly uncomfortable discussing his recent action further.

"*Valkyrie* is doing quite well." Tina made a sour face as she said this. "Despite being stuck on permanent courier and VIP duty. We're pushing back in eighteen hours to head Coreward," she added with a heavy sigh. "I am afraid yet again we are tasked with VIP duty. The last one I hauled, a low-level politico on some fact-finding mission, was a pretentious prick. Her only concern, which she voiced at every conceivable opportunity, was the inadequate size of her quarters and the dismal food that Cook kept dishing out. Only when I showed her the size of my own quarters, which are smaller than the VIP quarters, and gave her a personal tour did she cease most of her incessant whining."

There was some chuckling and amusement around the table.

"Somewhere between seventy-four to seventy-six hours from now, the *Valkyrie* should be 'jump drive active,' with Midway all but a memory. Our ultimate destination this time is the ocean world of Sera."

"Sera? Really?" Julia asked. "I've always wanted to go there and take a cruise or spend some time on the beach."

"The comforts of the Core," Tina said. "We will be on station long enough to get a few days of planetside R and R, some fun in the sun, which will be a nice break from the routine. I'll send you pictures."

"You're evil," Julia said. "Have I ever told you that?"

"At least you get to leave the system and stretch your legs a bit," Jason spoke up. "Garrison duty is boring. With such a strong Fleet presence here, there's not much going on, other than continual training and the occasional patrol, and those are far from exciting."

Commanding the battlecruiser *Achilles*, Jason was part of the Twenty-First Fleet. Positioned at Midway and the backbone of the Fleet out along this region of the Rim, the role of the Twenty-First was to provide depth and backup for those fleets and other elements which were posted forward.

Jason had been the commanding officer of *Achilles* for the past four years. During that time, Garrett had finished three separate Jobs. He knew that Jason's current assignment would be soon coming to an end, as it was very rare to command a single ship for more than five years. His friend would most likely receive a promotion and another command, probably a pocket battleship. He might even be sent to the Staff College.

"Seems you two are kind of stuck here—together." Julia smirked, glancing between Garrett and Jason. "I thought I noticed a certain stench when I came aboard station. Perhaps you both should bathe more."

"Seems we are both stuck," Jason acknowledged, managing to look a tad bit forlorn as he held up his drink in salute to Garrett before addressing the table. "Jim and I manage to dine together whenever I happen to make it stationside, which isn't very often. Our dinners provide me a good excuse to obtain an unabridged inside track on his latest Job. You might call this a perk of our friendship and side effect of being stuck in the ass end of nowhere together."

"Well?" Julia asked, the focus shifting over to Garrett. "Have at it. Any fool on final approach to Midway could hardly miss that monstrosity you call a Job."

Garrett let go a breath. He had known the subject would

eventually come up no matter how much he had attempted to remain silent on it. Almost everyone whom he met in a social setting, upon discovering who he was, wanted to know more about his current Job. There were some who even considered him a local celebrity. Whenever stationside—which was a rare event, as his duties kept him quite busy—Garrett could count on being stopped at least a half dozen times by the curious, mostly fellow officers.

"Come on," Tina demanded, "out with it. Spill the beans."

"She's coming along quite well," Garrett began slowly, hoping they would accept a quick summary. "At the minimum, we have another nine months of work ahead of us. General construction is complete. Most major systems are installed and operational. We're in the process of putting the finishing touches on things. Two days ago, we test-fired the engines, drives, and maneuvering thrusters in preparation for trials. I'm pleased to report everything functioned better than anticipated. If I wanted," he chuckled, "we could even maneuver under our own power and take her out for an unauthorized spin."

"I bet that would get Admiral Isabel's attention," Jason said.

"When are trials due to begin?" Julia asked.

"Within the next two to three months, though I bet for the most part we could pass most of them today. Fleet has been talking about delaying them, but after they occur—well, at that point I will be handing her off to her new captain and remaining on for a few weeks to help with the transition of command."

"That's fantastic news," Tina breathed excitedly. "It must be a tremendous experience to be responsible for the completion of a ship of such revolutionary design and concept. I can't imagine what it must have been like to watch her go from near skeleton to complete starship."

"Like watching a baby grow to adulthood," Garrett said with a chuckle.

"She's your baby, Jim," Tina said, "the largest starship ever constructed. You know you're doing something historic here? You realize that, right? Tell me you get it?"

"Feels more draining than historic," Garrett said with a slight grin. He had long since moved past the excitement stage. A grueling work schedule coupled with a host of never-ending problems and people continually wanting his attention had seen fit to temper any sense of exhilaration. "And here I thought delivering a Specter class dreadnaught was difficult. This Job has been an absolute bear. I swear, the workload is slowly killing me, one report and meeting at a time. When she's done, I am going to sleep for a week, maybe more."

"I have an admission to make," Jason announced. "Last time I was stationside I made a point to take a train over to get a close-up look at your ship."

"Really?" Garrett asked, finding himself genuinely surprised. "I would have given you a tour had you asked."

"I know and I did not want to bother you. You're a busy guy." Jason paused and ran his gaze around the table. "On a data pad it's easy to read her size, specifications, and scope, but in person—to actually see her, with your own eyes—she's crazy large. It's a shame the slip covers up a good portion of her hull."

"I think I might have to go look for myself," Tina admitted, "before I leave."

"Jim, did you know they installed an exhibition port and information center specifically for your ship?" Jason asked. "It's almost a mini museum. They even have an augmented reality tour. You can walk the corridors of your ship without ever going aboard." He paused, barking out a laugh. "I swear, I never would have imagined you commanding a damned tourist attraction."

"Maybe I should sell tickets for tours." Garrett was aware that there was a keen interest in his Job, not just here on Midway, but far beyond. He was already routinely required to interrupt his work to provide VIP tours or answer longwinded

message traffic from distant politicians, not to mention his correspondence with senior flag officers and the War College. It had
gotten so bad and distracting, Construction Command had
assigned a public relations officer to handle most of the basic
inquiries and tours.

"How many are under your command?" Julia asked.
"Surely it has got to be a considerable number."

"Not counting the ten thousand plus civilian engineers and
techs commuting and working aboard daily," Garrett said,
mentally tallying, "roughly five thousand Fleet personnel."

Tina about choked on her drink, which she had just brought
to her lips. They all looked at him with astonishment, except
Jason. He was a bit more familiar with Garrett's command and
the responsibilities Fleet had saddled him with.

"Fifteen thousand?" Tina almost gasped, setting her drink
down next to the menu. "Are you serious? You have fifteen
thousand people under your command, including civilians?"

"Well, the civilians really report to their bosses, who then
coordinate with me." Garrett had never given it much thought.
His command dwarfed those of his friends' combined. He had
begun with around one hundred fifty naval personnel, and over
the months, the crew had steadily grown. He laughed lightly
and decided to continue to roll on and deliver the real kicker.
"In about a month, we're scheduled to take on another five thousand personnel in preparation for trials and roughly around
three thousand shortly after. But honestly, we have people
reporting aboard all the time."

"I thought skippering a crew of eighty was bad enough,"
Tina breathed, still eyeing Garrett with clear newfound respect.
"How do you manage all those personnel?"

"Yeah, how do you do it?" Julia pressed. "Two hundred and
eighty is almost too much for me."

"I have an excellent support staff, some really good people,"
Garrett responded. "In all transparency, I must admit we hold

entirely too many staff meetings. They consume my day, eating time like you'd not believe. My department heads are quite good at what they do. Fleet assigned only the best for this project, and they take a lot of the pressure off, and I mean a lot. They really do. That allows me to focus on important tasks."

"I bet," Julia agreed. "Ships like yours will make the difference during the next Push. She is a game changer for sure."

"That's the idea." Jason sat forward, drawing each word out, always one eager to talk about tactics. "That is the general idea."

"This time when the enemy makes their next Push, we will finally be ready to take the war to them for a change, turn the tables." Julia paused, glancing around the table. "Ships like Jim's will shift the dynamic by allowing us to hit the enemy behind the lines. This is only the beginning. Give it a few years and no longer will we be confined to jump points like the enemy, at least with ships that are capable of mounting a gripper drive."

"I don't know about that, the dynamic shifting," Tina said. Such conversations were frequent fodder here on Midway and elsewhere. Though, unlike the last Push, Midway, at some point, was sure to be on the front lines this time around. "She's only one ship, and they cost a lot, some would say too much."

"What is expense when it comes to the defense of our people?" Julia said. "Right now there's just the one, but more are being built, one here at Midway and another two in the Core. Each will be able to transport an entire strike force to hit when and where we want."

"She's one ship among thousands," Tina said. "Each and every Push, when the enemy shoves their way forward into our space, humanity has been arrogant enough to believe we were better prepared than the last time. What happened? At the cost of billions of lives, we were thrown back again and again. What did we do? We built larger fleets, with more powerful weapon systems. Each time they weren't enough. So, what's to say this time will be any different?"

"We have vastly improved our weapons and ship systems since the last Push that happened forty-five years ago," Jason stated firmly. "In addition, we have more hulls deployed than ever before. The Fleet is larger, more powerful. We also have at least another four to five years to prepare. Think how strong we will be when the fifty-year Push finally comes. Command has already deployed the Third and Twenty-Ninth Fleets to the Outer Rim, with well over six hundred ships between them. The Twenty-First, stationed here at Midway, numbers at least another four hundred ships, but more importantly, included with them are two hundred forty ships of the line, big fat bastards. These include our new Specter class dreadnaughts. There are also plans to bring up Fifth and Seventh Fleets. And that doesn't count the numerous system garrisons and jump point defenses already in place. Hell, we are now stronger than we've ever been. By the time the next Push comes, we will have the largest fleet ever assembled, and more importantly, we will be ready." He drummed his fist down on his menu lightly. "We have a real shot at stopping them this time."

"That's my point," Tina asserted. "Each Push, for the last two hundred years, was expected to be stopped cold, halted dead in its tracks. They weren't. The enemy is an unrelenting tide that may not be able to be stopped. Yes, we're stronger. Yet with each Push they show up in greater and greater strength. They've also shown significant weapon systems development, not quite up to our levels, but close enough. We should expect nothing different this time. In fact, we should really expect the unexpected."

"Bah." Jason waved his hand dismissively. "That's defeatist talk."

"You feel our fight is hopeless?" Garrett asked quietly, drawing everyone's attention. "Is that what you're saying?"

"Talk like that might be considered dangerous," Julia said, glancing around at the other patrons of Little Hill. None of them were paying any attention to their conversation. "I would not let a political officer hear me say that."

"There is always hope and determination," Tina asserted firmly. "Hope is why I wear the uniform. Determination is why I am not raising a family somewhere safe in the Core. I sacrifice so that humanity may one day prosper and thrive again." She paused. "So I hope I am wrong."

"We have to figure something out soon, or it will be too late," Eric said. "If we do not halt their progress—either this Push or the next—the enemy will be on the edge of the Core, and then, as a species, we are in real trouble."

"You're talking extinction?" Julia breathed.

"We need to find a way to stop them—if not, the end will surely come when the Core is invaded," Eric said.

"The news and faxes are always filled with wonder weapons under development," Julia asserted. "Maybe this time R and D will come up with something that will make a real difference and give us an edge."

"Have they come up with anything like that yet?" Eric asked quietly, looking around at each person.

Ears perking up, Garrett said nothing. He knew of one such weapon, but declined to speak, as it was classified and none of those at the table had been cleared or read in.

"Besides Garrett's ship?" Eric continued. "They improve our basic weapons, systems, and ships, but have you seen anything really spectacular, revolutionary—barn-busting?"

Again, Garrett remained silent. He felt his ship was barn-busting, especially with the tactics he'd been helping to develop. In his own opinion, the enemy was in for a rude surprise.

"Old doom and gloom," Jason said, but Eric was having none of it.

"Not one of you, save Garrett, has ever been in combat where you are directly responsible for the lives of those under your command and those you are defending." Eric paused before continuing. "When the next Push comes, our responsibility does not end with our ships and crews. Think of those populated systems and worlds beyond Midway and those out on the Rim, the ones Fleet is not able to evacuate. If we fail, they all die."

No one said anything. It was a sobering thought.

"Good thing the enemy operates like clockwork," Garrett said. "Every fifty years they come at us. We have another four or five years to prepare before the next Push begins in earnest."

"I will drink to that." Jason raised his glass. There was a moment of hesitation, then the others did the same. They all took a drink.

Garrett moved the menu before him with a finger. He had not even glanced at it yet. "What bothers me is that we do not know who they are or what they look like, their ultimate objective, why they started the war. No one's ever seen a live enemy and lived to tell the tale, let alone got their hands on a dead one."

"That proves my point, doesn't it?" Tina said. "Once they force their way through the jump point defenses and break into a system, they advance. They come at us with thousands of ships. We may cause them horrendous casualties, but they've shown themselves to be an unstoppable force. They take the system, forcing us out, and all we do is fall back. They just keep coming and coming."

There was another moment of silence around the table, this one more uncomfortable than the last.

"From the ships we've destroyed," Eric said, "we do know they are hydrogen breathers. Sensors have told us that much."

"That and we know the capability of their ships," Julia added. "They are not too dissimilar from ours."

Garrett had grown tired of the conversation. He had come here to relax and renew old friendships. Someone cleared their throat, drawing their attention. The waiter had returned.

"Captains, have you had a moment to look over the menu? Are you ready to order?"

"Well." Garrett sat up. He grabbed his menu like it was a lifeline and really looked at it for the first time. "I don't know about the rest of you, but I am famished. I could use some real steak, not the simulated stuff I get shipboard. I came here for some good company and food. How about we focus on that and move away from weightier discussions?"

"Jim's right," Julia said. "Let's enjoy our evening."

With that, Garrett relaxed a little. He glanced back at the menu, which only had a few items on it. He looked up at the waiter. "I will take the porterhouse, cooked medium rare and I think a baked potato. That's real grown right?"

"It is, sir. The potatoes being served tonight were grown on Taylor's World."

"Excellent," Garrett said, "I will take it. Extra butter, please."

SEVEN

TABBY

"Ma'am, time to wake up," Sanchez called.

Tabby opened her eyes, blinking rapidly to dispel the grogginess that clung to her like a veil. The displays and control panels of her pilot's seat gradually swam into sharp focus. She rubbed her temples and then stretched, feeling the stiffness throughout her body from sleeping awkwardly in her seat. There was a foul taste in her mouth. A quick glance at the chronometer confirmed that she had managed to snatch a mere four hours of restless sleep.

"Ten minutes till the beacon," Sanchez said, her tone steady and professional. "We're entering the initial approach pattern now."

"Roger that," Tabby replied, her voice a mix of fatigue and authority. She twisted slightly in her chair, the material creaking under her movement, and called out to the rear of the cockpit where the bunk was located. "Chen, still with us?"

"Here," came the slightly muffled response from the compact bunk situated just behind her seat. The sound of Chen stretching and a yawn punctuated his words. "Mom, are we there yet?"

"We're almost at the beacon," Tabby confirmed, her eyes scanning the readouts on her console. "Hey, while you're back there, could you grab me a coffee? I need a serious caffeine hit."

"Aye, ma'am," Chen replied, his voice now clearer. There was the sound of him shuffling in the small space. She could hear Chen opening a compartment.

"I could use one as well," Sanchez chimed in from her station, her voice tinged with a hint of weariness.

The compartment closed with a heavy thunk, followed by a click as it locked into place. Tabby stretched again in her seat, trying to work the ache and stiffness out.

Chen navigated through the narrow confines of the cockpit with practiced ease, the ambient hum of the boat's engines and hiss of the air handlers a constant backdrop. As he reached Tabby's station, he extended his hand, offering her a squeeze tube emblazoned with the label COLOMBIAN COFFEE, LIGHT ROAST. The container, simple yet functional, bore the personal touch of a handwritten "For Mom" in permanent marker.

Tabby accepted the tube with a nod of thanks, her fingers brushing against Chen's in the brief exchange. The coffee, though synthetic, was crafted to her exact liking, two sugars with a splash of hazelnut cream, a flavor profile she thought perfect. It was a small luxury, but in the deep reaches of space, such things took on greater significance. She placed the unopened tube in a designated holder on her armrest.

Upon reaching his own station, Chen casually tossed another tube to Sanchez. The precision of the throw and catch spoke of their time spent in close quarters, a well-rehearsed dance of small, shared spaces. Sanchez caught the tube with a deft movement, quickly activating the chemical heater within by pressing a tab on its surface. The tube emitted a faint hiss as the heating process began, and Sanchez set it aside to warm. With a sense of routine, Chen slid into his seat, the familiar click of buckles and straps sounding as he secured himself.

Tabby's eyes methodically scanned the various displays, each flickering with the vital statistics of their spacecraft. Her trained gaze searched for any anomalies or warning signs among the myriad readouts. The screens, bathed in a soft glow, reflected back a status of normalcy; everything was operating within expected parameters. There were no red flags, no urgent alerts, just the steady rhythm of a vessel in good operation.

Their trajectory toward the jump beacon remained unwavering. Tabby's attention shifted to the power plant diagnostics, her eyes flickering over the readouts that indicated the health and efficiency of their main sources of energy. Satisfied, she moved on to inspect the drive systems, ensuring that the engines that propelled them through the vastness of space were functioning optimally.

Next, her focus turned to the life support systems. These were crucial, the lifeline that sustained them in the harsh and unforgiving environment of space. She scrutinized the oxygen levels, the waste recycling systems, and the temperature controls, finding all in order.

Returning her attention to the HTD, Tabby observed the plotted course. The autopilot had performed flawlessly, adhering to their path with precision, navigating through the waypoints she'd programmed seamlessly. It reported no anomalies. She had come to expect such reliability from their advanced navigation systems, yet she never took it for granted. It was always worth double-checking.

As they approached the beacon, the autopilot had already initiated the deceleration process, reducing the output of the gravitic drive, exerting force in the opposite direction to slow their advance. The readout indicated they were down to five gravities, a significant deceleration, but thanks to the inertial compensators, the sensation was entirely negated. In this moment of calm, as the boat hummed softly around her, Tabby felt a profound connection to the vessel, to *Max*.

Tabby's focus was still on the HTD, her eyes narrowing slightly as she surveyed the space around their vessel. The display offered a comprehensive three-dimensional view of their surroundings. She was immediately reassured to see her squadron maintaining their assigned positions, using their station-keeping autopilots, keyed upon her boat. It was a comforting sight, her little chicks or ducks.

With practiced ease, she manipulated the controls of the HTD, zooming out to gain a broader perspective of the space around them. The jump beacon, their immediate destination, appeared prominently on the display. It was an immense struc-ture, spanning several kilometers, one of many such gateways that connected distant points across the system.

The area between their spacecraft and the beacon was clear, free of any immediate traffic that could pose a naviga-tional hazard. Her attention was then drawn to a fast transport, indicated by its civilian tag and Identification Friend or Foe (IFF) signal, which appeared on her display.

The vessel was a significant distance behind them, approxi-mately five hundred thousand kilometers away, rapidly moving toward the Nikura jump point. Its formidable speed and course, clocking in at seventy-five gravities, suggested it had recently completed its transit through the beacon, likely coming from Midway Station, an event that had occurred while she was asleep.

The fact that Sanchez hadn't deemed it necessary to wake her during the transport's passage was telling. It meant that the vessel hadn't presented any threat or navigational obstacle.

The soft chime of an alert from the HTD drew Tabby's attention back to the present. The sensors had detected a mounting surge in power emanating from the beacon. This was a routine indicator, one she had come to expect and understand. The beacon, a structure capable of manipulating the very fabric of space, was initiating its preparatory phase for their transit. The complex process of bending and twisting space-time was no small feat, and the power surge was a byproduct of this monumental task.

Tabby toggled the communication system, bringing the squadron's channels into view on her console. The display lit up with a series of green lights, each representing a different channel currently in use. She noted that several of her pilots and crewmembers were engaged in private conversations. These small interactions were vital for maintaining morale and camaraderie among the crew. They were far from home, and these connections, however brief, were a lifeline to normalcy and fellowship, friendship even.

Her gaze lingered on three craft that were tied into a single conversation. It was not uncommon for her crew to share moments of leisure together, finding solace and entertainment in each other's company. They might even be watching a show, one of the many updated entertainment packages downloaded from *Neptune*. These shared experiences, whether they were watching a beloved series or engaging in group discussions, helped forge stronger bonds among her people, making them more than just colleagues. They were a family, united by their shared journey through the stars, and she was their leader— Mom.

"All Oscars, report status," Tabby's voice cut through the various calls with authority, activating the main squadron channel. This direct call to action immediately overrode any ongoing private conversations or broadcasts. One by one, the responses began to come in. Tabby listened intently as each pilot reported. It was a roll call of readiness, a confirmation that her team was alert and prepared for the operation ahead, the transit jump.

Glancing once more at the time displayed on her main console, Tabby initiated a ping to the jump beacon, alerting it that they were on final approach. The beacon was an automated and unmanned device. While a jump point enabled interstellar travel connecting distant solar systems across vast expanses of space, a beacon facilitated limited faster-than-light (FTL) travel within a single system. It was, in essence, a tool for point-to-point mini-jumps within the confines of a solar system. Unlike a jump point, with a beacon, a jump-capable drive was not required. The beacon did all the work for them.

Tabby remembered a time when someone had tried to explain the intricacies of the beacon's operation to her. The explanation had been overly detailed and technical, but she had only been half listening, her attention fragmented by the ambiance of the bar and the effects of alcohol. Also, he had been quite attractive to the point of distraction, even if he'd been a civilian engineering tech and she an officer in the Confederation's Navy.

From what she had managed to grasp, the operation of these beacons involved massive amounts of power on a magnitude that was challenging to not only harness but also to stabilize when they brought two points of space-time together. Despite ongoing efforts by scientists and engineers to enhance their range and efficiency, the beacons had seen no significant advancements in the last hundred years.

They also had to be spaced out at considerable distances from each other, likely due to the immense power they generated, wielded, and released, along with the potential risks involved with the manipulation of the fabric of space-time. Tabby had heard stories of beacons that had been placed too close to one another failing catastrophically, but she had neither witnessed such an event nor known anyone who had.

Her time in flight school had not been very enlightening when it came to the technical operation of such machines, only that they worked and the expected result. Each beacon could warp space-time to transport a vessel slightly more than twelve light minutes, equivalent to almost one and a half astronomical units. This technology, while not as far-reaching as jump points, significantly streamlined inter-system travel, making trips like the one they were making feasible. By utilizing a chain of these beacons, traversing across star systems became considerably more efficient and faster.

"Oscar Flight," Tabby's voice carried clearly over the comms, her tone firm and commanding. "Make ready for transition. We will treat this as a hot jump, as if we are dropping into combat. Nothing like getting the practice in." She allowed a brief pause, ensuring her instructions were absorbed. "Once on the other side, we will conduct a series of simulated combat exercises as we cruise to the next beacon."

Tabby could almost hear the collective groan from her pilots and crew. Her lips curled into a slight grin at the thought, for once, as a junior officer, she would have had the same reaction. The idea of jumping and then going straight into a simulated combat scenario wasn't particularly appealing after a long stretch of travel. That said, it was essential to keep her team ready for anything, and these exercises were critical for maintaining their combat readiness, keeping the point of the spear sharp.

"Arm weapons, point defense," she instructed Sanchez, switching off the squadron-wide comms. It was time to shift into a more combat-oriented mindset.

"Missiles armed," Sanchez responded without hesitation. "Laser and maser turrets charged and ready, ma'am. Weapons going hot."

"Charge defensive screens. Prep and arm the electronic warfare suite for action," Tabby continued, her voice calm yet authoritative.

"EW suite online and armed," Chen reported back promptly. "Defensive screens active."

"Button up," Tabby commanded with an air of finality. She reached to her left, retrieving her flight gloves from the mesh restraints beside her seat. She slipped them on, feeling the familiar click as they automatically locked into place, seamlessly integrating with her suit's systems.

Next, she grabbed her helmet and pulled it on, the connection points clicking as they locked into place. She pulled down her visor, sealing her helmet. A soft hiss signaled the pressurization of her suit, a sensation accompanied by a gentle popping in her ears as the pressure normalized.

Tabby noted that, as expected, her crew had followed suit. Gloves on, visors down, they were a picture of disciplined readiness. The final step before the jump was to secure the cockpit by creating a vacuum inside. It was a standard safety procedure before utilizing a jump beacon.

Precaution was vital. In the event of a collision or other mishap during the jump, the absence of an atmosphere inside the cockpit would mitigate the risk of explosive decompression, a scenario they were trained to avoid. Space travel, for all its advancements, still carried inherent risks, ones that could easily be lethal. Collisions, though rare, were a grim reality in the vast expanse of space, and something she wanted to avoid at all costs.

The knowledge that laxness or small errors and oversights could be fatal was always at the back of her mind. History was littered with stories of spacefarers who had met their end due to a miscalculation or a momentary lapse in judgment, or simply slacking off. Tabby was determined not to add her name, or those of her people, to that list.

As the cabin pressure dropped to zero, she felt the familiar sense of isolation that came with being sealed in her suit. It was never a good feeling.

Tabby's focus shifted to the squadron status displayed on the left side of her console. The indicators glowed green across the board, signaling that every craft in her squadron was weapons hot and ready for combat. This visual confirmation of readiness brought a sense of assurance to Tabby; her team was prepared.

Her gaze moved to the HTD. She noted the presence of the other squadron, which had launched from *Neptune* after them, escorting the two shuttles. The display showed the relative positions and trajectory of the two groups, hers and theirs, indicating a flight time differential of about five minutes between them. She quickly reviewed their speed and confirmed that they too were decelerating in preparation for transit through the beacon.

"Chen, kindly ping the beacon," Tabby instructed. "Confirm we are good to transit and the other side's clear."

"Pinged and good," Chen responded promptly after a few seconds' delay. "Handshake is good. The clock is ticking. Thirty-five seconds to jump activation. The beacon is waiting on us to hand over control."

Acknowledging the countdown, Tabby took the necessary steps to facilitate the transit. "Releasing control to the beacon," she announced to her crew. Her fingers danced over the controls as she inputted the command to cede navigational control to the beacon's automated system.

Almost instantly, the HTD screen began to flash with new information, indicating the beacon's takeover. The autopilot system on her boat, now under the structure's direct guidance, expertly adjusted their trajectory, bringing the boat down to a smooth one gravity. Within moments, the gravity drive was completely disengaged.

As the beacon assumed command, guiding them toward the transit point with maneuvering thrusters only, Tabby felt a familiar rush of anticipation. They were on the brink of another jump, a leap through space-time. The seconds ticked down, each one drawing them closer to the moment of transition, a moment that, despite its routine nature, never ceased to evoke a sense of awe and wonder.

Chen began counting the last ten seconds. As his countdown reached its final moments, Tabby braced herself for the imminent jump, tensing her body.

"Four... three... two... one."

At the count of one, the familiar yet always unsettling sensation of a beacon jump enveloped her. Her stomach lurched in a disorienting flip-flop, a physical reaction to the abrupt manipulation of space-time. The sensation was intense, more visceral than the smoother transitions facilitated by jump points. It was a reminder of the raw power and somewhat crude execution involved in the beacon's operation.

The screens in front of her flickered and flashed erratically as they momentarily lost sync with the surrounding reality. It was a brief but jarring experience, one that left her panting in discomfort as she tried to regain her bearings. The nausea induced by the jump was always an unpleasant side effect, a stark contrast to the more refined process of the ancient jump points. She had always thought there was something inherently inelegant about the beacons' operation, a brute-force approach to space-time manipulation. It was like using a hammer when a screwdriver was required.

As her senses stabilized, Tabby's eyes quickly refocused on the HTD. The display was now populating with contacts around their spacecraft, indicating their new position post-jump. Her primary concern was her squadron; a quick scan confirmed that all craft had successfully made the transition. Relief washed over her as she saw their familiar signatures and tags on the display.

The beacon, having successfully transported them, powered the twin coiled gravitic drives back up and began ramping up the speed to ten gravities. This swift increase in acceleration was necessary to move them clear of the jump point, creating a safe zone for the following squadron to transit.

The movement away from the beacon was a critical safety measure. The unpredictable and sickening nature of beacon jumps meant that crews could suffer severe adverse reactions, ranging from simple nausea to temporary incapacitation, essentially passing out. This could potentially pose a serious risk, especially if a spacecraft lingered near or in the transit zone, with other vessels preparing to jump in. Automatically moving and clearing spacecraft to a safe distance after the jump was a standard protocol, designed to mitigate any potential hazards.

A moment later, as they cleared the controlled space around the beacon, a confirming beep sounded from Tabby's console. *Max* seamlessly transitioned back to her own autopilot systems. The smooth handover of control marked their successful exit from the immediate vicinity of the beacon's control, allowing them to proceed onward.

Tabby quickly reviewed the course she had plotted earlier. The next segment of their journey to the subsequent beacon was set to take a little over fourteen hours. This stretch of space travel, while long, was a necessary stride in their mission to reach Midway. Once they arrived at the next beacon, they would have completed half of their journey to Midway Station.

Feeling the need to reacclimatize after the jump, Tabby stretched out her legs, the simple motion bringing a measure of relief. Once settled, she initiated the process to reintroduce air back into the cabin. The hissing was a welcome one.

"Stand down weapons," Tabby commanded as she raised her visor.

"Powered down and safed," came Sanchez's prompt confirmation, indicating the deactivation of their boat's weapons systems.

Tabby reached over and pushed the tab on her coffee, activating the heating process. When her stomach fully settled from the jump, she would have some. By then, it would be hot, which was how she preferred her coffee.

Turning her attention to the squadron, Tabby activated the communication channel to address her people. "Listen up, boys and girls," she transmitted. "As I promised, we're going to conduct some simulated exercises."

Simultaneously, she pulled up a file on her screen, one she had designed earlier, and dispatched it to every member of the squadron. The file contained the details of the simulated exercises they were about to undertake. At her command, half of the screens on *Max* shifted over to simulator mode. The other half remained focused on their journey and the boat's operations.

Though the craft of her squadron would remain on autopilot, maintaining their course and speed toward the next beacon, following the waypoints she'd loaded, Tabby had planned a series of mock fights and attack runs.

"We will start with simulation one," Tabby transmitted.

"I like this one," Lieutenant Ackerman, call sign Ghost, announced back. "I do believe it will be fun."

"That's because you're in a fighter," Husky retorted with a dry humor, acknowledging the advantage that Ghost's Raptor would have in this kind of exercise. The Typhoons would do their best to protect the slower Hawks while they made a torpedo run on an enemy heavy cruiser.

"Damn right I am," Ghost shot back, his tone brimming with confidence and a touch of playful bravado. "For those who are about to die gloriously—not the fighters, of course—I salute you."

The mock challenge set the stage for an engaging, and spirited, exercise. Tabby was ready to initiate the drill. "On my mark," she announced, her voice cutting through the chatter with authority. As if in anticipation, the comm line fell silent.

She tapped on her display, setting the parameters for the

exercise. The simulation was designed to test both offensive maneuvers by the fighters and the defensive capabilities of the larger boats.

"Engage," Tabby commanded, activating the exercise. She smiled as she allowed herself to drop fully into the simulation. Ghost was right. "This is going to be fun."

EIGHT

GARRETT

Leaving Little Hill was always an experience, one Garrett enjoyed—a journey through time. The restaurant was nestled deep in Section Two, one of the earliest modules of the space station. It harkened back to the pioneering days of space exploration. Affectionately termed the Egg, or the Yolk, or heart of the station, it was not uncommon for the visitor to feel a sense of the module's age.

Having said goodbye to his friends, Garrett moved through the corridors outside the restaurant. He couldn't help but feel a profound connection to the history. Each step on the antiquated deck plating was a reminder of the countless individuals who had traversed these very paths before him.

Despite the station undergoing centuries of technological advancements and upgrades, vestiges of its original architecture remained visible. The sight of the station welds was particularly striking. These manual welds, crafted by the hands of pioneering space engineers, stood as a statement to human determination in the early days of space colonization.

The current state of station construction and maintenance showcased the leaps in technological evolution. The era of manual labor in building and repairing most space structures had long since passed, giving way to advanced methodologies that relied heavily on cutting-edge chemical compounding techniques. These modern methods predominantly utilized a diverse array of adhesives, tailored to the unique demands of space construction and assembly.

"And yet, the screw is still used." Garrett almost grinned as he spoke to himself. A marine lieutenant, clearly having heard, looked at him funny as Garrett passed him by.

The actual construction work was no longer the exclusive domain of humans alone. Under the guidance and meticulous oversight of highly skilled engineers and technicians, nanoids and construction bots had taken center stage in the ongoing expansion and direct upkeep of the station. These robotic workers, guided by humans, performed tasks with a precision and efficiency that was once beyond imagination.

Navigating the congested corridors of Section Two was like traversing a labyrinth from a bygone era. The passage was quite different than the spacious and modern designs found elsewhere on the station, especially in the newer modules. The overhead lighting, an archaic feature when compared to the paneled area effect lighting of the newer modules, cast a dim, yellowish glow, enhancing the corridor's sense of antiquity.

Midway Station had been originally constructed during a golden age of exploration and expansion, a time when humanity's gaze was firmly fixed on the stars, driven by an insatiable hunger for discovery and the thrill of venturing into the unknown.

That had been before the Push.

The current reality was a grim shadow of those days. Humanity's grand dreams had been eclipsed by a more pressing and ominous agenda: survival. The station, once a beacon of human achievement and interstellar ambition, a midway point to the Rim, now stood as a bulwark against an aggressive, expansionist alien species.

The nostalgia-laden corridors of Section Two always had a profound effect on Garrett. Whenever he came here, it ignited his innate sense of wanderlust. Each step through these historical passageways resonated with dreams of exploration, of embarking on journeys to realms untouched and unseen by human eyes. While he recognized the nobility in his current role of defending humanity, there was a part of him that yearned for something more, something transcendent.

Garrett's heart harbored a deep-seated desire to venture beyond the confines of known space, to lead a mission not of war, but of discovery. In his mind's eye, he saw himself encountering strange new worlds, deciphering the secrets of distant galaxies, and contributing to a wealth of knowledge that could propel humanity to new heights of understanding and achievement.

In these moments of reflection, walking through the echoes of history in Section Two, Garrett's aspirations seemed both tantalizingly close and frustratingly distant. The reality of his current duties clashed with his innermost desires, creating a rift between the world as it was and the world as he wished it could be. Yet even in the face of these challenges, his dreams remained undimmed, a beacon of hope in a universe fraught with uncertainty and strife.

"Captain Garrett." A familiar voice pulled him abruptly back to the present. Garrett looked up and saw Admiral Yenga.

"Sir?" So engrossed had he been in his thoughts that he hadn't noticed the admiral until their shoulders almost brushed in passing. Garrett halted in his tracks, a smile breaking across his face as he reached out to grasp the outstretched hand of his old friend and ally.

"Good to see you, Garrett."

"Admiral," he replied, his tone still infused with both

surprise and genuine pleasure at the unexpected meeting. The
admiral stood before him in his informal day uniform. This
attire, less formal than the standard uniform, subtly signaled to
Garrett that a relaxed demeanor was appropriate for their
interaction.

The admiral was accompanied by two aides. These, clearly
recognizing the personal nature of the encounter between the
two senior officers, maintained a respectful distance, standing
back to give them space.

Yenga's handshake conveyed both warmth and professionalism. Their encounters, though infrequent since Garrett's
posting to Midway Station, had always been brief, limited to
quick exchanges amidst the hustle of station life. Garrett understood all too well the demands placed upon someone in Yenga's
position. Holding a high command within the Fleet required an
unwavering commitment and often left little room for extended
social interactions. Still, Yenga was most definitely a friend, of
which Garrett had few, with even fewer friends in high-level
positions.

The sector was overseen by Fleet Admiral Michelle Isabel,
who commanded a significant portion of the space forces out on
the Rim, including the Third, Twenty-First, and Twenty-Ninth
Fleets. Yenga's role was pivotal in this hierarchy, serving as the
right hand of Isabel. A two-star, his primary responsibility was
the oversight of Midway Station, ensuring that it remained a
fully functional, efficient hub in this strategically crucial area of
operations.

"You know, it has been too long, my boy." Yenga offered a
hearty smile. "When was the last time we saw each other?"

"About two months ago, sir," Garrett said, "when I gave you
that tour."

"Ah, yes, I remember." Yenga gave a curt nod. "And how is
that Job of yours coming? I follow your summary reports with
great interest, but how is she really doing?"

Garrett appreciated the genuine interest in Yenga's eyes as he inquired about the progress of Garrett's current project. The admiral's demeanor, a blend of approachability and astute intelligence, made it clear he was seeking an honest insider's perspective, despite likely being well-versed with the official reports.

"Coming along nicely, sir," Garrett responded, matching Yenga's directness. He knew the admiral valued succinct yet informative updates. "I am confident we could successfully conduct our movement and operational trials as of today. However, as you're probably aware, we're currently grappling with a shortage of crew for such an exercise. Additionally, there's a significant amount of work still pending, a long punch list to work through, including a comprehensive systems test."

Garrett's gaze briefly swept over the bustling crowd around them. He was acutely aware of the need for discretion, especially in such a public setting. There were aspects of the project, like the gripper drive, that were highly classified and not suitable for discussion in the open corridors of Section Two.

"That said," Garrett continued, "it looks like the trials will be delayed so that Admiral Isabel can personally attend."

"I understand. Regardless of any delays, the trials will be here before you know it. Just keep doing what you are doing. There's no one better at completion than you. It is why you were handpicked for this task."

"Yes, sir." Standing together in the center of the corridor, they formed a distinct presence, a focal point amidst the steady stream of those passing by. While some might have initially been irritated by the obstruction, a quick glance at the admiral's stars was enough to quell any discontent, and they continued on their way without complaint.

"Admiral Gray insists you be part of the full trials for the ship, and that includes the system target," Yenga said. "That destination seems quite interesting, quite interesting indeed. In truth it will be the first bit of real exploration the Confederation has done since the Push began."

"Yes, sir," Garrett said again, suddenly seriously interested in what the admiral knew. Yenga's mention of the destination, codenamed 66-Lima, for their first superluminal transit was intriguing. Garrett had no idea where the star system was, as it was classified, but Command wanted the Mothership to go there, and badly. The destination and course was already loaded into their navigation system, but it had been locked out pending the arrival of the person who would replace him as captain. He'd asked but had been bluntly told that it was not important to his current duties.

"I understand the science teams have already arrived and are setting up shop," Yenga said. "Doctor Pascal has sent me a considerable number of requests for equipment, additional personnel, and supplies."

"He has, sir, and I am aware he has gone outside of the chain of command. I apologize for that." Garrett resisted a scowl. Pascal, like most of the other scientists they'd been saddled with, was a civilian. The man was the lead scientist, and since he'd come aboard, he had been nothing but a pain in the ass. "We are doing our best to accommodate his needs."

Yenga gave an understanding grunt. "I suppose that is only to be expected. Regardless of which strings the doctor pulled to head your science department, your trial run is deemed so important by Command that the ship was assigned additional science personnel, some of the best and brightest the Confederation has to offer. This is not done lightly, but with clear intention. When the time comes, more will be shared with you."

Garrett absorbed the gravity of Yenga's words. He gave an understanding nod. In the current climate, allocating such a vast array of scientific talent to a single vessel was unprecedented, reflecting the high stakes and expectations placed on their upcoming endeavor.

"I understand, sir."

"Good, then do your best with them."

"I will, sir," Garrett said, "but they don't get along with the crew, and hell, sir, not even with each other."

"I can imagine, big egos and all, especially Pascal. He has some powerful patrons."

"Shaw is running most of the interference for me, sir," Garrett responded dryly. "Even so, they still get in the way. But we'll manage."

"Lucky for you that your Job is large enough for you to hide from them," Yenga said.

Their lighthearted exchange was interrupted by one of the admiral's aides, a full captain, who had been observing Garrett with a discernible measure of displeasure.

"Admiral," she interjected with a sense of urgency, "we really must go. The fast packet has just docked. Admiral Isabel is expecting your presence on the flagship."

Yenga's expression soured slightly at the interruption. He glanced back at the captain, acknowledging the importance of the summons with a slow nod before turning his attention back to Garrett. For a moment, he appeared contemplative, as if weighing his next words carefully. Then, leaning in closer, Yenga placed a comforting hand on Garrett's shoulder, ensuring their conversation was private. He lowered his voice. With the background noise of the packed corridor, no one else could hear but them.

"Garrett, I know that Jobbing someone else's starship is not what you had planned, for a variety of reasons. Your work on this Job has been more than outstanding, exemplary. I might add, even more so, considering your collaboration with the War College on tactics and strategy. There is a future for you beyond Construction Command. Trust me on that. It will only take time."

"Yes, sir." Garrett felt a mix of appreciation and resignation.

He interpreted the admiral's words as an attempt to offer encouragement but not a promise.

The aide interjected once more, her tone insistent. "Admiral, we must get going."

Yenga, visibly irked by the interruption but acknowledging the urgency, replied, "I know, I know."

"Is something up, Admiral?" Garrett asked.

"I am not sure," the admiral confessed, his brows furrowed as he glanced down the corridor in the direction he had originally been headed. "A fast courier came in this morning from the Core, from Fleet HQ. Admiral Isabel was out on her flagship, and I've been summoned. The fleet is being put on alert. Beyond that..." Yenga shook his head.

"Another readiness drill?" Garrett asked.

"I am hoping that is what it is," Yenga replied, though his tone suggested a hint of uncertainty. Then the man's demeanor changed and he smiled. "We must really get together for a meal sometime, to catch up properly. It's been too long. Send your schedule over to my aide, Commander Dillon. He will block us out some time."

"Yes, sir," Garrett responded, though both men understood the unlikelihood of this plan materializing. This wasn't the first time such an invitation had been extended, and Garrett knew it was nothing personal. The admiral's schedule was notoriously packed, and such informal engagements often fell by the wayside in the face of pressing responsibilities.

With a final handshake, the admiral and his aides disappeared into the throng, quickly absorbed by the ceaseless flow of people through the section. Garrett was left standing in the corridor, their conversation lingering in his mind.

He exhaled a breath, glancing in the direction Yenga had gone, then continued on his way through the bustling crowd. He could have called Shaw for a boat to be sent, but he had decided he wanted to take the long way home. That he always enjoyed.

His path soon led him to the section's train terminal, a hub that, despite its sizable layout, felt somewhat cramped compared to the grander, more modern terminals in other sections and modules of Midway. The scene was typical: long queues snaking their way through the platform, with passengers patiently waiting for the arrival of outbound trains.

Section Two had a rich history within the framework of Midway. In its early days, it was a nerve center, housing critical command components vital to Midway's operations. However, as the station expanded and evolved over the years, the needs of Command grew. It was eventually decided to relocate Command and Control to Section Six, which offered a larger and more suitable space for the growing complexity and scale of operations.

The transformation of Section Two into a zone dedicated to rest and relaxation marked a significant shift. Where once it had buzzed with the serious business of Command and Control, it now thrummed with a different kind of energy.

The section had been repurposed and now boasted some of the finest amenities on Midway. Renowned for its high-quality restaurants, entertainment, and vibrant clubs, Section Two had become a popular destination for those off duty and looking to unwind and escape the rigors of stationside life.

Garrett couldn't help but notice the increase in foot traffic, particularly from those in uniform. Each visit stationside seemed to reveal an even denser crowd, a sea of faces from various branches of the military, many adorned with unit patches and uniforms unfamiliar to him. These patches represented a diverse array of commands, revealing the wide-reaching mobilization efforts of the Confederation.

The influx wasn't just limited to military personnel. There were many civilians about too. Massive convoys had become a regular sight, orchestrating a vast movement of resources and manpower to the frontline systems.

These convoys, on their return journey, carried a different cargo: civilian evacuees. Men, women, and children, uprooted from their homes and their lives, were being transported to safer locations across the Confederation. These evacuations painted a stark picture of the realities of the coming conflict, the human cost.

The line moved forward as one train left and another arrived, and in a short time Garrett was boarding a car. He settled into his seat, a rare find in the crowded car, right by the window. His momentary companion, a nursing assistant dressed in a ship's uniform, took the seat next to him. They shared the space in a comfortable silence, typical of many who traversed the busy routes of Midway, each absorbed in their own thoughts.

As the last of the passengers squeezed into the car, it became standing room only, with people gripping the straps that hung overhead. The doors of the car sealed with a soft hiss, followed by a series of toncs and an announcement over the speakers indicating the next stop.

The train began to move, but the transition was so smooth, so devoid of any jolting motion, that it was almost imperceptible. It accelerated swiftly, gliding through the vacuum tube, the train's speed only discernible through the window.

Outside, the utility lamps, placed every ten meters along the tube, created a dull strobe-like effect, flashing by in a rapid, almost dizzying blur. It was a surreal experience, feeling stationary while hurtling forward at incredible speeds.

Some of the newer trains had replaced windows with entertainment screens, a modern touch aimed at providing distractions or information to passengers, along with Confederation propaganda. However, he preferred the old-fashioned windows, enjoying the connection to the outside world they offered.

Watching the lights zip by was a grounding experience, a reminder of the station's scale and the incredible technological advancements that had become commonplace in their daily lives.

A tone sounded, followed by an announcement of the next stop's imminent arrival. The train began rapidly decelerating as it pulled into the terminal and came to a halt. The doors opened with a hiss, the differing pressurization levels between the train and the station causing a slight but noticeable pop in Garrett's ears.

The opening of the doors initiated a fluid exchange of passengers. Some disembarked and were swiftly replaced by others waiting to board. This ebb and flow of people was a well-orchestrated dance of daily commute, a routine yet normal part of station life.

The nursing assistant beside Garrett, who had remained quiet throughout the journey, retrieved a reader from her duffle bag. She immersed herself in its contents, finding solace or perhaps distraction in whatever material it displayed.

With each stop, the train inched closer to the outer edge of Midway Station. Garrett's destination was Section DE1. There, his Job awaited him, securely moored in her construction slip.

As the train made its stop at the second terminal in Section Five, the nursing assistant sitting next to Garrett stood up and made her way out. With each subsequent stop, the congestion within the car gradually thinned out. This pattern was typical as the train approached the Edge, a part of Midway where the focus shifted from residential and administrative areas to zones dedicated to construction and maintenance.

With the gradual thinning of the crowd, Garrett found himself with more space to relax. He took advantage of the additional room, stretching out his legs and resting his feet on the seat in front of him, a small luxury. The change in the train's population reflected the shift in the station's functional zones,

from the densely populated central areas to the more spacious
and industrially oriented outskirts.

The entrance of two military police into the car introduced
a momentary shift in the atmosphere. The MPs, as they moved
from the front to the back with their authoritative presence,
quickly set about enforcing decorum within the train. One of
them addressed a naval rating, another passenger who, like
Garrett, had his feet propped up on the opposite seat. The interaction was a reminder of the strict standards often upheld
within military environments, even in seemingly mundane
settings like a train car.

As the MPs continued their slow walk down the aisle,
studying each person intently, their gaze inevitably fell upon
Garrett and his similarly relaxed posture. One of the MPs
scowled slightly. However, the dynamic shifted upon their
recognition of his rank. The insignias on Garrett's shoulder bars
spoke volumes, as did his command stripe, silently communicating his status and authority within the station's hierarchy. It
was a clear indication that, unlike the rating, Garrett's actions
were not subject to the same level of scrutiny or intervention.
Garrett could have removed his feet, but he chose not to and
instead met their gazes levelly, for in his view there had been no
real need to hassle the sailor.

Recognizing his rank, the MPs altered their approach.
Instead of admonishment, the one closest offered a respectful
nod and a polite "good evening, sir," before continuing on,
passing him by. Then they were gone, moving onto the next car.

As the train journeyed from the bustling heart of Midway
toward its outer edges, Garrett observed a notable shift in the
demographic makeup within the car. The number of officers
gradually dwindled, and those who remained were predominantly ship's officers, distinct from the station-bound officers
typically encountered closer to the center. This change was a
reflection of the train's route, moving away from administrative

hubs and toward areas focused more on direct Fleet operations, construction, and maintenance.

Alongside this shift in officer presence, there was a noticeable increase in the number of noncommissioned officers and enlisted personnel. These men and women represented a different segment of the military workforce, each with their own unique backgrounds and motivations for joining the Fleet.

Many of the enlisted personnel were volunteers. For some, it was an escape from the challenging conditions of economically depressed systems within the Confederation. They saw service in the Fleet as a pathway out of the slums and a chance for a better life. For others, the motivation was more patriotic, a desire to defend humanity and contribute to the greater good.

The Fleet offered these volunteers not just employment, but a suite of opportunities and benefits. A steady salary was just the beginning; they also received access to higher education and the development of new skill sets. Furthermore, for those who served long enough, a healthy pension waited, adding a layer of long-term security to their service.

The completion of a twelve-year term in the Fleet often resulted in the acquisition of two or more higher educational degrees, qualifications that were highly valuable and sought-after in the civilian sector. This aspect made service in the Fleet an attractive option for many, a stepping stone to future success. For a significant number, their time in the Fleet was a transformative experience, providing them with the tools and education necessary to excel in their post-military careers.

The contemplation of the demographic changes in the train car led Garrett to reflect on the broader implications of military service, especially in light of the upcoming Push. This represented a period of heightened risk and sacrifice for those in the Fleet. It was a time when the realities of military service came sharply into focus, where the commitment to defend humanity often meant putting your life on the line and, if you came face to face with the enemy in battle, the real prospect of losing it.

Garrett was aware of the traditional patterns that emerged as the Push approached. Enlistment rates typically declined, a natural response to the increased danger. In response, the Fleet often had to take measures such as extending existing enlistments to maintain necessary personnel levels. Additionally, the Confederation would start implementing conscription, a move indicative of the desperate need for manpower during such critical times.

For officers like Garrett, life in the Fleet was more than a job; it was a way of life, a path chosen with full awareness of its demands and sacrifices. He had foregone the possibilities of a traditional family life and the comforts of civilian existence for the sake of his service.

Garrett's observant gaze fell upon two sailors seated toward the front of the car. The presence of their full kits, complete with yellow travel tags, indicated their recent discharge from service. These tags, a common sight on the belongings of those transitioning out of active duty, signaled the end of their current enlistment period. They were on their way home, perhaps to reunite with family and friends, or to embark on new ventures in civilian life.

Despite the apparent conclusion of their service, he knew that their departure from the Fleet would likely be short-lived. With the looming Push, there was a high probability that these sailors, along with many others who had recently completed their enlistments, would be recalled to service.

What role would he play when the Push unfolded? Would he continue as a Job captain, safely overseeing the construction and commissioning of vessels from behind the lines?

The idea of remaining in a comparatively safe position while others faced the dangers of direct conflict stirred a sense of unease within him. While some might find comfort in such a role, Garrett felt a deeper calling. There was a part of him that yearned for more than the security of a rear echelon position. He harbored a sense of being destined for something greater, a feeling that his life was in a holding pattern, waiting for a moment of significant action or decision.

Yet despite these internal yearnings for a more active role in the Fleet, Garrett recognized the realities of his situation. His current position as a Job captain, vital as it was for the operational readiness of the Fleet, might very well continue to be his assignment. He understood that the decisions regarding his role were not his to make. Construction Command, evaluating his skills and the needs of the Fleet, would determine where he was most needed.

In military service, individual desires often took a back seat to the greater needs and strategic decisions of the command structure. Garrett's destiny, as much as he might wish to shape it, was largely in the hands of his superiors. It was a reality that he, like many others in the Fleet, had to come to terms with.

The train pulled into Edge Terminal E2-14-A, known as the Big E2. The naming conventions of the stations within Midway were a mix of formal titles and informal monikers, reflective of the pragmatic approach to station life and the human tendency to personalize one's environment. While some stations boasted names rich in heritage, like Ripley or Nelson Transit Terminals, others were identified by more straightforward alphanumeric designations or, as in this case, endearing nicknames.

The Big E2 stood out as a significant hub within the network, featuring twenty-two train platforms. Its size and the number of platforms underscored its importance, especially considering its location on the edge of the station. Terminals located farther from the center, like the Big E2, were fewer in number but played a crucial role in connecting the sprawling sections of Midway. Their larger size was a necessity, accommodating the diverse and often heavy traffic that flowed through these outer areas.

The terminal was not just a transit point, but a vital junction that facilitated the movement of personnel, equipment, and supplies across the station, particularly to and from the areas dedicated to construction, maintenance, and Fleet operations.

Stepping off the train, Garrett stretched his legs, grateful for the opportunity to move after the long journey. The platform was spacious and well organized, with clear visibility to four other empty platforms within the same terminal.

The platforms were grouped into self-contained components, a strategic design to mitigate risk. In the event of an unexpected decompression, each compartment was capable of sealing itself off from the others within seconds. This rapid isolation capability was crucial in preventing the spread of damage and minimizing the loss of life.

Scattered every few meters along the platforms were emergency suit lockers and shelters. These installations were a constant reminder of the ever-present dangers of living and working in space.

As Garrett started walking along the platform, he took note of the barrier-shielded vacuum tubes that facilitated the entry and exit of trains. These barriers, composed of energy fields, played a crucial role in maintaining the station's atmosphere. They effectively sealed the station environment, preventing the escape of air into the vacuum of space while allowing the trains to move seamlessly in and out.

At the moment, the platforms were relatively quiet, with no other trains in immediate sight. Garrett, however, was aware that this lull was temporary. The constant flow of traffic in and out of a major hub like this one meant that trains would soon be arriving and departing again.

He joined the stream of passengers making their way toward the escalator, moving in unison with those who had disembarked from the train. Simultaneously, a new group of passengers, those who had been waiting on the platform, began boarding the train he had just left.

Descending on the escalator, Garrett passed through the open blast doors, entering the main terminal of the train station. The terminal was a vast, cavernous space, bustling with activity and offering a plethora of amenities. Benches lined the area for those waiting for their trains, while various shops, including auto-shops and newsstands, catered to the diverse needs of the passengers. Fast food restaurants provided quick meals for those on the go, and information booths stood ready to assist with inquiries. Entertainment monitors dotted the area, adding to the lively atmosphere. Music played softly in the background, one of the singers popular at the moment. Garrett recognized the song but did not know the band.

The terminal was also filled with a barrage of advertisement screens and holograms, each vying for the attention of the passersby. For Garrett, this sensory overload was more bothersome than engaging, very different than the more utilitarian and focused environment to which he was accustomed.

Checking his internal chronometer, he noted he had about ten minutes before his next train departed. With some time to spare, he stopped at a newsstand, idly scanning the advertisements for papers and magazines. However, he quickly abandoned the idea of purchasing anything for entertainment download, realizing he hadn't brought his tablet or a reader with him.

Feeling the weariness of the day press upon him, he decided against any distractions. The dinner he'd had earlier, a more pleasant part of his day, lingered in his thoughts, especially the moment with Tina. Her goodbye hug, lasting longer than expected, brought a momentary warmth to his reflections.

"I will see you when I see you," she had said and given him a peck of a kiss upon his cheek. He could almost still feel where she had kissed him and smell her perfume. Her touch had been intoxicating.

Letting go a breath, he consciously turned his thoughts away from her. His next ride was set to take about an hour and twenty minutes, a perfect duration for a much-needed nap.

Garrett paused briefly at a small kiosk to pick up a bottle of water. The panel on the kiosk displayed the temperature of the water, chilled to a "refreshing" 3.33 degrees Celsius. The variety of temperature options catered to individual preferences, a small but thoughtful touch in the station's amenities. Some of these kiosks were even advanced enough to anticipate a person's needs based on their purchasing history.

As he walked away from the kiosk, the cost of the water was automatically debited from Garrett's wallet, a seamless transaction that epitomized the efficiency and convenience of the station's commercial systems.

It was time to catch his train, which was specially designed since it would be exposed to the hard vacuum of space. He knew time was running out and he did not feel like waiting twenty minutes for the next one. Following the directions on the signs overhead, he found the appropriate escalator to platform twelve and rode it up to the top.

The platform was well lit, casting a calm, somewhat sleepy ambiance at this late hour. The train, having arrived, stood ready, its doors open in a welcoming gesture, humming with contained energy, almost as if it too was eager to embark on its journey.

Joining Garrett, a trickle of people emerged from the escalator and spread out across the platform, some heading straight into the train cars. A few passengers were already seated inside, settled in, and patiently waiting for departure. This quiet, subdued atmosphere was a stark contrast to the hustle and bustle of the busier hours, offering a more tranquil travel experience.

Garrett made his way to the last car, an area reserved for ship's captains. The distinction of this car was immediately apparent. It was more luxuriously appointed than the others, featuring separate compartments with comfortable seating arrangements that resembled couches more than the standard seats, all upholstered in high-quality, simulated leather.

Upon entering, Garrett noted that the car was almost empty, save for one other officer occupying a compartment in the back. This officer, unknown to Garrett, was absorbed in a reader. The intensity of his focus suggested that he was likely perusing a ship's report.

Garrett was all too familiar with the endless stream of reports and paperwork that accompanied a command position. It was a routine yet critical aspect of leadership within the Fleet, ensuring that all operations were meticulously documented and reviewed.

The officer's position made it impossible for Garrett to identify the ship's patch on his right shoulder, a patch that would reveal which vessel he commanded. Garrett's own shoulder patch bore the insignia of Construction Command, reflecting his current role in overseeing the construction and preparation of vessels, rather than commanding a commissioned starship.

Garrett's choice of the captain's car was not just a matter of preference, but also a matter of protocol. The Fleet's decision to require all commanding officers traveling along the Edge to use this specially designed car was rooted in practicality and safety considerations. Command-level officers were deemed too valuable to risk in the event of an accidental decompression.

The captain's car was distinct from the other cars in several key aspects. Most notably, it was divided into separate compartments, each equipped with its own emergency air supply. This design provided an added layer of safety, ensuring that in the event a breach, the occupants of each compartment would have access to a critical, independent supply of air.

As Garrett entered his chosen compartment, the door closed and sealed automatically with a soft hiss, affirming the compartment's isolation and security. This feature was particularly important given that this train traveled through sections directly exposed to the hard vacuum of space.

As he settled into the comfort of the couch, the material contoured to his form, creating a sense of relaxation and ease. This small luxury, a couch that adapted to its occupant, was a welcome feature, especially after a long and taxing day. He uncapped the water bottle, taking a refreshing pull, and gazed out of the compartment window.

The view from his compartment offered a clear perspective across to platform fourteen. Garrett's attention was drawn to a significant gathering of marines on one of the platforms, numbering at least a hundred. They were fully equipped, their kits indicating that they were in the midst of an organized transit.

This scene was a common one on Midway, yet it never failed to remind him of the vast and complex machinery of military operations. The constant movement of personnel, the logistics of managing equipment and supplies, and the coordination required to maintain readiness and efficiency were all part of the station's daily rhythm.

As Garrett watched from his compartment, a new train arrived, efficiently unloading its passengers in a swift, coordinated manner. Almost immediately, those waiting on the platform boarded, the marines included. Moments later, the train departed with the same speed and precision.

In the six years that Garrett had been stationed at Midway, he had witnessed firsthand the station's ongoing expansion, with three new module sections added during his tenure. This growth was indicative of Midway's strategic importance and its role in the broader scope of space operations. Garrett could easily envision the station doubling in size and capacity over the next twenty years, a projection that spoke volumes about the Confederation's long-term plans and the coming fight.

The station was also far from helpless, with significant defenses. If the enemy made it all the way to Midway and attacked the station, they would have a hard go of it.

Midway's current capabilities were already impressive, with the infrastructure to support the operations, maintenance, and repair of several fleets. Its strategic location and extensive facilities made it an ideal logistics and command center for operations on the Rim.

If they were successful in halting the enemy's advance, Garrett speculated that Midway could play an even more crucial role. It could become the springboard for humanity to transition finally from a defensive stance to an offensive one, taking the battle to the alien aggressors. The strategic advantage of having a major station like Midway, so well positioned to provide direct support to the front lines, was unparalleled in the planners' history.

A soft tone chimed, signaling imminent departure. Garrett settled more comfortably into his seat. He was familiar with the routine procedures, knowing that the outer doors of the car would have sealed automatically, even though he couldn't see them from his compartment.

The train's automated system began to relay a series of messages over the speaker, detailing upcoming destinations and providing instructions for transfers to other trains. Garrett, well-versed in these announcements and focused on his own journey, paid little attention to this stream of information.

The train itself began to stir to life, its energy transforming from a passive hum into a more palpable vibration. This change marked the transition from a stationary state to readiness for movement. The train levitated slightly above the track, a feature of its advanced magnetic propulsion system, minimizing friction and enabling the smooth, efficient travel for which it was designed.

As the train commenced its journey, Garrett experienced once again the unique sensation of high-speed transit devoid of the physical feeling of motion. The only indication of their rapid movement was the changing view outside his window. The platform, with its flurry of activity, swiftly passed from view, replaced by the monotonous blur of utility lamps lining the vacuum tube.

As the train left the confines of the vacuum tube, it emerged out and onto the outer surface of Midway Station, transitioning into a dramatically different environment. The window tint of Garrett's compartment automatically darkened to compensate for the intense brightness of Midway's sun, a necessary adjustment to maintain a comfortable viewing experience.

Outside, the expansive, smooth, white hull of Midway Station stretched out in all directions, creating a vast, curved landscape. The train glided effortlessly along this surface, giving the illusion of skimming the station's exterior and not following a track. This view offered a unique perspective of the station's impressive scale and design.

Garrett noticed a faint haze encircling the station's curves, a phenomenon known as the Baz Effect. This was the visible manifestation of the station's passive energy field, an essential protective feature. The field served a dual purpose. It shielded the station from micro-meteorites, debris, and particles that could cause damage. It also acted as a containment system.

The energy field gently attracted any extraneous material, drawing it back toward the station to designated collection points. Once gathered, these materials were transported for recycling or disposal.

The station was a beacon of light in the darkness of space, its exterior adorned with an array of illuminations. Viewing ports glowed like constellations, work lights punctuated the hull, and powerful floodlights were trained on the ships docked or tethered to the station. Flashing beacons added to the visual symphony, marking the positions of ships moored in the slips, their rhythmic patterns cutting through the void. This profusion of lights was so intense that it obscured the stars themselves, turning the station into a self-contained universe of activity and life.

The mooring slips, extending outward from the station's hull, resembled colossal skyscrapers reaching into the cosmos. They disrupted the smooth continuity of the hull, branching out in various directions. Docked to these slips were starships of all kinds.

Garrett could see several battleships in nearby slips, their massive hulls a harsh reminder of the coming conflict. Lined up in orderly fashion, these behemoths were imposing in their size and capability. Adjacent to them, a series of smaller frigates was also moored. Despite seeming small in comparison to the colossal battleships, Garrett knew that these vessels were still substantial in scale.

As usual, Garrett found himself enjoying the view. As he gazed out the window, a particularly awe-inspiring moment unfolded. A destroyer, her running lights blinking rhythmically, began to decouple from the station. The process was slow and methodical, the ship gradually moving away from her berth, assisted by a pair of automated tugs. These tugs, their red lights flashing in the darkness of space, expertly guided the large vessel, shepherding her outward.

The sight of the destroyer backing away from the station was a captivating spectacle. It was both majestic and graceful, reminiscent of a colossal creature gently disengaging itself from its resting place. The ship's powerful maneuvering thruster pods glowed a vibrant blue, signaling readiness for free movement and the beginning of a new journey.

Garrett watched, his breath caught by the grandeur of the

scene. The detachment of the massive ship resembled a piece of the station itself coming to life and venturing out into the unknown.

While he had no knowledge of the destroyer's destination or mission, he felt a surge of camaraderie and goodwill toward its crew. Their journey, wherever it led, was a part of the vast tapestry of tasks and missions that kept Midway Station and the wider Confederation functioning.

The dynamic scene that unfolded around the departing destroyer and beyond captivated Garrett. It was a mesmerizing ballet of movement and color, a vivid display of the intricate orchestration of space traffic around Midway Station. Shuttles and small automated support craft, expertly navigated by their pilots or onboard computers, weaved their paths around the massive moorings, moving above or skirting around the slips in well-organized traffic patterns. Automated ministering craft, purposeful in their movements, buzzed around several nearby ships, busy with the task of delivering supplies.

For Garrett, the view was more than a visual spectacle; it was a source of deep inspiration and a reminder of humanity's incredible achievements in space. As the train continued its journey, the mooring slips drew closer, gradually obscuring the once-open view. Then the train was passing through the slips.

With the grand vista now hidden, Garrett closed his eyes, allowing himself to drift away from the thoughts that had occupied his mind, the responsibilities of command, the looming Push, and the complexities of life. In the quiet comfort of the captain's car, he sought to embrace the rare opportunity for a peaceful nap, a treasured respite amidst the relentless pace of his duties.

The couch's responsive design subtly adjusted to Garrett's deepening relaxation, cradling him in a more encompassing embrace as he succumbed to sleep.

The door to his compartment hissed open. Startled awake,

Garrett opened his eyes, momentarily disoriented. Wondering who had interrupted him, for there were plenty of compartments, he propped himself up and was surprised to find Tina standing there, gazing down on him like a hungry predator.

"Hello, stranger," she greeted him playfully.

Garrett, still gathering his wits, managed to ask, "What are you doing here? How did you get here?"

"I told you I'd see you when I see you. I took a boat back to my ship, checked in, and decided everything was in order. Besides, I have some time before my ship pushes back. I figured you wouldn't mind showing me your Job and"—her gaze flicked downward, before running from his feet back up to his face as she locked gazes with him—"perhaps a little more?"

Garrett couldn't help but grin back at her. "I think that can be arranged."

NINE

STROUD

Two marines, in standard shipboard fatigues, stood guard at the entrance to the ship's brig. Both were armed, their weapons securely holstered against their right thighs. They snapped to attention as Stroud approached. The hatch, equipped with advanced recognition technology, identified his implants and smoothly slid open, granting him access.

Inside, he was greeted by the sight of a severe, unadorned waiting room. Staff Sergeant Osman, seated at the duty desk, was deeply engrossed in his tasks, his fingers dancing over the holographic interface of the station display. Stroud supposed he was writing a report on the night's activities.

The room was silent except for the faint hum of the ship's air handlers hissing in the background. As Stroud entered, Osman's sharp gaze lifted, immediately recognizing the figure of his superior. With practiced precision, the sergeant rose to his feet, his posture snapping to rigid attention, a mark of respect and discipline ingrained in every marine.

The hatch, with a soft hiss, sealed shut behind Stroud, encapsulating him in the somber atmosphere of the brig's lobby. The space was compact, and functional to a fault. Six chairs, stark and uninviting, were lined up against the right wall. Each was bolted securely to the floor. Across from them, Osman's desk stood against the left wall, a solitary island in an otherwise spartan space. The decor was minimal, the walls bare, the air tinged with a sterile, impersonal feel.

Stroud recalled his previous visit here, a rare occurrence, prompted by a disciplinary issue with one of his marines who had been involved in bar fighting stationside. His marine, Private Cain, had sent five sailors to the hospital. That memory lingered briefly in his mind before it was pushed aside by the present.

Directly ahead, a single hatch, solid and unyielding, marked the threshold to the deeper confines of the brig. It was firmly closed, a silent sentinel guarding the secrets and tales of those held beyond its steel embrace. Stroud's eyes briefly traced its contours, pondering the stories it concealed before turning his attention back to Sergeant Osman, ready to address the matter at hand.

"Morning, Sergeant," Stroud greeted, his voice echoing slightly in the sparse room.

"A bit early, sir," the sergeant replied, his voice rough, almost a growl. The years had etched themselves into Osman's face, a statement to his more than two decades in the Corps. His demeanor was that of a man who had weathered countless storms, a marine as tough as they came, hardened by service and experience. Over the years, he had earned not just Stroud's respect, but also a reputation for unwavering commitment and grit. He was someone who never gave up, no matter how difficult it got.

Stroud nodded slightly, understanding the unspoken words behind Osman's terse reply.

"I was led to believe Sergeant Major Burns is here."

"He is, sir," Osman confirmed, his hand motioning toward the hatch. "And he's been expecting you. Major Ramirez is here too, arrived not too long ago. It's a bit of a mess, sir, to put it mildly."

"I imagine so," Stroud responded, a hint of dryness in his tone.

Indeed, the situation had to be serious to have summoned him at such an early hour. The unfolding scenario seemed to be escalating beyond the usual run-of-the-mill issues, a fact that didn't escape his seasoned judgment. You don't wake the colonel unless it's important. Knowing it had the potential to ruin his day, Stroud braced himself, mentally preparing for whatever lay beyond the hatch.

"Open it," Stroud said.

Osman's movements were precise and practiced as he leaned forward, his fingers deftly inputting a sequence on the touchscreen display at his station. With a heavy clunk, the hatch unlocked and hissed open, revealing a corridor stretching about twenty meters long. The hallway, lined with numerous hatches to either side, was eerily empty, its stillness punctuated only by the faint hum of the ship's life support systems.

"Last one on the left, sir, interrogation room six," Osman directed, his voice carrying a note of finality.

Stroud, acknowledging the instructions with a brief nod, stepped past the sergeant and entered the hallway. As the hatch slid shut behind him, the sound of its seal echoed briefly in the confined space. Stroud's boots thudded hollowly against the deck, each step resonating off the corridor walls as he made his way forward.

He passed several hatches, noting their reinforced nature. These weren't ordinary rooms; they were holding cells. His gaze was steady, his mind focused, as he approached the end of the corridor.

The hatch he sought was conspicuously open, a silent invitation. The interrogation room was starkly utilitarian, its simplicity underscored by the sole presence of a single table and a pair of chairs. Inside were Major Ramirez and Sergeant Major Burns.

Both stood before the table, their expressions etched with concern. They had been engaged in a deep, presumably grave conversation, which ceased abruptly as they turned to face Stroud. The atmosphere in the room was charged, a sense of unease hanging in the air.

Burns, the very embodiment of marine discipline and prowess, stood with grim determination. His fatigues were neat, the folds crisp to the point of sharpness, so much so Stroud could imagine them cutting. His boots were shined to an impossible mirror finish. He wore blue disposable gloves, an unusual detail that did not escape Stroud's notice.

On the table behind them lay a medium-sized package, already opened. Its contents, though not immediately visible, seemed to be the focal point of their concern.

"Sir," Burns greeted, concern underlying his respectful tone. "Sorry for disturbing you at such an hour, but we felt it was necessary."

"I was planning on getting up early to work out," Stroud replied, maintaining a composed demeanor. He chose not to mention that his actual wake-up time was still more than an hour away. A glance at the digital clock on the wall confirmed the hour, 0332 in the morning.

"Yes, sir," Burns responded.

Stroud shifted his focus to the matter at hand. "What do we have here?" he inquired, his steps taking him closer to the table and the opened package resting upon it. The seal had been broken but the lid had been flapped closed. "What did you find?"

"Bad stuff," Ramirez stated bluntly, his gaze shifting to the package. "It was intercepted in a delivery pallet during one of our random security sweeps. Corporal Desaris found it before it could be brought aboard."

"Drugs, I take it?" Stroud ventured, his expression turning into an unhappy scowl. This was not the first time he had encountered such issues. Usually it was minor stimulants, like mind blaze or scorpion brain sting. The security protocols of their operations included rigorous screenings precisely to prevent the smuggling of illicit substances and contraband aboard ship.

The problem with his current assignment was that the ship was far from complete. So much was coming aboard at any one time that it was difficult, if not outright impossible, to screen everything. That included personnel.

"Yes, sir," Burns confirmed, his tone laced with displeasure. He carefully stepped forward and gingerly opened the top of the package, pulling the flap back to reveal its contents. Inside, hundreds of injection vials, each filled with a menacing red liquid, were meticulously arranged in holders.

"What is it?" Stroud took another step closer.

"Bloom, sir," the sergeant major said.

The revelation hit Stroud with the weight of a silent bombshell. Bloom was a dangerous substance. Its presence here, aboard their vessel and within reach of their crew, was a matter of serious concern.

Stroud's scowl deepened as he took in the sight of the vials. The discovery of bloom not only indicated a breach in their security but also hinted at deeper, more sinister undercurrents that could jeopardize the safety and integrity of the ship. His mind began to race, considering the implications, the necessary actions to be taken, and the investigation that would inevitably follow. This was more than a mere disciplinary issue; it was a significant threat that needed to be addressed with utmost urgency and precision.

Stroud let out a low whistle. He turned his attention to Ramirez. "Are we sure about this?"

"We are, sir," Ramirez replied with certainty. "We've conducted a thorough scan. The results are conclusive."

"Desaris's dog, then?" Stroud queried, referring to the method of detection. "She found this?"

"The beagle, Molly," Major Ramirez confirmed with a curt nod.

Stroud reflected on what he'd just been told for a long moment. "No matter how far we've come, technology-wise, it simply amazes me that we still rely on dogs to sniff out things like this."

"Yes, sir," Burns agreed, his expression grave.

"One taste of this stuff and you're hooked," Ramirez said with evident distaste. "The fact that it's even here bothers me greatly. It makes me wonder what else might be getting aboard that we haven't caught."

Stroud's nod was slow and contemplative, his mind churning over the implications. Bloom, a substance known for its ability to enhance cognitive abilities, was a double-edged sword. It allowed individuals to hyper-focus on complex tasks, which made it popular among professions that required intense concentration, such as scientists, engineers, and artists.

The drug created a state of heightened focus and relaxation, transforming challenging tasks into seemingly effortless endeavors. Users experienced an altered perception of time, with moments stretching out, allowing them to process information and react at speeds that appeared superhuman. This temporary enhancement of memory recall was particularly invaluable for tasks that demanded a vast repository of knowledge or intricate problem-solving skills.

Yet the presence of bloom here, in this environment, was deeply troubling. Stroud was all too aware of the dangers such substances posed, not only to the individual but to the safety and integrity of the entire crew and mission. The risk of dependency, the potential for impaired judgment, and the ethical implications of its use were all critical considerations.

If bloom had been smuggled aboard, especially in the quantity that lay on the table, it indicated a demand for it among the crew. This wasn't just a security issue; it was a matter of health and discipline. The discovery raised questions about the mental state, fitness, and stress levels of the ship's personnel. Were they resorting to such measures to cope with the demands of their work? How widespread was its use?

He had a lot of questions.

"This is really bad shit." Burns's words carried the weight of experience, his tone grave. "The euphoric state induced by bloom, coupled with its performance-enhancing effects, makes it extremely addictive. But worse, prolonged use wreaks havoc on neural pathways, leading to long-term cognitive impairments. I've seen what it does. Users gradually lose their grip on reality, struggling to differentiate between the bloom-induced focus state and normal perception. It leads to disorientation, social withdrawal, isolation... and ultimately severe clinical depression, hopelessness, suicidal thoughts... that sort of thing." He paused, exhaling a heavy breath. "At first, users think it's a blessing, a gift—but by the end..."

"The number of users who end up committing suicide... is quite high," Ramirez chimed in, his voice somber. "As the sergeant major said—it's really bad stuff."

"Yeah," Stroud echoed, his agreement laden with concern. "From the first hit, you're hooked. From there it's a dangerous and slippery path downward." He eyed the box, scanning it for labels or markings. There were none other than a simple shipping label in machine code. "Do we know who brought it aboard or who it was meant for?"

"Yes, sir," Burns said, and Stroud watched intently as Ramirez activated the screen built into the table. It revealed the image of a young woman in a green engineer's work suit, confined in a holding cell. Her posture suggested restraint, with her hands cuffed behind her back. The smeared makeup around her eyes, a telltale sign of tears, indicated the emotional turmoil she was experiencing. For her, he knew well, it would only get worse from here.

"Who is she?" Stroud inquired, his gaze fixed on the screen, studying the young woman's features for any hint of familiarity or insight into her situation. He could not recall having ever seen her before, but that was not unusual. At any given time, there were thousands of civilian techs working aboard.

"Technical Assistant Donna Mester," Ramirez said. "Civilian, twenty-six years of age from Avalon. Ironically, tomorrow is her birthday. She's part of the medical installation unit team and has been on the job for the last six months. No prior arrests or incidents on record. We think this is her first run-in with the law."

Stroud's mind began to weigh the possibilities. Was she an isolated case or a part of a larger network within the ship? Her lack of a criminal history suggested either a first-time offense or a careful avoidance of detection until now.

Stroud's gaze lingered on the image of Donna Mester, the young engineering assistant whose life had taken a drastic turn. He felt an undeniable sadness in acknowledging the consequences she now faced. Her youth and the potential she might have had sharply clashed with the grim reality of her situation and the likely consequences of her arrest. The prospect of spending a significant portion of her life on a penal colony, followed by the daunting challenge of reintegration into society, was a heavy price to pay.

The consequences of involvement in the transport and distribution of a substance like bloom were severe and far-reaching. Stroud knew all too well that the rules and regulations in place were not just for maintaining order; they were crucial for the safety and well-being of everyone on board.

As his gaze shifted back to the vials of bloom on the table, Stroud felt a hardening resolve. The gravity of the situation was undeniable. Bloom wasn't just an illegal substance; it was a catalyst for destruction, capable of derailing lives, ruining families, not to mention compromising the integrity and safety of the ship.

"She claims she doesn't know what's in the crate." Ramirez's statement suggested a possible defense, but the truth of it remained to be seen.

"Once they drug her, the interrogation unit will get to the bottom of that," Burns added, his tone suggesting a reliance on more intensive techniques to uncover the facts. "Whether she wants to or not, she will tell them everything."

"Have you called station security?" Stroud asked, ensuring that the necessary protocols were being followed in handling the situation. "Have you notified them?"

"Yes, sir," Ramirez replied. "They are on their way over now and should be here within the hour to collect her. I figured you'd want to see this before they arrived—in case you wanted anything done beforehand."

Stroud nodded in approval. It was a prudent decision to inform him first, allowing him to grasp the situation before it escalated to higher command. This foresight would enable him to prepare a report for Captain Garrett, maintaining the chain of command and ensuring that the captain of the ship was not blindsided by the incident.

The matter, while serious, did not warrant waking the captain himself, but it certainly required Stroud's attention at the earliest appropriate time. He would compose a brief but comprehensive report, detailing the incident and the initial steps taken. This report would be ready for the captain's review before the morning briefings and department head meetings. Stroud would make sure to mark it as a priority security matter so it came immediately to the captain's attention.

Looking ahead, Stroud anticipated that the captain would likely seek a personal discussion regarding the incident. The focus would not only be on the immediate handling of the situation but, more importantly, on the measures to prevent such an occurrence in the future. This meant that Stroud needed to formulate a robust plan, enhancing the screening processes for personnel and materials coming aboard.

"She's clearly a mule," Burns stated, suggesting that Mester was a courier in a larger operation.

"Fast cash," Ramirez added. "I could see that. Pick a young, stupid, but pretty girl for transport, someone who works in medical, a person who's easily overlooked." He gestured at the table. "Even if she was stopped carrying this, without a scan, it would likely not draw attention. That red liquid in the vials looks like blood."

"There has to be a dealer aboard, not to mention on the station," Burns continued, "and a network for transport and distribution. I can hardly imagine this is an isolated incident."

"How'd you catch her?" Stroud inquired, seeking to understand the sequence of events that led to the discovery. That would help him develop a future plan of attack when it came to screening.

"Desaris's dog hit on this package in the transfer terminal before the pallet was brought aboard. Once we knew what we had on our hands, we allowed the pallet onboard and then waited for the crate to be picked up. It didn't take long, sir, less than a half-hour."

"Why didn't you wait until she delivered it to the dealer?" Stroud asked. "You could have followed her using the ship's internal surveillance system."

"That was my call, sir," Ramirez interjected, capturing Stroud's full attention. "Where the package was delivered, where Miss Mester picked it up—the surveillance system in that section of the ship had an outage. At the time, it was down."

"Someone brought it down, sir," Burns said. "That's our guess."

"I couldn't let this stuff get distributed," Ramirez said. "I did not want to take that chance."

"Good call, then," Stroud acknowledged, appreciating the quick thinking. He then turned his attention to a broader issue. "Did you check the surveillance logs to see how many times the system had either failed or had an outage previously?"

"We did, sir," Burns responded. "The system has been experiencing technical outages on average every two to three weeks. Maintenance has been on it multiple times, but the issue persists. They've been unable to pinpoint exactly where the problem lies. They're now considering replacing the entire core unit."

"This is no coincidence," Ramirez said. "Someone either has the manual ability to bring it down, or they've programmed a backdoor into the system."

"Neither possibility makes me feel comfortable," Stroud admitted. "Let's get our techs and hackers on it. See if they can find some electronic fingerprints or evidence that will lead us to who is responsible."

"Yes, sir," Burns affirmed. "I will make that a top priority."

The situation called for a thorough investigation, not just of the bloom smuggling, but also of the surveillance system's integrity. Stroud knew the importance of identifying and neutralizing this internal threat. It was imperative to safeguard the ship's security systems against such vulnerabilities to prevent future incidents. This would require a coordinated effort from their best technical minds, combining expertise in technology and security to uncover and address this hidden danger. Stroud's mind was already strategizing the broader scope of their investigation and how he could better attack it.

"I also want to determine if any other areas have had similar security outages. We may be facing a larger drug and smuggling problem," Stroud said, considering the possibility that the issue extended beyond the bloom-smuggling incident.

"We'll get right on that," Ramirez responded.

"When I speak to the captain about this matter, I'll request Fleet resources to assist us in our investigation."

"That would be helpful, sir," Burns agreed. "We'll need the extra hands."

Stroud's gaze returned to the screen, his eyes lingering on the image of Donna Mester as he considered her role in this complex puzzle.

"Has she talked?" Stroud inquired.

"Yes, sir," Burns replied. "As I said, she claims she didn't know what was in the crate. After picking it up, she takes it to medical stores. From there, someone else retrieves it. She insists she doesn't know who that person is."

"Do you believe her?" Stroud asked, weighing the likelihood of her story.

"Yes, sir, I do," Burns responded confidently. "But the station interrogation unit will confirm whether she's telling the truth. Either way, it doesn't matter much for her now, does it?"

"No, it doesn't," Ramirez said. "The court won't care. Her fate is sealed."

"All right, let's get this crate to medical stores, then," Stroud decided, "and see who comes for it. I want plenty of security around so it does not disappear. Add a motion-delayed activation tracker to the case. That way, it won't be lost. Once it begins moving, we can pounce."

"Sir," Burns interjected. "I would like permission to approach Doctor Neelan, to secure his assistance."

"The chief medical officer?" Stroud questioned, curious about this new angle.

"Yes, sir. I want him to replace these vials with something harmless," Burns explained. "That way, if our suspect or suspects are more sophisticated than we think and somehow manage to elude us and get away with the goods, no one gets hurt by the contents."

Stroud nodded. "I understand. See that it is done quietly and quickly."

"Aye, sir," Burns said.

Stroud glanced back at the monitor. He let go a long breath. "Stupid girl. A waste of a good life."

"Station security will interrogate her thoroughly," Ramirez said. "She will tell them all she knows and then some. We should have some additional answers before the end of the day."

"Though I doubt it, hopefully they will get something actionable." After a brief pause, Stroud made a call. "Let's test our own people while we are at it."

"All of them?" Burns queried, sounding slightly taken aback. Their current protocol involved random checks, but Stroud's suggestion was far more comprehensive.

"Let's hit all our people this time around." Stroud turned to Ramirez. "Coordinate with medical, get it done in the next forty-eight hours—hair, blood, urine. If anyone's using anything, I want to know." He gestured at the crate with a hand. "The last thing we need is someone hyped up on something worse than bloom while using powered armor or handling a weapon."

"I'll get on it, sir," Ramirez responded promptly.

"Do you wish to speak to her?" Burns asked. "Before station security gets here?"

"I see no need." Stroud shook his head, then looked between both men. "Good work, both of you. Also, tell Desaris the same."

"Thank you, sir," Ramirez said.

A comm chimed in Stroud's ear, signaling an inbound call. He turned away and with a thought accepted the connection. Whoever was calling him, it was still bloody early and was sure to be more bad news.

When it rains, it pours.

"Stroud here," he answered, his voice steady.

The response came quickly, tinged with a hint of nervousness. "I am sorry to disturb you, sir. This is Lieutenant Smith at boarding post 331-A. I have something to report."

Stroud's brow furrowed slightly, a scowl forming as he processed the unusual nature of the call. Boarding post 331-A was a specific entry point, one primarily used by the yard dogs, maintenance, and repair personnel. It was not a location typically involved in high-priority security issues. The fact that the lieutenant was contacting him directly, bypassing the usual chain of command, suggested something out of the ordinary.

"How can I help you, Lieutenant?"

"Ah, sir, there is something going on stationside," Smith explained, a note of concern in his voice. "I'm not sure what the problem is, but several civilian personnel have debarked from the ship. They weren't scheduled to do so until their shifts end, several hours from now. At first, I thought it was nothing, but... well—"

"Why didn't you bring this matter to your immediate superior? Why are you breaking the chain of command?" Stroud cut in, seeking clarification on the breach of protocol. At the same time, he found himself wondering if the word on the drug seizure had gotten out. If so, there was nowhere for those involved to flee but the station, and that would be a wasted effort. Station security would simply conduct a station-wide bioscan, seeking the individuals' implanted identity tags and finding them in short order. Removing the tags would trigger alarms.

There was a brief, telling silence before Smith replied. He could hear the lieutenant suck in a breath. As he spoke, he let it out. "I did, sir. I talked to my captain a short while ago."

"And what did he say?" Stroud prodded further.

"That it was nothing to worry about, sir," Smith answered cautiously. "He said that civilians come and go at unexpected times and not to hassle them. That it was likely nothing more than a scheduling issue... or an important meeting they were late for..." The lieutenant fell silent.

As Stroud processed this response, he pondered the dynamics at play. He knew Smith was new to his role, a junior officer in Charlie Company on his first deployment. The decision to bypass his captain and reach out directly to Stroud suggested a level of concern that Smith must have felt was not adequately addressed by his superior. Stroud found himself quietly impressed by the lieutenant's initiative and audacity, despite the coming backlash for stepping outside the chain of command. His company commander would be irate when he found out. At the same time, Stroud felt a niggle of irritation at Smith's immediate superior.

Still, the situation was peculiar. The unscheduled departure of civilian personnel might not be alarming under normal circumstances, but given the current context of the bloom discovery and security concerns, any irregularity warranted closer scrutiny and attention.

"Captain Kesty is your company commander?" he asked, though he already knew it to be fact.

"Yes, sir, he is," Smith confirmed.

"And you don't believe this is nothing?" Stroud probed further, seeking to better understand Smith's perspective. "Explain yourself."

"No, sir, I don't," Smith replied with conviction. "Those leaving the ship seemed panicked, on edge, anxious. And they weren't just regular civilian techs or yard dogs; they were the bosses—supervisors and foremen. Also, our stationside security counterparts have left their posts. I don't like what that suggests, sir."

Stroud was taken aback. It was like someone had slapped him in the face.

"What?" he asked sharply. Ramirez and Burns, only hearing

Stroud's side of the conversation, looked at him with curiosity and growing concern. "They left their posts?"

"They have, sir. I sent my people out into the terminal for a look. They're all gone, sir. We took up their positions, assuming their posts. I am concerned... something is going on that we don't know about, sir. Whatever it is, it can't be good."

"You are at post 331-A?" Stroud was already strategizing, picturing the ship's layout in his mind and the quickest path there. The post was not far off.

"Yes, sir," Smith confirmed.

"Lieutenant, I will be there shortly. Hold your position," Stroud instructed with authority. "Anyone else attempting to disembark before their assigned shift ends is to be detained and held until I arrive and can question them. Do you understand me?"

"Yes, sir, and thank you, sir," Smith responded, a noticeable tone of relief in his voice as Stroud ended the call.

"Is there a problem?" Ramirez asked.

"I don't know," he replied to Ramirez. "Something may be up stationside. The civilian bosses are leaving the ship early, and the security contingent stationed opposite 331-A has abandoned their posts inside the station embarkation terminal."

"They did *what*?" Ramirez asked, his shock evident. "That's not good. This could be a prelude to a terrorist strike."

"If I recall the duty schedule, sir, Lieutenant Smith has that post," Burns said.

"He does," Stroud confirmed.

"That boy has a good head on his shoulders," Burns said.

"That's a compliment if I ever heard one," Ramirez said to Burns, who gave a noncommittal grunt in reply.

Stroud agreed, for the sergeant major never complimented anyone.

"Sir." Burns glanced at Ramirez before turning his attention back to Stroud. "Concerning terrorists, if they brought a bomb to that transfer terminal, our detection gear would have spotted it straight off. I cannot imagine anyone spoofing our gear—the ship's maybe, but not ours."

"Right, I'm heading to 331-A," Stroud announced, already moving toward the hatch with a sense of urgency. "Burns, check on all our active boarding posts. Ensure there's no trouble or strange things going on elsewhere."

"Yes, sir, I'm on it," Burns responded promptly.

Half out into the hallway, Stroud paused at the hatch, his hand resting on the frame as he turned back to Ramirez. "Roust the ready platoon. If there's some sort of trouble stationside, a coming terrorist attack or riot, whatever, I want to be prepared." He paused and looked directly at Burns. It was an effort to keep his tone steady when he spoke next, for his irritation was great. "And kindly get Kesty moving for me. I want him to meet me at Smith's post. The man has some questions I want answered, such as why he blew off his lieutenant's concerns and forced a junior officer to go over his head."

"I will find him and get him there on the pronto, sir." The sergeant major grinned with near glee, if he was capable of joy. "If I have to kick him out of the rack, I will."

Though Ramirez was Stroud's second in command, as the senior-most ranked noncommissioned officer, the sergeant major was just as important. In fact, when he gave his opinion, both Ramirez and Stroud listened.

"Good." Stroud turned and swiftly made his way down the hallway. His mind was already racing ahead to the challenges awaiting him at the boarding port.

TEN

GARRETT

Garrett emerged from the shower, droplets of water cascading down his body. He was immediately enveloped in a strong gust of hot air, a comforting embrace that rapidly helped dry his skin as he briskly toweled off. After thirty seconds, the warm air subsided, and he wrapped the towel securely around his waist and moved over to the sink and mirror.

Standing there, he allowed himself a moment to study his reflection with a critical eye. Time, it seemed, had been a double-edged sword for him. On one hand, the years had graced him with a certain distinguished air, an undeniable mark of experience and resilience. He was also fit and in shape. He made a point to set aside time to work out each day.

Yet there were undeniable signs of the passage of time, the fine lines etched more deeply around his eyes, the rebellious strands of gray weaving through his once uniformly brown hair. He had pondered the idea of coloring them but had dismissed the thought. It was a pretense that didn't align with his nature.

Garrett ran his fingers through his short, damp hair. He reached for his preferred styling product, applying it skillfully. With a few deft movements, he arranged his hair into its familiar style, a slight part to the left adding a touch of order to his otherwise rugged appearance.

Next, he picked up his electric razor. The hum of the machine was a familiar morning symphony as he expertly shaved off the prior day's growth, leaving his skin relatively smooth and refreshed. Once satisfied with his shave, Garrett moved on to his oral hygiene routine, brushing his teeth thoroughly.

His attention shifted to his ship suit, which hung neatly beside him from the back of the hatch. Slipping into the suit, he admired its precision fit as it shifted and conformed to his body, contouring to his physique, thanks to the advanced technology that went into its design. The material was not only comfortable but lightweight and durable, perfect for the demands of his profession. He then reached for his boots, sliding his feet into them with practiced ease. They automatically tightened around his ankles and feet, formfitting like his suit had.

As he rose to his feet, the boots audibly clicked into position with his suit, creating a secure and airtight seal. This design was far more than a mere stylistic choice; it was an essential safety measure. In the event of an accident where part of the ship became exposed to the harsh vacuum of space, the suit's sophisticated emergency response would activate. The helmet, crafted from a durable, non-fabric nano-material, would swiftly deploy, unfolding and enveloping his head in a protective embrace. Following this, the suit would begin to pressurize, providing him with a precious few minutes of breathable air. This brief window could be the difference between life and death in the unforgiving environment of space, granting him just enough time to reach a locker and secure an additional external oxygen supply.

Garrett took a moment to adjust the suit, ensuring everything was in perfect working order. His implants told him the power supply was fully charged and the suit was functioning as expected.

Satisfied, he carefully opened the hatch, stepping back into the tranquility of his cabin. The room was steeped in a soft, muted light, casting a serene glow over everything.

Sleeping peacefully on his bed was Tina. She lay on her side, the gentle rise and fall of her breathing speaking to her deep slumber. The sheet that partially covered her had slipped, revealing her delicate form in a moment of unguarded vulnerability.

For a brief moment, Garrett stood motionless, allowing himself to admire her beauty in the stillness of the cabin. The soft lighting accentuated her features, highlighting the curves and contours of her lithe body in a way that was both artistic and intimate.

He was struck anew by her allure, the memory of their shared passion from the night before lingering vividly in his mind. A familiar warmth stirred within him, tempting him with the thought of rekindling their earlier intimacy. He knew she would be open to more...

But then, with a resolute shake of his head, Garrett snapped out of his reverie. He reminded himself of the responsibilities awaiting him, the tasks he had put off the night before in favor of their amorous escapade. There was work to be done, duties that couldn't be neglected any longer, even if it was a little earlier than usual.

With a last, lingering glance at Tina, Garrett silently moved toward his office. His steps were measured and quiet, careful not to disturb her peaceful rest. As he closed the hatch behind him, he shifted his focus fully to the tasks at hand, the image of Tina lingering like a sweet afterimage, a private memory for a later time. The professional part of him took over, ready to dive into the world of reports, analyses, and decisions that waited.

With a mere thought channeled through his neural

implants, Garrett activated the lights in his office. The space was instantly bathed in a soft, efficient glow, revealing the neatly organized chaos that was his personal workspace. His eyes fell upon the pile of mail on his desk, a seemingly unending stream of communications and responsibilities that came with his position. The pile seemed to have grown overnight.

Among the assorted envelopes and data pads, he noticed the secure bag, its presence standing out. Settling into his chair, Garrett powered up his tablet with a swift motion. The screen came to life, displaying the time: 0434 in the morning. It was a stark reminder of the early hour, a little less than thirty minutes before his usual waking time. He quickly accessed his mail, his eyes scanning the digital inbox. More than three hundred new items awaited his attention, a daunting addition to the physical mail already lying neatly stacked upon his desk.

Suppressing a yawn, Garrett contemplated calling for his steward to bring him a coffee. However, mindful of the early hour, he quickly dismissed the idea. His steward would still be asleep, and he was not one to disrupt the rest of others for a mere convenience. He had iced coffee in his cabin, but he did not want to disturb Tina. Garrett would wait.

Resigned to face the mountain of work unaided by caffeine, he leaned forward, his fingers beginning to navigate through the emails, rapidly scanning their subjects. Each message was a puzzle piece in the vast tapestry of his responsibilities, ranging from routine updates to critical decisions that required his immediate attention. Those, he decided after a moment, could wait.

As Garrett scratched an absent itch on his arm, his attention was irresistibly drawn back to the secure bag from Admiral Gray. There was an air of intrigue about it, for it was larger than normal. He reached out and pressed his thumb against the sensor lock. The bag responded with a satisfying click, signaling the security measures in place. Any unauthorized attempt to access the bag would have resulted in the destruction of the contents within.

Pulling back the flap, Garrett found his curiosity piqued as he discovered a small tablet inside, a departure from the typical data cubes he received from the admiral. He extracted the device, examining it with a practiced eye before activating the tablet, pressing his thumb to the sensor.

The tablet sought confirmation of his identity, interfacing seamlessly with his implants. Satisfied with the verification, the device unlocked, revealing a still image of the admiral on the screen, accompanied by an icon indicating the presence of three distinct messages, all of which were marked as top priority.

The prioritization of the messages was clear, with the most important one loaded first and ready to go. Garrett felt a mix of anticipation and apprehension; communications from Gray were seldom without significant implications, especially when she sent a tablet. He pressed the play button, his focus narrowing as he prepared himself to absorb the contents of the message.

The screen came to life, and Admiral Gray appeared, her expression solemn. Garrett couldn't help but notice the toll that time and stress had taken. Her face was more lined than he remembered, and her hair had turned fully silver. She also appeared tired, weary. Yet despite the visible signs of fatigue, her voice carried the unmistakable timbre of authority, strength, and resolve.

"Garrett," she began, her tone leaving no room for doubt about the seriousness of the situation, "this is a war warning. Intelligence has reason to believe the Push may come early, much sooner than anyone anticipated. By the time you receive this message it may already have begun." Her words were measured, deliberate, conveying a sense of the impending threat. Shocked, Garrett listened intently, his mind already racing through the implications of her statement. "I cannot go into why they have come to that conclusion. Accept it as fact. Admiral Isabel has been notified. She will receive a more comprehensive update than yours. As you can imagine, the Fleet is unprepared for the fight to come. Should the Push at some point arrive at Midway, under no circumstances are you to allow your current and uncompleted Job to fall into enemy hands. Consider this a direct order to scuttle your ship and ensure the gripper drive is destroyed."

"What?" Garrett asked aloud, leaning back. It came out as more of a gasp. He could not believe what he'd just heard.

"I have issued a direct order for the trials of your vessel to be expedited, giving it priority," Gray continued. "Make all possible haste in getting your ship ready for action. With the current emergency in mind, I recommended and personally requested you be promoted to full command of your vessel upon commissioning. There will not be time to get another officer up to speed on your ship. Unfortunately, Isabel is close to Omaga. I do not know if she will accept my recommendation—but you never know." Gray's tone softened. "I hope she does, for at the moment, you are the most qualified candidate available and my personal choice. At the very least, you will end up as the ship's first officer should you desire the position. However, if you find yourself relieved, I have left standing orders for you to commandeer a fast transport and report immediately to my headquarters for reassignment. Those orders cover taking Shaw with you. Whatever happens in the days and weeks ahead, I wish you good fortune. Admiral Gray out."

The message ended.

The reality and full import of Gray's message settled over Garrett like a cold fog, leaving him stunned. He leaned back in his chair, his mind grappling with the enormity of the situation. The shock of it all rendered him motionless as he struggled to process the implications of what he had just heard and learned.

Yenga's earlier summons now clicked into place, a puzzle

piece fitting into the larger picture of unfolding events. Isabel's receipt of the message explained the sudden alert status of the fleet, a response to the impending threat.

Garrett shook his head, trying to clear the fog of disbelief. He had been recommended as the ship's first captain. He could scarcely believe that. But now, the weight of his current responsibility felt heavier than ever. The prospect of facing an early offensive by the enemy, coupled with the revelation that the Confederation was unprepared, was a jarring reality check.

The strategic disadvantage was clear: the main power of the Fleet was badly out of position. Worse, it was spread out over multiple systems, diluting its power, a vulnerability that the enemy could exploit with devastating effect. The thought of scuttling his own ship, as per the admiral's direct order, was a scenario he had never envisioned confronting. The intentional destruction of the Job he had come to love was hard to conceive, impossible even.

Needing to hear the message again, to absorb every nuance and detail, Garrett pressed the play button. He listened intently, his mind working overtime to anticipate, plan, and strategize the road ahead. As the message concluded for the second time, a profound sense of gravity settled over him, as did a feeling of terrible worry.

Sitting back in his chair, Garrett closed his eyes. If he was to speed up the commissioning process, there was a lot of work ahead of him, and time might not be on his side. In fact, he was certain it was not.

"Holy shit."

He almost jolted in his seat, not having heard Tina open the hatch. There she stood, completely naked, her expression one of utter astonishment. Her eyes, wide and unblinking, were fixed on him.

"Holy fucking shit," Tina breathed out, her voice barely above a whisper.

"You were not supposed to hear that," he said, feeling a twinge of concern and regret.

"You think?" Tina retorted, her voice rising slightly in both volume and intensity. "I knew you swam in big circles, you'd have to to be assigned to this Job, but that"—she pointed at the reader—"was Admiral Gray briefing you directly, one of the joint chiefs."

In the silence that followed, Garrett powered off the tablet and carefully placed it back on his desk. He found himself momentarily at a loss for words, not just because of Tina's unexpected presence and her exposure to classified information, but also due to the gravity of the situation he—everyone—now faced. The war was on their doorstep and the enemy was knocking.

His thoughts shifted to his ship, the vessel he had dedicated so much of himself to. The idea of scuttling her, as per the admiral's orders in the worst-case scenario, was something he could not conceive doing, ever. The thought was almost unbearable.

As he grappled with the situation, practical considerations began to take shape in his mind. Time was clearly now of the essence; how much of it did he have before the potential early arrival of the enemy? The possibility of accelerating the ship's trials was critical. He pondered the feasibility of convincing Yenga and Isabel to allow these trials to proceed immediately, even as the final touches were being put on the ship. Could he manage it with just a skeleton crew? The logistics were daunting, but not wholly insurmountable. He might just be able to pull it off. In fact, he would have to. The alternative was something he did not wish to consider.

"What was that bit about Omaga and Isabel?" Tina asked. Garrett could read the genuine curiosity and concern in her eyes. "What did she mean?"

He hesitated for a moment, considering how much he could divulge. Finally, he gave a shrug and decided to come clean.

"It goes back to *Repulse* and Antares Station," Garrett began, his voice carrying the weight of the past. "I was sidelined for what happened there." He paused, memories of those events casting a shadow over his thoughts. "Omaga wanted to put me out to pasture. Gray saved my career. I was given a second chance in Construction Command."

Tina's next question was almost inevitable, reflecting her confusion about the situation. "Why would they do that? Why would they sideline you?"

Garrett sighed, the complexity of the answer stretching beyond the simplicity of the question. "It's not always about what you do or don't do in these situations. Sometimes, it's about politics, perceptions, and the need for someone to take the fall for another's mistakes. My actions aboard *Repulse* were controversial among Command. Some saw them as necessary, others as a failure. Omaga was one of those who took it negatively and wanted me punished."

Tina's eyes narrowed.

Garrett sucked in a breath and continued. "Admiral Gray, however, believed in me, saw the potential and the circumstances differently. She advocated for me. It's rare to get a second chance like this, and I worked hard to make the most of it, to pay her back."

"Why would they do that? Why would they sideline you?"

Garrett paused, his gaze lingering on the surface of his desk. The memories of those events began to resurface. Omaga had worked to conceal the true nature of what had transpired. Even though it had happened more than twelve years before, rumors still circulated. They were a dark cloud that hung over his head, but for most, the full story remained shrouded in mystery and conjecture.

He leaned forward, the leather of his chair creaking under his weight, and lightly tapped his knuckles against the desk, a rhythmic sound that seemed to echo the tumultuous beat of his thoughts. His gaze met Tina's and he found himself hesitating.

"You received a commendation," Tina continued, her voice tinged with a mix of admiration and skepticism. "The *Gazette* heralded you as the hero of the hour, who not only saved your ship but also quelled the mutiny. They wrote that you were the highest-ranking officer left standing." Her eyes searched his face. "Tell me the rest of the story... please."

Garrett sighed; a faint, bitter smile played out on his lips. "You can't believe everything you read." His voice was barely above a whisper. The weight of unspoken truths hung heavily in the air between them.

"Then what really happened?" Tina pressed, leaning in closer. "What truly happened out there, Jim?"

"Surely you have heard some of the rumors."

"I have," Tina admitted. "They spoke of cowardice under fire—your cowardice, losing your head for a time before getting command of your faculties. There were others that told of unfitness for command, mistakes made. I never believed any of them, especially after the commendation you received. More importantly, I know you."

Garrett's gaze drifted away, lost in the past. He knew the time had come to unveil the curtain of secrecy, to reveal the harrowing reality of those dark hours aboard *Repulse*.

Still, he hesitated, finding himself engulfed in a maelstrom of emotions as he gazed back over at Tina. The night they had just shared flickered through his mind like a poignant memory, casting a ghostly glow on the moment. Tina, more than just a beautiful woman, was the captain of her own vessel and one of his oldest friends. Would she understand? A wave of trepidation washed over him as he pondered how she would react to the harrowing truth he was about to unveil.

Her skin bathed in the soft light of his office, Tina moved toward him with the grace of a predator. As she approached, her naked form seemed almost surreal, like a vision crafted from the sea mists. She knelt beside his chair, her presence both comforting and unsettling. Her hand came to rest upon his forearm. He almost jumped at the contact. Her brown eyes, deep and probing, searched his face for clues, silently urging him to divulge the secret weighing heavily on his conscience, his soul.

Garrett's voice was barely above a whisper, strained with the burden of his confession. "I shot and killed my captain."

"What?" she gasped, her voice a mix of horror and disbelief. Removing her hand, she rose to her feet, her movements hesitant, as if the gravity of his words had suddenly made the air around her dense and oppressive. "You killed Captain Marlowe? In our first year, she was one of our instructors. She wrote me a recommendation letter and got me my first billet on a ship. Heck, she handpicked you, Jim—personally—when she assumed command of *Repulse*."

"She did," Garrett confirmed. "In hindsight, I wish she hadn't."

The intensity in Tina's eyes as she looked down at Garrett was almost too much for him to bear. Her gaze, fraught with horror and disbelief at this revelation, seemed to pierce through him. It was a look that spoke volumes of the shock, the disgust, and the turmoil within.

Garrett, feeling the weight of each second, continued his explanation, his voice laced with a mixture of sorrow and resolve. "We were ambushed. The ship was in pieces, the bridge shattered," he began, his heart beginning to race as if he was reliving the harrowing experience, which, in a manner of speaking, he was. There were still nights where sleep eluded him or he was plagued by nightmares. "Most of the crew were dead, and all other senior officers were gone but for me and the captain. Many who survived the attack were injured, isolated, and trapped. The ship was dying." He paused, sucking in a breath while gathering his thoughts. "Captain Marlowe was hurt badly and wasn't thinking clearly. The fight had ended. We had already destroyed the enemy ship. There was no need for further bloodshed, but she... she was determined to kill every single person on that station, all ten thousand civilians, guilty or not. She wanted to make them pay for what they had done to her ship, and *Reprise*. In that moment, she wasn't the person who had earned my respect." Garrett's voice cracked slightly as he continued. "The mutiny had been quelled. The threat was over. But she... she shot the helmsman dead, right in front of me, simply because she refused to obey her order to murder innocents."

Tina remained silent, her expression unreadable. The revelation had clearly shaken her to the core. Garrett's gaze met Tina's, his expression a complex mix of resignation and resolve.

"I was cleared by a Navy board," he stated, his voice steady and firm. "But much of the truth about that day was swept under the rug. It's the reason why I've been sidelined, kept away from any command position besides what I can find in Construction Command."

Tina's hand had gone to her mouth, a gesture of shock and perhaps a subconscious attempt to stifle the emotions threatening to overwhelm her.

"You killed Captain Marlowe?" she repeated, her voice tinged with disbelief. It was as though the gravity of his confession had only just fully registered with her... that she hadn't heard his explanation. "You killed your captain?" The question echoed again in the small office, carrying with it a weight of accusation and patent disbelief. "You shot her."

"I did," Garrett admitted, his eyes not leaving hers. "It is something that I have had to live with and, truth be told, would do again were I given the opportunity. I saved lives that day and that is what matters."

A heavy silence settled between them, thick with unspoken thoughts and emotions. Then, Tina's gaze shifted to the reader lying on Garrett's desk. Her expression, previously a mask of shock and confusion, now tightened.

"Why didn't you tell me sooner?"

That seemed to have hurt her more than anything. Garrett did not have a good answer. Instead, he gave a shrug of his shoulders as a reply.

"I think I had best report to my ship," she said, her voice steady but carrying an undercurrent of hardness.

Or was it betrayal?

Garrett understood plainly enough. What they'd had was gone—forever.

"What you heard is classified," he said firmly, gesturing at the tablet. "You cannot share what you learned about the Push with anyone."

"I won't," she assured him, her voice low and steady.

The blare of the buzzer, unexpected and jarring, broke the tense atmosphere between them. They both flinched, momentarily startled by the intrusion of the outside world into their fraught conversation. Garrett, realizing the significance of the sound, a rarity outside of routine tests, quickly leaned forward to manually activate the intercom.

"What is it?" he asked, his voice now adopting the authoritative tone of command.

"Captain," came Shaw's voice, urgent and laced with an undercurrent of concern. "I think you had best report to the bridge. We have a developing situation."

"What's the problem?" Garrett asked.

"Something is happening stationside. I am not sure what, sir."

"I will be right there." Garrett's response was immediate, the call of duty overriding all other considerations.

He stood.

The hatch to his cabin clicked shut. Tina had retreated into his cabin, the hatch now closed, a physical barrier echoing the emotional distance that had suddenly emerged between them. For a fleeting moment, Garrett considered going to her, to offer some form of solace or further explanation, to try to make her understand and get things right between them. But the compelling pull of his responsibilities as captain quickly over-shadowed this impulse.

"So be it." Duty, as always, came first.

Garrett's eyes fell upon the reader on his desk, the one sent by Gray. There were two additional messages waiting for him, their contents unknown, but potentially critical. However, they would have to wait. The urgency in Shaw's tone was clear.

With a final glance at the closed hatch to his cabin, Garrett turned for the bridge.

ELEVEN

GARRETT

The marine sentry, standing with impeccable posture and a disciplined gaze focused straight ahead, instantly snapped to attention as Garrett strode past her. Behind him, the hatch to his office slid closed with a soft hiss as the ambience of the bridge rolled over him, a buzz of focused activity and the soft glow of numerous displays illuminating the area, along with various pings and chimes.

Shaw occupied the first officer's station, strategically positioned to the immediate right of the captain's chair. His attention was riveted on a screen as he engaged in a dialogue with an unseen party.

Two other stations on the bridge were notably filled: engineering and communications. That was only to be expected. The rest of the duty stations were unoccupied. At engineering, McKay was focused on the screens before him, but he did glance over at Garrett, his eyes conveying concern, before hastily returning his attention to his station and the work that lay before him.

Keeli, the communications officer, was particularly engrossed in her tasks. She leaned forward intently at her console, her fingers dancing swiftly over the sleek surface of one of the advanced touch displays. Her eyes flicked rapidly across the screen, studying whatever was displayed there. She was biting her lower lip.

Garrett felt a growing sense of unease as he made his way over toward Shaw, his eyes searching for answers. As he approached, he could sense the gravity of the situation reflected in the furrows of the commander's brow and the rigid set of his shoulders.

"Shaw, what's going on?" Garrett inquired.

"Pence, I will be back in a few minutes." Shaw paused and muted the channel on which he had been communicating. He turned to Garrett, worry plain in his expression. There was a brief, weighted silence as he collected his thoughts. "We are receiving reports from multiple boarding posts. Something is happening stationside, some sort of disturbance, sir," he explained, his eyes flicking back to the screens displaying an array of incoming data.

"Disturbance?" Garrett echoed.

Shaw nodded gravely, his attention briefly shifting to a blinking console display. "It's not entirely clear yet, but the situation appears to be escalating rapidly. Several of our marine sentries at boarding posts have requested not only help, but reinforcement."

"What?" Garrett asked, becoming alarmed. At the same time, he felt a wash of relief as he grasped that the disturbance was confined to the station and not aboard his own ship.

However, his relief was tinged with a sense of vigilance. Station-bound trouble, particularly on Midway, was a rarity. The station was renowned for its harmonious blend of living and working conditions. The comfort and convenience offered here made it a jewel among the Confederation's space stations, a place where discontent was a rare, but not unknown, visitor.

No matter how good things were, there were always agitators, malcontents.

Protests and riots, while not commonplace, were not unheard of in some of the more remote space stations or outposts, especially penal colonies. Such riots, when they did occur, could be particularly dangerous. However, Garrett struggled to recall any such incidents occurring on Midway. Life on this station was generally too easy and good.

"I just got off with Stroud," Shaw continued. "He's already in the process of mobilizing his battalion and dispatching additional security forces to trouble spots he's designated as requiring priority."

Garrett pondered the possibilities, his mind at work. "Some sort of accident or protest at one of the neighboring slips?"

"I don't know," Shaw admitted with a shrug of his shoulders.

"You said there are multiple reports," Garrett pressed, seeking clarity.

"Yes, sir," Shaw confirmed. "We're receiving alerts from several of our posts."

Garrett's mind raced as he connected the dots. "Which means trouble is occurring across a number of station decks and levels."

This revelation was worrying. In a typical riot or localized disturbance, the chaos would usually be contained within a specific area. Stationside security would have acted fast to contain it as well. The fact that the trouble was spreading to multiple levels, affecting several boarding posts, indicated something far more serious.

"That's correct, sir."

"What do we know?" Garrett asked, keeping his tone firm yet calm. His job was to set the example for others to follow, to be the rock in the middle of the storm.

"The station has gone to high alert, sir. Our marines have

confirmed that the station's 1MC announcements are stating that the alert is not a drill. All military personnel are to report to their posts or return to their ships."

"Really?" Garrett responded, a hint of surprise evident in his voice.

Shaw nodded, his expression grave. "Yes, sir. And there's more. According to Corporal Tauhid, who is stationed at boarding post 22-B, the situation stationside is chaotic. He described it as 'they have gone apeshit.' He also reported some individuals have attempted to force their way aboard our vessel."

Garrett felt himself scowl.

"Why?" Garrett asked. "Why do they want to get aboard?"

Shaw shook his head, the lines of his face etched with concern. "We don't know yet, sir. The information is still coming in, and the situation is evolving rapidly."

Garrett processed this, his mind racing with possibilities. The lack of clear answers only added to the complexity of the situation, the puzzle to which he was missing key pieces. It was imperative that they gain a better understanding of the events unfolding stationside.

"What's the alert about?" he asked, hoping for some insight into the nature of the crisis. "Do we know?"

Shaw shook his head, his expression reflecting the frustrating lack of information. "None of the marines can tell me, sir. The announcement didn't specify the nature of it. We also didn't receive a copy of the alert."

Garrett nodded, understanding the implications. The lack of details in the announcement could mean that the situation was either too chaotic to be clearly understood or too sensitive to be openly communicated. Either scenario was troubling.

"What did Stroud have to say?" Garrett inquired.

"The colonel is on his way to post 44-B. He's been visiting the embarkation and debarkation points since the trouble started about an hour ago. It began with one post. Initially we thought it a brewing riot, then—well, it spread to the others within the last twenty minutes or so. That's when I called you."

Garrett gazed about the bridge. The engineering officer was casting concerned glances their way. Keeli had ceased her work, her attention fixed on the unfolding discussion between him and Shaw.

"Keeli," Garrett asked, "have you reached out to Station Command?"

Keeli's response was hesitant, revealing concern that was uncharacteristic of her usual composed demeanor. "I've tried to reach them..."

"You can't get through?" Garrett asked, incredulous.

"No, sir, I can't," Keeli breathed out, her voice tinged with a nervousness that Garrett understood all too well. The inability to establish contact with Station Command was deeply troubling. In their line of work, constant and reliable communication with Command was a given, a cornerstone of their operational protocols. They were the central hub for coordination, information, and direction during any crisis or routine operation. The fact that they were unreachable was not just highly unusual; it was almost inconceivable.

"I've tried myself, sir," Shaw said, drawing his attention. "No one over there is answering."

Garrett's mind raced, evaluating the situation. The combination of a station-wide alert, reports of disturbances, and now the communication blackout with Command painted a picture of a potentially grave situation.

"I have the bridge." Garrett's declaration was a clear assertion of command.

"I stand relieved, sir," Shaw replied. His tone of voice carried a subtle note of relief. Only someone like Garrett, who knew Shaw well, could detect the slight change in his usually steady tone.

Garrett thought for a moment. "Keeli, why do you think you can't get through to Station Command? Is it possible there is a problem with our external communications?"

"No, sir." Keeli's response came with a shake of her head, ruling out the possibility of a technical fault on their end. "I believe the communication ports are operating normally. They're just overwhelmed."

Garrett approached the captain's station, a space he had become intimately familiar with, especially after spending hours assembling it. He paused for a moment, reflecting on the irony of the situation. His intent had been to take proper time to test the new setup.

With a focused thought using his implants, Garrett activated the station, bringing its systems to life. The technology responded seamlessly, screens flaring, lines of data scrolling as it began a rapid self-diagnostic. Settling into the seat, he adjusted himself comfortably.

Garrett's fingers moved with practiced ease over one of the displays, calling up the readouts on the communication system. He scrutinized the information carefully and confirmed Keeli's assessment. The systems were operational; there was no technical fault or malfunction to speak of, nothing out of the ordinary.

Keeli's voice broke through his concentration. "Too much chatter across the station, sir. That's my guess. It has overwhelmed the system."

"Anything on the TFC?" Garrett asked, speaking of the tactical flow channel used by the Twenty-First Fleet and the Midway System defense forces. The TFC, a dedicated communication line, was an invaluable tool for sharing intelligence and maintaining a tactical overview of the star system as a whole. In a situation like this, where standard communication channels were overwhelmed, the TFC could provide a crucial lifeline to real-time updates and strategic insights.

"We do not have the go codes for access yet, sir," Keeli explained. "We're supposed to get them within the next month, prior to trials."

Garrett felt a stab of frustration. The absence of the go codes for the TFC access was a significant oversight, albeit an understandable one. Codes to such a secure and specialized channel were typically provided only to active-duty forces, a status that their vessel, still in the final stages of construction and testing, had not yet achieved. In the normal course of operations, this wouldn't have been an issue, but in the current emergency, it was a notable handicap.

"What about the civilian net?" he asked. "Have you tried it?"

"No, sir. I will get right on that." She quickly turned to her display, expertly navigating the interface. Her fingers moved, tapping on the screen, while she listened intently through her earpiece, her head slightly cocked to catch every nuance of the transmissions she was intercepting.

Garrett looked over at Shaw and met the other's gaze.

"I don't know what the hell is going on," Shaw admitted in a low tone so only the two of them could hear. "What I do know is that whatever it is, it's serious."

"Agreed," Garrett said.

Keeli looked up and around, her gaze fixing upon her captain, her expression conveying the seriousness of what she had discovered. "The civilians are jabbering on numerous channels, sir. Something about an attack, perhaps terroristic in nature. It's hard to make out what's going on. Everyone is talking over one another. But the civilian ship chatter seems to be focused on getting out of the system."

"They're getting out of Dodge," Shaw said in the same low tone. "That can't be good."

Garrett felt himself scowl at that as his mind continued to search for viable communication alternatives.

"How about the 2-1 comm?" Garrett asked, referencing the sophisticated FTL communication array used for long-distance communication by Fleet units. The 2-1 comm was a critical asset for communication, especially in situations where immediate and wide-reaching contact was necessary.

He was aware of the limitations and regulations surrounding the use of such advanced technology near a station or structure. FTL communication arrays, while incredibly effective, were expensive to operate and required substantial power. This high operational cost was a deterrent for civilian ships, which often opted for less powerful sub-light communication methods to maintain profitability.

Additionally, the use of FTL communications near a station like Midway was restricted due to the potential for disruption of standard station communication networks and the risk of damaging sensitive systems.

"We already tried the 2-1," Shaw said, a shrug accompanying his words. "I thought it worth a try."

Garrett felt a surge of appreciation for Shaw's initiative. It was reassuring to know his team was proactively seeking solutions.

"We were told to stand by... an automated attendant," Shaw added after a moment.

Garrett's reaction was a mix of frustration and understanding. "They told us to hold? Is that it?"

Shaw gave a nod.

Garrett rubbed his jaw, his mind whirling in disbelief. The idea that a ship, regardless of the hour or urgency, couldn't reach Fleet Command was unthinkable. His fingers had danced over the comm console countless times before, always, when needed, connecting seamlessly to a living, breathing operator at Command. This deafening silence was a first, an eerie void that filled him with a sense of foreboding.

His heart began to race as Admiral Gray's message echoed

in his mind, words that now seemed like a premonition. A shiver, sharp and sudden, sliced through him, chilling his very core. The possibility loomed like a dark cloud—was the attack underway? Had the enemy reached Midway? Logic argued against it. Any offensive action would have been detected weeks earlier as the enemy advanced one system at a time, shoving and forcing their way down the chain of star systems that led to Midway. They would have to batter their way through a string of systems and their defenses long before even nearing this star system.

But Garrett couldn't shake off the gnawing dread that something unexpected had occurred. He stood from his station and paced, thinking, each step a drumbeat in the quiet. The weight of command had suddenly pressed down on him, weighing upon his shoulders heavily.

What to do?

He paused, taking a deep breath, trying to still the turmoil within. His mind sought clarity amidst the chaos of possibilities. He needed to act, to move beyond the paralyzing grip of uncertainty. He had to know what was going on.

"What is it, sir?" Shaw's voice, tinged with concern, sliced through Garrett's thoughts, bringing him back to the present.

For a brief moment, Garrett remained silent, his gaze drifting toward his office, thinking on the secure bag and the reader it had contained.

"Sir?" Shaw's voice grew more insistent. "What would you like done?"

Breaking free from his reverie, Garrett's eyes focused on Shaw and held the other's gaze for a long moment. Then, in a swift motion, he swung about and marched back to his command station.

Seating himself, Garrett shifted his demeanor back to one of commanding authority. It was time to set an example, to take action. He faced forward, his eyes scanning the array of screens and controls that formed the nerve center of the ship's operations.

"Keeli," he called out, his voice steady and clear, "send an E-COM-1 to Admiral Yenga's attention."

Keeli's face registered shock as she turned from her station to Garrett, her eyes wide with disbelief. "Sir? What shall I declare?"

"Declare a core reactor emergency," Garrett instructed, his voice unwavering. "When someone with a pulse responds, tell them I want to speak with Admiral Yenga immediately."

"But, sir," interjected McKay, glancing down at his displays, rapidly scanning them, then turning back with a look of confusion. "All reactors are functioning normally."

"That's an order, Lieutenant Keeli." Garrett's voice brooked no argument, a firm edge slicing through any potential dissent.

Shaw leaned closer, his voice a low murmur meant only for Garrett's ears. "Are you certain about this? That might be a career-ending move."

Garrett had a flash of the bridge of *Repulse*, the gun in his hand, and Captain Marlowe dead.

"Do it," Garrett commanded, hardening his tone and leaving no room for doubt. His career concerns were a distant thought, overshadowed by the urgency of their situation. In the silence of unanswered calls and the absence of normal communications, such a risk seemed necessary, a gamble in the face of an unknown threat that loomed just beyond their current understanding. Besides, the skills he possessed were too critical to be easily dismissed by Construction Command.

Keeli hesitated a moment more, the gravity of the command weighing on her. Then, with a nod, she began executing the order, her fingers moving with practiced efficiency.

As she sent the signal, Garrett turned his attention to the comm nodes, keying in the codes to bring up internal communications. The screen before him lit up with various connections, showing that several posts had attempted to contact the bridge and were awaiting responses. He quickly keyed into one, establishing a direct line with post 201-C. This post was primarily responsible for bringing aboard civilian technicians and engineers, a crucial link in their current operations.

"Captain here," he announced as a small screen flickered to life, revealing the face of a young female marine. Under her image was the text *CPL SNEED*. In the chaotic background, indistinct shouting echoed.

"Get the fuck back!" someone was shouting. "I said, get back or I will stun you!"

Garrett's eyes quickly noted the purpling bruise forming under the marine's eye. "Report your situation."

The marine, visibly shaken at finding herself in direct communication with the captain, struggled to find her words.

"Spit it out, marine," Garrett pressed, his patience thinning. He allowed a hint of irritation to seep into his voice.

The marine collected herself, her words spilling out in a rush. "Everything's gone to hell down here, sir. People are panicking, running wild stationside. We've had incidents of individuals trying to force their way aboard. I—I had to resort to physical restraint and stunners, sir." She paused, her gaze flickering over her shoulder as numerous people began shouting at once. Garrett could not make out what was being said. "There's a growing crowd on the station, sir. They're angry, scared, and stun pulses won't hold them back if they decide to charge us."

Garrett softened his tone, understanding the gravity of her report. "Any idea what's causing this panic?"

"Mostly rumors, sir. But the prevailing fear is that the star system is under attack. Someone just told us that a few moments ago. Everyone wants off the station, thinking we're their escape route, that we won't be sticking around for long."

"Heads!" someone shouted.

The marine glanced away and ducked. Something flew past

the screen and clattered as it landed out of view. The shouting seemed to intensify. A moment later, she was back in the frame.

"Thank you, marine. Seal your port and activate the automated defense systems," Garrett ordered.

"Yes, sir," she replied, notable relief in her tone. "Right away, sir."

Garrett cut the connection. His frown deepened in contemplation, the pieces of a complex puzzle swirling in his mind. Was the system under attack? By god, he hoped not. After a moment of thought, Garrett opened a channel to Stroud.

"Stroud here," came the response, the marine's voice gruff and punctuated by heavy breathing. The sound of his labored breaths painted a clear picture for Garrett—Stroud was in motion, and he wasn't walking. The lack of video only reinforced Garrett's suspicion that the colonel was on the move.

"Captain here." Garrett didn't waste time on pleasantries. "You're probably aware that all hell is breaking loose stationside."

"I had heard something along those lines, sir," Stroud said, his voice strained from physical exertion. "I'm receiving trouble reports from almost every post. The most critical situation is at 223-H. We've got alarms even at closed ports. In short, believe it or not, we're being boarded by civilians and station service personnel. Any idea of what's happening and why they want on the ship?"

"Nothing concrete yet," Garrett replied. "One of your marines reported the possibility of a system-wide attack by the enemy. I've ordered her to seal her entry post. I want you to do the same for any other posts you deem necessary. Activate all nonlethal defenses at closed posts to deter anyone from attempting entry."

"Yes, sir." Stroud's next question cut through the tense air, his voice steadying as if he had momentarily ceased his hurried movement. The marine's breathing was still labored. "Are we under attack? Has the enemy arrived?"

"We're unable to contact Fleet Command," Garrett admitted. "I want you to begin arming your people with combat loads."

The silence on the other end of the line stretched out as Stroud processed the command. "Did I just hear you right, sir?"

"You did. That includes battle and powered armor. I don't need panicked people forcing their way aboard my ship. There's no telling what damage they could do or what harm they might inflict upon our personnel. Mobs don't think rationally, so let's force them to second-guess their choices. If things go south, we could have half the station trying to force their way aboard. I want to discourage that or at least manage the situation—if that's even possible. Nothing says 'behave yourself' more than an armed marine in full battle rattle."

"And if people do continue to force their way aboard? Say they try to subvert the defenses or attack my people?"

Garrett, feeling the surreal nature of the circumstances they were in, didn't hesitate. "Use whatever force you deem necessary to control the situation and protect the ship. That's the priority."

The reality of issuing an order that might lead to the use of deadly force was not lost on him, but the urgency and potential danger of their situation demanded such decisiveness.

"Understood," came Stroud's tight response. "We will control the situation, sir, and keep the ship safe."

"I expect nothing less," Garrett acknowledged. "I won't keep you any longer, Colonel."

"Thank you, sir. I need to get moving. I have a post in trouble and I'm almost there."

With a soft beep, the connection terminated, leaving Garrett alone with the heavy responsibility of his decisions.

"Captain, the admiral's on the line for you." Garrett's attention shifted immediately as Keeli's voice cut through the room. Without a glance back, she transferred Admiral Yenga's call to the captain's station.

The display in front of Garrett flickered, and the image of Yenga materialized. Garrett couldn't help but notice the stark change in the admiral's appearance. The normally composed figure now bore the marks of acute stress, his face etched with fatigue and worry, as if the weight of countless burdens had suddenly descended upon him.

"Jim," the admiral began, his voice terse, each word heavy with urgency. "Tell me this is a mistake or some sort of joke. Please tell me I don't have to worry about one of your reactor cores taking out a large portion of the station."

"Sorry for the false alarm, Admiral. Our reactors are functioning normally."

He watched as a visible wave of relief washed over Yenga, who slumped back into his chair, the tension momentarily draining from his posture. The admiral appeared to be on a ship. He was clearly sitting at some sort of duty station.

"Admiral, can you tell me what the hell is going on?" Seizing the opportunity, Garrett pressed for answers. "We can't get anyone from Station Command or Fleet. I have people attempting to force their way aboard my ship. I've just authorized the arming of my marines and the use of force to help control the situation. What's happening?"

Yenga's expression shifted to one of surprise. "You didn't get the AF-1 flash traffic?" The admiral's surprise quickly turned to realization as he nodded to himself, a sudden understanding dawning on him. He snapped his fingers. "Your ship has not been commissioned—no go codes."

Garrett immediately understood the implication. Not being commissioned meant he was excluded from priority Fleet transmissions and action notices. This exclusion had left them in the dark, unaware of the broader context of the crisis unfolding around them.

"I don't have much time. This is what we know." Yenga leaned forward, his eyes locked onto Garrett's through the screen. "One of our jump point fortress defense networks, on the Haier Chain, is under full assault by the enemy. As we speak, the Fleet is being mobilized to respond."

"The Haier Chain?" Garrett interjected. "But that doesn't even lead to the frontline. It's a dead-end chain."

"We're aware," Yenga acknowledged, his expression grim. "Nevertheless, it's happening. Early reports indicate that this is not a mere probe, but a full-scale assault. They've come in strength. The Push is here on Midway's doorstep."

A chill ran down Garrett's spine as he processed the admiral's words. For the first time in the war, the enemy was deviating from their predictable patterns. They were not only being unpredictable but also prematurely aggressive.

"How did they get to Midway without word reaching us from higher up the chain?" Garrett questioned. "There are ten settled systems along that route."

Garrett felt like he might be sick to his stomach. If the enemy had reached Midway, it meant they had either bypassed or obliterated the defenses of those settled systems farther up the chain. More than six hundred million civilians living in those systems could have been wiped out.

There had been plans for evacuating them, as they were far from the frontlines, but now it was too late. The strategic impact was immense, but the human cost was even more devastating.

Shaw had left his station and positioned himself close to Garrett, just out of the admiral's line of sight. He was clearly listening to the exchange. The horror on his face matched what Garrett felt.

Garrett's mind continued to whirl with the implications of

the admiral's news. It was clear that the Fleet had been blind-sided, unprepared for such a direct and forceful strike. The usual safeguards and strategies seemed to have been rendered ineffective. How the enemy had achieved this surprise was a question burning in his mind. Standard procedures dictated that ships were always stationed at jump points to serve as emergency couriers, yet this mechanism had evidently failed or been subverted.

He pondered over the unsettling rumors that had been circulating about the enemy's capabilities, particularly regarding cyber-weapons powerful enough to disable entire ships and stations. Until now, these had been unconfirmed reports, nothing more than rumors, but the current situation lent them a terrifying credibility.

"We do not yet know how they managed to force their way down the chain without word being passed ahead," Yenga said. "We can only assume they somehow achieved complete surprise. Intelligence thinks we might have missed a jump point, one far enough out that our survey ships didn't detect it. But, honestly, they are just guessing. That said, we've sent warnings to all chains along our nexus. They will not be caught off guard like we were."

Someone off-screen called for Yenga's attention, and he momentarily muted his mic, turning to address the issue. This brief pause gave Garrett a moment to process what he'd just learned. A few seconds later, Yenga returned to the conversation, his face reappearing on the screen.

"What would you like me to do?" Garrett inquired before the admiral could speak. "Can we help in any way?"

Yenga paused, his gaze dropping as he clearly contemplated what he wanted to say. When he looked up again, his expression was resolute, hard, unforgiving.

"I know you don't want to hear this—but I believe you received Gray's note. It is time to scuttle your Job. The enemy cannot take the gripper drive intact," Yenga stated firmly. "I will arrange for you to be towed away from the station to a safe distance. We're preparing to evacuate the station and save as many personnel as we can. I want you and your key people, along with any experts you deem necessary when it comes to Mothership construction, ready to transfer to a fast transport as soon as you've set the scuttling charges. We will get you all out of the system before the enemy can make significant progress."

Garrett felt a jolt of disbelief. Though Admiral Gray had issued similar orders, hearing it from Yenga made it all the more real and somehow irreversible. The idea of scuttling the ship he had devoted so much effort to was a bitter pill to swallow.

The ship, his Job, was more than just a vessel; she was a culmination of hard work, dedication—blood, sweat, and tears. To contemplate her deliberate destruction was agonizing, yet he understood the strategic necessity. The gripper drive was a critical asset in the Confederation's arsenal, one that couldn't, under any circumstances, fall into enemy hands.

Garrett's mind wrestled with the emotional toll of the order and the logical understanding of its importance. The safety of his crew and the larger strategic picture had to take precedence, but that knowledge did little to ease the sting of what he was being asked to do.

"You don't think we can stop them here at Midway," Garrett stated more than asked, needing to vocalize the grim reality.

Yenga's response was tinged with sadness, his admission heavy with the weight of the situation. "No, the power in the vanguard and the number of enemy vessels continuing to transit into the system suggests a vastly superior force to what we have stationed here. At best, we can hope to delay them, to buy some time and whittle them down some. Admiral Isabel is working to concentrate the Twenty-First for a fleet action, but most of our ships are scattered across the system, far from the Haier Network and not within rapid response range. We never anticipated an attack from that direction, especially a surprise assault. The bottom line is, we will not be able to get significant assets into position to assist in the defense of the jump point before it's too late and they are overcome."

Garrett found himself shaking his head, struggling to digest the enormity of what Yenga was saying. The scenario unfolding was almost beyond belief. The strategic implications were staggering.

"The current thinking is to assemble the fleet somewhere in the enemy's path," Yenga continued, "fight a defensive and delaying action, and buy time to evacuate as many as we can to Nikura. We'll try to make a stand there... but I have my doubts about our ability to manage even that. After we engage the enemy in a fleet battle, we may not have the strength to do more than delay their advance through Nikura and beyond."

Garrett was staggered by the admiral's words. The Twenty-First Fleet, stationed at Midway, was the Confederation's crown jewel, a formidable force meant to be the backbone of their defenses along the Rim. Its dispersion across the system, though strategically sound under normal circumstances, now left it vulnerable and ill-prepared for a concentrated and surprise assault.

His mind raced with the fallout. When Midway fell, the Outer Rim, along with the fleets stationed there, would be cut off, isolated without support. It was a scenario that hadn't been seriously considered. It was a disaster of unprecedented scale, and Garrett was at the epicenter, witnessing it unfold in real time.

"I will appoint a liaison to coordinate the evacuation of your personnel to transports," Yenga assured him. "Your people will have priority. You have my word on that. We will need their technical expertise in the years to come. Jim, your Job must be thoroughly scuttled, especially the gripper drive and computer cores. Make sure it is done right."

The weight of the admiral's instructions pressed down on Garrett with an almost physical force. As he sank back into his chair, a tumult of emotions swirled within him. He had devoted years of his life to this Job, pouring his heart and soul into every detail. The thought of destroying her, so close to her completion and commissioning, was unbearable. It was simply wrong.

Garrett sat up. "Admiral, I will not scuttle my ship."

"Jim..." the admiral began. "I know you—"

"Our drives are fully functional," Garrett insisted, cutting off the admiral. "We can spin them up, disengage from the station, and proceed under our own power to the Nikura jump point. We can use our jump drive to escape. Later, we can put the finishing touches on the ship and bring her to action."

"Jim," Yenga sighed, a mix of frustration and understanding in his voice. "I realize you're deeply attached to your Job, but—"

Garrett, fueled by a blend of desperation and conviction, interrupted again. "Sir, I know we can do this. The jump drive is operational. So too is our gravitic drive. Based on our tests, the gripper drive should work as well."

"You only just test-fired your main drive units a few days ago," Yenga snapped, pointing at Garrett through the screen. Yenga's patience clearly began to fray, his exasperation evident. "She's not even attempted to maneuver. Every Job has major problems, systems failures that emerge during trials and the shakedown cruise. You of all people should know that. You don't know what problems you might encounter. If your engines fail once you're clear of the station and halfway across the system, there's no guarantee we could evacuate your crew. Frankly, we don't have the transport capability to get everyone off the station, and we'll be leaving far too many behind as it is."

The admiral's words were a stark reminder of the harsh realities of their situation. The dangers of proceeding with an untested ship were clear, yet Garrett's proposal offered a glimmer of hope, at least in his mind. It was a chance to save not only his ship, but potentially more lives. His gut feeling told him this was the right move. They had to make an attempt to save the ship. It was wrong not to.

"We can do this, sir," Garrett urged, his resolve becoming unshakable. "Trust me."

"Damn it, man, you could be condemning everyone aboard your ship to a senseless death. Are you prepared for that possibility?"

"I understand the risks, Admiral," he replied without a hint of doubt in his voice, "and this ship is worth the risk. We've come too far with her, and in the days ahead, the Confederation will need every hull to hold back the enemy. Besides, you just pointed out you can't evacuate everyone. More importantly, we have room, a lot of space for extra personnel, and we're only going to be traveling a few jumps Coreward, until we can unload all nonessential personnel at a friendly planet or station. It's not like we're planning to use the gripper drive, an untested technology."

"You barely have a skeleton crew aboard," Yenga pointed out.

"I know."

A long silence followed, filled with the weight of the decision at hand. Garrett could almost feel the pressure bearing down on Yenga, a visible manifestation of the stress and responsibility that came with leadership in such dire times. Finally, the admiral exhaled deeply. At that moment, someone off-camera called for Yenga's attention. The admiral muted the channel and replied. When Yenga faced the screen again, his expression was one of resignation.

"Be sure about this," Yenga said, a simple yet profound directive. "You know that ship better than anyone. Be very sure."

"I am," Garrett affirmed, though he did harbor doubts about what he was going to attempt. "To pull this off, sir, I will need access and priority to supplies, fuel, food, ammunition, and time to spin up the drives and engines. We can be underway in a matter of hours."

At that moment, the admiral's attention was drawn off-screen again, the voice calling for his attention almost a shout. The admiral muted his mic, turning to respond with a pointed finger and speaking with animation.

Garrett turned his gaze to Shaw, who still stood by his station. "We can do this, right? I'm not overpromising?"

"You already know my answer," Shaw said. "You told the admiral so. Come hell or high water, we will pull it off."

Garrett gave a nod and glanced down at his hands. They were rock-steady, though his heart was hammering a furious beat in his chest. In truth, what he was about to attempt scared him. No matter what Shaw said, the decision ultimately rested with him. It was his responsibility, no one else's.

As he contemplated further, the practicality of the decision solidified in his mind. The maneuvering thrusters, main drive systems, and the jump drive were all technically operational. Although various sections of the ship were offline or nonfunctional, he was confident in her ability to maneuver and, if necessary, engage in limited combat.

Yenga was back. Someone off-screen was talking in a raised voice. But this time, it was not to the admiral.

"I don't have time for this," Yenga said. The admiral leaned forward with a serious demeanor. "Do you honestly believe you can pull this off? We're old friends, Jim. Don't bullshit me, not on this."

Garrett met the admiral's gaze with unwavering determination. "I will pull it off, or I will die trying."

Yenga sighed. "That is my fear." He paused, seemingly lost in thought for a moment. "Do you at least have a name picked out for her?"

The question caught Garrett off guard, sparking a flicker of excitement. "For the ship?"

Yenga nodded. "What do you want to name her?"

"*Surprise*." Garrett sort of blurted it out. As soon as the word left his mouth, the name felt right. The enemy had caught them off guard, and in a twist of fate, this ship, his Job, was poised ultimately to do the same. Once fully operational, she would be a formidable asset, a symbol of humanity's resilience, creativity, and unexpected strength in the face of adversity.

The name encapsulated not just the ship's potential, but also the current state of the war, a conflict marked by unforeseen developments and shifting tides. It was a fitting moniker for a vessel that represented a glimmer of hope and a tactical advantage. Garrett's choice reflected both his defiance against the odds and his belief in the ship's capabilities to turn the tables in their favor. At some point, he knew she would prove to be quite the surprise. He was certain of that.

The admiral's reaction to the chosen name was a welcome respite from the tension of the moment. His tired face lit up with a weary, yet genuine grin, and a chuckle escaped him.

"Very well then, on this date I commission your ship the Confederation Navy Starship *Surprise*," Yenga declared.

The admiral busied himself with a few off-screen keystrokes.

"I am entering this commission into the log as we speak. I will have her formally registered within the next few minutes," he said, his tone turning more serious. After a brief pause, he looked at Garrett with a rueful expression. "Congratulations, Jim. You are the first commanding officer of a commissioned Fleet-class Mothership. Effective immediately, I am field promoting you to the rank of senior star captain." He paused, his gaze steady. "Do not make me or Gray regret this."

Garrett felt a surge of pride. It came with a feeling of intense satisfaction that he'd finally achieved his goal. At the same time, it was mixed with the heavy responsibility of his new role and the burden that came with it.

"You won't, sir," he replied, his voice almost gruff.

Yenga, about to terminate the connection, paused as Garrett held up a hand to interject.

"Admiral," Garrett said urgently. "We need supplies, food stores, fuel, water—that sort of thing."

"We are opening up the depots to everyone, though most, especially the civilians, seem intent on simply pushing back from the station and running. Take whatever you need. I will make sure to grant you priority. Once your ship is ready, make best possible speed toward Nikura."

"We can also accommodate evacuees," Garrett suggested, aware of the ship's capacity to aid in the evacuation efforts.

"I will begin steering personnel your way."

"Point them in Shaw's direction," he instructed. "He will coordinate such efforts."

"I will direct my aides to make it so. They will reach directly out to him in the next few minutes."

"Admiral, how much time do we have? How long do I have to get the ship moving?"

Yenga paused, clearly thinking. "I would suggest not waiting longer than sixteen hours to break away from the station. It's a long way to the Nikura jump point. As I said, Admiral Isabel is assembling the fleet to contest the enemy. Should that effort prove unsuccessful—well, delay any longer and you risk not making it to the jump point. You might find yourself cut off." He leaned forward, tapping something off-screen. "I will have your ship immediately tied into the TFC. Official orders will follow shortly from my office."

"Thank you, sir," Garrett responded, his gratitude genuine. "I appreciate it."

A sad expression passed over Yenga's face. "I wish we could have had that lunch and reminisced on old times."

"Me too, Admiral."

"Good luck, Jim." Yenga terminated the connection.

Garrett leaned back in his chair, his mind a whirlwind of thoughts. He scratched his jaw, contemplating his next steps. The magnitude of what had just transpired hit him fully. In a span of a brief conversation, the fate of his ship had taken a dramatic turn. From being on the verge of being scuttled to now being an active participant in a critical evacuation.

Garrett realized the enormity of the task ahead. Not only did he have to oversee the final preparations of his ship for departure, but he also had to manage the intake of evacuees and coordinate with the supply depots, all within a tight sixteen-hour window.

Yet, amidst the challenges, Garrett felt a surge of determination. *Surprise* was no longer just a project. She was now a ship of the line. With the clock ticking, Garrett understood he had to act swiftly and decisively. The lives of his crew, the evacuees, and the potential impact on the war effort depended on his next actions. It was a moment of truth, a test of his leadership and the capabilities of the newly commissioned Mothership. At the same time, the effort before him seemed daunting.

"What have I just done?" he whispered to himself, still staring at the screen where Yenga had been.

"What needed to be done, sir," Shaw said.

Garrett looked up at Shaw and gave a firm nod. "Let's get to work."

TWELVE

GARRETT

"Shaw," Garrett said, "I need you to start compiling a comprehensive list of necessities—consumables we will need in the days ahead. We have to think beyond just the essentials. Yes, food, water, medical supplies, and additional atmospherics are all critical, but let's dive deeper. Consider ammunition, aviation fuel for our ship's boats, and other such resources."

"I can do that, sir," Shaw said, still standing by Garrett's station. "I'd also recommend taking on crates of unassembled ship's boats, assault craft for the marines, maybe even some fighters. Even if we don't have pilots for them currently, we have the storage space and it'd be a waste to leave them behind. Eventually, Fleet will assign us squadrons of fighters, interceptors for close-in protection and the like. Having the physical craft already aboard may make that process easier. I will grab the ammunition and fuel for them too and do my best to make sure all storage tanks are full."

"Good idea. There's no telling when we might see a fully stocked supply depot. It may be months. Anything else we might conceivably need, let's take and bring aboard. We must be thoroughly prepared for all eventualities. Once you've drafted the initial list, the department heads can further refine and expand it as they see fit. You will have to be point on that, to make sure we get all we can take."

"Understood," Shaw responded with a firm nod, a glimmer of readiness in his eyes. "I'll get right on that. May I ask, sir, what you will be working on?"

Garrett's gaze drifted slightly, his mind already racing ahead. "First, I'll be talking to Tam. I will break the news to him and make sure I've not overpromised."

"You haven't," Shaw reassured him confidently before turning back to his station. Just as he settled into his chair, he cast a sideways glance at Garrett, a hint of a grin playing on his lips. "But I'll tell you this, sir, your call is going to brighten our chief engineer's day. Trials are going to be a crash course, one that hopefully will take us out of this star system."

"No doubt." Fingers moving deftly on the display before him, Garrett opened a communication channel to engineering. He was seeking his chief engineer, Commander Sing La Tam.

In Garrett's experience, Tam was always there, a constant presence in the engineering bay. No matter the time of day or night, he was seemingly on duty, usually immersed neck-deep in his work. It was a level of dedication that Garrett had not seen in anyone else, himself included.

"Tam here," came the chief engineer's lilting voice, crisp and clear, yet his face on the screen was slightly averted, his attention caught by something or someone just out of the camera's view. This was typical for Tam, perpetually in the midst of something critical, his focus split between multiple tasks. His work ethic was legendary, putting even the most dedicated workaholics to shame.

Although not tall in stature, Tam possessed a commanding presence. His posture alone spoke volumes of his confidence and authority. His age was somewhat ambiguous, his appearance hinting at late forties, but it was hard to pinpoint exactly from just a glance. The subtle signs of aging only added to his distinguished demeanor. Garrett knew from the man's service record that he was fifty-three years of age.

His skin bore a rich olive tone, a gift from his home world, Irdella, setting off his sharp, angular features, which radiated determination and intelligence. His hair was jet-black, kept short and neat, while his piercing black eyes seemed to miss nothing and catch everything. Despite his presence, Tam's physique was lean, almost to the point of being wiry.

"Sit tight, Lieutenant," the chief engineer instructed someone just beyond the camera's view, his voice firm, yet not without an underlying note of assurance. "I'll be there shortly to review your work and then we can discuss it, along with ways to improve upon what you have done."

"Tam," Garrett interjected. "I need your attention."

The man's focus swiftly shifted to the screen. He blinked.

"Ah, Captain," he responded after a moment, a slight hint of surprise in his tone. "It's a pleasure to hear from you directly. I've just forwarded the latest diagnostic reports on the power intermix ratios, along with a requisition request for additional coolant, a backup supply. It's crucial for the upgrade of our secondary reactors. I was about to ask if you could perhaps expedite our needs with Command—put in a good word. It would not be—"

"Tam," Garrett cut in, his voice carrying an edge, momentarily derailing the engineer's train of thought, for the other suddenly frowned, eyes narrowing. The slight scowl that formed on Tam's face was telling; he was not accustomed to being interrupted, especially mid-discussion about his domain, his responsibilities. However, Garrett's tone left no room for the usual protocols, the leeway that he usually gave the man. Given the opportunity, Tam would go on and on, badgering until he got his way or was firmly told no. There was no time for that now. "I need to know how rapidly you can get us ready to depart and underway. When can we be ready to move the ship?"

Tam's scowl deepened as he weighed Garrett's words. "Captain, we're scheduled for trials in a little over three months. I could possibly expedite that by cutting some corners, though it's not ideal, nor do I recommend it. As you no doubt understand, there are certifications and warranties that I need to personally make and sign off on. Is Fleet pushing for an early deployment for trials, sir? The last I heard, they were thinking of delaying them so that Admiral Isabel could be on hand."

"We need to move the ship now, Tam, not in a few weeks or months—now." Garrett paused as he sucked in a breath. "Listen, the situation is critical. The enemy is in the process of breaching the defenses of the Haier Chain. Fleet has been blindsided. They've ordered a general evacuation. Midway is lost. We have to get this behemoth of a warship operational and underway as soon as possible. Every moment counts."

Tam's skepticism was evident as he squinted further at the screen. "Is this some kind of joke, Captain? Because if it is, I must say, it's not in the best taste."

"This is no joke, Tam. Command has assessed the situation as critical. If we can't get our ship to safety, I have orders to scuttle her."

"Scuttle?" Tam blinked rapidly and drew back slightly from the camera. The horror on the man's face was plain. "Scuttle her? You're not kidding with me? You mean to say the Push has come? The enemy are here at Midway?"

"That is exactly what I am telling you. I've just had a conversation with Admiral Yenga. I convinced him we could get this ship moving and evacuate the system ahead of the enemy. They've commissioned us, granting access to whatever resources we require from the depots—and I mean anything. But here's the catch: we have a limited window of twelve hours. Beyond that, we'll be left to fend for ourselves." Garrett, seasoned in his interactions with the chief engineer, intentionally tightened the timeframe, aware that these types of situations often required more time than initially anticipated. It was like when you were told that a task would take five minutes... and it took twenty.

Tam stared intently at the screen, processing the information. His jaw clenched tightly, then relaxed as he opened his mouth, only to close it again. Finally, he asked, a hint of incredulity still in his voice, "You're serious? This isn't a joke?"

Garrett could read the shift from disbelief in Tam's expression, the dawning realization of the reality which now faced them all. The Push had arrived—and it was early.

"I wish it were a joke, Tam. Fleet's gearing up to engage the enemy in a delaying action while the system is being evacuated. I need to know we can make good on getting this ship moving. I can't afford to have overpromised on this. There is just too much riding on us, especially when we begin taking on evacuees from the station."

Tam let out a heavy sigh, a physical manifestation of the weight of the situation bearing down on him, clearly coming to rest heavily on his shoulders. As Garrett began to speak again, Tam raised his hand, signaling for a moment's pause. He sucked in a rapid breath and let it out. "Just to be absolutely clear— you're not pulling my leg?"

"This is very real," Garrett affirmed, his tone grave.

Tam's response was a slow, deliberate nod. His eyes, which had been locked onto Garrett's image on the screen, now drifted downward betraying a moment of deep contemplation. He ran a hand through his short-cropped hair. When he raised his gaze again, there was a newfound intensity in his eyes, a spark of resolve to meet the coming challenge and overcome it.

"Seven hours," Tam stated firmly. "That's the earliest I can promise. We've only recently tested the main drives. If fortune favors us, and I think it will, I might be able to shave off some time"—he wagged a finger at the screen—"but no guarantees. The gravitic coils take a while to fully spool up and go hot. They are the largest that have ever been constructed." He rubbed his jaw absentmindedly, his gaze momentarily shifting off-screen, perhaps to the mountain of tasks now awaiting him. "Eight hours would be safer, especially since I'll have to cut corners to pull this off—and you know how I feel about cutting corners."

"You don't like taking shortcuts."

"Exactly."

"You also know the ship's drive systems better than anyone else," Garrett acknowledged, conveying both his confidence and reliance on Tam's expertise.

"I helped to design them."

"If anyone can make this happen, it's you, corners cut or no."

Tam, absorbing the gravity of the responsibility, gave a resolute nod. "I'll make it happen," he affirmed, his voice carrying a tone of unwavering commitment. "I will get her moving for you, but I don't want to hear any more talk of scuttling my baby. You and I have worked too hard on her to let it come to that."

"Excellent," Garrett responded, a hint of relief in his tone. "And you won't, not by me."

Tam glanced away again, clearly still in problem-solving mode. He turned back to the screen. "Once we're underway, I'd advise against pushing the ship beyond twenty gravities until I've confirmed the drive coils are functioning optimally."

Garrett frowned slightly. "That's rather slow, isn't it?"

"I need to calibrate the drive coils while under power and ensure there are no resonance issues, unexpected vibrations, that could lead to a fault, one that might leave us without power and adrift. I don't think either of us want to see that eventuality, especially with the enemy in-system."

Garrett's mind already raced ahead. "How long will the calibration take?"

Tam paused, clearly considering the variables. "Maybe an hour at most before I will feel confident the drives can pull more of a load. Based upon what I discover, there may be further restrictions, limits upon which you can push the drives."

"Very well," Garrett conceded, understanding the necessity of the precautions. He paused a moment, thinking. "Might as well warm up the gripper drive too."

"The gripper drive?" Tam was surprised by that.

"In the event something happens to the gravitic drive, I want all options on the table. As you said, we both worked too hard on this project to see her scuttled."

"All right, then. I have a lot to do, more than I expected when I awoke this morning."

"Did you even go to sleep?" Garrett asked.

"What day is it?"

"Thursday."

"I've never liked Thursdays." Tam gestured behind him with a hand, indicating the urgency to get started. He moved to terminate the connection but hesitated, his hand hovering over the key. "You mentioned we've been commissioned? What have they named my girl?"

"*Surprise*," Garrett revealed, "and I named her. It was my choice."

"*Surprise—Surprise*," Tam repeated, mulling over the name. A flicker of recognition crossed his features. "If I'm not mistaken, that name has a history, doesn't it? Several ships going all the way back to Old Earth have borne it before, yes?"

"You're not wrong," Garrett confirmed.

"I like it," Tam said, a sense of approval washing over his face. "It's a name with a legacy, something to live up to, but also, given our circumstances, oddly appropriate. But now, there's no time to lose." With a nod that conveyed both his determination and a sense of the immense workload awaiting him, he severed the connection.

Garrett exhaled a deep breath of relief and leaned back in his chair. The call had gone better than he'd expected. With Tam's assurance, he had no doubt that the ship would indeed move under her own power.

He turned his attention back to the bridge. It took him a moment to register the unusual quiet that had settled around him. Then, it dawned upon him—this was his bridge. He was now the commanding officer of a fully commissioned starship, albeit on a brevet promotion, but he was captain nonetheless. The realization brought a moment of awe, a silent acknowledgment of the awesome responsibility that came with this role.

His thoughts were broken as he noticed his bridge crew's eyes fixed on him, excluding Shaw, who was hard at work building a list of what they would need. Including the two marines, there were only six crew present, but their attention was upon him. Garrett straightened in his chair, adopting a more appropriate posture of command. He locked his gaze on Keeli, his communications officer.

"Put me through on the 1MC. I want a ship-wide broadcast," he ordered.

Garrett had learned early in his career, ironically from Captain Marlowe, that projecting confidence and issuing clear, concise orders during a crisis could and would instill a sense of control and capability in the crew. It was about leading by example, providing a beacon of steadiness in the tumult of uncertainty, lending the crew strength, his strength. Now, more than ever, his crew needed that leadership, and he was ready to provide it.

Garrett felt the weight of the situation pressing upon him, a burden that, for a moment, threatened to overshadow his resolve. Yet he pushed these concerns roughly aside, understanding the vital role his demeanor would play in this critical moment when he set the tone for what was to come.

His crew's faith in him and their belief in the possibility of success were paramount. He was acutely aware that he was about to ask them to venture into uncharted waters, but he also knew that he had to frame it not just as feasible, but as the only logical course of action... the only path to follow.

"You are on, Captain," Keeli's voice broke through his thoughts, signaling that the ship-wide broadcast system was now live.

Garrett took a moment to compose himself, gathering his thoughts. He knew the importance of his next words, the mission he was about to give his people.

"This is the captain speaking," he started, steadying his voice. "I'll cut to the chase. The Push has begun. The enemy has emerged from the Haier Chain jump point. Our system forts are currently engaged in heavy combat. Command has assessed that the enemy force is potent enough to overwhelm our fixed defenses at the jump point. A general evacuation of all nonessential personnel from the system has been ordered. Our ship has been officially commissioned as the CNS *Surprise*. In roughly seven hours' time, we will depart from Midway Station and head toward the Nikura jump point. There, under the protection and cover of the fleet, we will safely exit the system."

Garrett paused for several seconds to allow that to sink in.

"There's a significant amount of preparation needed before we can disengage from Midway and push back. While I do not expect direct engagement with the enemy, we will be ready for that eventuality. Additionally, before we depart, we will be taking on evacuees, along with additional supplies from the station. You will shortly receive orders from your department heads. I trust each of you to fulfill your duties to the utmost and not let your shipmates down." Garrett paused again, a sudden inspiration striking him. "Stand to your duty, stand to your responsibility to your comrades, your brothers and sisters, the ship, and the *Surprise* will see us all safely through this challenge." Garrett paused again, almost dramatically. "That is all."

"You are off, Captain," Keeli said.

He looked forward to his communications officer.

"Keeli, sound general quarters," Garrett ordered, his voice firm.

At once, the alarms began to blare, and the ship's automated system announced, "General quarters... general quarters. All hands to your stations. This is not a drill. General quarters."

Garrett turned to Shaw, who had temporarily stopped working as Garrett had addressed the crew. Their eyes met. Shaw gave him a nod of approval.

"Well said, sir."

"Commander," Garrett said, "we're going to be taking her out much sooner than anticipated. I need a helm officer and navigation team on the bridge. Once they're here, plot the most efficient and fastest course to the Nikura jump point."

"Quickest possible course, sir." After a brief pause, Shaw queried, "Do you mind if we cross some of the civilian shipping lanes in the process?"

"No matter the lanes, quickest possible course. Ensure we're ready for pushback as soon as Tam gives us the go-ahead."

"Aye, aye, sir. We will be ready."

"Good," Garrett acknowledged with a nod, then turned to Keeli. "Keeli, I need a conference call set up with all department heads. Schedule it within the next ten minutes. Make sure they're all on standby for that. When I am ready, I will take it in my office."

"Yes, sir," Keeli replied promptly, her fingers moving swiftly over her console to send out the necessary communications.

A movement to his left caught his attention. Turning, he saw Tina emerging from his office. She was dressed, but her appearance was slightly disheveled, her hair not quite in place, and her complexion notably pale. Her eyes, wide with a mix of surprise, concern, and horror, fixed upon him. It was evident she had overheard his ship-wide address. The gravity of the situation was clearly not lost on her.

There was a moment where their gazes met, a silent exchange that spoke volumes. Garrett could sense the emotions and unspoken words hanging between them. He knew there was much he wanted to say, to explain, perhaps to reassure, but the urgency of the moment and the presence of the crew around them made it neither the time nor the place for personal conversations.

Breaking the moment, Garrett turned back to Shaw, maintaining his professional demeanor, catching the other's gaze.

"Shaw," Garrett said, loud enough for Tina to hear, "please arrange for one of our boats to transport Captain Martin directly back to her ship. Like us, I am certain she has a great deal to do."

Shaw eyed Tina for a moment, his gaze flicking briefly to Garrett, then nodded. "I will make that happen immediately." Shaw looked to the marine guarding Garrett's office. "Marine, kindly escort Captain Martin to the admiral's boat dock." Shaw shifted his attention to Tina. "Ma'am, I will have you on a boat within the next twenty minutes and on your way."

"Thank you, Commander," Tina said, her tone stiff and hard. "I appreciate it."

"This way, ma'am." The marine indicated the hatch at the back of the bridge with an outstretched arm and bladed hand. She started to lead the way.

Garrett caught Tina's gaze. She eyed him for a moment more, then turned and followed the marine off the bridge, walking briskly.

With the arrangements for Tina being handled, Garrett shifted his focus back to his station. He began to compile a brief agenda for the meeting with his department heads. Top of the list was what they would want drawn from the depots. Next was processing and quartering the evacuees they'd be bringing aboard. How many could they safely take in? There would undoubtedly be personnel with skills they could use in the hours and days ahead.

Garrett went to add a third item to his agenda and found himself hesitating. He glanced back at the hatch through which Tina had just departed and let go a heavy breath. That had not ended how he'd wanted it to.

Would he see her again? With the Push on, nothing was certain.

He shook himself. Soon, he knew, the bridge would be humming with activity as his crew arrived and he'd have no time for idle thought or action. Heck, he did not have time for that now. Forcefully putting Tina from his mind, he turned his attention back to the agenda and got to work, for he had a job to do, and Garrett meant to do it right.

THIRTEEN

TABBY

The comm's alert shattered the silence in the cockpit with a jarring urgency, yanking Tabby from the depths of her light sleep. She jolted upright, feeling the sharp tug of her restraints against her chest.

This sound was alien to her ears, something far removed from the routine drills she'd grown accustomed to. It was an ominous harbinger, a sound that spelled uncertainty and potential danger.

Tabby's heart raced as she blinked rapidly, trying to dispel the last vestiges of sleep that clouded her vision. She rubbed her eyes vigorously, a futile attempt to prepare herself for whatever crisis waited. The alert blared again, its harsh, insistent tone impossible to ignore, a relentless siren demanding immediate action. It was a sound that cut through the calm of the spacecraft, as disconcerting as it was imperative.

She saw the source of the alert was the tactical flow channel, a critical communication line reserved for matters of utmost importance, such as system defense. Sanchez and Chen turned their heads toward her, curiosity and concern in their expressions.

Tabby leaned forward. She tapped the flashing display icon. By acknowledging the alert, she initiated the sequence to bring up the message on the same display.

"Was that the TFC, ma'am?" Sanchez asked.

Tabby, her focus entirely absorbed by the gravity of the message before her, responded only with a terse nod. She couldn't spare the words; her eyes were riveted to the display, where the message glowed ominously in a stark, alarming red:

THIS IS NOT A DRILL. ENEMY FORCES HAVE ENTERED MIDWAY STAR SYSTEM AND ARE ACTIVELY ENGAGING THE DEFENSIVE FORTS GUARDING HAIER CHAIN. ALL UNITS... NEW ORDERS TO FOLLOW. THIS IS NOT A DRILL.

The words seemed to leap off the screen, each one a hammer blow to her sense of security.

An ice-cold chill slithered down her spine. Dread gripped her heart and held it fast. She read the message again, hoping against hope to find some error, some sign that this was just a miscommunication or that she had misread the message. But the reality was undeniable, as harsh and as cold as the void of space itself.

This was no bad dream, but a nightmare come to life. The chill in her bones deepened, accompanied by a sudden gnawing fear that settled in the pit of her stomach.

The Push had begun.

But what sent a fresh wave of dread through her was the realization that the enemy was early. This was an unexpected move, a deviation from the predictions and strategies the Confederation had been planning and preparing for. Tabby felt the weight of the moment, the burden of command, and the looming specter of war that now threatened to engulf them all.

The timestamp on the message was a glaring detail Tabby couldn't ignore. It was more than two hours old, a significant delay from sending to receipt. The forts had been under assault for an unknown duration, likely longer before the word had gone out. How long could they withstand the attack? How long before they were overwhelmed? How long before the enemy broke into the system proper?

Tabby's mind raced with tactical considerations. Her vessel, while equipped to tap into the faster-than-light constellation chain, had limitations in its communication capabilities. It was not designed to directly receive long-range FTL comm traffic or send messages through this advanced network. Instead, their system was reliant on a more indirect method of communication —a chain of relay stations.

These stations, strategically seeded across the vast expanse of the Midway Star System, served as critical links for transmitting messages across the immense distances of space. However, this relay system, while functional, was not instantaneous, at least not for her boat. It had taken more than two hours for the message to bounce from station to station, traversing the void before reaching the one that had transmitted directly to her boat.

Tabby felt a sense of urgency welling up inside her. The situation was evolving rapidly, and they were operating on delayed information. It was a dangerous disadvantage, leaving them blind to the current state of the conflict and what was happening on a broader scale. Worse, the TFC only showed her information critical to her situation and not the strategic picture of the entire system. She was not cleared for that, only for what her current orders entailed, and that was nothing more than a simple flight from *Neptune* to Midway Station.

"Two bloody hours," Tabby muttered under her breath. Realizing her unfamiliarity with the Haier Chain, she instinctively turned to her left, her fingers moving with practiced ease to pull up the star system map on her display. She swiftly entered her query, and the Haier Chain materialized on the screen, highlighted against the backdrop of the entire star system. The location was alarmingly clear—it was situated across the vast expanse of the system, a considerable distance from their current position.

As she studied the map, Tabby noted the strategic positioning of Midway Station, which lay between them and the jump point leading to Haier Barber. Haier Barber was a system with a dangerously active neutron star. The information displayed on her screen painted a vivid picture of the star's lethal nature, underscoring the risks of navigating near such a volatile celestial object.

She quickly learned that transit along the Haier Chain was highly regulated, restricted to specific types of ships. Only vessels that had been hardened with specialized shielding could safely endure the intense radiation and magnetic fields emitted by the neutron star.

Tabby's gaze lingered on the display, absorbing the unfamiliar details of Haier Barber. It was a name that had never crossed her path before, a remote and seemingly insignificant location in the vast canvas of the galaxy. According to the data tag accompanying the map, Haier Barber was devoid of permanent human settlement. Its only sign of human activity were a few automated asteroid mining stations, likely operated remotely due to the hostile environment.

The reason for this absence of human presence was clear. The neutron star at the heart of the Haier Barber System was a source of intense radiation, a maelstrom of deadly energy that made prolonged and sustained human habitation impossible. Even ships with augmented shielding, designed to withstand such harsh conditions, were advised against lingering in the system for any extended period of time. The risks were simply too great, the star's lethal radiation a constant threat.

Beyond Haier Barber, the Haier Chain stretched out, linking several settled systems. These systems, in contrast to the barren and hostile Haier Barber, were hubs of human activity and civilization. Yet what caught Tabby's attention was an unusual detail on the map. Several jumps up the chain, the route was marked as a dead end. This was an oddity in space navigation, where routes and chains typically connected various systems in a complex web of travel paths.

Tabby's mind whirred with strategic calculations, trying to piece together the puzzle that lay before her.

"How?" she whispered to herself. How had the enemy managed to infiltrate the Haier Chain, a route that, until now, had seemed a dead end?

Her eyes were drawn back to the display, focusing intently on the depiction of the jump point. As she scrutinized the map, a realization slowly began to take shape in her mind. There had to be an undiscovered jump point hidden somewhere along that chain. It was a chilling thought—the Fleet, with all its resources and vigilance, had missed something crucial, and the enemy had capitalized on this oversight. Perhaps, she theorized, this hidden jump point was lurking somewhere in the Haier Barber System.

This possibility opened up a troubling new front in the conflict. If the enemy had indeed found an unknown jump point in Haier Barber, they now had access to not just one, but two jump points leading into Confederation space.

Could the intense radiation from Haier Barber's neutron star have played a role in concealing the jump point from the survey ships? It was a plausible hypothesis, but Tabby wasn't a scientist. Still, she thought the hellish conditions around the neutron star could easily interfere with sensors and equipment. It was a sobering thought, nature's own ferocity aiding the enemy in a way no one had anticipated.

Tabby was momentarily lost in the whirlwind of her thoughts, her mind racing with the implications of the unfolding situation. The war, it seemed, had abruptly reignited with a vengeance. This realization hit her with the weight of a star collapsing upon itself. The quiet before the storm had ended and what had seemed so far off was now at hand.

"Ma'am?" Sanchez's voice cut through her thoughts, a hint of concern lacing her tone. Meanwhile, Chen had already redirected his attention back to his station and was working on something. "What's wrong?"

Still Tabby did not answer as her mind raced. One of the Confederation's largest fleets, a formidable force in its own right, was based at Midway. She pondered the current disposition of the Twenty-First. She did not know much about how the fleet was dispersed around the system, especially since the TFC did not give her that information. She supposed they were likely scattered, some docked at Midway Station, others deployed at what were considered to be strategic points, but likely most far from the Haier Chain. There had been no reason to post ships near that jump point.

Despite being dispersed, the Twenty-First remained a force to be reckoned with, a powerful formation, a hammer that could present a challenge to any adversary, including the enemy.

"Ma'am?" Sanchez repeated, her voice pulling Tabby back from her strategic contemplations. "What's wrong?"

Tabby's gaze met Sanchez's, and for a brief moment, she could not speak. Then, she blinked, her mind refocusing on the present, forcibly regaining command of her own faculties. She drew in a deep, steadying breath, then exhaled slowly, gathering her thoughts before breaking the news.

"The Push is on." Her voice sounded hoarse and hard to her ears.

Chen, who had been absorbed in his station, whipped around at her words. "What? What did you say about the Push?"

"They are here in Midway," Tabby replied, her voice steady but laced with the weight of the revelation. "The enemy. They are here."

"How?" Chen asked.

Tabby simply shook her head.

"What do we do, ma'am?" Sanchez asked.

That indeed was the pivotal question. Tabby sat there, feeling the eyes of her crew upon her, looking to her for guidance and leadership. The responsibility weighed heavily on her, but she knew hesitation was a luxury they couldn't afford. Displaying weakness and indecision was not an option either. Tabby was the commander of her squadron, the Nighthawks. They were hers and would be looking to her for direction, just as her own crew was doing at this moment.

Tabby's attention shifted momentarily to the HTD. The course to the next beacon was clearly outlined. There had been no deviation. The autopilot had them firmly on course. They were about an hour away from the initial point and steadily approaching their destination.

The autopilot had already initiated the deceleration phase, a necessary precursor to their final jump to Midway Central. Once they completed this transition, they would be four hours away from the station, an easy hop.

As she contemplated their approach to Midway Central, the TFC shattered the brief lull with its insistent blare, demanding immediate attention again. Tabby quickly pulled up the incoming message, her eyes scanning the text for the new information it contained. A look of incredulity crossed her face as she read, prompting her to go over the message again. The content was so unexpected that she found herself grappling with its implications.

An itch on her jaw drew her hand momentarily, a subconscious gesture as she processed the startling directives. The orders were clear, yet they represented a dramatic shift in their plans. With a slight hesitation, Tabby considered the ramifications of this new directive, weighing its potential impact on the hours ahead. She replied to the message, acknowledging the change in orders.

"We have new orders," she announced to her crew, her voice steady as she spoke. She found herself surprised at how calm she was as she programmed their new destination, setting the waypoints for her squadron to follow. "Give me a minute. Inputting the new course now," she said, her fingers moving deftly over the controls.

As Tabby worked, she glanced over at the HTD, studying the area immediately around her boat and eyeing her squadron, their positioning and spacing. A sense of reassurance washed over her. Her "chicks" remained precisely where they should be. The station-keeping equipment had maintained their formation flawlessly.

Her gaze then returned to the plot, her eyes tracing the new course she had charted. With meticulous care, she double-checked each parameter and waypoint, ensuring that every detail was accurate. Satisfied with the thoroughness of her work, she transmitted the new course to her squadron.

Tabby opened the squadron channel, cutting through any ongoing communications.

"Listen up, all Oscars," she began, her tone hard, her words transmitting across the channel to every pilot under her command. Tabby's voice was rock-steady, betraying not a hint of the adrenaline that surged through her veins nor her heart pounding a rapid rhythm in her chest. "We have a change in plans. I've set a new course. We are being redirected to a different beacon. Stand by to change track on my mark."

She paused for a moment, giving her squadron time to receive and process the new track. Tabby knew that her pilots would already be analyzing the implications of the course change.

"That will add another four hours to our flight," Ghost protested, his tone conveying the weariness of prolonged confinement in a fighter. "I'm already beginning to feel like a sardine packed in a can here."

"More like an oyster," Punkster replied, "one that's spoiled."

"Why the change?" Husky asked. "That specific beacon will put us on the far side of Midway Station, well away from the entertainment. I've just pulled up the station's map and that's Construction Command territory."

"Those are our orders, and it can't be helped." She took a deep breath before continuing, knowing the importance of transparency in such critical moments. "The Push has begun. Worse, the enemy are in-system. They came down the Haier Chain. Someone screwed up and apparently missed a jump point. At least, that's my guess, but I don't have any additional information on that point."

Tabby did her best to keep her tone calm and authoritative, despite the racing of her own heart. She allowed a moment for her words to sink in among the squadron.

"Holy shit," Buster exclaimed softly, the gravity of the situation dawning on him. "The Push is on?"

"I don't believe it," Ghost added, his voice revealing a mix of surprise and skepticism.

"We have been assigned to the CNS *Surprise*," Tabby announced. "We are to make best possible speed to link up with her before she pushes back from the station. That means we are going to go to max military power all the way to the beacon and then beyond."

"The *Surprise*?" Husky questioned. "I've never heard of that carrier. Is she a main line unit or an escort CV?"

"We've been assigned to the Mothership." The simplicity of her statement underscored the significance of their new assignment. "Beyond that, our orders don't specify what comes next. I suppose the CAG will tell us what's what at that point. So speculate all you want. But sure as shit, there is going to be fighting in our near future, and we will be part of it. I'd recommend checking all systems over to make certain everything is functioning optimally. If it's not, be ready to tell the deck chiefs when we land."

As Tabby glanced down at the HTD, she noticed the squadron trailing them was actively executing a course adjustment. She watched as their craft turned to a new heading and began to accelerate, gathering speed rapidly as they aligned themselves toward the same beacon Tabby's squadron was now tasked to navigate. It was evident that they too had received new orders, a sign that the wider strategy was rapidly evolving in response to the enemy's unexpected attack.

The shuttles the other squadron had been escorting were now gradually fading into the background, steadfastly maintaining their original course and speed. These shuttles, once under their protective wing, were now left to continue their journey independently.

Tabby keyed in the "go" command for her own boat, *Max*. The vessel responded instantly, her movements precise and swift. *Max*'s nose swung around almost elegantly, aligning itself with the new trajectory as the drive's intensity surged, the gravity field around the boat changing as it was manipulated in response. Tabby could feel the deep hum and the subtle vibration through her seat as the boat adjusted her course. The power plant was now operating at near-maximum capacity, propelling them forward at incredible speed. She felt none of it.

As Tabby monitored the change in course, she noted with satisfaction that the rest of her squadron were seamlessly falling into formation. They were expertly slotting into their designated positions, each craft mirroring the maneuvering of her own boat.

The HTD pinged for her attention.

Tabby glanced down at it and observed a change at the last beacon they had transited through hours earlier. Two destroyers had made their entrance, emerging from jump. Their presence was marked by a sudden surge in their power signatures, an unmistakable sign of rapid acceleration as they powered out of the safe zone surrounding the beacon.

The plot on the HTD flared with the intensity of their activity, capturing the raw power of these warships as they ramped up their drives, slicing through space with purposeful haste. No sooner had they cleared the jump area than a battleship followed, making its grand entrance. That surprised Tabby, for capital ships rarely utilized beacons. The power requirements needed to transit such a behemoth taxed the beacon's reactors. It was also reputedly not the safest thing to attempt.

The battleship wasted no time, immediately beginning her acceleration away. As Tabby watched, another battleship jumped in seconds later, almost before the first could clear the field.

Husky's voice crackled over the transmission. "That's a lot of muscle coming in behind us."

Tabby could only nod in agreement, even as she remained focused on the display. The Confederation Fleet was responding in force. Two more destroyers transited in after the battleship. The sheer scale of the movement she could see was impressive and she was certain more was on the way.

In her mind's eye, Tabby pictured the controlled chaos that must be unfolding across the system: ships, previously engaged in routine patrols or stationed at various strategic points, their crews scrambling to readiness, to adapt to the new directives and movement orders Fleet had issued. The network of communications would be buzzing with orders and confirmations, each vessel a cog in the larger machine of the Confederation's military response.

Tabby's thoughts instinctively turned to her "people" as she considered their mental state. The atmosphere within the squadron, she knew, would be a mix of shock, fear, worry, and determination to do the jobs for which they had been trained. It was a natural response; after all, the reality of their situation was stark. They were now in a combat zone, a notion that would unsettle even the most seasoned pilots and crew. And Tabby, despite her position as their leader, was not immune to these feelings. She too felt the grip of fear, a silent companion in the midst of the unknown and what lay ahead in all of their futures.

They had named her Mom for a reason. With a deep sense of responsibility toward her people, Tabby keyed in to transmit a message, her voice steady, a beacon of reassurance in the tumultuous sea of uncertainty.

"Stay calm and in control. Midway is a big system, and there are a lot of Fleet assets here. More orders will be forthcoming once we reach *Surprise*. I have no doubt about that. Until then, let's stay frosty. Midway is now a combat zone. Keep weapon systems hot and ready, unless otherwise ordered. Mom out."

FOURTEEN

STROUD

Stroud's footsteps echoed faintly off the walls as he turned into a broad, gun-metal walled corridor. Looming ahead, he found what he'd been coming to find: more than two dozen marines. They were armed with sleek M95 rifles and clad in light yet resilient black armor. The marines were aligned along either side of the corridor, their expressions taut with anticipation, like predators coiled and ready to spring into action at a moment's notice.

The air was thick with tension. In their midst, Sergeant Major Burns, hands on his hips, stood like a steadfast sentinel. His imposing figure was complemented by the presence of Lieutenant Dixon from F Company. Both men had been talking among themselves. They turned simultaneously as Stroud approached, their faces etched with determination and solemnity.

"I brought you this, sir." Burns extended his hand to reveal a P-55 personal sidearm attached to a holster and belt. The weapon, known for its reliability and precision, was meticulously coiled with the belt around the lethal pistol, complete with extra ammunition clips securely attached. The sidearm was more than just a tool—it was a potential lifeline when things got dangerous, a means to strike directly back at those who meant you harm.

"Thank you." Stroud accepted the sidearm with a practiced ease. He quickly strapped the weapon around his waist, feeling the familiar weight settle comfortably against his hips. It was a weight that brought a sense of assurance, a reminder of his training and experience that had over the years carried him through countless violent encounters. As he secured the weapon, his gaze drifted toward the airlock at the end of the corridor. The massive door stood sealed, an imposing barrier between them and the unknown challenges that waited on the other side.

"Are we ready to go?" Stroud asked, his gruff voice cutting through the silence with a clear, commanding tone.

"We are, sir," Burns affirmed with a measured confidence, his gaze shifting to the heavy hatch that loomed at the end of the corridor. Next to the airlock, a control panel was embedded into the bulkhead wall. A solitary light on the panel pulsated with a foreboding red glow. "No one's trying to come aboard from this access point. We made sure to activate the automated defenses, and that chased anyone with half a brain away."

"And this is next to post 66-A, right?" Stroud's insistence on double-checking facts had become more than just a habit; it was a survival tactic honed through years of commanding troops in high-stakes situations. In the military, it never hurt to check twice. "That post is still open?"

"It is, sir, and yes, we're right next to that boarding post, perhaps no more than a hundred meters away," Dixon chimed in. "Lieutenant Borne is in command over there, and from the latest reports, they are barely hanging on. There is apparently quite the crowd and they're very agitated. He says it's becoming a near riot."

Dixon's report painted a vivid picture of the situation at

post 66-A, one Stroud was quite familiar with since he'd just finished a call with Borne. The marine and his platoon were blocking anyone from making their way across the umbilical and boarding the ship. That was intentional.

"It's a bit frisky, sir," Burns commented with a wry tone that hinted at the underlying tension of the situation. His choice of the word "frisky" seemed almost understated in Stroud's opinion, but that was the sergeant major in a nutshell. "I believe we can all understand why, sir."

Stroud was acutely aware of the escalating urgency with the few posts he'd left open to the station. He knew that an increasing number of people were desperate in wanting to board the ship. Fleet Command had redirected everyone from this station component and the adjacent sectors to their location. This influx, if not managed efficiently, threatened to spiral into chaos. It was Stroud's responsibility, his duty, to instill order amidst the brewing storm, to navigate the fine line between control and pandemonium.

A commotion echoed through the corridor behind them, drawing their attention. Another platoon from F Company was rapidly approaching, their arrival marked by the rhythmic cadence of their hurried footsteps and clattering gear.

Leading the group was Captain Devennis, his presence at the head of the column commanding and assured. The men, including their company commander, exhibited signs of exertion, their chests heaving from the effort of their run from the marine barracks. Running such a long way while wearing unpowered armor was not an easy task.

"I want two lines yesterday. Move up to Second Platoon." Devennis barked orders with the precision and clarity of a seasoned leader.

His men, well trained and disciplined, responded instantaneously. They swiftly arranged themselves into two orderly lines, augmenting the ranks of those already in position with Lieutenant Dixon's platoon.

"Sir." Devennis greeted Stroud with a mixture of respect and a hint of amity, his face flushed from the exertion of the rapid journey to this crucial meeting point. Sweat ran down his face in beads. They had history, and the good kind. Devennis had been Stroud's first executive officer, back years ago, when he'd been a company commander. "A fine morning for a jog, don't you think?"

Burns responded to the comment with an amused grunt. "Every morning is a good morning for a run."

Knowing he had little time, Stroud dove straight into the heart of their mission as he spoke directly to the two officers and the sergeant major. "This is where we establish control. We are going to open that airlock and move out into the transfer terminal. We secure both exits and establish a perimeter out into the corridors beyond. Once we have control, only then will we close the other post, 66-A, and direct the people over there our way. We bring them aboard in an orderly manner. Every person, no matter their rank or standing, gets scanned and logged. They get assigned a spot on the ship. If it's an admiral, we scan them too. I don't care who comes before your men. Even if it's the CNO, everyone is scanned, logged, and accounted for. Those are our orders directly from the captain. He's the boss. We need to know exactly who is coming aboard. Is that understood?"

The two officers nodded, a silent but firm agreement to the direction they'd just received.

"We will escort evacuees in groups of twenty to their designated place on the ship. Once there, they will remain under guard and will not be permitted to roam." Stroud was doing his best to convey the importance of maintaining order amidst the potential chaos. He wanted to impress that upon all his people. "The sergeant major has already seen to a standing guard. We can't have them wandering the ship and getting into trouble. Got that?"

"Understood, sir," Devennis responded promptly, his acknowledgment reflecting his readiness to execute the orders without hesitation.

"You both studied the floor plans for the transfer terminal and the corridors beyond, yes?" Stroud asked, directing his question to Devennis and Dixon. He already knew the sergeant major had, for the two of them had selected this spot specifically due to the transfer terminal beyond the airlock having only two exits. It would be easier to control, and the knowledge of the layout was crucial for the effective movement and direction of the crowd that was sure to come.

"I did, sir," Dixon replied confidently.

"I looked 'em over too, sir," Devennis affirmed.

"Good," Stroud said, pleased.

"Food, water?" Dixon inquired. "How do you want to handle that, sir?"

"Our immediate and only concern right now is taking people aboard. Once the ship is underway, we can attend to such other matters." Stroud thought for a moment. "However, if anyone requires medical assistance, have the corpsman attached to your platoons see to them. If care is immediate and needs demand escalation in care, send them onto the med bay."

The nods from Devennis and Dixon signified their understanding. Though the planning was on the spot, Stroud hoped his leadership had set the stage for a coordinated and efficient operation. The coming hours would tell whether or not he had succeeded. He also trusted his people. Devennis was one of his best company commanders.

"What about security beyond the perimeter?" Burns asked, jerking a thumb at the airlock. "How do we handle the areas past the transfer terminal, and deeper into the station?"

"What about it?" Dixon asked. "That's not our responsibility."

Burns turned an unhappy look upon the lieutenant. "The lines are going to get quite long, *sir*, stretching beyond our area of immediate control. Therein will lie and fester the chaos just waiting to spread."

Stroud turned his attention to his sergeant major. Burns's concerns about the lines extending beyond their area of control were valid. "Go on. Speak your mind."

"It's likely to get ugly out there," the sergeant major said, waving a hand in the direction of the airlock. "People pushing and shoving others aside to get to the head of the line. Panic brings out the worst in human nature—fear, anxiety. If we allow it, the chaos will spread rapidly, making our job of keeping a lid on things more difficult."

"What do you recommend?" Stroud asked.

"That we put a handful of marines in powered armor out in the corridors beyond the transfer terminal. The prospect of marines in powered armor patrolling the corridors will be both a deterrent and a stabilizing presence. When the lines form, and they will, we send them out to reassure those waiting and convince people to behave themselves in the strongest possible manner. Let them range and patrol a bit as well."

"I see," Stroud said and glanced over at the lieutenant, who looked slightly abashed, for his cheeks had colored. Stroud understood this was a learning experience for Dixon. "Anything else, Sergeant Major?"

Burns paused, glancing down at the deck, clearly thinking. He looked back up after a moment. "We can also employ automated flying drones with speakers to help patrol and spread the good word about people waiting their turn and that we will take everyone aboard. They just need to be patient to allow us to work."

"The use of drones will amplify our reach and presence,"

Devennis agreed, "providing a constant reminder and reassurance to those waiting. It's a smart use of technology to manage large crowds, offering a non-threatening method to help maintain order. I like it."

"The good old carrot and the stick," the sergeant major said.

"The carrot being a ride and the stick being the Marine Corps?" Devennis asked.

"You got that right, sir," Burns said.

Stroud considered Burns's recommendations thoughtfully. The combination of powered marines and spreading the word via drone would likely be effective in maintaining order and preventing a general panic where lethal force might be required. It was a multifaceted approach, addressing not only the immediate task of boarding but also the psychological aspects of crowd control. This multi-layered strategy would also help ensure the safety and efficiency of their operation.

"How many are you thinking?" Devennis asked. "How many of our people in powered armor?"

"A fire team or two should be sufficient," Burns responded, his eyes briefly meeting Devennis's. "Eight-foot hulking mechanical giants, each armed with a maser rifle, should prove convincing enough to get people to listen."

"I like it," Stroud said with a nod. "Make it happen. Get them up here and deploy any drones we have that are readily available." Stroud then turned to Devennis. "Once we're in the terminal, see if you can also tie in to the station's speaker system. We can address people that way too."

"Yes, sir," Devennis acknowledged.

Burns took a couple of steps away from the group, then activated his internal microphone and began to speak. His voice, though inaudible to the others, was undoubtedly issuing commands to summon the powered marines.

"What do we do with people that cause trouble?" Dixon

asked. "I'd like some clarification, sir. Do we send them to the brig?"

"No," Stroud said firmly. "We don't let them get aboard. We turn them away, with force if needed."

"That's a little harsh, sir," Devennis commented. "Doing that will likely be consigning them to their deaths."

"If they can't handle waiting their turn to board," Stroud countered, "what happens when the ship comes under fire? Do they panic, interfere with operations, hurt someone? I don't think we can take that chance. In fact, I know I don't want to take that chance."

Devennis's discomfort was palpable as he shifted his stance.

Stroud, sensing the unease coming from both officers, continued. "Listen, we're not playing games here. The Push is on, and things have gotten only too real. We're not taking risks we don't need to make. If someone becomes violent, shows dangerous tendencies, they get left behind. They can find a ride somewhere else, but not on our ship. Understand me on this point?"

"Yes, sir," both officers said in unison.

Stroud softened his tone. "This is a test case for opening additional boarding posts from the station to the ship. Right now, we have four planned openings, but depending upon how well it goes, we may open more embarkation posts to bring personnel aboard at a faster pace. Whatever we learn here, what works best, you make sure to pass on to the sergeant major and he will tell me, understand? We will pass it on."

"Yes, sir," Devennis responded. "You can count on us, sir."

"I know I can," Stroud said.

"And what if we're fired upon?" Dixon asked. "Station security is armed. They may try to cut the line and force their way aboard."

This query highlighted the potential for a hostile engagement, not just with unruly civilians, but with armed and trained personnel as well. The situation would be rapidly evolving into a scenario that could require Stroud's marines to make split-second decisions under fire. The lieutenant simply wanted direction if it came to that.

"If fired upon, we return fire," Devennis said matter-of-factly before Stroud could answer. "We look after our own first and kill anyone who proves hostile."

"Exactly," Stroud said, reinforcing the point.

Burns, rejoining the conversation, added a strategic perspective. "Quite right. We kill them with prejudice if they take shots at us. That said, if the chance arises, we should try to get station security to work with us, to help keep order out into the station component. We should promise them a ride if they make themselves not only helpful, but useful. That is, if they've already not lost all discipline and gone panic mode."

Stroud, weighing the input from his team, made a decisive call. "Do it," he instructed, and then, with a sense of urgency, directed his attention to the task at hand. "We've talked enough. Captain Devennis, you have your orders. Get that airlock open and your people out into the transfer terminal. Let's get this show on the road."

Devennis immediately took charge, turning to Dixon. "Lieutenant, open the hatch."

"Listen up." Devennis, embodying the role of a company commander, turned to address his marines with authority and clarity as Dixon moved off to engage the control panel. His voice, firm and commanding, captured the attention of the waiting troops, instantly silencing any background chatter. "We are going to move out into the transfer terminal and secure it," he announced, his voice resonating through the hallway, ensuring every marine was acutely aware of the mission ahead. Devennis's instructions were straightforward, yet they carried the weight of responsibility and the urgency of their task. "No one gets by us. There are two feeder corridors to either side of the terminal. Sergeant Hayes, Sergeant Bents, sound off."

"Sir?" A sergeant from Dixon's platoon, identified as Hayes by his nameplate on the right breast of his body armor, promptly stepped forward, distinguishing himself from the line on the left side of the corridor.

"Here, sir," another voice rang out, belonging to Sergeant Bents, who raised a hand but maintained his position in the line.

"Hayes, once inside the terminal, you will take your squad and push out into the corridor on the left and set up a blocking position. Bents, you have the right."

"Aye, sir," Hayes said.

"Got it, sir," Bents said. "No one gets by us."

"Once the transfer terminal is secure," Devennis continued, gazing around at his marines, "we will extend our control beyond and farther out into both corridors. Our goal here is to take people aboard in an orderly and proficient manner. At no point will we tolerate disrespect or disorder." His words were firm, setting the tone for their conduct during the operation. "Powered marines are on their way to assist with crowd control. People are likely to be scared and frightened. Expect that. They may not realize it, but we're here to help them."

"Help-me-help-you kind of thing, sir?" Hayes asked.

"That's right." The captain paused a moment to allow that to sink in. "Be firm and use all possible restraint to control the situation. Work to de-escalate any hostility. Only utilize force if it becomes required. Anyone who is armed and wanting to come aboard is to be disarmed first."

"That point is nonnegotiable," Stroud asserted firmly. "There will be no exceptions. I don't care their rank. They are not coming aboard armed." His directive left no room for ambiguity, underscoring the priority of safety over hierarchy or status.

Just then, Dixon's voice cut through the tension. "Airlock

door is opening," he shouted. The announcement marked a pivotal moment, transitioning from planning to action.

The time for talk had ended.

Stroud felt his heart begin to beat faster. A light over the airlock started to flash, signaling the activation of the hatch. A whooping alarm sounded next, and with a mechanical pop, the heavily reinforced door started to slide slowly aside, revealing the threshold between the safety of the ship and the uncertainty of the station and potential chaos that lay beyond.

Dixon, positioned by the control panel, moved to the head of the line where the airlock door was opening. He cautiously peered through the growing gap, assessing the situation beyond. Though his marines were equipped with rifles, Dixon himself was armed only with a P-55 sidearm, holstered at his hip. He did not draw the weapon or appear alarmed by what he saw on the other side of the door.

"Are we ready to scan people?" Stroud asked, turning to Burns. This step was essential to ensure that everyone boarding the ship was identified and accounted for.

"We are, sir," Burns confirmed, gesturing toward four marines who stood prepared off to the side. Each was equipped with a personal reader, a device capable of scanning and logging identity tags.

"Anyone with a skill useful to ship's operations is to be reported immediately to Commander Shaw's attention," Stroud instructed, reiterating what they had discussed earlier.

"I know, sir," Burns said. "I've already briefed them on that requirement. The commander has created a mailbox specifically set aside for that purpose. Lieutenant Daster from supply has been assigned to direct people with useful skill sets to the appropriate department head. We've been requested to provide shipboard guides to get them there and make certain they don't get lost. I have set aside people for that job."

"Sounds good." Stroud gave a nod. "What would I do without you, Sergeant Major?"

"Probably fail upward, sir," the sergeant major said with a trace of a grin.

Stroud gave a chuckle.

As the airlock door widened enough to allow passage, Dixon's command, "Go, go, go," echoed with urgency. He led by example, swiftly moving through the opening and leading his marines forward. His proactive approach set the tone, emphasizing speed and decisiveness, just what Stroud wanted and expected to see.

The door continued to slide open, creating ample space for the marines to move through. They sprang into action, each marine going forward, one after another, pouring through the airlock. Captain Devennis went with them.

Meanwhile, Burns and Stroud momentarily stood aside, allowing the marines to pass. Once the last had gone by, without a word, they followed, passing through the airlock. They moved through the elastic tube connecting the ship to the construction slip and station. The environment was reminiscent of an umbilical cord, a lifeline connecting two entities. The tube, thirty meters in length, was illuminated by overhead lights, creating a clear path forward.

The absence of windows in this connector emphasized its utilitarian purpose, which usually catered to freight. Its primary function had been to bring aboard supplies and consumables, delivered by mech or bot, such as rations for the ship's mess.

As Stroud and Burns continued their advance through the connector, the hollow echo of their boots sounded off the scarred and heavily used deck plating. Utilizing his implants, Stroud initiated a comm call with Major Ramirez, who was in the process of organizing another boarding post five decks below them.

"Ramirez," Stroud called, his voice steady and focused. "How is your embarkation operation going?"

At the same time as they were setting up these posts, the ship was also actively taking on equipment and supplies. Stroud had had to detach more than seven hundred marines to help with that effort, and now, he was possibly shorthanded to properly handle the embarkation process. It was not a good feeling, but he'd make it work. He had good people to rely upon.

"We are setting up now, sir," Ramirez reported. "I expect to have the airlock open within the next ten minutes. I'm getting my people into position as we speak. Everything so far is under control here."

"Excellent," Stroud responded, his reply brief yet filled with approval. "As we planned, establish control before you begin taking anyone aboard."

"Yes, sir. I'm on it."

"Should you have any problems, give me a call," Stroud offered.

"I will, sir," Ramirez confirmed, solidifying the understanding between them.

"Stroud out." With that, he terminated the call, his focus returning fully to the task at hand.

As Stroud and Burns emerged into the transfer terminal, the scale of their challenge ahead became starkly evident. The terminal, resembling a loading dock, was cluttered with pallets of dry goods stacked in a disorganized manner. There were several deactivated supply bots that sat haphazardly about with a forlorn look. The air smelled strongly of lubricant and ozone. The entire terminal was massive.

Corralling the evacuees once they got inside the terminal would be difficult with the numbers he had on hand. Unhappily, Stroud understood they'd have to limit the numbers allowed in. That meant the loading of personnel would take additional time, something he was certain they did not have.

"It is what it is," Stroud said to himself after a moment. He'd just work with the deck he'd been dealt.

The sight of his marines swiftly deploying toward the two exits, with sergeants issuing directives, added a sense of controlled urgency to the scene. Despite the activity, the terminal was notably devoid of anyone other than Stroud's marines, a temporary calm before the inevitable influx of people seeking to board the ship, the coming storm.

"You know this is going to be a shit show," Burns said in a blunt, yet realistic assessment of the situation.

"A shit show?" Stroud repeated, their eyes meeting in a moment of shared understanding. Both men, seasoned veterans, had experienced their share of difficult and messy situations. "Sergeant Major, perhaps you haven't noticed, but it already is a shit show."

FIFTEEN

GARRETT

Sitting at his station on the bridge, Garrett was engrossed in a report that detailed the progress of atmospherics acquisition, a vital life support task to ensure the crew had enough breathable air before they separated from the station. The numbers were promising; they were at eighty-three percent capacity and rising, swiftly approaching full holding tanks, which, with recyclers, would allow the ship to sustain more than fifty thousand people for a prolonged period of time. Well satisfied, Garrett closed the report and soaked in this scene around him.

As his gaze swept across the bridge, he took in the sight of over a dozen crewmembers, all diligently at their posts. The bridge space was teeming with activity, and even the auxiliary stations along the walls were manned, as Shaw had called upon more of the crew to help carry the load.

The air fairly thrummed with the buzz of conversations as they worked. The background was punctuated by the occasional pings of alerts and the melodious chimes emanating from various stations.

In this last hour, *Surprise* had transformed from a mere construction Job into something almost alive. Garrett could feel her awakening in his very bones, a sensation transmitted through his chair. It was as if the ship's heart had started beating, and rapidly too, the deep, resonant hum of her powerful reactors coming to life, the subtle vibration from the gravitic drives spinning into action. The atmosphere felt charged, an excitement that coursed through the air, as palpable as the anticipation of a great adventure about to begin.

To Garrett's right, Shaw momentarily detached his attention from the display he had been scrutinizing. His eyes, sharp and observant, flicked across the bridge with a practiced awareness, studying everything before eventually locking onto Garrett's. In that brief exchange, a silent understanding passed between them, a shared excitement barely contained beneath their professional demeanors.

"I know," Shaw said. It was as if he could read Garrett's mind, sharing in the mounting atmosphere that had taken hold of the bridge. The corners of his mouth twitched, betraying the effort it took to suppress a grin. "I know it."

Feeling a surge of mutual enthusiasm, Garrett acknowledged the moment with a slight nod. He recognized the same thrill mirrored in Shaw's eyes—they would soon be taking her out to space.

With a deep breath, Garrett turned his focus back to his own duties. There was an undercurrent of urgency now, a recognition that despite his excitement, there remained a multitude of tasks to complete before they could set *Surprise* in motion, push back from the station, and power away toward Nikura.

Even at this very moment, a logistical ballet of preparation was unfolding outside the ship. Thousands upon thousands of automated supply drones and bots, resembling a swarm of industrious insects, buzzed around *Surprise*, each carrying a precious cargo, docking, unloading, and then heading back to the depots for more. They were ferrying tons of supplies and equipment, a veritable mountain of resources that had been requested by each of Garrett's department heads. These essential provisions ranged from mundane necessities to ammunition to specialized equipment, all vital for the journey ahead.

Amidst this orchestrated chaos, a large portion of the crew was deeply engaged in the monumental task of managing these incoming supplies. Among them, a sizable contingent of marines was helping to catalog each item, methodically storing them in the designated areas of the ship and securing everything in preparation for departure.

The enormity of the task could not be overstated. It was a Herculean effort, requiring coordination and dedication from everyone involved, and he was doing it all with a skeleton crew. Each drone that docked, each crate that was stowed away, brought them one step closer to the success of the mission, pushing back and making best possible speed for Nikura and safety. It was a race against time, but one Garrett was determined to win.

No, he *would* win it. There was no other option.

Garrett's attention shifted from the bustling activity of the bridge to the tactical feed displayed on a backup monitor to his right. This feed, a crucial link provided by the TFC, was currently focused on the Haier Barber jump point, where a fierce battle was raging.

As he immersed himself in the analysis of the fight, a cold shiver crept through his being, muting the excitement he'd felt moments before. The data relayed on the screen painted a grim picture of the ongoing struggle. The enemy had not yet succeeded in breaching the jump point's defenses, but their relentless assault told him that it was only a matter of time.

The Haier Barber jump point had been guarded by a chain of four asteroid forts, each a formidable bulwark. However, these fortifications were smaller and less capable compared to those at the other jump points, a vulnerability that the enemy was mercilessly exploiting.

Only one of these asteroid forts remained operational, still fighting valiantly against overwhelming odds. The other three had been reduced to nothing more than wreckage and expanding debris fields, the once-mighty structures now tagged as destroyed. The areas surrounding these fallen guardians were marked as navigational hazards.

Studying the tactical feed, Garrett felt a profound sense of urgency and foreboding. The situation at the jump point was not just a distant battle; it was a harbinger of the challenges that lay ahead for the *Surprise* and her crew.

The tactical feed displayed a scene of intense fighting as Garrett observed with a critical eye. The battle at the jump point had escalated into a chaotic maelstrom of destruction. Amidst this, four enemy combatants stood out, their presence dominating the battlefield. These ships were maneuvering through the massive debris field created by the ongoing conflict. They were heavily shielded and armored, designed to endure the harshest of battles, and they were doing so with a terrifying efficiency, shrugging aside much of the fire thrown at them.

As Garrett watched, a grudging respect for the enemy's resilience surfaced within him. Despite being under constant and intense attack, these enemy ships fought back. Maser and laser fire relentlessly lashed out at them from the sole surviving asteroid fortress, streaks of deadly light cutting through the void. Shielded and heavily armored gun battery satellites, scattered around the jump point, joined in this desperate defense, their barrages adding to the harshness of the battle.

In addition to these, stealth satellites, once hidden and dormant, were now engaged in the fray. Invisible assassins in the expanse of space, these satellites dropped their stealth fields and unleashed their deadly payloads, launching volleys of missiles and torpedoes at the enemy. As soon as they revealed their positions, they became priority targets themselves and often were swiftly destroyed by the enemy in retribution.

Garrett's eyes absorbed every detail of this harrowing scene. The tactical feed not only provided him with crucial information but also was a stark reminder of the brutality and unforgiving nature of space warfare, something he knew only too well.

Studying the plot, his thoughts were consumed by the human cost of the conflict unfolding before him. The jump point, now a vortex of destruction and chaos, was not just a strategic location; it was now a war grave for countless souls. He pondered the number of personnel who had been stationed in those asteroid forts, each now reduced to debris or trapped and hanging on the edge of oblivion. Had thousands perished? Tens of thousands?

His mind lingered on the fate of those aboard the last standing fortress. They were undoubtedly aware of their impending doom, yet their resolve did not waver. They continued to fight, with a fierce determination, a resolve to make their inevitable end as costly as possible for the enemy. This act of defiance, while heroic, was tinged with profound tragedy.

The realization that there were no Fleet assets, no mobile units within range to assist, added a deeper layer of helplessness to the situation. This isolation, this lack of hope for rescue, rendered their struggle even more poignant. Garrett felt a pang of sorrow for these brave souls.

His attention snapped back to the tactical feed as a new blip erupted onto the screen, signaling the arrival of an additional enemy combatant at the jump point. Intelligence data immediately tagged it as a capital ship, likely a super dreadnaught.

The feed was marred by the distortion caused by the relentless exchange of weapons fire, making it difficult for intelligence to discern the exact class or type of the newly arrived ship. However, her size and the manner of her entrance left no doubt about her capabilities and the threat she posed. The new arrival was a big one.

As Garrett watched, this formidable enemy capital ship made her presence felt almost immediately. She unleashed a massive barrage of missiles toward the already beleaguered fortress, each projectile streaking through space with deadly intent.

With a practiced gesture, Garrett manipulated the controls, zooming out on the tactical display to gain a broader perspective of the situation unfolding across the Midway Star System. He sought a comprehensive view, a strategic assessment of the space that stretched between Midway Station and the Haier Barber jump point.

The system map came alive with a myriad of markers and indicators, showing rally points that had been designated for the gathering of warships. These points, strategically placed, were beacons calling the scattered system defense forces to assemble, to form a unified front against the enemy.

Warships responding to this call were burning at maximum military power toward these rally points. Remarkably, capital ships were even utilizing jump beacons, a maneuver fraught with danger, but necessitated by the urgency of the situation. Garrett observed that several of these rally points already boasted a serious assembly of forces, dozens of frontline ships, all preparing themselves for battle.

His attention then shifted to Midway Station itself. The space around the station was a flurry of activity as starships, both civilian and military, were pushing back and away from their docks and slips. Some moved to join the burgeoning ranks of their comrades at the rally points, while others—perhaps less equipped for combat, burdened with civilians, or civilian ships themselves—were retreating and running toward the Nikura jump point at the best speed they could make.

The sight of so many starships in motion was a spectacle

Garrett had never witnessed before. The array of vessels, each moving with purpose, whether to fight or flee, was a sight both awe-inspiring and sobering. This grand scale of movement, a dance of survival and determined resistance, showcased the enormity of the situation they had all been thrust into.

"Sir," Shaw called for his attention. "Might I have a moment of your time?"

"Go ahead." Garrett looked over. "What's up?"

"I've got a military transport that may be of interest to us. She's nearly twenty slips over. They put in for repairs to their gravitic drive. Somehow"—he gave a shrug of his shoulders—"they managed to crack a coil."

"What of it?" Garrett asked curiously. "What's she transporting?"

"The ship is carrying over seventy million liters of aviation fuel, originally destined for Third Fleet. I'd like permission to have her towed to one of our hardpoints. We can manually load the fuel and then jettison the ship when done and underway. It will be quicker than bringing fuel aboard through automated drone deliveries from the depots."

"I don't believe the captain of that vessel will be too happy to lose his ship," Garrett said.

"He isn't, sir," Shaw said, "but I just spoke with him, and he and his crew are more than a little anxious since they can't get under power themselves. The entire coil array has been disassembled. They're not going anywhere and are willing to accept a ride in exchange for the fuel. I will need to requisition a few marines for labor to pull this off, but I recommend we take advantage of the situation."

"All right," Garrett said. "How many do you need—marines, that is?"

"A platoon," Shaw said, "to help set up the fuel transfer. Once it's in place, we will be good and they can return to whatever they were doing before."

"Do you need marines for the towing job?"

"I do not, sir. I just need them ready for when we mate the transport to our own ship."

"What's the name of this transport?" Garrett asked curiously.

"The *Celestial Fire*."

"Kind of ironic considering what she's carrying," Garrett said ruefully.

"I know, right?"

"What about the tugs?"

"I have automated tugs on standby," Shaw said. "I'm just waiting for your go-ahead at this point. Since we're still docked to the station, I will mate her on one of the hardpoints that's not blocked by the slip."

"Very well, make it happen. I will speak to Stroud and ask him to spare some labor."

"Thank you, sir."

Garrett opened a channel to the colonel. A moment later, the colonel's image flickered onto one of the screens before Garrett, fatigue etched into his features.

Despite his apparent weariness, there was an undeniable strength in his demeanor, a resilience born from duty and experience.

"Sir," Stroud greeted. "What can I do to help?"

"How is the boarding operation going?" Garrett asked, looking for an update.

"It's going," Stroud growled. "This is all ad hoc, sir, but we've already embarked more than four thousand people and gotten them settled."

"That many?" Garrett found himself surprised. It had been only an hour since the operation had begun.

"I now have six boarding posts opened," Stroud said, "and am working to activate two additional embarkation points. There are a lot of people wanting to get on the ship. The more we can bring on, the better, but I won't compromise security for quantity, sir."

The sudden commotion in the background of someone shouting momentarily diverted the colonel's attention. Stroud cast a brief glance away from the screen, his focus on whatever urgent matter had arisen out of view. When he returned his gaze to Garrett, his expression had subtly changed; it was now tauter.

"Any trouble?" Garrett asked.

"Yes, sir, but we're handling it. So far, there's been no need to bother you. When there's time, I will write up a full report concerning our actions, along with the results, and forward it to your attention for review."

Garrett decided to cut to the chase. "I need a platoon of men."

A pained expression crossed the colonel's face. It was as if Garrett had asked for one of the man's kidneys. "I am stretched thin at the moment."

"I know it," Garrett admitted. "We're going to mate a transport filled with aviation fuel to the ship and effect a transfer before pushing back. We need that fuel for flight operations, as our tanks are almost dry. There's no telling when we might see more. Yes, we technically have the ability to manufacture more on our own, but that takes time and finding a gas giant. Everything right now comes down to time."

Stroud nodded gravely. "When do you need my people?"

"Shaw," Garrett asked, looking over and away from Stroud, "when will you need that platoon?"

"In about an hour, sir," Shaw responded. "The tugs are already moving into position to extract the transport from her docking slip. It will take that long to get her moved and mated."

Garrett turned back to Stroud. "An hour."

"I'll have them ready," Stroud said, clearly resigned to the inevitable. "If there's nothing else, I'd like to get back to my job, sir."

"Let me know if you need anything," Garrett said.

"I could use more marines, sir," Stroud said. "But unfortunately, I don't have any more to draw upon."

Garrett's mind briefly wandered, a vivid memory surfacing unbidden. He recalled the sight of the marines standing at the train terminal. They had been there when he had returned from Little Hill. This flash of memory, seemingly trivial, sparked a realization in Garrett. He snapped his fingers, an instinctive gesture that accompanied the moment of clarity.

"What about marines barracked on the station? Can we bring some of those aboard? I am sure there are units not only stationed on Midway, but some that were likely in transit and are now finding themselves potentially stranded and looking for a way off the station."

Stroud blinked, the look of exhaustion dropping from his face. "That's not a bad idea, sir. Do we have orders to pull them off?"

"No," Garrett answered, "but I will ask forgiveness later."

Stroud let go a light chuckle, just as more shouting erupted off-screen. He did not look this time. "If there are any, those marines would be quartered in marine country on the other side of the station. That's a long distance from where we are, sir. I understand it is complete chaos on the station. They may not be able to get to us. Things are beginning to break down stationside."

Garrett could only imagine. He looked at the commander. "Shaw, how many personnel transports do we have, shuttles, boats, and the like?"

Shaw looked over at him, his brows drawing together. He'd clearly not been following the conversation with Stroud. "I'll have to check with the CAG, but I believe thirty-two boats, sir. They're big birds and can handle a few hundred each. Some of the engineers have been using them to move from the ship to other parts of the station and back again as needed. Why do you ask?"

"Are we using them currently? Are they in use?"

"Not that I am aware. The automated supply bots and drones are bringing everything aboard. In fact, I reassigned the pilots and crew to help with the settling in of the evacuees."

"Get the pilots and crews back to their boats and ready to go immediately," Garrett ordered. "I have a job for them."

"Yes, sir," Shaw said and turned back to his station.

Garrett looked to Stroud. "If you can contact any marines on the station looking for a ride off Midway, I've got boats that can pick them up on their side of the station. We can transport several thousand before pushback."

Stroud gave what Garrett took to be a pleased nod. "I'll make some calls, sir, and see what I can do, maybe even reach out to the station commandant himself—if that's all right?"

"It is," Garrett said. "Contact Shaw when you have people ready for transport. He will make it happen for you and send the boats."

"I will, sir."

Garrett ended the communication with Stroud, his mind already shifting back to the tactical situation at hand. As he glanced down at the HTD, a somber update confronted him. The last fortress defending the Haier Barber jump point had fallen. The destruction of the fort was not just a strategic setback; it represented the loss of countless lives, brave souls who had fought valiantly to the end.

A heavy weight settled over Garrett's heart as he processed this grim reality. The situation was rapidly deteriorating. The HTD now showed twelve active enemy ships within the system. At great cost, the enemy had successfully breached the initial line of defense. These ships were beginning to maneuver away from the jump point, pushing out and deeper into the system with ominous intent. As he watched, two more enemy capital ships made their entrance, jumping in.

"Mister Tyabni," Garrett called, tearing his gaze away from the display to look over at his weapons officer.

"Sir?" Jared Tyabni, a striking figure with his dark skin and contrasting, crystal clear blue eyes, held a look of inquiry and readiness as he gazed over at his captain.

"How are the ammunition loads coming?" Garrett asked.

"I'm working on filling our magazines, sir." The slight lilt in Tyabni's voice was distinctive. It hinted at a cultural heritage from a far-off place, a unique inflection shaped by the nuances of his home world's dialect.

Although Tyabni was a recent addition to the ship's roster, his presence had already become an integral part of the bridge crew's dynamic. He was confident, capable, and skilled. More importantly, he knew his job.

"We're at about twenty percent for all types of offensive missiles and torpedoes," Tyabni continued. "The same for point defense charges and kinetic weapons. However, I am happy to report we now have something with which to shoot. Ammunition and weapons loads are being distributed as we speak to all point defense batteries and missile tubes—in the event we need them."

"Very good," Garrett said. Thankfully, that process of loading ammunition and missiles was mostly automated and would not require additional human resources. "How about maser and laser batteries?"

"Ready to charge on your mark, sir. I've run diagnostics on all systems. We're at about eighty-five percent functionality on the turrets. The rest either have not yet been installed or are in the process of final assembly and therefore out of action. We do have three assembled turrets that have registered faults. I've tagged them for engineering to look at, but they can't get to them for some time."

"Understandable, as the chief engineer's people have their hands full." Garrett gave a pleased nod with the report. "Now that the reactors are hot, let's make that happen. I want to be ready for the unexpected. You have permission to prime and charge the functioning batteries and turrets."

"Aye, sir," Tyabni said. "And what about the main battery? That takes a while to load and charge, sir. It might come in handy for the fleet to call upon."

There was almost an eagerness in the weapons officer's gaze as he looked at his captain. It was something he too felt. Garrett pondered the tactical possibilities, his mind analyzing the potential of deploying the *Surprise*'s main battery. This weapon was a closely guarded secret within the Fleet. The prospect of utilizing it presented a strategic opportunity that could significantly impact the unfolding situation, perhaps even help it.

Heck, Garrett couldn't see it hurting.

He considered the scenario: if Fleet Command authorized the use of the weapon, and if the enemy ships ventured within its targeting range, *Surprise* could lash out, offering a chance to defend and retaliate even as they prepared to move toward the Nikura jump point.

He knew that any decision to engage the main battery would come with its own set of risks and consequences. It would reveal one of *Surprise*'s key capabilities, possibly drawing unwanted attention from the enemy. Moreover, the authorization from Fleet Command was crucial, as the use of such a classified weapon would have broader implications. By observing its use, the enemy might be able to replicate it. That was a serious and real concern.

"Do it," Garrett said after a moment's thought. When the weapon was charged, he'd reach out to Yenga and make the offer. Command might want to keep the cannon under wraps, but then again, the situation was desperate. Better to have it ready than not.

"Yes, sir," Tyabni said eagerly.

Garrett turned to another officer. "Cassidy, how are the sensors coming along?"

Lieutenant Junior Grade Jennifer Cassidy was also a new addition to his crew. With her blonde hair and youthful demeanor, she embodied the enthusiasm and potential of an officer fresh from the academy. Her presence on *Surprise* spoke to her academic excellence, having graduated at the top of her class, a distinction that earned her a position aboard his prestigious ship. She had clearly impressed someone.

As Cassidy looked over at him, Garrett could perceive the undercurrent of nervousness and unease in her posture and expression. It was a natural response for someone in her position, young and relatively inexperienced, suddenly thrust into a role of significant responsibility. The upcoming days were poised to be challenging, especially considering that she was temporarily heading the sensor, scanner, and electronic warfare department, a critical segment of the ship's operations.

The senior officer, a Commander Warren, who was originally designated and slated to run this department, had not yet arrived, leaving Cassidy to shoulder the responsibilities in the interim. This scenario, while daunting for a junior officer, was also an opportunity for her to demonstrate her skills and adaptability under pressure. Failure for her was not an option, and Garrett was sure she understood the stakes.

Garrett recognized the importance of providing support and guidance to his younger officers. As captain, he knew that the success of their mission relied not only on his decisions but also on the collective capabilities and growth of his team, being the entire crew. He made a mental note to speak to Shaw about providing not only her, but everyone else additional training and support. Once they were away from Midway, an aggressive training schedule would have to be drawn up. That was the best and fastest way to get everyone up to speed and working as a true team.

"I've finished my diagnostics and am now calibrating the sensors." Cassidy paused and glanced down at a screen at her station. "Once that's done, sir, I will begin charging all systems, say, maybe an hour."

"What about EW?"

"Electronic warfare is on my list for after that, sir."

"Very good and carry on," Garrett said as his attention then shifted toward the helm station, where the navigation team was deeply engrossed in the task that Shaw had assigned. Observing them, he appreciated the complexity of their work. Plotting a course for *Surprise* was no small feat, especially given the ship's immense size and mass.

Surprise would behave like a beached whale in space, slow to maneuver and challenging to navigate. Her sheer mass was such that she generated a minuscule gravitational field, a unique characteristic that added another layer of complexity to her handling. The ship's drives and inertial dampeners were designed to counteract and compensate for this gravitational influence, but it was still a factor that always required consideration.

Garrett watched as one officer sat diligently at the helm, fingers moving deftly over the controls, while another stood beside her, pointing at a display screen and speaking, likely discussing trajectory adjustments or course options. Garrett understood the importance of their work; the correct plotting of the ship's course was crucial, especially when time was a constraint.

He considered asking for an update on their progress but reconsidered. Their focus was evident, and he didn't want to interrupt their concentration. In his experience, trust in his crew's professionalism and expertise was often more beneficial than constant oversight and interference. Besides, after they finished, both he and Shaw would review their work and verify that the course they'd plotted was acceptable.

"Shaw," Garrett said, suddenly thinking on his conversation with Stroud.

"Sir?" Shaw looked up from his station and over at Garrett.

"With the personnel we are taking aboard, primarily from Fleet, how many have we identified with a useful skill set?"

Shaw glanced over at one of his displays and tapped upon it for a moment. "A little over a hundred, sir. I have someone assigning them to the appropriate departments. We are putting them to work."

Garrett felt a stab of disappointment. "That's all?"

"Most of those we are taking aboard are civilian engineers and construction techs, which is understandable, given where we are moored. I am certain we will pick up more from Fleet in the coming hours."

Garrett gave an unhappy nod. Turning his attention to his own station, he was immediately confronted with a slew of messages in his mailbox, each marked urgent. These were from his department heads, likely requests for additional resources or updates on the logistics of provisioning the ship. Under normal circumstances, fully stocking a vessel could take days, if not weeks for the larger ones, and *Surprise* was the largest starship ever built. They had only hours.

Garrett knew he needed to address these requests promptly. Efficient provisioning was critical for their mission's success, and his role in coordinating and responding to these needs was paramount.

"Oh, and Shaw," Garrett said, glancing around the bridge once more. There was also something important to consider that had not been addressed, at least not yet.

"Sir?" Shaw looked up.

"Send to the galley for some coffee and sandwiches to be run up to the bridge." Garrett knew the importance of keeping his people fed, watered, and caffeinated. They could eat while they worked, for once they were underway, there was no telling when watch relief would come for those stuck on the bridge. "In addition, get them working on precooked meals and distributing rations for not only the crew, but those we are taking aboard, the evacuees. If they need additional resources, we are bringing on plenty of personnel that won't have anything to do, those civilian engineers and construction techs. They can assist with the effort."

"Yes, sir. I will get right on that."

Satisfied, Garrett prepared to delve into the pressing matters in his mailbox. His instincts prompted him to take one more look at the TFC and what the enemy were doing by the Haier Barber jump point. His eyes quickly scanned the display, and he noted an increase in the enemy's presence. More than twenty-five enemy ships were now within the system, all capital ships.

These warships were maneuvering strategically, fanning out around the jump point in a pattern that suggested a defensive posture. This tactical arrangement hinted at a larger scheme. As Garrett watched, yet another enemy warship emerged at the jump point, reinforcing the growing enemy fleet. It was another dreadnaught.

If history was something to go by, the ships currently in-system were likely just the vanguard, the first wave of what would soon be a much larger force. Garrett understood this was only the prelude. The enemy's main body was on its way. Once it arrived, the invasion would fully commence. As Admiral Isabel brought the Twenty-First Fleet to bear, soon after the real fighting would begin.

But that wasn't his job or worry. He had a ship to save for a day when she would be able to strike her own blows. He turned to the display with the urgent messages and got to work.

SIXTEEN

STROUD

"Here you go," Burns said, extending his arm to hand over a steaming mug of coffee, the scent wafting through the air of the dimly lit control room. Several of the lights overhead were out. The walls, adorned with glowing screens, some of which were static-filled, and blinking control panels, cast a soft light on Burns's face. He held a similar mug himself, the steam gently rising in the cool air of the station. "Two sugars, no cream—just how an alcoholic takes it," he added, a faint smirk playing on his lips, reflecting a camaraderie born from countless hours working together, not to mention more than a few shared hard experiences they had both survived.

Stroud felt a frown crease his forehead at the comment. He took a cautious sip of the hot beverage, feeling the warmth spread through him. The coffee was good, exactly how he preferred it. He studied his sergeant major, observing Burns closely.

"I thought alcoholics take it black," Stroud replied, his voice tinged with amusement.

"That's just what they want you to think," Burns replied, his expression innocent. The gentle hum of the space station's life support systems provided a soft backdrop to their conversation.

"Uh-huh," Stroud responded skeptically, his eyes narrowing slightly as he continued to observe Burns over the rim of his mug. The steam from the coffee blurred his vision momentarily. The sergeant major took a leisurely sip from his own mug, the aroma of the coffee mingling with the sterile air of the station. "And how do you take it, Sergeant Major?" His tone was playful yet inquisitive as he lowered his mug.

"Black," Burns answered, maintaining a straight face. His response was delivered with a stoic calmness.

Stroud merely shook his head, a wry smile briefly crossing his face as he took another sip of his coffee. The warmth of the drink was welcome in the cold environment of the small control room. Just meters away, one of Stroud's embarkation posts bustled with activity.

The half-platoon assigned to this post had scrounged up a coffee machine and dispenser from somewhere nearby, trans- forming this neglected control center into an impromptu break room.

The control room itself was a relic of the past, clearly unused for years. Dust coated every surface, creating a ghostly sheen in the dim light. Clutter was everywhere. Old screens flickered with unneeded data. Panels were missing in places, leaving cables hanging in tangled heaps. Buttons blinked with sporadic, aimless patterns.

In the corners and along the back wall, worn-out furniture was stacked haphazardly, chairs with peeling upholstery and tables with chipped edges, silent reminders of a bygone era. It seemed someone had been too lazy to recycle them and had simply shoved them into this forgotten room, adding to the sense of abandonment and decay.

Exhaustion weighed heavily on Stroud as he released a weary breath, leaning against the sturdy, cold metal table where the coffee machine sat. He took another sip from his mug, combatting the fatigue he felt.

He had briefly entertained the idea of taking a stimulant pill, a common practice among the Corps to maintain alertness during extended duties. But the very thought of the inevitable comedown, the post-stim hangovers that left one feeling worse than before, was unappealing.

Stroud had always had an aversion to relying on drugs, even those deemed safe and standard-issue like the stims provided to keep fighters awake, on task, and focused. He preferred to tackle his fatigue head-on, without artificial aids.

On a nearby table lay the remnants of a ham and cheese sandwich, now just an empty wrapper with crumbs amidst the dust. The sandwich was a simple yet satisfying meal after the long hours spent moving from post to post. After having nothing for much of the day, it felt good to have finally eaten.

Here, Stroud was taking a precious moment to relax, drawing comfort from the small pleasures of a simple sandwich and a freshly brewed mug of coffee.

Amidst the relentless pace of managing crises and maintaining order during the evacuation process, Stroud hadn't even noticed the gnawing hunger until he'd devoured the sandwich. With another sip of coffee, he felt its warmth spread from his throat down to his belly. The chill in the air was noticeable, almost biting, leading Stroud to wonder if there was a glitch or malfunction in the station's normally efficient heating system.

He took another long pull, feeling a renewal of spirit with each sip. In this moment, the coffee was more than just a beverage; it was a small but significant source of comfort and rejuvenation.

"It's the little things in life," Burns commented, as if he could read Stroud's thoughts, a mix of wisdom and care in his voice. "Besides, it's my job to look after you, sir. Sometimes you forget to care for yourself."

Stroud couldn't help but feel a surge of warmth toward the crusty old salt. "You're mothering me again."

"I believe the words you are looking for are 'thank you'," Burns retorted, the hint of a smile in his voice.

Stroud rubbed the back of his neck and glanced toward the open door that led to the transfer terminal where his marines were processing evacuees. "It's not over yet, but I am shocked we've managed to pull this off without a major incident, like facing a full riot, given the circumstances."

"So far there have only been a few violent episodes," Burns conceded, "caused by unruly individuals. Those were dealt with harshly and rapidly enough to suppress others from trying something similar or to allow any chaos to spread. Setting the proper tone from the get-go helped, especially our marines in powered armor."

"There was only one death, right?" Stroud inquired.

"Yes, sir. The offender drew a projectile weapon when we found contraband in one of his bags and shot Corporal Sing in the chest. The body armor held. Sing returned fire and killed him instantly. Our man has a bruise, nothing more, from the experience, beyond regrets. We also had one minor injury, a twisted ankle, Private Marks. He hurt it while trying to break up a fight in one of the lines. I think he was shoved and fell awkwardly."

Stroud nodded, understanding the gravity of the situation and the thin line they walked between maintaining order and potential chaos. The fact that these incidents had been contained with minimal casualties was a relief, yet the weight of every life ended or put in danger under his command was not lost on him. They were all Stroud's responsibility.

Burns's attention shifted as his earlobe glowed subtly, indicating an incoming communication on his implant.

"Burns here. Go ahead, Corporal, report," he spoke into the comm, his voice taking on a professional, attentive tone.

Stroud observed as Burns's expression turned focused, listening intently to the report from the other end. The sergeant major's face remained impassive, giving away nothing of the conversation.

After a moment of deep listening, Burns responded, "Are you certain?" His question hung in the air, suggesting the importance of the information being relayed and confirmed. Again, Burns fell into a silent, attentive stance, absorbing the details from the caller. "All right, head on back to the barn and report what you found to the major. Good job. Burns out."

The glow on Burns's earlobe faded, indicating the end of the comm call.

"Good news or bad news?" Stroud took another sip of his coffee, his eyes on Burns, trying to gauge the situation from his reaction.

"I am not sure," Burns admitted as he set his mug of coffee down on the table. "I was wondering why the lines had fallen off and fewer evacuees were arriving."

The decrease in the number of evacuees had been an unexpected development, one that hadn't immediately fit into any straightforward explanation.

"Yeah, me too," Stroud echoed, finishing his coffee and placing the empty mug alongside Burns's. He moved toward the open control room door, his gaze sweeping over the transfer terminal. The initial pandemonium that had marked the first three hours of the evacuation had subsided considerably. The dwindling number of people waiting to board the evacuation ship was a contrast to the earlier mad rush of scared people they had processed. Stroud noted that some of the evacuees even had luggage with them, indicating a certain level of preparedness and calm amidst the crisis, as if they had gone home first.

The sight of civilians in line, particularly a mother with two young children, girls, one barely more than a toddler, struck a chord with Stroud. The vulnerability of these individuals, especially the children who were likely struggling to comprehend the upheaval in their lives, was a poignant reminder of the human aspect and cost of what was happening.

Stroud reflected on the reports from other posts, all indicating a similar drop in the number of evacuees seeking to board the ship. He had sent marines to scout the nearest parts of the station, confirming that much of it had become eerily quiet, almost a ghost town. This unexpected turn of events raised several questions in his mind.

Where had everyone gone?

This was Construction Command territory, not densely populated, but with a few residential blocks. Could it be that many had retreated to their quarters, perhaps to gather personal belongings in the hopes of a more organized evacuation? Or had a significant number of people already found alternate means to leave the station and taken it over an untested ship?

"Well, sir," Burns said, "I had a suspicion and took the liberty of sending out a patrol to the nearest train terminal about three kilometers away. It's empty, not even station security about. The trains are not running. There were even two sitting idle in the station. Our people confirmed they were offline."

Looking back at Burns, Stroud processed this new information, connecting the dots. "They've finally locked the station down. Stopping the trains is the only way to control the chaos and isolate trouble spots," he deduced, his voice reflecting both understanding and a hint of frustration. It was a drastic measure, but in light of the circumstances, an effective way to manage the situation to help control the spread of the chaos.

"That's my assessment," Burns confirmed.

"Well, it took Station Command long enough to make that decision."

Picking up a reader he'd placed on the table, Stroud tapped at it, accessing the latest data and total count of evacuees processed thus far from all posts. His eyes scanned the screen, absorbing the numbers.

"Between all eight embarkation posts, we've taken aboard forty-two thousand and then some."

"A good day's work," Burns said.

"A very good day's work."

"With the announcements we've been making on the component's speaker system, there can't be very many more left for us to take off," Burns said.

"I think so too." Stroud set the reader back down.

"Does that include the additional marines we've brought aboard?" Burns asked.

"It does. Four thousand of that number are our people, a mix of companies and replacements in transit."

"But no senior officers," Burns said. "For the time being, you are it, sir."

Stroud let go a heavy breath. "At least until we get to the next star system. I am certain Fleet will find someone senior."

"It's not all that bad," Burns said, "at least, not until then."

"No, it is not," Stroud agreed, understanding the sergeant major's meaning. Not counting the captain of *Surprise*, this was essentially an independent command for him. Stroud's thoughts shifted. "With the trains shut down, finishing early is not a bad thing for us. I was worried we'd be turning people away. I was not looking forward to doing that."

"There are still going to be people left behind," Burns said. "That can't be helped."

The sudden outburst of "I said put it down!" followed by a scream and a flurry of shouting shattered the relative calm of the moment. Stroud and Burns, instantly alert, moved swiftly to the door.

Peering out, Stroud's eyes widened at the scene unfolding just outside. A man in a station security uniform was gripping a young girl, one of the children Stroud had noticed earlier. His heart dropped at the sight of the pistol, muzzle pressed against the girl's head, her face etched with fear. The situation was every commander's nightmare: a hostage scenario, an innocent life at immediate risk.

A squad of marines, their rifles trained on the security officer and the child, were tense and ready. Lieutenant Mike Zepper, commanding the squad's platoon, was in a precarious position. Standing closer to the gunman than the rest, one hand rested on his holstered pistol, a sign of readiness and restraint, while his other hand was extended toward the security officer in a gesture that was both calming and commanding.

"Fuck me." Stroud felt a surge of anger at the sight of the young girl in danger, her life threatened by someone who should have been a protector, not a perpetrator. His years of experience in crisis situations kicked in, even as his emotions roared with rage.

The marines, well trained and disciplined, were in a stand-off, their focus unwavering despite the high stakes. Though they weren't typically trained for this, Zepper's posture suggested he was attempting to de-escalate without resorting to violence. Stroud knew the importance of maintaining control, of finding a resolution that would save the child without bloodshed.

The gravity of the situation demanded swift yet calculated action. Stroud's mind raced through possible scenarios and outcomes, assessing the risks and the best course of action. His gaze shifted between the frightened child, the desperate security officer, and his own marines, poised for action yet restrained by the need for caution. Marines by nature and training were killers, not hostage negotiators.

"Put it down," Zepper ordered the security officer. "Put the pistol down before things get out of hand and someone gets hurt."

Amidst this chaos, the mother's screams pierced the air, a raw sound of terror and desperation to save her child. A marine sergeant, acting quickly, took hold of her as she tried to rush forward. With some effort, he pulled her back to safety, away from the immediate danger. In a swift, protective move, another marine, a woman, scooped up the mother's younger daughter, the toddler, removing her from the line of fire. She set the child down at a safe distance and then positioned herself as a shield between the gunman and the young girl.

The rest of the evacuees, who had been waiting to board, scattered. Some backed away hastily, while others sought cover behind pallets of equipment and any available shelter in the terminal. The atmosphere was one of panic.

The security officer, his voice strained with desperation and anger, shouted at the marines. "Get back!" he yelled, his words laced with threat and fear. "You listen to me. You fucking marines are going to let me get on that ship, or so help me I will blow her brains across this bay."

His threat was terrifyingly clear, the life of the young girl hanging precariously in the balance.

Zepper maintained a calm, soothing tone. "Everyone's getting aboard," he assured the man. "Just relax and hand over the weapon. Then you can board like the rest."

The security officer, however, was not swayed, his response laced with defiance. "Not a chance," he snarled, his grip on the weapon and the girl unyielding.

Zepper persisted, his voice still composed. "There's no need to do this," he reasoned. "We're not leaving anyone behind, including you."

The man countered with a desperate proposal. "You let me aboard, and when the ship pushes back, you can have the gun and the girl."

It was at this moment that Stroud intervened, stepping out from the office. His voice, hard and commanding, cut through the tension like a blade. "That's not happening," he declared, his presence demanding attention. All eyes, including those of the man with the gun, turned to him.

Burns followed Stroud out.

Stroud, without turning to Burns, triggered his comm unit and opened a channel to Burns via his implants. Subvocal, he spoke, issuing a tactical command. "Work your way to his side and then behind the bastard."

"Yes, sir," Burns replied in a whisper, understanding the gravity of the situation and what his colonel wanted. "You keep him occupied for me and I will take him out."

Stroud advanced with a confident stride, his approach calculated to draw the gunman's full attention. The man's eyes, filled with desperation and fear, remained locked on Stroud, tracking his every move. Stroud's presence was authoritative and composed.

As he passed the first of his marines, Stroud made a crucial decision. He was acutely aware of the potential for a tragic mistake in such a high-tension situation, especially with nervous fingers on triggers.

"Lower your weapons," he commanded firmly, his voice carrying the weight of his experience and authority.

"Sir?" the lieutenant questioned, his focus still on the gunman. "I am not sure that's a good idea." His concern was palpable, reflecting the risk involved in lowering their arms in such a volatile situation.

"You heard me," Stroud reiterated, his tone leaving no room for doubt or argument. His order was clear and unequivocal.

Reluctantly, the marines began to comply, pointing their rifle muzzles down toward the deck. This gesture, a significant lowering of their defensive posture, was a gamble, but Stroud's decision was grounded in his understanding of the situation and his aim to de-escalate the tension. His move was strategic, intended to reduce the immediate threat felt by the gunman and create an opening for a peaceful resolution, if one could be found. If not, Burns would end it.

"Now let me aboard," the officer, his voice laced with desperation and agitation, demanded.

Stroud, unfazed and resolute, responded simply, "No. You are not going anywhere."

"What do you mean, no? I have the gun."

"I am not letting you aboard the ship armed," Stroud stated firmly, halting less than five paces from the gunman. In his peripheral vision, the colonel noted Burns discreetly moving to the side, skillfully navigating around a large pallet stacked with assembly equipment.

"I'll kill her," the security officer threatened, his eyes wild. Stroud, assessing the man's unstable state, considered the possibility of drugs, alcohol, or extreme fear driving his actions, perhaps a combination of all three.

In this critical moment, Stroud understood he had to maintain control of the situation, balancing the need to de-escalate with the urgency of disarming the man without harm to the young girl. The longer it went on, the more dangerous and volatile the gunman would become.

"Do that," Stroud said, "and my men will kill you dead."

The gunman, still clutching the girl, took a step backward, dragging her with him, his movements erratic as he scanned the surrounding marines immediately to either side.

"Get back," he demanded. "Get back. I'm warning you all."

The young girl, caught in this terrifying situation, was visibly shaken. Tears streamed down her cheeks, and her eyes, filled with fear and confusion, looked imploringly at Stroud. In that moment, Stroud felt a powerful urge to draw his weapon and end the standoff, but he knew that doing so could endanger the girl's life. The risk of a stray round or a sudden move by the officer made any aggressive action too perilous.

"Back off," Stroud commanded his men, signaling for them

to give the security officer more space. He held his hands out, a gesture of non-aggression.

His men, trained to respond to his commands, took several steps back, creating a wider buffer between themselves and the gunman. Zepper stepped back as well.

"What's your name?" Stroud asked, his tone calm and direct.

The question caught the man off guard. "What?" he exclaimed, confusion momentarily overriding his panic as his eyes narrowed.

"I am Colonel Stroud. Your name, what is it?" Stroud pressed on, attempting to establish a personal connection.

"Lieutenant Bennet of station security. It is my right to carry this gun. Your men tried to take it from me. It is my right."

"Not aboard my ship," Stroud countered firmly. "You don't have a right to carry it there." He held up his hands in a placating gesture. "Now, Bennet, drop the weapon. There will be consequences—there have to be after this—but you will be brought aboard when the ship pushes back. We won't leave you here. More importantly, you will be alive."

Bennet's distrust was evident as his face twisted with patent disbelief. "I put this down and your men will kill or leave me. You're lying!"

"I'm not," Stroud said, taking another calculated and careful step forward, closing the distance between them. "I am a man of my word. We will take you with us."

The girl began sobbing. At the same time, she attempted to struggle free from Bennet's grip. Stroud couldn't help but admire her bravery and spirit in such a terrifying situation. She was a fighter, that was for sure. Meanwhile, Bennet, reacting to her movements, tightened his grip on her, his arm constricting around her chest in a desperate attempt to maintain control.

"Stay still, damn you," Bennet hissed at the girl. His anxiety was clear as he glanced around, his eyes darting to the marines positioned throughout the terminal to his front. In his height-ened state of panic, he failed to notice Sergeant Major Burns stealthily maneuvering behind him, inching closer with the precision and focus of a skilled predator.

Stroud intensified his approach, adopting a harder tone to command Bennet's full attention. "Look at me," he demanded, taking another step forward.

Bennet glanced sideways at Lieutenant Zepper.

"I said, look at me!" His authoritative voice cut through the chaos of the moment, forcing Bennet to meet his gaze.

Bennet's eyes, filled with a mix of fear and defiance, locked onto Stroud's.

"I am giving you my word. Put the gun down before this gets worse for you." Stroud's words were firm, a clear ultimatum that left no room for misunderstanding.

As Stroud engaged Bennet, Burns had completed his silent approach, now directly behind the man and only steps away from striking. Stroud took another deliberate step forward, ensuring that Bennet's attention remained fixed on him, providing Burns with the opportunity to act.

The tension was at a breaking point. Every second counted, and the precision of their actions could mean the difference between a peaceful resolution and a tragic outcome.

Bennet's desperation escalated, his voice strained as he threatened, "No. You stop. Come closer and I will kill her. I swear, I will kill her."

"You kill her, and as I said, you die." Stroud remained unyielding. "That is a promise."

In a sudden and dangerous shift, Bennet redirected his threat directly at Stroud, moving the gun from the girl's temple to aim squarely at Stroud's unarmored chest. Since the crisis had begun, neither he nor Burns had had time to collect their body armor. That, in hindsight, was clearly a mistake, for the dilation of Bennet's pupils and his erratic behavior reinforced Stroud's suspicion that he was under the influence of drugs.

Despite the acute danger he was now in, Stroud recognized the critical need to keep Bennet's focus on him, especially as Burns was closing in from behind, nearly within reach to make an attempt to disarm the man.

"It may surprise you, but this is not the first time someone has pointed a weapon at me," Stroud said.

Bennet, fueled by a manic energy, seized on this. "Have you been shot before?" he asked eagerly, his eyes alight with a kind of crazed curiosity.

"I have," Stroud confirmed gravely, his response measured and deliberate. His admission was not just a statement of fact, but a psychological tactic, aimed at keeping Bennet engaged and distracted from Burns's final approach. "I'd not recommend the experience. Have you?"

The girl stopped sobbing and bit her lower lip, her eyes hardening as she looked up at Bennet. The gun was no longer to her head but still pointing at Stroud. With a swift, determined motion, she drove the heel of her boot down onto Bennet's foot. His reaction was immediate and pained.

"Bitch!" he cried out and pulled her even more tightly against him. Her efforts intensified. Fighting like a she-wolf, she bit down on his forearm, a desperate bid for freedom, but Bennet's response was brutal. Crying out, he struck her on the side of the head with the butt of his pistol. The girl went limp, her body's sudden weight pulling Bennet forward and off balance, as he still had an arm around her chest.

Seizing this fleeting opportunity, Stroud lunged forward. He grabbed Bennet's pistol hand and forced the weapon's muzzle away and toward the ceiling. The pistol cracked as it discharged. With his free hand, Stroud delivered a powerful blow to Bennet's jaw. The fist slammed home and Bennet fell to the ground.

Sergeant Major Burns was there, just a moment later, his actions swift and precise. He took firm hold of the gun, wrenching it roughly from the dazed and disoriented man. Almost instantly, marines converged on the scene. One marine quickly scooped up the girl, who had fallen to the floor, and carried her to safety, away from the incapacitated gunman.

Meanwhile, two other marines stepped forward to handle Bennet. They pulled him up to a sitting position and with efficient movements secured his hands behind his back using plastic ties. Their actions were methodical and swift, ensuring Bennet was restrained and no longer a threat.

Once he was secure, they conducted a thorough search, patting him down, discovering and confiscating additional weapons, a knife and a smaller snub-nosed pistol hidden in the lip of his boot. The pistol was unloaded and then promptly cast aside, safely out of reach. The knife followed a moment later.

Letting go a breath, Stroud allowed relief to wash over him as he stepped back, shaking his hand to alleviate the pain from his forceful strike. The immediate danger was over but his heart was still hammering in his chest.

"Nice move, sir," Burns commended, his voice a mix of respect and concern.

"Thank you," Stroud responded, his focus shifting to the next steps in handling the situation as he rubbed his hand, which ached painfully.

Burns, noticing the colonel's discomfort, asked with no little amount of amusement, "That hurt, sir?" Waiting for his answer, the sergeant major raised a curious eyebrow.

"It did," Stroud admitted. "It was like punching steel. He's got a hard jaw."

"Maybe you are just out of practice, sir," Burns said.

Meanwhile, the girl's mother rushed past them and to her daughter's side, her voice filled with panic and maternal concern. "Help her, please. Someone help her." Her plea was urgent, a mother's instinct to protect her child overriding everything else.

Glancing over, Stroud quickly assessed the girl's condition. She was dazed and had a thin trail of blood running from her right temple, where she had been struck, but she seemed to be moving, albeit weakly. He turned to Lieutenant Zepper. "Get her medical attention."

"Yes, sir," Zepper responded immediately. "Corpsman. Corpsman!"

"Here, sir." The corpsman moved quickly to the girl's side, dropping his aid kit and kneeling to assess and provide the necessary medical assistance.

In the background, two marines, each grabbing an arm, dragged Bennet away, handling him with a no-nonsense efficiency. They placed him against the wall of the terminal, near the airlock leading to the umbilical, ensuring he was secure and no longer a threat to anyone else. Then, they both stood aside, keeping their eyes on him.

Stroud, his gaze fixed on Bennet, couldn't hide his disgust at the man's actions. He lowered his voice. "I tell you, Burns, some people—I just don't understand what goes on in their heads."

"Some are just plain fucking morons, sir," Burns said. "They were born that way and you cannot fix them no matter how hard you try. Others are marines like us. We fight and struggle for what's right."

Stroud nodded, his response concise but emphatic. "Damn straight."

The corpsman, focused on the task at hand, spoke with urgency while he applied a bandage to the girl's temple. "I need a stretcher and some bearers." He pointed at two marines. "You two, there's one just inside the airlock on the ship."

In response, the two marines jogged off and into the umbilical, and back toward the ship.

"I told you this, sir, would be a shit show," Burns remarked.

"You did, Sergeant Major, you did," Stroud agreed.

The sudden tone sounding in Stroud's ear and the opening of a communication channel indicated an urgent message.

"This is the captain."

Stroud, already bracing for potentially challenging news, responded promptly. "How can I help you, sir?"

"We are pushing back early," Garrett informed. "The station is charging their shields and defensive screens. If we delay—well, we will be stuck here when they go up. All ships that are capable of departing have been advised to put some distance between themselves and the station as soon as practical."

This development presented a significant complication. The activation of the station's shields and defensive screens would effectively lock down the station, preventing any ships from leaving or entering. Stroud wondered what had changed. Surely the enemy were hours away from even coming within striking distance of the station.

"How much time do I have to wrap things up, sir?" Stroud asked, understanding the critical importance of every minute now.

"The tugs are on their way—maybe half an hour, before we seal up. We're talking to Command now. We will know more when they tell us."

The information set a tight deadline for Stroud and his team, but not an impossible one, especially with the station being locked down and the crowds having fallen off. With only about thirty minutes at their disposal, they would still need to expedite the evacuation process and ensure that all personnel were safely aboard the ship.

"Don't worry, sir, half an hour will be plenty of time," he said, projecting calm and control, at least on his end. He had no idea what things were like on the bridge. "The station is locked down and the trains are no longer running. We've almost got everyone from this component aboard. We're about done here."

Captain Garrett, on the other end, sounded audibly relieved by Stroud's update, for he let go a breath. "That's good to hear, Colonel, really excellent work. Notify the bridge as soon as the last embarkation post is closed. We will push back once your people are clear."

"Will do, sir," Stroud affirmed, ready to coordinate the final phase of their operation.

"Captain out," Garrett concluded, and the communication channel terminated, going dead.

"What's up, sir?" Burns asked.

"We have thirty minutes to wrap everything up and then the ship's pushing back and away from the station," he said, keeping an eye on the situation around him. He noticed the girl being carefully placed on a stretcher. Once she was on and strapped down, the two marines who had fetched the litter carefully raised her. His focus shifted back to Burns. "Inform the other posts to immediately take everyone still waiting aboard. There are so few now, they can be scanned, searched, and processed once inside the ship. Then, they are to close up shop. Any issues with that, they are to report in immediately."

"Aye, aye, sir," Burns responded promptly, turning away and speaking in subvocal tone, clearly relaying the orders.

Stroud then addressed the crowd, ensuring his voice carried across the terminal. "Listen up," he shouted as the girl was carried away toward the airlock, her mother and younger sibling following. "Everyone inside now. We are closing this post. Anyone not yet scanned, searched, and logged will have it done on the ship itself. We're leaving, people. Get a move on."

Lieutenant Zepper, supporting Stroud's orders, echoed the urgency. "You heard the colonel," he called out, "everyone move, now."

The terminal, which had been the scene of a tense standoff

moments ago, transformed into a hive of activity as marines and evacuees quickly responded to follow Stroud's directive. Within five minutes, the evacuees had been safely boarded onto the ship, and the marines began their own pullback.

As the operation drew to a close, Zepper approached Stroud, his expression apologetic as he gestured toward Bennet.

"Sorry about that, sir," Zepper said. Bennet sat a short distance away, conscious, his demeanor sullen, his eyes still betraying a hint of wildness. "Before we could search him, he pulled out the pistol and took the girl. We had no idea he had it or that he'd act that way. The security officer before him handed over his weapons readily enough."

Declining to answer, Stroud acknowledged Zepper with a nod, his gaze shifting to the subdued security officer. Words were unnecessary as he contemplated Bennet's actions. The disdain Stroud felt was strong; witnessing such a flagrant disregard for human life and safety was a harsh reminder of the darker aspects of humanity. In the expanse of space, where survival hinged on cooperation and trust, such actions were particularly egregious and, in the colonel's mind, unforgivable.

"You two." Stroud indicated the marines standing guard over the prisoner. They were among the last still in the terminal. He jerked his head toward the airlock. "Get on the ship—now."

They did not need to be told twice and set off, jogging rapidly away, clearly eager to be off the station.

"What do we do with him?" Zepper inquired, thrusting his jaw at Bennet.

"Throw him in the brig?"

Bennet's eyes snapped to Stroud, clearly understanding that his fate was in the colonel's hands. He had a bruise forming on his chin, where Stroud had hit him.

"You promised," he said desperately, looking up at the colonel, "to not leave me behind."

"I told you to lower the pistol and let the girl go," he

reminded Bennet. "You did not do that. Therefore, my promise is no longer binding."

Zepper, seeking clarification, pressed further. "Do we take him, sir?"

"No," Stroud said, his voice reflecting a hard resolve. He then turned and started toward the umbilical. Over his shoulder, he said, "We leave him behind. Get moving, Lieutenant."

"Aye, sir." With that, Zepper turned and jogged past Stroud, moving toward the umbilical, where the last of his men had already gone inside, to make their way over to the ship.

"Sergeant Major, with me."

"Aye, sir." Burns turned and followed, hastening to catch up.

"You can't leave me!" Bennet fairly screamed as it dawned upon him what was happening. "You promised! Bastard, you will not leave me here." Struggling with effort to his feet, hands still secured behind his back, he began a desperate attempt to run toward the airlock. "I won't let you leave me."

Just as he was passing the sergeant major, Burns turned, intercepting Bennet. With a swift, decisive motion, the sergeant major brought his fist around and delivered a powerful punch square into the man's face. There was a sickening crunch as his nose broke and his momentum was checked, like he'd run into a brick wall. He went down again, collapsing in a heap.

He did not rise.

"That was for putting a gun to a little girl's head." Burns spat upon the man, his rage plain. "Fucking idiot."

"Let's go," Stroud said, having stopped, looking back. "We've wasted enough time on him, don't you think?"

"Yes, sir," Burns said. "I believe we have."

As they prepared to leave the transfer terminal for the final time, the colonel paused, stopping at the airlock hatch, casting a final glance over the now empty stationside space. Bennet's form was the only sign of the recent turmoil that had unfolded there. He was just beginning to stir groggily. The rest of the terminal was deserted.

There was not another soul in sight.

Zepper and the other marines had already moved ahead, making their way through the umbilical toward the safety of the ship's airlock. Burns, joining Stroud, rubbed his hand, a small physical reminder of what he'd just done.

"He has a hard jaw, doesn't he?" Stroud commented, with a hint of amusement.

"He does, sir, just like you said—made of steel." Burns had a note of satisfaction in his voice as they entered the umbilical together. The sergeant major triggered the stationside hatch, which began to close rapidly behind them. "But decking that bastard was so worth it."

SEVENTEEN

GARRETT

"Helm, is the ship ready to move under her own power?" Garrett asked, turning his attention to Lieutenant Senior Grade Heller, who sat at one of the helm stations, his fingers dancing over the buttons with a practiced ease.

Heller, a man with sharp features and keen eyes that seemed to miss nothing, swiveled to face Garrett. The overhead lighting on the bridge had been lowered slightly and the dim light from the man's displays cast a flickering glow across his face, highlighting the eagerness in his eyes.

What they were about to undertake was unprecedented. No one had ever attempted to move a ship as colossal as *Surprise*, a behemoth that represented the pinnacle of human engineering.

Over the last few months, numerous simulations had been run, analyzed, and rerun, but they were just shadows of the challenge they now faced. Reality, with its unpredictable nature and unforgiving consequences, was a different beast altogether. She would be the true test.

"She's ready, sar. Just give the order. We are good to begin the undocking procedure," Heller added, his Irish accent a rare

and melodic relic from Old Earth. Garrett found this enthusiasm not only reassuring but also comforting.

He took a deep breath, feeling the weight of the moment
settle on his shoulders. The undocking of *Surprise* was more
than just a technical maneuver; it was a leap into the unknown.
Today, they were not just operating a ship. They were charting
a course into history.

"McKay, do you concur?" Garrett asked, seeking confirmation from the engineering officer posted to the bridge.

Without hesitation, McKay responded, "I do, sir. All lights
are green—well, most of them. The ones that matter." His voice,
tinged with a blend of professionalism and a hint of dry humor,
conveyed a confidence to match Heller's.

"Commander Shaw?" Garrett felt his heart rate pick up, a
natural response to the gravity of their undertaking.

Shaw, who had been engrossed in his own set of tasks,
ceased his work to meet Garrett's gaze. The commander exuded
a calm, collected demeanor, his expression betraying none of the
pressure that the moment imposed upon him. "Sir?"

"Are the tugs in position?" Garrett asked.

"Captain," Shaw replied smoothly, his eyes flicking over the
screens that displayed the requested information. "The tugs are
in position and ready to assist. However, due to our size, we will
have to utilize maneuvering thrusters. They will only assist with
station-keeping—if we require it."

Garrett nodded, having anticipated this response. *Surprise*
was a leviathan among starships, and the standard procedures
were inadequate for her scale. The use of maneuvering
thrusters was a delicate task, requiring not only preplanning,
but skill and precision to guide the massive ship without
incident.

"Very good, XO," Garrett said calmly, his voice resonating
in the quiet of the bridge. He was acutely aware of the eyes
suddenly upon him, the weight of expectation and responsi-

bility resting on his shoulders. This was a historic moment, the maiden voyage of the largest starship ever built by human hands. "Begin undocking procedures."

"Aye, aye, sir," replied Shaw, his voice equally composed. Turning back to his station, Shaw moved his fingers deftly across a touchscreen display, initiating a complex sequence of commands. Garrett watched, knowing that throughout the ship, with the exception of the bridge, an alarm and announcement were echoing, a herald of their imminent departure. "Engineering," Shaw called to the engineering station on the bridge, his voice cutting through the quiet hum of the ship's systems and background sounds of the bridge. "McKay, initiate full switchover from station to ship's power."

At the engineering station, McKay was a picture of readiness. His eyes turned to an array of indicators before him, each one a vital sign of the ship's beating heart, the lifeblood flowing through her. With a decisive motion, he stabbed a button.

The lights on the bridge flickered ever so slightly, a subtle indicator of the massive power shift taking place within the depths of the ship. It was a transition from reliance on an external power source, Midway Station, to the ship's own, as they shifted from preparation to action.

To the untrained eye, the flicker was barely perceptible, but the seasoned hand would have noticed. To Garrett, it was an important moment. He felt a surge of pride and excitement. This was more than a ship; it was a culmination of human ingenuity and spirit, a vessel that carried not just people, but the hopes and dreams of a civilization struggling mightily for a future among the stars.

"Switchover complete," McKay announced, his voice carrying a note of satisfaction. He continued to study the display before him, clearly assessing the status of the ship's systems following the power transition. "Minor failures reported throughout the ship because of the switchover.

Nothing serious. Rebooting those that failed. Major systems are unaffected, online, or functioning as before."

"Do you anticipate any problems?" Shaw asked.

"No, I do not," McKay responded, his confidence in the ship's capabilities evident in his tone.

"Thank you," Shaw said. He turned his attention to Keeli. "Communications, kindly notify Station Command and Traffic Control of our intention to undock and push back from our construction slip. Given the circumstances, inform them we will not be asking nor seeking clearance."

"Yes, sir," Keeli responded, her fingers flying over her console as she crafted the message.

As the final preparations were underway on the bridge, Garrett could feel a surge of excitement building within him. The culmination of months of relentless work and meticulous planning were finally at hand.

"Helm," Shaw called out with authority, "confirm running lights, IFF, and avoidance collision systems are active and online."

From the second seat chair, nestled beside Heller, Helmsman Bob Foster responded promptly. "Confirmed," he replied, his voice steady and assured. "Running lights, IFF, and avoidance collision systems are online."

"Cassidy," Garrett said, addressing the officer responsible for the ship's sensors and detection systems, "confirm sensors are operational and in good working order."

"Confirmed," came the crisp reply from Cassidy.

"Message from Midway Station, sir," Keeli announced. "They have advised all traffic in the area of our impending movement. We are clear to push back anytime we desire."

"Thank and wish them luck," Garrett said. His words were not just a formality, but a gesture of appreciation and solidarity with those they were leaving behind.

"Retract boarding and ministerial connections," Shaw

ordered crisply. Like a baby's umbilical cord, the physical bonds that had connected the ship to the station during her final construction and preparation phase were about to be severed, permanently.

"All connections retracting," McKay reported from his station. His fingers moved across several displays and consoles, orchestrating the retraction of the various umbilicals that provided life support, power, and data connections to the ship, along with the ability for personnel to come and go. "Successfully retracted."

"Helm, release docking clamps," Shaw continued.

"Docking clamps released," confirmed Foster, his voice steady but tinged with the excitement of the moment.

Shaw's next command came promptly. "Decouple magnetic locks and moorings."

"Decoupling magnetic locks and moorings," Foster acknowledged. His hands were steady as he initiated the sequence. There was a brief pause, a moment of tension, as the system worked to release the locks and moorings that held the ship in place.

Garrett, sensing the slight hesitation, turned to one of the screens at his command station, observing the progress of the decoupling process. The visual feed showed the locks and moorings disengaging, their indicators transitioning from red to green in a steady progression. However, a snag in the seamless procedure became apparent and remained red.

"Lock thirteen failed to decouple, sir," Foster reported, a hint of concern in his voice. Garrett's eyes fixed on the stubborn red light on his screen, marking the one remaining tether binding the bow of *Surprise* to the construction slip.

"Engineering," Shaw snapped, his voice cutting through the charged atmosphere, "get a damage control and repair team to that lock on the double. Cut the ship from the station if need be."

"On it, sir," McKay responded, his hands moving rapidly over his console, coordinating with the engineering teams scattered throughout the ship.

Shaw's brief, unhappy glance toward Garrett conveyed the seriousness of the situation, but Garrett's response was simply a calm nod. He maintained his composure, a necessary anchor for the crew in moments of uncertainty. Garrett was fully aware that the ship's departure hinged on resolving this issue. Yet he also recognized that in the grand scheme of things, such obstacles were to be expected. If this was the most challenging problem they faced this day, he would count it as a fortunate beginning.

Garrett's eyes swept across the bridge, taking in the scene of everyone at their stations, focused and intent. It struck him, almost with a sense of irony and disbelief once more, that this was his bridge. This realization carried a weight of responsibility and pride.

Garrett, with the undocking and pushback procedures momentarily on hold due to the issue with lock thirteen, took the opportunity to shift his focus to the TFC. His eyes scanned the latest intelligence reports from Fleet Command, seeking an update on the broader strategic picture across the system. He was particularly interested in what the enemy was doing, for he'd not had time to check on it in over an hour.

The data on the screen quickly subdued the burgeoning excitement of the ship's imminent departure. The report outlined a grim scenario: the enemy had brought through into Midway a formidable force that now totaled over two hundred major combatants, with a large number of smaller vessels. That was a significant presence that guaranteed them a foothold in the system.

The size and disposition of the enemy were cause for concern as well. A substantial portion of this force, comprising more than a hundred fifty ships, was steadily advancing toward

Admiral Isabel's assembly point, nearly halfway between the Haier Barber jump point and Midway Station.

The admiral had managed to gather a force of around seventy-five ships of the line, escorted by fifty smaller combatants, at this location. The disparity in numbers was stark.

Garrett, momentarily distracted by an itch on his arm, contemplated the tactical situation. The TFC indicated Isabel's fleet was more than five hours away from potential contact with the enemy. This was assuming, of course, that she maintained her current position and speed. Reinforcements were en route to bolster her forces, including ten battleships, six cruisers, and four destroyers. These additional ships, burning at maximum speed to join the admiral, were less than four hours away from the assembly point.

However, the rest of the fleet, really the bulk of it, was still spread across the system. They were too far out to provide immediate support, hence these ships were moving to various other rally points, to form separate task forces that could mutually support one another. All of these rally points were on the other side of Midway Station and closer to the other jump points, leading to the Rim and Core.

Station Command, in a seemingly preemptive move, had begun the process of activating the station's shields and defensive screens, a quarter of which were now up and online. This action struck Garrett as peculiar, given the current disposition of enemy forces. There was still time to get more ships away. So why the rush?

The nearest enemy combatant was still a significant distance from the station, more than twenty-seven hours from being within extreme weapons range. Isabel's main fleet, which posed a considerable obstacle, stood square in the enemy's path. The activation of the station's defenses at this stage suggested an abundance of caution or, more likely, the presence of an unseen threat, one Garrett was not privy to.

Pondering this anomaly, Garrett narrowed his eyes on a particular segment of the report, a detail he had initially overlooked. Fleet Command had noted the disappearance of more than three dozen enemy ships from their scopes, all identified as capital ships.

The implication was clear and troubling: these ships had likely engaged stealth fields, effectively vanishing from traditional detection methods. But still it would take them a considerable amount of time to reach the station, and operating in stealth mode, their speed, along with their emissions, would be reduced, to help hide and mask their gravity signature.

This development introduced a multitude of questions and concerns. The whereabouts and intentions of these stealthed capital ships were unknown. The disappearance of such a significant number of enemy units was a strategic move that couldn't be ignored. There was no doubt in Garrett's mind those ships were moving deeper into the system. Eventually, they would pass a sensor platform where their presence would be revealed. The enemy had to know that as well. So why were they attempting to hide this force?

As Garrett delved into the tactical data, his focus homed in on the enemy ships closing on Isabel's fleet. These represented the immediate threat. Intrigued, Garrett clicked on one of the tags, bringing up a summary report of a particular enemy starship. The data painted a picture of an unknown adversary; the ship was of a type previously not encountered by Fleet intelligence. Designated as a battleship, the lack of concrete information on its capabilities suggested that Fleet Command was operating with a mix of educated guesses and assumptions based upon past encounters with the enemy, ones that had occurred more than forty years prior.

The battleship was estimated to have at least twelve maser cannons, perhaps a dozen missiles tubes, and torpedo launchers. Point defense and electronic warfare were estimated to be strong. The ship was expected to have defensive screens and be heavily armored. Confidence in that report was forty percent.

Curious, Garrett opened another tag, hoping for more substantial information. However, as he glanced through the report, he realized that this too was rife with assumptions and educated guesses, and a low confidence score, further high-lighting the gaps in their knowledge about the enemy's current capabilities.

Zooming out on the display, Garrett sought to grasp the broader tactical and strategic picture. He scrutinized the positions and movements of the enemy ships, looking for patterns or strategies that might reveal their intentions, how they were going to go about their assault on Midway, despite the imminent engagement of Isabel's fleet. Each tag on the display represented a piece of the larger puzzle, and Garrett was intent on understanding the enemy's overall plan, which seemed to involve simple brute force.

Pulling back the view even further, he surveyed the entire star system, taking in the expanse of space. His gaze settled on the Haier Barber jump point. Enemy ships were still emerging. Within a span of a minute, more than a dozen new warships entered the system. Garrett had to assume that many more were still on the way. He found that thought mildly depressing.

The strategic implications were clear. Currently, the Confederation had more warships in-system. But that would not last. The enemy would continue to grow their numbers until they were capable of overwhelming any defense.

Garrett considered the other rally points, where the Twenty-First Fleet was forming. He suddenly understood the Confederation's strategy. Isabel was positioning the bulk of her fighting forces to cover as much of the evacuation as possible. Then, when everyone who could got out, the rest of the Twenty-First would fall back upon the Nikura jump point and leave. They would undoubtedly set up a defense on the other side and kill anything that came through after them.

His attention was drawn to a long string of enemy ships behind their main force, which was advancing on Isabel's forward rallying point. These ships were making a fast burn in a clear effort to catch up.

However, what truly caught Garrett's attention, causing him to blink in surprise, was the presence of more than a dozen enemy starships of colossal size. These massive vessels, each estimated to be more than a hundred kilometers in length, had emerged from the Haier Barber jump point and moved a short distance away, a few hundred thousand kilometers, where they had come to a relative halt. The sheer size of these ships, each dwarfing Garrett's own Mothership, signaled a formidable and potentially game-changing element in the enemy's arsenal.

Garrett opened a tag on one of these behemoths to access more detailed information. The data contained within was sparse and troubling. Fleet intelligence had little to no information on what type of ship it was, much less its capabilities.

One key detail, however, stood out: like its counterparts, the ship was generating a massive amount of power. This fact alone was enough to raise concerns about the potential threat these vessels posed. The power generation on such a scale could imply advanced weaponry, strong shielding, or other unknown technologies.

In the event of Isabel defeating the enemy's advance force, were they there to guard the jump point? It was an intriguing line of thought.

As Garrett read, he saw that there was a speculation by Fleet intel that each was some type of command ship or control platform, but with a low degree of confidence, labeled as "unlikely." There were a number of additional guesses on their purpose, including that they were also potentially mobile forts designed to defend the jump point.

After pondering the situation for a moment, Garrett sent the screen displaying the information over to Shaw's station. The commander spotted it, an unspoken question in his eyes as he momentarily paused his work and looked up at Garrett. He turned his attention back to the data now on his screen.

"What's this?" Shaw inquired, his voice tinged with curiosity.

"I don't know," Garrett admitted candidly, "and neither does Fleet. But they are big."

"They are," Shaw agreed, "and the power they're generating is off the charts, like the amount of energy a beacon generates during transition, but more powerful."

"We really need a combat information center to analyze data like this," Garrett mused, thinking aloud about the necessity of a dedicated space for information gathering, processing, and threat analysis.

"We're a little shorthanded, sir," Shaw responded with a pragmatic acknowledgment of their current limitations. "We've got the space and an actual CIC, but not the trained and qualified personnel to properly staff it, at least not yet."

"I know, but it is something to work on once we're underway and burning for Nikura. When you get a moment, see if you can find anyone that we can assign to the CIC and get it up and running. Something is better than nothing."

"Agreed. The more eyes on a problem, the better. Perhaps some of the scientists we have aboard can help. I think they will be very fascinated by the opportunity. After the pushback, when there's time, I will get on that and see if we have anyone who has CIC experience."

Garrett gave a nod. "Engineering, how is that work on lock thirteen coming?" he asked, shifting his attention and striving to keep his growing impatience from seeping into his voice. The minutes were burning away, one after another.

"Damage control team is on site," McKay said. "There is a

failure in the control unit motherboard. The manual release is frozen too. They are reporting it will take ten minutes to replace."

"Nothing takes ten minutes," Shaw growled, returning his attention to the task on hand. "Tell them to step on it."

"Yes, sir."

The comm chimed at Garrett's station, signaling a priority incoming call. He recognized the identifier of the Commander Air Group, Lieutenant Commander Knox. He promptly accepted and opened the call.

Knox appeared on one of his screens. Knox was tall, a brunette with short hair and pleasant features, though her appearance was marred by an unmistakable scar on her chin, a remnant of an earlier incident in her piloting career, which had ended her flying days. The scar, rather than detracting from her character, added to it.

Garrett held Knox in high regard. Over the last few weeks she had taken over the job of air boss and made it her own. He had since come to value her intelligence, dedication, and, most importantly, her competence, which had been proven repeatedly.

At the moment, however, Knox displayed signs of fatigue and stress. Managing the automated and rushed supply and provisioning operation was a mammoth task, especially at this crucial juncture when the *Surprise* was preparing for departure. Based on their payload, she was responsible for directing where the ministerial and supply craft should dock for unloading, a logistical challenge that required constant attention, vigilance, and adaptability.

The task had been so demanding that Shaw had found it necessary to assign additional personnel to assist her in the Herculean effort of provisioning the ship.

"CAG, how can I help you?" Garrett asked.

"Sir, I wanted to report Fleet has assigned us two squadrons that are inbound," Knox said. "They were on a transfer flight from the carrier *Neptune* to Midway Station when the balloon went up. Currently, they are about thirty minutes overdue."

"Overdue," Garrett repeated. "Did something happen to them?"

"No, sir, not at all," Knox responded. "There is so much jump traffic through the local beacon they've been forced to wait for clearance to jump in. I expect that to happen within the next few minutes. If possible, I'd like to make sure they have a place to land."

"Ah," Garrett said, understanding, "you are concerned we may leave them behind? Is that it?"

"Yes, sir. After the ship pushes back and gets underway, that is exactly my concern."

"There will be plenty of time for them to catch up," Garrett said. "We will be moving under reduced power for more than an hour before ramping things up while the chief engineer calibrates the drive coils and makes sure there are no issues that might create complications for us. We will be moving so slowly I do not anticipate there will be a problem with them catching up to us."

"That's good to hear, sir." The relief in Knox's voice was plain. She paused, clearly thinking, and then brightened. "I'd like to request permission to keep the ministerial operation going while we are under reduced power. The supply craft will have farther to go—but we will be able to take on additional supply and equipment, stuff we might need in the coming days."

Garrett thought about it a moment, then gave a nod of approval. "Granted. Is that all, CAG?"

"Yes, sir."

"Good, let Shaw know when both squadrons are aboard and secured. Send him a note that they are on the way as well."

"I will, sir."

Garrett, after concluding his call with Knox, turned his attention back to the broader picture of his ship's readiness. He was keenly aware of the urgency to get the *Surprise* underway, a feeling that was more a product of his own impatience than any external pressure, at least for the moment. Everything he saw on the TFC told him he had plenty of time. But if something went wrong with the drive, that might change, and in a hurry too.

He glanced toward McKay, tempted to ask for another update on the troublesome lock thirteen. However, he checked himself, recognizing that repeatedly inquiring would only betray his growing anxiety to the crew and undermine their trust in him. Garrett could not have that.

Acknowledging that the issue with the lock would be resolved in due course by the capable hands of his engineering team, Garrett decided to focus on other pressing matters. He diverted his attention to the list of items that had accumulated in his mailbox, immersing himself in the routine yet crucial task of reviewing updates from his department heads. Responding to each message, he addressed concerns, replied and provided guidance when required, and made decisions, mostly granting them whatever they requested, as long as it was within reason.

There were even a series of messages from the lead scientist, Pascal. The man was demanding access to the sensor feed they were receiving. He wanted to see the enemy, for his team to study them. Garrett felt a stab of frustration. From the moment they had met, he and Pascal had not hit it off. The man simply rubbed Garrett the wrong way. Then, he thought back to Shaw's suggestion about the CIC and utilizing some of the scientists, employing them.

"Shaw?"

"Sir?"

"Pascal wants access to our sensor feeds," Garrett said. "Give it to his team, along with the TFC. See if they can come up with anything useful on the enemy's capabilities. Perhaps they might be able to assist Fleet intel."

"Aye, sir. I will get it done immediately."

After clearing out five more items from his inbox in rapid succession, Garrett brought up the status board for *Surprise* on one of his monitors. He studied it intently, taking in the myriad of readings and indicators that displayed the ship's current condition and readiness. To Garrett, *Surprise* was more than just a vessel; she was akin to a living creature, the largest self-moving machine ever constructed by human hands. She was a marvel of engineering, a symbol of human ambition and capability.

As he reflected on his role, Garrett felt a mix of awe and responsibility. Being the master and commander of the largest warship ever built by his people was a role he still found somewhat surreal. The ship represented the pinnacle of human ingenuity and martial prowess, a moving fortress equipped for the challenges of deep-space operations and interstellar conflict. For Garrett, commanding *Surprise* was not just a duty; it was a privilege and a lifelong ambition realized.

As he scrutinized the status board of his ship, a sense of exhilaration, like electric fire, coursed through him. For the first time, he was witnessing his ship fully powered up and soon operating under her own propulsion. This moment was a significant milestone, diverging from the previous tests and operations that had relied on stationside power sources. The ship's reactors, now independently powering the massive vessel, marked a turning point in *Surprise*'s journey from construction to a living, breathing entity, one that lived in space.

Each completed Job in Garrett's career had brought with it a sense of accomplishment, but this experience was different, more intimate and personal. He watched the status board, noting the mix of red, amber, and green lights. While some systems were offline or functioning at minimal capacity, the predominance of green lights indicated that the ship was funda-mentally operational.

This sight filled him with a deep sense of satisfaction and confidence. In his bones, Garrett felt an unwavering belief that *Surprise* would not fail them. She was ready to move, ready to face whatever challenges lay ahead, and so too was he.

Leaning back in his chair, Garrett laid a hand on the armrest, allowing himself a moment to take in the full scope of the bridge. For the first time, he could really sense the subtle vibration, or more accurately, feel the underlying hum of the ship—a sensation that spoke of power, readiness, and life. *Surprise* was no longer just an assembly of metal, composites, and technology; she had become a commissioned starship, a warship of the Confederation, with a life and presence all her own.

Perhaps it was partly his imagination, but to Garrett, the ship felt different now. She seemed to possess an essence, a soul, a character that transcended her physical components. Yes, she was truly alive, primed for action, and ready to carve her way through the stars to walk the path of destiny.

The realization then dawned that there was something crucial he needed to do.

"Keeli, put me on the 1MC."

"You are on, Captain."

"This is the captain speaking," Garrett began, his voice steady and assuring. He knew the importance of projecting certainty and calm to his crew and the evacuees they had taken aboard. In times like these, the crew's morale and confi-dence in the captain hinged on his ability to communicate effectively. "We are going to shortly push back from the station and begin making our way toward the exit jump point to Nikura. Fleet is currently preparing to engage the enemy in an effort to delay. We should have no trouble making our way out of the system."

His words were chosen to reassure and inform, outlining the immediate plan and the broader context of their mission.

"That said, *Surprise* is first and foremost a warship, the largest and most powerful vessel ever constructed by our people. I have no doubt we can stand up to anything the enemy tries to throw at us. Our primary purpose will not be to stand and fight, but to escape the system so that this ship may live to fight another day. Today, that is our mission, our only focus."

He paused as he took a breath to allow what he'd said to sink in.

"We have taken aboard a large number of evacuees from the station. To those evacuees, please be aware that we are operating under a skeleton crew. We need the help of all able-bodied personnel. If you have not been assigned a task and feel that you can be helpful in some way, please make yourself known to a crewmember. I will provide further updates as I am able. Stand by for pushback. That is all."

"You are off, sir," Keeli reported, then paused as she studied something on one of her displays. "We just received a communication from the station asking us to immediately push back and away. They want to raise the defensive screens over the Construction Command component. They've already activated the defense grid, sir."

Feeling frustration, Garrett turned to Shaw. "Commander, if we pulled away from the station with that lock still in place, what would we lose? How much damage would it do to the ship?"

Shaw studied that problem for a moment, working one of his displays. He looked over at Garrett with a grim expression. "Such an action would cause significant damage to the outer hull and expose at least a portion of one, possibly up to three decks to space. There are no critical systems housed in those areas. I have already ordered all personnel evacuated, with the exception of the damage control team. We would need some time to pull them out. Worst case, we would lose two point defense batteries."

Garrett nodded and opened his mouth to give the order.

"Captain," McKay spoke up. "Lock thirteen is disengaged. We are free to push back."

"Very good," Garrett said evenly, keeping the relief he felt from his voice. "Commander, if you would be so kind, push us back."

"Aye, aye, sir," Shaw said. "Helm, maneuvering thrusters, push back five meters per second."

"Thrusters firing," Helmsman Foster reported. "We're moving."

There was no discernible movement other than what the display screens said.

"Five meters per second," Foster reported.

"Steady as she goes," Shaw ordered.

"Aye, sir, steady as she goes," Foster replied.

The spontaneous cheer that erupted from the bridge crew was a reflection of collective relief, excitement, and pride. Shaw's glance toward Garrett was marked by a tight, satisfied grin that conveyed a shared sense of accomplishment and readiness. It was a moment of unspoken understanding between the two of them, acknowledging the significance of what was happening, of what they were finally doing.

Garrett, maintaining his composure and leadership demeanor, refrained from displaying any outward emotion. His focus shifted immediately to the task at hand as he brought up the navigational plot on his console. His eyes tracked the progress of *Surprise* as she began to pull back from her slip.

The space around the *Surprise* was bustling with activity. A virtual fleet of automated shuttles, drones, and ministerial craft swarmed around the ship, engaged in a carefully orchestrated dance of docking and mating procedures. Many more craft, in the hundreds, were queued in meticulously managed traffic patterns, each awaiting their turn to approach the starship, land in a bay, or dock at an airlock. All of it was the work of the CAG, and Garrett found himself impressed.

Expanding the view on the navigational plot, he observed the broader traffic situation around Midway. The scene was chaotic, with an overwhelming number of ships by the hundreds and of all sizes, both civilian and military, in motion, amidst the backdrop of space. The presence of numerous hazard tags and markers indicated points of collision or disabled ships. Such sights around Midway Station were highly unusual and indicative of the heightened tension and activity in the area —the panic to get away.

Returning his attention to *Surprise*, Garrett watched intently as the ship continued to clear the slip. This was a critical phase of departure, requiring careful navigation by his helm crew to avoid any incidents amidst the crowded and busy space around the station. As the ship steadily crept backward, gradually distancing herself from the station, Garrett felt a mix of relief and anticipation for what was to come.

"Increase speed to thirty meters per second," Shaw ordered.

"Speed increased to thirty meters per second and holding. All maneuvering thrusters functioning nominally."

As the minutes passed, Garrett remained quiet and intently focused on the navigational plot, watching closely as his ship gradually pushed back and away from the station. From an external perspective, the sight of such a colossal ship moving from the station must have resembled a lumbering mountain slowly detaching itself from a mountain range.

However, for Garrett, the perception was markedly different. To him, there was an elegance in her movement, a grace that belied her immense size, her bulk. Watching her push steadily back, Garrett felt a sense of pride akin to that of a loving parent. In his eyes, every line and contour of *Surprise*, every subtle maneuver as she navigated away from the station with the assistance of more than a dozen automated tugs was a display of her beauty. In a way, this moment was more than just a physical detachment from the station; it was a symbolic severing of the umbilical cord, marking the beginning of *Surprise*'s journey as an independent entity in the vastness of space.

"Captain," Shaw reported. "Ready for roll maneuver."

"Detach tugs," Garrett ordered promptly.

"Tugs uncoupled," Foster said, "and backing away." There was a long pause. "They are clear."

What was coming was the real test. Garrett waited a moment more. He watched as the tugs fell back and farther away from his ship.

"Helm. Come to a full stop," Garrett ordered.

There was another long pause.

"Full stop," Foster reported. "We are stationary, Captain."

"Do you want the honors, Commander?" Garrett offered.

"I do," Shaw said.

"Go for it."

"Roll the ship ninety-two degrees and come onto bearing 331.34.1," Shaw ordered without hesitation, studying his plot as he read the course. Garrett checked himself from what had been plotted. So far, everything looked good.

"Rolling ninety-two degrees and coming onto bearing 331.34.1," Foster repeated, entering in the commands.

Garrett's pride in *Surprise* was strong as he observed the ship executing the maneuver, a neat slow roll and turn that began to align her with the plotted course to the Nikura jump point.

However, this moment of admiration was interrupted by a sudden beeping from his console. The alert, originating from the TFC, indicated an urgent message from Fleet Command. Garrett's attention shifted immediately to the new information.

The alert concerned the large enemy ships at the Haier

jump point, which had become noticeably active. The power emanating from these ships was surging, an ominous sign that suggested some sort of escalation.

Fleet Command's analysis, though uncertain, speculated that this surge could be indicative of a weapon activation or some other unknown capability, as whatever the ships were doing, they were beginning to warp and bend space-time.

Garrett felt a stab of frustration that they did not know what the enemy was up to. This development cast a shadow of concern over the situation, adding a layer of complexity to the already tense strategic environment. He studied the enemy formation, noting the presence of dozens of smaller ships, classified as carriers and dreadnaughts, surrounding the larger hulking vessels.

"What are you up to?" Garrett murmured to himself, his mind racing with tactical assessments and possibilities. The movements and actions of the enemy were a puzzle for certain, one that needed solving, but for the moment, his focus had to remain on his ship.

Turning his attention back to the navigational plot, Garrett resumed his watch over *Surprise* as she continued her rolling maneuver.

"All station-keeping and maneuvering thrusters are functioning nominally," Foster reported.

Garrett opened a channel to his chief engineer. Tam's face appeared on one of his screens. There was a fierce look of excitement on the man's face.

"Are the gravity drives ready?"

"They are," Tam said. "Just remember to take it slow for the first hour or so to allow me to calibrate the coils and make sure there are no issues or faults."

"Very good," Garrett said and terminated the call.

The seconds and minutes ticked on, passing one after

another as the ship continued to maneuver into the desired position.

"Roll maneuver complete. We are aligned onto bearing 331.34.1," Foster reported. "Ready for gravity coil acceleration."

"Captain?" Shaw asked, looking over. Excitement danced in the commander's gaze. "We are off Midway Station and are free and clear to navigate."

Garrett rechecked the course that had been meticulously plotted. In the vastness of space, even minor miscalculations could lead to significant issues, especially for a ship of such size as his. He scanned the space ahead, ensuring that their path was clear. In normal circumstances, Station Command would have ensured all space traffic was well clear and stood off, but not now when everyone who could leave wanted out of the system.

"Bring us to five gravities, Commander," Garrett ordered, his voice steady and authoritative. Despite the calm exterior, he felt a twinge of nervousness, a natural reaction given the stakes and the newness of the ship's systems. *Surprise*'s gravity coils had been built on an unprecedented scale. Although they had been recently tested, there was always the uncertainty that came with new and unproven technology.

Garrett's thoughts briefly turned to the possibility of unforeseen issues, the proverbial specter of Murphy's Law lurking in the background of his mind. What would that bastard throw at them? Would he take a swing?

"Aye, sir," Shaw responded. "Engage warp bubble."

"Warp bubble engaged and operational," Heller reported from the helm. "We are ready to rock, Commander."

"Helm, bring us to five gravities."

"Main engines engaged," Foster reported, "coming to five gravities."

"We're at five gravities, eleven point two kilometers per second," Heller reported.

A gravity, based upon Old Earth normal gravity, had become a standard unit of measurement for speed. It was not a constant acceleration, but instead a constant speed. The gravity coils manipulated space-time around the ship, making movement possible.

Garrett, with his extensive experience in space travel, had long come to terms with the peculiarities of starship dynamics. Despite the immense power generated by the main engines of a starship like the *Surprise,* the sensation of movement, even if they were going incredibly slow, was virtually absent, thanks to the marvels of inertial dampening technology. This absence of physical feedback was somewhat anticlimactic for those who expected a tangible sense of acceleration and power, but Garrett had become accustomed to it.

As *Surprise*'s engines engaged, propelling the ship away from the station, Garrett could only rely on the readings from his sensors to confirm their movement. The HTD system indicated their successful departure, a moment that marked the beginning of their journey and mission.

Seeking to check on the status of the engines, Garrett opened a channel to his chief engineer, Tam. The face that appeared on the screen was not one of routine professionalism, one that Garrett had become accustomed to, but of overwhelming emotion. Tam's eyes were brimming with tears that ran down his cheeks. It was an unexpected sight that took Garrett a moment to comprehend and process.

Realization dawned that these were tears of joy, a deeply human response to the culmination of immense hard work and dedication, perhaps even to the realization of one's life achievement. The successful engagement of the engines was not just a technical achievement; it was a personal triumph for Tam and the entire engineering team.

The chief engineer wiped away his tears with the back of his hand.

"How are the engines?" Garrett asked.

"Hardly puffing, Captain," Tam said. "They're performing beautifully. Isn't she—just magnificent?"

"She is," Garrett breathed. He felt a moment of emotion overcome him and forced it back. It would not do for the bridge crew to see their captain shed a tear. "I am going to keep her at a sustained five gravities for a bit, to allow the supply and provisioning process to continue. Will that be enough of a load for your tests?"

"It will be sufficient. You can hold them there, if you wish, for an hour."

"Excellent. I will do just that."

Garrett terminated the communication. Settling back into the embrace of his chair, he permitted a fleeting smile of triumph to grace his lips. They were underway and on course for Nikura. Everything, for the moment, was good.

"Oh my god," Cassidy blurted out, her voice slicing through the calm. Garrett's head snapped toward his sensor officer, noting the pallor of shock on her face as she gaped at her monitor. Concern knotted his stomach, but before he could formulate a query, the TFC and HTD erupted in a cacophony of shrilling alarms, shattering the illusion of tranquility.

Pivoting sharply toward the HTD, Garrett's eyes were immediately drawn to the glaring red alert icon blinking ominously around the nearest jump beacon, no more than a hundred fifty thousand kilometers distant. A gasp of astonishment escaped him as he straightened in his seat, his relaxed posture forgotten.

The impossible was happening right before his eyes.

There, perilously close to the beacon, was an enemy vessel —massive, imposing, and bristling with hostility. It was an enemy dreadnaught, and she was under power, veering away from the designated safety zone with a purpose that sent ice-cold chills down Garrett's spine.

Then came the shrill, unmistakable sound of missile warnings. The enemy was launching, but not against them. Dozens of missiles were hurtling toward those Confederation starships, all unprepared for a fight, that had been idling in line to wait to utilize the beacon for a strategic jump downrange toward Nikura.

Garrett's heart pounded in his ears, his gaze fixed on the HTD as another enemy ship burst into the fray, jumping in behind the first aggressor. This one was some sort of an assault carrier almost as large as the dreadnaught. She immediately began launching craft, spitting them out by the hundreds.

The dreadnaught began to fire her masers, as missiles slammed home into the unprepared. The screen before him depicted a scene of unfolding chaos, a nightmare scenario.

And *Surprise* was easily within engagement range.

EIGHTEEN

GARRETT

Unable to believe what he was seeing on the HTD, Garrett sat there staring in utter disbelief. He remained motionless, frozen stiff, unable to move, his eyes wide with shock as he processed the surreal scene unfolding before him. The display, a kaleidoscope of colors and symbols, showed an unexpected and chaotic battlefield.

The enemy had infiltrated the very heart of the Confederation's transportation network, the jump beacons. Garrett shook himself of the paralysis that had momentarily gripped him, his fingers clenching into fists, his knuckles whitening as he realized the full extent of the breach.

It was a masterstroke of strategy, something the planners had not foreseen. The enemy was not just using the beacons, but had also twisted and manipulated the technology, pushing beyond the Confederation's capabilities, warping the jump distortion fields to leap across vast distances of space, far beyond what anyone on his side had deemed feasible, let alone possible.

As this realization thundered through his mind, a critical piece of the puzzle clicked into place. The ships loitering near the jump point, the ones emitting an almost inconceivable amount of energy, for lack of a better term, they were bridging ships, monstrous constructs designed to bend space and create pathways for their fleet units to surge through, using the Confederation's beacons as endpoints.

This epiphany, sharp and clear, struck Garrett like a bolt of lightning. Yet there was no time to dwell on it. He knew that. He had to act. The moment of shock shattered as the first wave of enemy missiles began to slam into the hulls of the nearest friendly ships.

"Mister Keegan." Garrett's voice, sharp and commanding, sliced through the tense atmosphere of the bridge like a laser beam. His gaze fixed on the young officer who was staring at his own display and appeared lost in the maelstrom of chaos that had unexpectedly engulfed them. The bridge had transformed into a scene of shock and disbelief. Everyone, it seemed, was stunned to immobility.

Keegan, his face illuminated by the soft glow of his console, seemed frozen, his eyes wide as he stared at the cascading data and images depicting the enemy. The young officer, barely out of the academy, still had the look of someone not quite seasoned by the harsh realities of space combat.

"Mister Keegan," Garrett's voice barked again, more force-fully this time, with an edge to it. The urgency in his tone jolted Keegan out of his stupor. He jerked upright, his eyes snapping to meet Garrett's, as did several others' on the bridge.

That was good.

He had gotten their attention.

For a brief moment, Keegan looked like a deer caught in the headlights, blinking rapidly, his mind struggling to catch up with the severity of the situation. Garrett understood the fear and uncertainty that must be coursing through the young offi-cer's veins. He knew that not just Keegan, but every soul on the bridge looked to him for guidance in this moment of peril. The weight of command lay heavy on his shoulders, a burden that demanded not just tactical acumen, but the ability to inspire and lead them out of this crisis.

It was time to take charge, to transform the shock and fear into action and resolve. With a deep, steadying breath, Garrett straightened his posture, his voice taking on a tone of unyielding authority.

"Mister Keegan, I would prefer to have our defensive screens and shields up before the enemy takes it into their head to shoot at us. If you would, kindly raise them."

"Ah, yes, sir," Keegan said and bent over his station, beginning to work frantically.

"Weapons, are we in maser range?" Garrett asked.

"No, sir," Tyabni said. "At this distance, their defensive screens, shields, and armor will shrug off any maser fire."

"Missiles it is then," Garrett said. "Target that dreadnaught, staggered pattern of attack. I want a full spread of shipkillers. Fire everything we have at them. We will see if they are able to withstand the weight of one of our full volleys."

"Aye, sir," Tyabni responded. "Working on the solutions now. Do you wish torpedoes in the mix?"

"No," Garrett said, "they're too slow and the distance is too far. They will be easily picked off as priority targets. Shipkillers only. Let's save the torpedoes."

"Sir, I can't raise our shields," Keegan said, "only our defensive screens."

"Why not?" Garrett demanded, his eyes narrowing as he turned back toward Keegan.

Keegan, visibly tense, responded with a note of anxiety in his voice. "It's the *Celestial Fire*, sir. She's—she's mated to the ship. We are still in the process of transferring aviation fuel."

The mention of the *Celestial Fire*, a transport ship vulnerable in her current state, added another layer of complexity to the already dire situation. By being attached to the hull, she was also now a liability and put *Surprise* herself at incredible risk.

Garrett's mind raced with the implications. The *Celestial Fire*, laden with volatile aviation fuel and moored in a vulnerable position, was a disaster waiting to happen. If the ship were to take enemy fire and explode, the consequences would be catastrophic, not just for the transport, but for their own ship as well.

"Her mooring point is facing the enemy," Shaw noted, his voice steady but laced with concern. "Recommend we move the ship, sir, bring her out of the line of fire until we can decouple and cast her adrift."

"Helm," Garrett barked, his voice cutting through the tense atmosphere like a whip. "Fast roll the ship to place the *Celestial Fire* out of view of the enemy and away from any incoming ordinance."

"Aye, sir," Foster replied. "Rolling."

"Shaw," Garrett said, looking over. "Do we have anyone aboard the *Fire*?"

"We do, sir," Shaw said. "Some of our people and much of their crew are still on board."

"Emergency evacuation, now," Garrett ordered. "As soon as they are off, jettison the ship."

"Yes, sir." Shaw turned to his station and began relaying the orders.

"Helm, once that ship is away, increase speed to ten gravities."

"Aye, aye, sir," Heller responded.

"Keeli," Garrett snapped, "sound battle stations."

"Sounding battle stations."

An alarm began to blare. Garrett understood it would be sounding throughout the ship. They were such a large target that it was only a matter of time until they drew fire from the enemy, especially with their energy shielding down.

"Targeting solution set," Tyabni said. "Missiles ready to fire on your mark, Captain, a full spread, sir."

"Fire," Garrett snapped, hammering a fist down upon the armrest of his command chair as if he were pressing the button himself and executing the command.

"Missiles launching," Tyabni reported.

"How many are in that spread?" Shaw asked.

"Two hundred nineteen," Tyabni answered. "One missile failed to launch. It's held up in the tube. A repair team is on the way." He paused as he leaned forward, studying one of his displays. "All missiles—good contacts—running, hot, true, and normal. Impacts beginning in thirty-five seconds. Reloading all tubes, one minute forty-five seconds."

Garrett's gaze was firmly fixed on the HTD. As he watched, the missiles, represented by green icons, fanned out in a massive wave, each missile charting its own course toward the enemy. The shipkillers were deliberately spreading out, increasing and decreasing their velocities in a staggered pattern. This tactic was designed to confound the enemy's point defense systems, making it exponentially harder for them to intercept multiple missiles simultaneously. It amplified the chances of good hits, or it theoretically did. Garrett knew they were about to find out.

Additionally, the onboard electronic countermeasures of the missiles were in full play, sending out a barrage of false signals and deceptive data to further throw off the enemy's tracking systems. The aim was to create as much confusion and chaos as possible, to give their missiles the best chance of breaching the dreadnaught's defenses and scoring a critical hit that would incapacitate or destroy the enemy ship.

Garrett couldn't help but feel a surge of grim satisfaction at the sight. The weight of the volley they had launched was massive, a display of firepower and tactical acumen that was, by far, the most impressive he had ever witnessed or personally orchestrated. He knew such a show of force would undoubtedly draw the enemy's attention and ultimately their ire.

As the missiles streaked across the void, Garrett's ship continued her steady roll to port, working to get the *Celestial Fire* out of the enemy's line of sight. Watching the plot, Garrett willed the ship to turn faster.

The station's defenses sprang to life, a few heartbeats behind Garrett's missile launch. Beams of masers and lasers cut through space with lethal precision, while particle cannons unleashed their fury, all converging on the two enemy ships.

The defensive platforms, a network of strategically placed, heavily armed satellites, unleashed a relentless barrage. These platforms, along with the battery arrays mounted directly on the station itself, created a rain of energy fire that fell heavily upon the enemy, even if some of it was at extreme range.

The impacts of this defensive onslaught began to hammer against the shields of the enemy dreadnaught and carrier. Each hit was a bloom of light against the dark canvas of space. Yet the enemy ships were clearly prepared for such resistance. Their shields appeared stronger than they should have been. Garrett realized they had likely been reinforced and enhanced specifically for this mission, to hold for as long as possible against the barrage by the station.

Meanwhile, both the enemy dreadnaught and carrier were in motion as they powered away from the beacon, adjusting their trajectory to bring themselves ominously closer to the station. The dreadnaught unleashed a continual barrage of masers, missiles, and torpedoes on the nearest Confederation ships, lashing out at them without restraint.

Another enemy dreadnaught made its entrance, flashing into existence with the abruptness that only a beacon jump could facilitate. It appeared alarmingly close to the carrier, which was still launching small craft in a seemingly endless stream. The carrier had only just maneuvered herself out of the safety zone. Garrett felt his heart sink at the sight of the new enemy combatant. He was certain more were on their way.

322 MARC ALAN EDELHEIT

A battlecruiser, positioned near the jump beacon, had been preparing for a strategic jump when the enemy had appeared. Caught in the deadly crosshairs of the first dreadnaught, she endured a torrent of scalding fire. Laser and maser beams, along with a missile barrage from the enemy ship, struck with merciless precision, overwhelming the battlecruiser before she could even manage to raise her defenses or fight back.

Unable to withstand the bombardment, she lost containment of one of her reactors. The failure was catastrophic and spectacular as the ship detonated in a blinding explosion, which broke her into two parts.

In the wake of this, a destroyer became the next target of the enemy's relentless attack. The destroyer, agile and swift but less fortified than a battlecruiser, faced the enemy's wrath as she tried futilely to escape. The smaller ship lasted less than ten seconds before she too exploded.

Farther back, a cruiser, which also had been waiting her turn to jump, began maneuvering, swinging around, and starting away from the dreadnaught. Unlike her ill-fated counterparts, she successfully activated and raised her shields, the energy barriers coming to life around her.

The cruiser launched a volley of six missiles. These projectiles, each a harbinger of destruction, streaked through space toward the enemy dreadnaught. The enemy began to fire on these missiles, knocking each rapidly out. Then, the dreadnaught shifted her fire onto the cruiser, lashing out with her powerful maser cannons in retaliation for the smaller ship's impudence. This wasn't an organized Fleet fight; it was a one-sided surprise strike, a slaughter of the unprepared.

"For the moment," Garrett said to himself, "I am going to change the dynamic."

"Impact in ten seconds," Tyabni reported. "Enemy point defense fire detected. They are reacting with too little, too late."

As Garrett intently watched the HTD, the enemy's point

defense systems, desperate and frenetic, blazed away in a valiant effort to intercept the incoming wall of missiles that *Surprise* had sent their way. On the tactical display, missile contacts began to disappear, one by one, as they were intercepted and destroyed by the enemy's defenses. The loss of each missile was marked by its icon changing from green to red, then vanishing from the plot, first one, then another, followed by a rapid succession of disappearances.

"It's too little, too late," Tyabni repeated, his tone tinged with a mix of grim satisfaction and resolve and hope, echoing the sentiment of all those on the bridge. The enemy's defensive efforts, though vigorous, were proving insufficient against the sheer volume and ferocity of *Surprise*'s assault.

The next moments spoke to the might of *Surprise*'s firepower. The missiles that had survived the enemy's desperate defense began to find their mark, striking the dreadnaught with punishing force. The compression warheads, engineered for maximum impact and penetration, detonated against the enemy's energy shielding, creating a dazzling spectacle of explosions that lit up the void. The sheer force of the detonations was so immense that Garrett could see the dreadnaught visibly stagger on the HTD as the hits piled on, as if pushed aside by some colossal force.

This staggering blow altered the enemy ship's course several degrees, a clear indication of the impact's magnitude and the violence he had just unleashed upon her. Then, in a moment of climactic triumph, the dreadnaught's shields, overwhelmed by the relentless assault, collapsed and failed as missile after missile detonated in rapid succession.

What followed was a catastrophic breach of the ship's defenses. The bulk of the *Surprise*'s volley arrived with unrelenting fury, vaporizing hull armor and plating upon impact. The missiles that followed penetrated deep into the hull of the dreadnaught, discharging within her core.

The resulting internal explosion was shattering. One or more of the dreadnaught's reactors lost containment, leading to a blast that tore the massive ship apart. The explosion sent a shockwave rippling through space, spreading debris and atmospheric gas in all directions. This wave of destruction pelted the carrier's shields and showered the nearby Confederation ships with fragments of the once-mighty enemy ship.

On the bridge, a spontaneous cheer erupted. This cheer was not just a celebration of the destruction of a formidable enemy, but a release of the tension and fear that had gripped them. It was a moment of triumph, one Garrett keenly felt.

"Good shooting, weaps," Garrett congratulated, his attention unwaveringly fixed on the HTD. The aftermath of the dreadnaught's destruction was playing out in a deadly cascade of events. The carrier, the dreadnaught's companion in this fierce engagement, was now bearing the brunt of the explosion's secondary effects.

The debris pelted the carrier's shields relentlessly in a lethal storm. These shields, once a reinforced and powerful barrier against assault, began to show signs of distress under the kinetic bombardment. In some areas, the protective energy fields started to buckle and fail, revealing the vulnerability of the carrier's hull beneath.

Garrett watched, his expression grim, as the carrier persisted on her course toward the station, undeterred by the barrage of debris. The ship continued her steady advance, plowing through the expanding field of wreckage and gas. She was still under fire from the station itself.

A sizable chunk of debris, hurled from the explosion of the dreadnaught, struck the Confederation cruiser with crushing force. It was the same vessel that had just launched the missile volley and was attempting to run. For a fleeting moment, the cruiser's shields strained under the force of the strike, shimmering as they attempted to absorb the blow, to shrug it aside and off. But the effort was in vain; the shields buckled and then collapsed entirely.

The unprotected hull of the cruiser, exposed to the full force of the collision, cracked catastrophically, reminiscent of an eggshell fracturing under pressure. Garrett felt a tightening in his stomach as he watched the friendly vessel die.

Dozens of escape pods ejected, shooting out into the void, like a swarm of fireflies seeking safety. However, their bid for escape was short-lived. Moments later, the cruiser succumbed to her mortal wounds, exploding in a violent burst of energy, debris, and fire that took everything within range with her into the next life.

Garrett felt sick to his stomach.

How many had just died?

"Inbound enemy fire," Cassidy reported. "Thirty-two missiles. Forty-nine seconds till impact."

Garrett's focus returned sharply to the HTD. The second enemy dreadnaught had trained her considerable firepower on Garrett's ship, unleashing a full broadside. The display lit up with the trajectories of the incoming missiles, a deadly salvo aimed directly at them, closing impossibly fast.

The volley from the dreadnaught was impressive, a demonstration of her offensive capabilities. Under normal circumstances, facing such firepower would have been a significant concern for any commander. Garrett could appreciate the threat level of the enemy's attack.

If he had been commanding a smaller vessel, the situation would have been dire. However, the size, strength, and defensive capabilities of his ship offered some reassurance against the coming onslaught, but it was far from a guarantee of safety.

Despite the robustness of his vessel, her heavy armor, Garrett felt a knot of apprehension tighten in his stomach. The reality of their situation was stark: their shields were still down, rendering them vulnerable to even a single well-placed shot from the enemy.

In the unforgiving environment of combat, luck could be as much a weapon as lasers and missiles. Garrett's eyes tracked the incoming projectiles on the display, calculating trajectories and potential impact points.

"Point defense," Garrett ordered, "fire when ready. Cassidy, EW now. Let's see if we can spoof and confuse their missile targeting systems."

"Aye, sir," Tyabni said. "Point defense firing."

"Electronic warfare active," Cassidy reported. There was a pause. "No discernible effect on enemy missiles. They are still coming in hot."

Garrett's mind processed this information rapidly. The lack of success from their electronic countermeasures suggested that the enemy had made significant advancements in their missile technology, particularly in targeting and onboard guidance systems.

"Sir," Cassidy said, "I am detecting multiple beams from the enemy dreadnaught. They are painting us."

"They're likely using the beams to keep their missiles on target," Shaw said. "That's why our EW is having no effect. We're also one big-assed bloody target—kinda hard to miss."

"Shaw," Garrett asked, "how are we doing on the *Celestial Fire*?"

"She's out of the line of fire, sir," Shaw reported. "Still working to get all crew off."

"How much fuel is left on that ship?" Garrett asked.

"Roughly ten million liters of aviation fuel. We've already stopped the transfer and cut the lines."

"Eject her now," Garrett ordered. "Separate her from us."

"Sir," Shaw protested in a pained voice, "we still have people aboard."

"Do it," Garrett ordered harshly, seeing no other alternative and hardening his heart. "Anyone left aboard can get to an escape pod. If we can, we'll send a boat for them after the engagement."

"Aye, sir," Shaw said and set to work at his controls. "Separated and—clear."

"Helm," Garrett ordered, "increase speed to twenty gravities. Let's put the *Celestial Fire* behind us."

"Aye, sir," Foster replied. "Coming to twenty gravities. The *Celestial Fire* is falling behind us. She's firmly in our wake, sir."

Garrett felt a wave of relief at that.

"Ten seconds to missile impact," Cassidy reported.

"Bring the shields up," Garrett ordered.

"They're already coming online now, sir," Keegan responded. "They're not gonna be fully up when those missiles arrive, but we will have some protection."

Garrett's response to Keegan's report was a silent, stoic return of his focus to the HTD. The gravity of the situation demanded his undivided attention, and he watched intently as the ship's point defense systems engaged the incoming missile volley with increased effectiveness. The display showed the once-formidable swarm of enemy missiles diminishing under the relentless hail of fire from their massed defenses.

The PDS, a sophisticated array of kinetic and energy weapons, was now demonstrating its true potential. Kinetic titanium rounds and maser beams lashed out into space, tracing deadly arcs of destruction toward their targets. One by one, the enemy missiles began to disappear from the tactical display. His stomach in knots, Garrett continued to watch as the missiles drove into contact.

At the last moment, a rapid succession of hits followed, with five missiles being neutralized almost simultaneously. Despite this success, a tense atmosphere enveloped the bridge. Garrett, gripping the armrests of his command chair, embodied the

collective tension. The remaining enemy missiles, though significantly reduced in number, were still a pressing threat.

As the final remnants of the enemy volley closed in and
struck home, the ship experienced a slight, yet perceptible,
shudder. The lights on the bridge flickered momentarily. The
sensation of the missile detonations was transmitted through the
structure of the ship, a distant rumble and vibration that Garrett
could feel through his chair.

"Two hits, aft quarter. The shields and defensive screens
held." Keegan sounded surprised by that. "Enemy's weapons
were low-yield compression warheads. We may have minor
damage to the outer armor hull, but I doubt more than that."

Relief washed over Garrett as he released a breath he hadn't
realized he'd been holding, a subconscious reaction to the stress
of the moment.

"Damage control teams are on their way to the site of
impact," McKay reported.

"Weaps, target the other dreadnaught. Let's return the favor
and see how he likes being on the receiving end," Garrett
ordered, his voice carrying a determined edge.

"We should target the beacon. We need to destroy it," Shaw
said.

Garrett paused, momentarily surprised by Shaw's suggestion. The beacon was a pivotal Confederation asset. Then
again, it was now an enemy asset. Destroying it would have
significant implications. It would prevent the enemy from
bringing in additional reinforcements, effectively cutting off
their ability to escalate the battle, at least on this spot of the
field. Garrett was certain the enemy was using this new capability to send warships throughout the star system.

"The beacon," Garrett echoed, acknowledging the shift in
strategic focus. He then gave a decisive nod, signifying his
agreement. His resolve hardened. He had to do what was necessary. "Weaps, target the beacon."

"Sir, I can split our spread, have half target the beacon and the other the enemy dreadnaught," Tyabni suggested.

Garrett considered the idea for a moment, then shook his head. "Focus all fire on the beacon. The enemy may try to intercept our missiles. We have to be certain we take it out and keep them from jumping in reinforcements. Once it's down, we can focus on the enemy combatants on the field before us and destroy them in detail."

"Aye, sir, targeting the jump beacon, working solutions now," Tyabni responded and then hesitated. "Torpedoes, sir?"

"No, shipkillers only, once more staggered formation. Fire when ready. No need to seek permission."

"Aye, aye, sir, staggered formation. Firing when ready."

As Garrett's gaze returned to the HTD, his mind was awhirl with tactical calculations and strategic considerations. The immediate concern, besides killing the beacon, was the enemy dreadnaught's reloading time. How long would it take for the behemoth to ready another volley at him? One minute? Two? She was already turning in their direction. Garrett thought she meant to close to energy weapon's range.

That was something he could not allow. He would have to kill her first.

His eyes scanned the HTD, taking in the broader picture of the battlefield around his ship. The station's batteries, relentless in their purpose, continued their assault on the enemy carrier, which was still doggedly advancing despite the pounding it was receiving.

Her shields were almost down. In a shift of focus, the station's guns had also started targeting the newly arrived dreadnaught, which was now powering her way out of the beacon's safety zone. Both enemy ships were enduring a severe beating.

Garrett's attention shifted to the enemy light craft, launched from the carrier. Initially, he had pegged them as a mix of fighters and bombers. However, their behavior was atypical. Instead of engaging in standard attack patterns, these craft were accelerating steadily, gaining velocity in a manner that was uncharacteristic. But—they were not matching the extreme speed of missiles, which meant they had crew aboard, biologics. There were thousands of them, a swarm of rapidly moving dots on the HTD, all converging toward the station.

This observation raised a critical question in Garrett's mind: what was the enemy's intent here? The unusual acceleration and the sheer number of these craft suggested a strategy of some kind. Was this a kamikaze-style attack? Or was it something else, a new tactic and capability that they had not encountered before or anticipated?

The possibilities raced through Garrett's mind. He sat up in his chair as several hundred abruptly veered away from their approach on the station and came onto a course that would bring them directly to Surprise.

"Sir," Cassidy reported a heartbeat later. "Incoming attack craft approaching, several hundred at least. I'm doing a count now."

"Point defense," Garrett snapped, feeling a chill run down his spine. "Focus all fire on those enemy craft. Kill as many as you can."

"Aye, sir, when they come into range," Tyabni said. "They are roughly seven minutes out."

"What's wrong?" Shaw asked, glancing over. "Our shields are up."

The unease in Garrett's stomach grew into a tangible sense of foreboding. He opened a communication channel to Colonel Stroud. Garrett hoped against hope that his growing apprehension was misplaced. But deep down, he knew it wasn't.

The channel crackled to life, and Colonel Stroud's voice came through, clear and steady. "Stroud here. How can I assist, sir?"

Garrett, however, was preoccupied with the HTD and did

not immediately answer, his eyes locked on the unfolding scenario. The first of the enemy craft, part of the massive swarm that had been accelerating toward the station, made contact with Midway's defensive screens. The shields were not fully up yet. The impact was immediate and dramatic. An intense burst of energy erupted as the craft detonated something upon collision with the defensive screens, unleashing a powerful explosion that tore a hole through the protective barrier. In the brief window created by the explosion, the craft, still in one piece and hurtling at high velocity, burrowed into the station's hull.

That told Garrett all he needed to know.

"Arm your marines and prepare to repel boarders," Garrett ordered.

"What?" Stroud asked, clearly surprised, shocked even. "Boarders? Are you sure, sir?"

"Colonel, I need you to secure engineering, the reactors, magazines and"—Garrett found himself pausing—"and the bridge. You have less than six minutes before the enemy assault reaches us and ship is boarded. Hundreds of enemy craft are inbound. We're going to have one hell of a fight on our hands. They are going to hit us on the starboard side."

"Aye, sir," Stroud replied. "We're on it."

Garrett cut the connection.

"Missiles away for the beacon," Tyabni reported tersely. "Reloading."

Garrett's intense focus remained locked on the HTD, the situation escalating with each passing second as the enemy assault craft continued their relentless advance on *Surprise*, closing the distance rapidly. He could feel the tension mounting on the bridge, a sense of impending threat permeating the air.

Raising his eyes from the display, he surveyed the bridge, noting the presence of two marines stationed strategically, one at the armored hatch leading onto the bridge, the other guarding his office hatch. Both were armed with sidearms, a standard precaution but one that now took on new significance.

"Commander," Garrett addressed Shaw, his voice carrying a decisive tone that cut through the growing tension on the bridge. "It's time to seal the bridge hatch. Bring the magnetic lock down."

The bridge, which had been buzzing with background noise, fell into a sudden, profound silence as the crew absorbed the gravity of Garrett's order. All eyes turned toward him, apprehension reflected in their expressions.

"Aye, sir," Shaw responded promptly, his actions following the command without hesitation. He triggered the mechanism to seal the hatch, and a heavy, resounding clunk echoed through the bridge as the magnetic lock engaged. This action effectively fortified the bridge, transforming it into a secure stronghold.

There was now only one way to open the hatch, and that was through force, to either blast or burn it open. There was no doubt in Garrett's mind that the enemy would come prepared to do just that.

"Marines," Garrett began, the calm in his voice belying the intensity of the situation, "break out the weapons and arm the bridge crew."

NINETEEN

TABBY

Groaning, Tabby shook her head, her senses muddled in a disorienting fog. Nausea churned within her, a relentless tide that threatened to overwhelm. Her own labored breathing echoed thunderously in her ears, as if she were trapped in a confined, echoing space.

Her head throbbed with a pulsating pain, a drumbeat that seemed in sync with the shrill, incessant squeal of alarms piercing the air. These alarms, sounding like a chorus of mechanical banshees, tugged at the edges of her consciousness, a distant yet insistent call to action.

A part of Tabby's mind—the trained, instinctual part honed by countless hours of simulation and real-space experience— screamed in urgent warning, alerting her that something was catastrophically wrong. Yet the rest of her battered psyche yearned for the sweet, numbing embrace of oblivion, an escape from the chaos that enveloped her. It was a battle of wills within her, and with a monumental effort, she fought against the seductive call of unconsciousness.

Her stomach cramped almost violently. For a fleeting moment, Tabby feared she might succumb to the urge to vomit.

Desperately sucking in a shallow, ragged breath, she forced her eyelids open. It was a Herculean effort, her lids feeling like leaden curtains refusing to rise.

The world that greeted her was a blurred, chaotic swirl of colors and shapes, as if she were viewing it through a distorted, fogged lens. Disoriented, she tried to piece together her surroundings, to anchor herself in the familiar. Yet her body was a map of aches and unexplained pains, each movement a new discovery of discomfort. The metallic, iron-rich taste of blood lingered in her mouth. Had she bitten her tongue, or was it a sign of something worse, internal injury? The questions spun in her mind, each one a thread in the tangled web of her thoughts.

As the alarms relentlessly continued their piercing cries, Tabby's mind struggled to emerge from the miasma of fuzziness that enveloped it. She blinked rapidly, a desperate attempt to clear the veil of disorientation clouding her vision. Gradually, the world around her sharpened, details coalescing from the blur into stark, alarming clarity.

She found herself in the cockpit of her boat, her command, her realm in the vast expanse of space. The familiar contours of the cockpit, with its array of blinking lights and complex control panels, her pilot's station, anchored her in reality. She knew where she was.

Ahead of Tabby, her crewmates, Sanchez and Chen, were slumped forward in their seats, their bodies unnaturally limp, unmoving, their helmeted heads lolled to the side. The sight was jarring. She hoped they were both unconscious and not worse.

Instinctively reaching up to rub her eyes, Tabby's hand met the unexpected resistance of her helmet's faceplate. A momentary wave of claustrophobia washed over her as she realized she was sealed in, encased in her protective gear, a necessary barrier against the unforgiving vacuum of space and the cockpit.

The squealing alarms, previously a distant nuisance, now

grew louder in her ears, insistently piercing through the fog of her dazed mind. They snapped everything into a sharp, urgent focus.

"Proximity alert!" The words echoed in her head, one of the alarms cutting through the cacophony with a desperate plea for attention. "Take evasive action. Proximity alert!"

Alongside it, a missile alert screamed its own dire warning. Was this a drill? The thought flickered briefly in her mind, a hopeful, naive wish quickly extinguished by the grim reality of their circumstances.

"Proximity alert. Take evasive action. Proximity alert."

What had happened?

"Proximity alert. Take evasive action. Proximity alert."

Tabby's gaze drifted down to the HTD. At first glance, the display's intricate web of data and trajectories seemed like an incomprehensible jumble to her dazed mind. However, as the fog gradually lifted, fragments of memory started piecing themselves together, each recollection snapping into place like a puzzle piece.

She remembered the arrival of the enemy, the alert that the Push was on. There was the unexpected redirection, a course change and reassignment—and then, the beacon jump, the last one to Midway Station. Yet something had gone drastically awry.

"Proximity alert. Take evasive action. Proximity alert."

With effort that seemed to drain the last reserves of her strength, Tabby focused intently on the HTD, studying it. The display now made a chilling kind of sense. The beacon had moved her boat out of the designated safety zone. The engines were still generating power, propelling them forward on the course the beacon had set. Tabby's eyes widened.

They were hurtling toward disaster.

Directly ahead lay another ship, a behemoth of a vessel that loomed large on the display. Their paths were converging at an alarming rate.

"Proximity alert. Take evasive action. Proximity alert."

Her mind, trained and honed for such emergencies, screamed at her to do as the warning demanded and take immediate action. Tabby reacted. Her movements felt abnormally slow, as if she were moving through a viscous, resisting medium. With trembling hands that betrayed her inner turmoil and the lingering effects of disorientation, she reached for the controls.

Her fingers moved over the display with precision, despite their shakiness, keying in a new course to veer away from the impending collision with the massive vessel. *Max* responded almost instantaneously to her commands. The boat changed course, turning and accelerating to port in a swift, decisive motion.

Her breath hitched in her throat as she spied the rest of her squadron. Like she had been, they too were unwittingly barreling toward the massive ship. Urgency surged within her, a desperate need to warn them to break off.

Instinctively, she attempted to trigger her neural implants. However, to her mounting horror, the implants remained unresponsive, a crucial part of her that lay dormant just when she needed it most. It was a disconcerting, almost alien feeling, to be cut off from a part of herself that had become second nature.

With no time to dwell on this alarming malfunction, she swiftly reached for the manual comm button, a backup system for such contingencies. As her fingers hovered over the button, a chilling realization dawned upon her, sending a cold shiver down her spine.

The large ship looming before them was no ally; it was an enemy, and not just any enemy. The HTD's readings unambiguously identified the ship as a dreadnaught, a titan of space warfare, bristling with armaments, shielded by layers of defensive systems, and protected by a powerful point defense network. The implications were dire: not only were her people on a collision course with the massive ship, but they were also plunging headlong into the maw of a formidable adversary.

Then, as if to add to her burgeoning dread, the missile alarms escalated in their urgency. They screamed a warning that was impossible to ignore. Tabby's eyes flicked to the relevant display, her heart pounding in her chest. A large number of missiles, a powerful volley, was incoming, but with a twist that turned her stomach into knots. These missiles had not been launched by the enemy, but from another source entirely.

They were friendly.

"All Oscars," she broadcasted, with a sense of urgency that bordered on panic. "All Oscars, evasive action! Take evasive action. Now, now, now."

Her eyes moved from her squadron to the missile trajectories on her display. Each missile was a shipkiller, a deadly projectile designed for one purpose, to annihilate enemy starships, and there were a lot of them inbound. They were closing in at an incredible speed, their approach a relentless countdown to potential destruction. Knowing every second counted, Tabby rapidly keyed in a new course and speed into *Max*'s control system. The spacecraft responded with the agility of a living creature, rocketing away from the looming threat of the enemy dreadnaught and the missiles.

But as she executed the maneuver, a sinking realization dawned on her. Her squadron was not following her lead. They remained on their collision course, seemingly oblivious to the impending danger. Why weren't they responding? Then she understood. Like she had been, they were incapacitated, and worse, the jump had cut the link to the station-keeping equipment. The system required manual resetting by the pilot.

With renewed urgency, Tabby sent another message, this time infusing her voice with all the command and clarity she could muster. "Oscar Flight," she broadcasted, "evasive maneuvers. There is a ship in our path. Incoming missiles. Wake up!"

Tabby watched, her heart racing with a mix of hope and fear, as one of the fighters in her squadron suddenly veered off course. It was a moment of triumph, seeing the fighter break free. The Raptor swerved sharply, carving a path away from the looming threat of the enemy dreadnaught. This act of defiance was quickly emulated by one of the boats, its pilot also awakening to the danger and reacting just in time. A torpedo bomber followed suit, its bulky frame maneuvering clumsily but effectively to avoid the imminent collision.

Despite these small victories, Tabby's relief was short-lived. Her voice, straining with desperation and fear, broke through the comm system. "Oh god, wake up!" she screamed, her plea both a command and an entreaty. "Wake up! Please." It was a call to action, a prayer for survival, voiced with the raw emotion of a leader watching her squadron teeter on the brink of disaster.

Her worst fears materialized in a series of heart-wrenching moments. One of her boats, propelled by the immense force of its drive maintaining over ten gravities, failed to alter its course in time. It collided with the dreadnaught's powerful shields with a ferocity that was both awe-inspiring and terrifying. The impact was followed by another, and then another, as more of her craft met the same fate.

Each collision resulted in a blinding flash of light, a burst of released energy, a brief but intense flare that marked the end of brave souls, her people. On her screen, the tags representing her squadron winked out one by one, until there were only four left, herself and those who had managed to come to their senses and take evasive action, breaking away.

"No!" Tabby screamed, her voice a raw, anguished cry that echoed hauntingly in the cockpit. Tears stung her eyes, a physical manifestation of the pain and despair that clutched at her heart. "Oh god no."

She stared at the HTD in horror, the screen that had just moments ago been a source of information and guidance now was a grim picture of loss and destruction. Her tears blurred the lights and numbers, transforming them into a kaleidoscope of sorrow and loss.

Their deaths were so senseless.

As Tabby powered *Max* away from the monstrous form of the enemy dreadnaught, the missile alarms continued their relentless, high-pitched wailing, a cacophony that underscored the urgency and danger of their situation and bad positioning. The dreadnaught was not just a passive target; it was actively responding to the incoming onslaught. The capital ship's point defense cannons were ablaze, firing rapidly in a frantic attempt to neutralize the inbound missiles.

In this maelstrom of destruction, Tabby found herself perilously positioned between the incoming shipkillers and the dreadnaught. The enemy's point defense reached out like the fingers of a desperate hand, attempting to swat away the missiles that threatened her existence. The space around Tabby was alive with ordinance, a display of firepower that she found suddenly terrifying in the extreme.

Pushing her spacecraft to its limits, Tabby demanded even more from *Max*. The boat was already operating at maximum military power, her systems stretched to their designed capacity. Undeterred, she pushed the drive into the red, demanding an output beyond what was considered safe or standard. The reactor and gravitic drive of the boat responded with a high-pitched scream, a mechanical cry of protest.

The force of the sudden acceleration slammed Tabby back into her seat, a physical manifestation of the raw power she had unleashed. The inertial compensators, sophisticated systems designed to mitigate the effects of such extreme maneuvers on the human body, struggled to keep pace with the demands being placed on them. They worked tirelessly to counteract the brutal forces that threatened to crush Tabby.

Under the immense strain of the acceleration, each breath was a strenuous exertion. The force sitting on her chest and pressing her into her seat felt like an invisible, unyielding hand, an indicator of the relentless physics at play. Despite this, concern for her crewmates spurred her to action.

"Sanchez, Chen," she groaned, the effort to speak almost as taxing as the maneuver she had just executed, "wake up."

The urgency in her voice was strong. She needed them now more than ever—their skills, their support, their presence in what was to come.

Finally, her boat cleared the immediate danger zone, slipping out of the lethal field of fire. The moment they were clear, Tabby released a breath she hadn't realized she was holding, a sigh of relief that was as much about personal survival as it was about mourning for those she'd lost. With deliberate care, she eased off on the acceleration, bringing down the power output to safer, more sustainable levels. The boat seemed to sigh in relief, the screaming of the reactor and drive quieting down to a more stable background hum.

Breathing heavily, once again, she called out to her crewmates, "Sanchez, Chen, wake up." The silence was heavy, an ominous void where she had hoped for signs of life, for any response.

Neither of them stirred.

Tabby's helmet was once again filled with the shrill sound of alarms, each one a herald of a new threat or complication. Her attention snapped back to the HTD, which now showed a new and immediate danger. Directly ahead lay a vast debris field, a chaotic graveyard of space wreckage that presented a lethal obstacle course. To make matters worse, *Max*'s shields were down, leaving them vulnerable to high-speed fragments that could tear through the hull like paper.

Tabby's reflexes kicked in. She pulled back hard on the speed, reducing their velocity to navigate the hazardous field more safely. Simultaneously, her hands flew over the controls, toggling several buttons with practiced ease to bring the boat's defensive screens and shields online. A wave of relief washed over her as they responded nearly instantly, flickering to life and providing a much-needed layer of protection.

With the shields now powered and coming up, she focused on steering *Max* through the minefield of debris. A large chunk of starship hull loomed suddenly in their path, a ghostly remnant of a once-mighty vessel. Tabby's maneuvering was precise and swift, guiding the boat around the obstacle with barely a moment to spare. Despite her efforts, the boat shuddered violently as something struck the shields. The ship shook again from another impact.

Once past the fragment of hull, Tabby piloted *Max* back out of the debris field and into the open expanse of space. Her gaze remained fixed on the HTD, absorbing the tactical situation with a glance. The display showed a chaotic battlefield: the enemy dreadnaught and a carrier, and several Confederation warships in a desperate retreat. The station was there too, a fixed point just beyond the chaos.

Among the myriad details on the display, one stood out to Tabby, the Mothership. She was under power and moving away from the station, a colossal presence on the battlefield. It was the largest starship Tabby had ever seen, easily dwarfing the dreadnaught, an awe-inspiring titan of space, and she was no more than two hundred twenty thousand kilometers distant—a mere stone's throw, tactically speaking.

Multiple alarms were still calling for her attention, a constant backdrop to the pandemonium unfolding outside the spacecraft. Tabby suddenly found herself in the near-center of a storm, a chaotic battlefield where violence erupted from every quarter.

The station's guns were actively engaging the enemy, unleashing a torrent of firepower that streaked across space in angry arcs of destruction. In response, the enemy dreadnaught was a platform of retaliation, directing her powerful arsenal against the smaller Confederation starships.

These vessels, dwarfed by the sheer size and firepower of the dreadnaught, were nonetheless fiercely returning fire, even as they tried to run. The scene was one of utter chaos, a dance of destruction where each participant was both hunter, and hunted.

Amidst this maelstrom, Tabby pieced together the origins of the missile barrage. The Mothership had been the likely source. A weapon platform of that magnitude would have the capability to launch such a devastating attack.

But then, a puzzling realization struck her as her gaze snapped back to the missiles on the HTD. The volley had completely missed the dreadnaught, blasting right by the ship. It was a shocking outcome, given the precision typically employed in space warfare.

"How?" Tabby murmured to herself, her mind racing through the possibilities. "How did they miss?"

In the realm of space combat, where advanced targeting systems and meticulous calculations were the norm, such a glaring miss by so many missiles was almost inconceivable. It raised a host of questions. Was it a targeting error? A malfunction? Or perhaps something more strategic was at play?

The answer hit Tabby with the force of a physical blow, a moment of clarity amidst the chaos. The missiles weren't aimed at the dreadnaught; they were targeting something else entirely. Her realization was confirmed in a dramatic fashion as another enemy dreadnaught blinked into existence, right in the midst of the battlefield, having performed a jump.

"They're aiming for the beacon," Tabby murmured, her voice a mix of horror and realization. The implication was chilling: the enemy had access to their beacons, the vital navigational aids used for precise jumps in local space. It was a strategic masterstroke by the enemy, and the Mothership was attempting to render the enemy's continued use of the beacon moot by destroying it.

As the new dreadnaught materialized, it was immediately engulfed by the missile barrage. The enemy ship was caught completely off guard and unprepared. Due to the beacon jump transition, even her powerful shields were down.

The missile warheads had no time to arm and detonate, for the dreadnaught had not been the intended target. It was the perfect example of bad timing, transitioning a mere second before the missile volley reached it.

The vessel was staggered by the kinetic force of the strikes, a brutal welcome to the battlefield. Her drive, which had just ramped up, faltered and then failed altogether.

Tabby's gaze was glued to the HTD. Not all of the missiles had been intercepted by the hull of the enemy dreadnaught. Several of them had slipped past, continuing their relentless trajectory toward the beacon. The realization that these missiles were still in play, hurtling toward their target with undiminished purpose, added another layer of urgency.

"Oh shit," Tabby breathed. Her voice was a whisper of dread. She quickly tabbed the mic, broadcasting a warning to her squadron. "All Oscars clear the area. The beacon is about to go up. I say again, clear the area. Get clear!"

As she issued this warning, Tabby's eyes were locked onto the HTD, scanning for a viable escape route for herself. The debris field, a graveyard of a once-mighty starship that had met a violent end, blocked the natural path away from the beacon, even with her shields up. And even if she went in that direction, there was no telling how the beacon's destruction might affect the debris, potentially making a successful navigation of the field more dangerous, perhaps even impossible. No, she needed to find an alternative course.

Amidst her focused calculations, a weak voice spoke in her ear. "What's wrong?" The voice was faint, barely more than a whisper.

Without diverting her attention from the plot, Tabby continued to work on the HTD, her fingers moving deftly to key in a new course that would turn the boat around and steer them clear of danger. That same course would bring them closer to the enemy carrier, and that was dangerous too.

The voice grew stronger, more coherent. "What's happened?" It was Sanchez, finally regaining consciousness, her voice a mixture of confusion and grogginess.

"Sanchez, get the specter shipkillers ready for action," Tabby instructed, her tone firm and commanding. "Spin up the point defense and arm the maser turret for action."

"What?" Sanchez's confusion was evident in her response. "Specters? Why?"

Tabby expertly maneuvered *Max* along the treacherous edge of the debris field. The situation was a pilot's nightmare: on one front, a field of death, and behind her, the dreadnaught that they had narrowly avoided colliding with, and behind that was the beacon. Just ahead, the enemy carrier loomed, vulnerable, with its drive having clearly failed and shields flickering uncertainly. This was no time for hesitation or confusion. She was choosing the lesser of evils.

"Wake the fuck up," Tabby barked. "We're in combat."

"Combat, ma'am?" Sanchez still sounded groggy.

Before Tabby could elaborate, the situation outside took a catastrophic turn. The missiles found their target. The HTD flared with blinding brilliance as more than a dozen shipkillers struck the beacon nearly simultaneously with devastating force.

In an instant, the massive structure, a vital node in the

network of Confederation jump technology and system transit, succumbed to the violent assault. The containment of its giant reactors, which powered the complex jump mechanisms and the ability to manipulate local space-time, failed spectacularly. In a nanosecond, the beacon was obliterated, annihilating itself in a colossal explosion that radiated outward in all directions.

The newest enemy dreadnaught, caught in the immediate maelstrom, was thoroughly consumed by the explosion. The vessel stood no chance against the unleashed energy of the beacon's reactors, not to mention the matter that was blown outward. On the HTD, the blast was a spectacle of destruction, a blinding, expanding sphere of light, matter, and energy that was both awe-inspiring and terrifying.

"Holy shit." The comm system crackled to life with a disbelieving whisper, echoing the shock and awe that every surviving member of Tabby's squadron must have been feeling. "Holy shit."

"Ghost, is that you?" Tabby queried, seeking to identify the voice amidst the chaos.

"I'm here, ma'am," Ghost reported, his voice a welcome sound in her ears. "My fighter got a little singed by the radiation blast, but the shields held. I am still capable."

"Anyone else with us?" Tabby sent on the squadron channel.

"Buster reporting in, Mom."

"Husky here too."

Hearing these responses, a wave of relief mixed with deep sorrow washed over Tabby. She almost sobbed as she keyed in the command to bring up information on her squadron. The display was a clear reminder of the cost they had paid. All that remained of her squadron, the Nighthawks, was one fighter, two boats, and a torpedo bomber.

Guilt and grief surged within her. Her people had trusted her leadership, and she had inadvertently led them to their deaths. They had died not in battle, but in a catastrophic event beyond their control, their lives snuffed out before they could even engage the enemy.

But then, as she grappled with this crushing realization, her sorrow morphed into a burning rage. She decided the enemy's interference with the beacon was the cause of the bad jump experience. Determination hardened within her, a resolve born of loss and the unquenchable desire for retribution. She was going to make the enemy pay for every life lost. This was no longer just a battle for survival; it had become a crusade for vengeance. Her gaze became fixed upon the enemy carrier. Her drive had failed and she was still under assault by the station's guns, her shields just barely managing to hold.

"Buster, see that carrier?" Tabby called.

"I do, Mom," Buster replied. "She's in bad shape."

"I am going to bring her shields down with specters," Tabby said. "Think you can put a few torpedoes in her, finish her off?"

"Drop her shield and she's all mine," Buster replied hungrily.

Tabby quickly reviewed her course and speed, her mind laser-focused on the task at hand as she brought *Max* to bear on the enemy ship. The readouts showed she was less than a minute from being within effective weapon's range of the enemy.

"Sanchez, are you with me? Come on, girl," she urged, seeking confirmation from her crewmate in these critical moments.

"Aye, ma'am," came Sanchez's response, her voice stronger but still tinged with the effects of their recent ordeal. "Chen doesn't look so good. There's blood running from his nose. I can't get to him with his suit on and the cabin depressurized."

"We will worry about him later," she ordered, hardening her heart. "Get those specters locked onto the carrier and activate our point defense system."

"Yes, ma'am," Sanchez acknowledged, shifting into action. "Locking weapons now—locked, solutions set. PDS grid up and set to automated mode."

As Tabby closed in on the battered carrier, the HTD showed the enemy ship still launching small craft. Most were headed toward the station, but some were angling toward the Mothership. The carrier's image on the HTD grew larger and more defined as their distance closed with every passing second.

The lack of return fire was telling. It indicated that the enemy carrier was clearly in a compromised state, either unable to retaliate due to damage she'd sustained or preoccupation with something else. Tabby did not care. This was an opportunity, and she was ready and prepared to exploit it.

"In weapon's envelope. Ready to release," Sanchez's voice came through, indicating that the shipkillers were primed and waiting for Tabby's command.

"Hold," Tabby said, her voice measured. She was playing a high-stakes game, allowing the distance between *Max* and the enemy carrier to diminish.

Two thousand kilometers, fifteen hundred.

Every meter closed was a calculated risk, a balance between maximizing the effectiveness of their attack and exposing themselves to danger, to the enemy waking up to her attack run and turning their guns upon her boat. When she released her ordinance, she wanted to give the bastards as little time as possible to react.

One thousand kilometers.

Still, she waited.

Five hundred kilometers.

"Fire," Tabby snapped when they were impossibly close.

Sanchez executed the command without hesitation. "Specters away!" she announced, her voice crackling with a mix of tension and excitement. "Good contacts, enemy acquired... missiles engaging."

As the specters hurtled toward their target, Tabby was already one step ahead. She executed a new course, a maneuver she had pre-planned and was holding in reserve for this exact moment. In a heartbeat, *Max* flashed past the carrier, skimming dangerously close to her flickering and failing shields. Then they were past, with open space stretching out before them.

"Hits!" Sanchez's voice conveyed both relief and triumph. "Multiple hits!"

Tabby's eyes were locked on the HTD, where the enemy carrier was displayed in stark clarity. The carrier's shields, already strained and weakened, collapsed under the assault of the six shipkiller strikes. Designed to shatter an enemy's shields, the warheads had detonated in a series of violent blasts, unleashing their destructive energy with lethal efficiency, seeking to overwhelm the enemy's shield emitters. A moment later, the carrier's shields failed, completely collapsing. The enemy vessel was now a crippled giant, her defenses thoroughly breached.

"Good job!" Tabby said, her eyes glued to the HTD, tracking the movements of Buster. In his torpedo bomber, he was closing in on the carrier and on final approach, with Husky and Ghost flanking him, providing him whatever point defense coverage they could.

The enemy carrier, though battered by the previous strike, sprang to life, seeming to become aware of this new threat, the torpedo bomber bearing down upon her. Defensive fire spat out at the approaching craft. The carrier's point defense fire was weak, likely a shadow of its former strength, and the torpedo bomber's shields easily shrugged off the ineffectual effort at defense.

"Torpedoes away," Buster reported coolly as he released three high-yield torpedoes at close range. Like Tabby's attack run, the maneuver was risky, requiring precision and timing, but it was a calculated gamble that could yield a decisive blow, minimizing the enemy's chance to shoot down the torpedoes. After releasing his ordinance, Buster began to angle and pull away from the carrier, evading the enemy's belated countermeasures.

Tabby watched, holding her breath, as the enemy's point defense shifted its focus from the bomber to the torpedoes. They managed to intercept one of the torpedoes, detonating the weapon, but their efforts were too little, too late. The remaining two torpedoes slammed into the carrier's hull with devastating effect. The impact was overwhelming, the twin blasts rocking the massive vessel as if it were a toy in a tempest.

The fusion-driven laser warheads of the torpedoes detonated with ferocious power, carving a vast path of destruction deep into the enemy's interior. Unable to withstand the brutal assault, the enemy starship began to break apart under the strain. After several moments, she split into two halves, both spinning slowly away from one another, a grotesque ballet of destruction playing out in the silent vacuum of space, while dozens of escape pods spilled out, a desperate attempt by the surviving crew to save themselves.

"Good shot, Buster," Tabby called out, her words echoing the triumph she was sure they all felt at the destruction of the enemy carrier. "Excellent shooting."

"Nighthawks 1-1, this is *Surprise* CAG. Do you read? I say again, Nighthawks 1-1, this is *Surprise* CAG. Do you read?"

Startled by the sudden call, Tabby quickly recalibrated her thoughts, remembering their assignment to the Mothership. "Copy, CAG. Nighthawk lead here, 1-1, go ahead," she responded, her tone professional and ready.

"Immediately proceed to grid alpha-three-zero. We have enemy inbound assault craft. They are attempting to penetrate our shields and effect a boarding. They are not fighters or bombers, but assault craft. Need immediate assistance."

"Copy, CAG. Rerouting to grid alpha-three-zero. Nighthawks on our way."

TWENTY

STROUD

The ship trembled violently, the deck quivering under Stroud's feet as if it were a living creature in terrible distress. Then the ship gave a sudden jolt, almost bucking like an unbroken bronco. Stroud was sent hurtling toward the reinforced bulkhead wall to his right. With a swift reflex and a hand pressed against the wall, he caught and steadied himself, narrowly averting a fall. Around him, several marines were less fortunate, tumbling to the deck with their gear clattering loudly.

The air was pierced by distant shouts and cries of alarm, echoing through the narrow corridors of the ship. The main lights flickered for a moment and then failed. The emergency lights kicked on.

"That's not a good sign," one of the marines said.

"Are you all right?" Burns asked, his tone laced with concern as he looked over at Stroud. The sergeant major stood unshaken in the center of the corridor.

"I'm fine," Stroud responded, straightening up.

"What was that?" The query came from one of the marines who had been unceremoniously sent sprawling across the deck.

He pushed himself upright, his armor rattling against the decking, then picked up his rifle and stood.

"Another breach," Sergeant Mayo responded curtly, her voice cutting through the tension. "Somewhere close, if I am any judge." Her eyes darted around, assessing her marines, clearly checking to see if anyone had been injured. She held her rifle ready.

"Yeah, that was close," another marine chimed in, his tone a mix of adrenaline and apprehension.

Stroud's eyes swept the scene. He was flanked by more than a dozen marines, two full squads. The marines were equipped with a mix of projectile and plasma rifles, their weapons glinting dully under the harsh emergency lighting. The air was thick with the scent of ionized metal and the faint electrical hum of charged weapons. The smell of smoke was on the air too. It was faint, but it was there.

Bringing up the rear were two towering figures in powered armor, their presence dominating the cramped space of the corridor. They were encased in layers of advanced armor plating that hummed with latent power. One had a menacing white skull painted across her faceplate. Each carried maser rifles, weapons of devastating power, capable of instantly frying an enemy clad in light armor.

Burns had insisted on their inclusion in the team, a decision Stroud silently commended, especially now that they had been re-routed to the bridge, navigating the labyrinthine corridors of the ship.

A burst of fire erupted around the corner ahead, punctuated by a harrowing scream. The sound was distant yet ominously clear, leaving Stroud with a sense of unease.

"That would be the enemy," Burns stated quietly with a grim finality, his hand instinctively moving to draw his P-55 pistol. The weapon, known for its reliability and power, seemed an extension of his steely resolve.

"Sergeant Major," Stroud replied, matching Burns's low tone, "your powers of deduction astound me."

"At least I astound someone," Burns retorted, the corners of his mouth twitching in a rare, fleeting smirk. "My ex-wife was never much impressed by anything I did."

"You were married?" one of the marines asked, aghast. "I thought you were married to the Corps, Sergeant Major."

"That's why she left me," Burns said.

"Are you sure it wasn't for that winning personality, Sarge?" another marine asked.

Stroud glanced in the direction they had been traveling. There were numerous places where the enemy had managed to breach the ship's shields and then the hull. Marines were rushing to each hotspot. The latest report he'd received indicated more than two dozen active firefights raging throughout the ship. It was a disagreeable situation. Stroud did not much enjoy reacting to the enemy. He preferred them dancing to his tune.

"Michaels, Simms, you have point," Stroud ordered quietly, deciding they had wasted enough time. He gestured with a bladed hand toward the corridor's bend just ahead. "Move out."

Both marines, two of his most reliable marksmen, instantly acknowledged the order. They brought their projectile rifles up to their shoulders in a smooth, practiced motion, aiming the muzzles forward and down the corridor. Moving, they hugged the walls on either side, advancing toward the critical bend ahead. Each step was measured, their boots making barely a sound against the deck plating, their movements a harmonious blend of caution and readiness for action.

There was another burst of firing off in the distance.

"Stay on their asses," Sergeant Mayo ordered on the squad channel, her voice subvocal, yet sharp and commanding. "Staggered formation. Make sure there's a meter separation between each of you. I don't wanna be writing any letters to your mammas because you meatheads are stupid and bunch up."

Spreading out, the rest of the marines followed. They moved with a fluidity and confidence that spoke of countless hours spent drilling and training for exactly such a scenario, close combat within the confines of a starship. Mayo followed after them, her rifle also held at the ready and pointed downrange.

As they neared the corridor's end, where it took a sharp ninety-degree turn, Simms stopped, and like an accordion, the group came to a synchronized halt. Burns and Stroud trailed behind.

The tension was almost a physical presence in the tight space. Simms cautiously knelt and peered around the corner, exposing only a fraction of his helmet to potential danger. In a heartbeat, he snapped his head back.

Still kneeling, Simms pivoted and locked eyes with Stroud, conveying a world of meaning in a single glance. He held up two fingers and then pointed to his eyes. The message was clear: two hostiles in sight.

The marines grew grimmer, clearly bracing themselves for Stroud's command. The air seemed to crackle with anticipation and the unspoken promise of violence.

"On three," Stroud instructed, his voice subvocal and barely above a whisper, yet carrying the weight of command through the communication system to the two squads. "We go and kill anything before us."

Stroud felt a momentary regret for not having taken the time to don his light armor, a fleeting wish overshadowed by the urgency of the moment. But in truth, there had not been time. Burns was still wearing his shipboard fatigues as well. Stroud drew his pistol, the familiar weight of the weapon a small comfort.

"Here we go. One... two..." Stroud counted down, his voice

steady despite the adrenaline surging through his veins. "Three!"

Simms, still in his crouched position, leaned around the corner with a fluid motion, his rifle coming up in perfect alignment. The weapon barked out a rapid, stuttering burst of fire, the sound echoing loudly back down the corridor as the other marines surged around the bend, several firing as they moved, sending death downrange at the enemy.

Stroud was just about to follow, his body coiled like a spring, when he felt a firm grip take hold of his left arm. Startled, he turned to see Burns holding him back, his hand like a vice. A surge of intense irritation flooded Stroud, his instinct to share the danger clashing with the unexpected restraint.

He looked questioningly at Burns, his eyes demanding an explanation. The sergeant major simply shook his head, his expression unreadable yet resolute, his grip not loosening.

Burns's stern voice on a private channel cut through the din of the firing. "Your job is to lead." The message was clear, a reminder of the weight of command and the responsibilities it entailed. "There are times when examples must be set. This isn't one of them."

The firing ceased a heartbeat later. All told, it had lasted less than ten seconds.

"Hostiles down," Sergeant Mayo's voice rang out, clear and authoritative. "Corridor clear. Move forward to the intersection ahead and secure it. Powered marines, check out that breach and see where it leads." Her command was followed by the rhythmic pounding of boots as the marines moved to swiftly carry out her orders. The two colossal figures in powered armor followed, their heavy steps thudding in a steady cadence.

Stroud, held back by Burns, shot the sergeant major an unhappy look, a silent protest against being restrained. His gaze then dropped to where Burns's hand still clamped his arm. Almost reluctantly, Burns finally released his grip.

From the corner, Mayo looked back at the two of them, then gave a nod to Burns before turning away to watch her marines. Stroud's expression tightened into a scowl as he looked between the two. Clearly, they had conspired to keep him back from the fighting. Moving forward, Stroud turned the bend in the corridor and surveyed the aftermath of the brief firefight.

Roughly thirty meters ahead lay two figures, clad in what appeared to be light body armor that was a dull matte black, almost inky. Stroud cataloged information about the fallen adversaries, the great bogyman that plagued humanity for nearly two centuries, noting they were unmistakably bipedal.

No one had ever set eyes upon the enemy and lived to tell the tale—until now.

Beyond these downed figures, Stroud could see his marines, already advancing. A sealed hatch blocked the way ahead past the intersection.

His marines moved with calculated precision as they advanced. Upon reaching the intersection, those in front took up positions at the corners and peered cautiously in both directions. The others stacked up behind them.

"It's clear," someone reported on the comms. "There are some crew who have been killed, but no enemy in sight."

Just beyond the bodies of their fallen adversaries, the corridor bore the scars of violent intrusion. Something had punched its way through the bulkhead wall on the left side, leaving a jagged maw that spoke of the ferocity of the enemy's assault. Stroud's eyes quickly assessed the damage. According to the ship's internal map, the armored hull should have been just beyond that ruptured wall.

Protruding from the breach was a section of gray, foreign-looking composite material, unmistakably a part of the enemy assault boat. Debris littered the area, a chaotic aftermath of the breaching process. Chunks of the bulkhead wall, torn asunder by force, lay strewn across the deck, which was also warped in places. A few jagged pieces were even embedded in the opposite wall, evidence of the explosive power used to penetrate the ship's hull.

The two marines in powered armor moved toward the breach. Maser rifles held ready, they disappeared around the corner, entering the enemy assault craft.

"It's a boarding craft all right, and it's clear," reported one of the marines from inside the enemy vessel. "No one left in here, not even a pilot."

"I don't think there was a pilot," the other marine said, the female. "There is no position for one."

A few heartbeats later, the two marines in powered armor clunked back out of the assault boat and breach, their heavy steps echoing in the corridor as they turned and moved to join the rest of the squad at the intersection. They left Stroud, Burns, and Mayo behind.

Stroud, driven by a mixture of duty and morbid curiosity, started down the corridor toward the two fallen enemy combatants. Burns and Mayo followed in step. The bodies lay face down. Some of the rounds had gone clean through the armor, emerging out the back. Stroud noted that each was not only bipedal, but they had two arms and five fingers on each hand, strikingly human-like.

As they approached, he studied the enemies' armor, which was clearly unpowered. It was self-contained and had been designed to operate in a vacuum environment. The armor bore a striking resemblance to the gear used by his own marines, yet with subtle differences that marked them as distinctly alien. He stopped a short distance away, with Burns and Mayo halting just behind him. A palpable tension hung in the air as Stroud gazed down at the motionless alien figures.

What horror was he about to uncover? How different were these beings who sought the extinction of humanity? These questions loomed in Stroud's mind.

"So, this is the enemy," Stroud murmured. As he spoke, his eyes caught sight of a startling detail—a pool of red liquid, unmistakably blood, seeping out from under one of the armored bodies.

Compelled to learn more, he knelt. With a concerted effort, he grappled with the heavy, foreign armor and turned the body over. The moment he stared into the enemy's facemask, a cold chill ran through him.

"Well, well, well." Burns's voice, tinged with disbelief and a hint of anger, broke the heavy silence. His words were a near growl. "Call me a monkey's uncle."

"I don't fucking believe it," Mayo added, her voice barely above a whisper, laden with pure astonishment. "What the fuck?"

Stroud couldn't tear his gaze away from the face inside the facemask. It was a human face, unmistakably so, staring back at him with lifeless blue eyes, pupils impossibly large, a kid no older than his early twenties. The realization hit him like a physical blow, sending waves of shock through his system.

"I thought the enemy was alien, hydrogen breathers," Mayo said.

"That's what we were told," Stroud replied, confusion and dawning realization in his voice. He reached out and tapped the enemy's armor on the right breast. There, stenciled in plain English, was a name: "Reid, Cpl."

Stroud's gaze shifted up the corridor, toward where his marines were positioned at the intersection, their presence a distant anchor in the surreal revelation they were grappling with. The implications of this discovery were profound, blurring the lines between their understanding of the conflict and its sudden, unexpected reality.

"What the hell is going on, sir?" Burns's question echoed the turmoil that Stroud felt. It was one without an easy answer.

"I don't know," Stroud growled, the frustration evident in

his voice. Despite the shock, his resolve was undiminished. "But what I do know is that, like anything else, this enemy can be killed."

"That's clear, sir," Burns acknowledged, his voice a mix of agreement and concern as he looked back down on the two dead enemy. "Do you think Fleet Command knows, the Confederation leadership?"

Stroud pondered Burns's query. The possibility that their own leadership might be aware of the enemy being human troubled him.

"I don't know," Stroud admitted, his mind racing with the implications of their discovery. He reached down and picked up the enemy's rifle, turning it over in his hands with a practiced eye, studying it critically. The weapon was familiar, yet subtly different. He held it out to Burns, his gaze questioning. "This looks like an old Hecker 5, don't you think?"

"Those are antiques," Burns remarked, taking the weapon and examining it with equal scrutiny. He expertly ejected the clip, peering at the ammunition inside. "It's been modified and upgraded. These here are armor-piercing pulse rounds. Like ours, they will tear right through light armor." Burns looked up, his expression troubled. "Does this mean we've been lied to?"

"Command had to know," Mayo interjected, her voice tinged with disbelief. "They hid this from us. How could they do that?"

Stroud pondered the possibilities as he stood, weighing each word the two sergeants had said. "If they did know, I think they would have told us," he said thoughtfully. "We've been happily killing our own for centuries, with no real issues. Why conceal this?" He shook his head, a gesture of both frustration and contemplation. "No, I am thinking this is something new, something Command has not yet encountered."

"You may be right, sir," Burns responded sourly, just as a distant stuttering of gunfire echoed from somewhere ahead.

"Perhaps the enemy, as they took our territory in prior Pushes, is not simply killing all those that fall into their hands. These could be slave soldiers or something worse, turncoats, collaborators."

The suggestion made sense. Stroud found the idea chilling, the notion that the enemy might be using captured humans as forced combatants, turning them against their own kind.

"Major Ramirez." Stroud opened a channel to the battalion command post. He included Burns in the call. Ramirez was coordinating the overall response and managing the tactical situation while Stroud got eyes on the action.

"Sir, I was just about to call you." Ramirez's voice came through with a hint of urgency. "We've discovered something rather unsettling. I have just confirmed it and have visual evidence—"

"The enemy is human," Stroud interjected, not waiting for Ramirez to elaborate.

There was a moment of silence.

"Yes, sir, how did you know?" Ramirez's response was one of surprise.

"We dropped two of them guarding an assault boat," Stroud explained succinctly. The facts were stark and needed no embellishment. "Spread the word. Make sure everyone knows we are fighting our own here and not aliens. It may settle some nerves."

"Yes, sir," Ramirez acknowledged.

"How many breaches do we have now?"

"Seven confirmed penetrations of the hull," Ramirez reported promptly.

"That's all?" Stroud asked. Given the intensity of the enemy's attack on the ship, he had braced himself for a much higher number.

"According to the bridge, the enemy is having trouble getting past the point defense batteries and shields," Ramirez explained. "I am not sure what, but engineering has done something to the polarity of the shields and defensive screens to make it more difficult to punch through."

"That's something," Stroud said. "Good news at least."

"There are also three squadrons out there chewing the bastards up," Ramirez continued. "Apparently, the enemy assault boats are not well defended and armed, a quantity over quality thing."

"How about those that have managed to get aboard? How bad is it?"

"They made a serious effort on engineering. We stopped them cold just moments ago and are now pushing back," Ramirez reported. "It was a close thing. The enemy is motivated and well led. In other parts of the ship, we're tracking them using internal sensors. They stand out like a sore thumb, no stealth fields, and limited electronics... we're beginning to get containment. Most were headed toward engineering and the reactors. How they knew where to go... your guess is as good as mine."

Stroud absorbed this, his mind racing with the tactical implications. The enemy's targeting of critical ship systems like engineering and the reactors was only to be expected. It indicated a level of planning and potential inside knowledge that was deeply troubling.

"And my bunch?" Stroud inquired, a suspicion already forming in his mind. As he spoke, he moved to glance into the breach and the enemy assault boat. The overhead lights in the craft were still functioning, revealing rows of seats that could accommodate around thirty occupants. The interior was starkly utilitarian, indicative of a vessel designed for a single-use assault rather than sustained operations.

"We think they're trying to find the bridge," Ramirez admitted, confirming Stroud's suspicion.

"So, they don't know where it is?" Stroud pressed further.

"I don't have that answer," Ramirez conceded. "But that would be my guess."

"And yet, they had no problem locating engineering," Stroud said. This painted a picture of an enemy that, while dangerous and determined, lacked complete information about the ship's layout. Their movements were driven by clear objectives yet seemingly hampered by incomplete intelligence. Still, the fact that they had some information on the interior layout of the Mothership was very troubling. When the dust settled, it was something that would need to be communicated up the chain of command, for the implications were staggering.

"Again, I don't have that answer. This ship is a literal maze of corridors. Maybe they just got turned around. I know I did when I first came aboard."

"Carlos, pass along orders. If at all possible, prisoners are to be taken," Stroud instructed. "I want answers and I think that's the only way we are going to get them."

"Will do," Ramirez responded promptly.

"Have you informed the captain about the enemy and what you know?" Stroud inquired.

"No, you were my first call," Ramirez admitted.

"Do it," Stroud commanded firmly. "Make sure Captain Garrett is brought up to speed and kept in the loop."

"I will get on it."

The ship shuddered once more, a less violent but still unmistakable tremor rippling through her structure. Stroud felt the vibration through his boots.

"We have a new breach," Ramirez reported. "Near the bridge, three decks down. Your people are the closest. I can tell you the bridge is secure... for the moment. They are in fortress mode."

"Got it," Stroud responded immediately. The proximity of the breach to the bridge added a new level of urgency to the situation. "It's gonna be a race to get there."

"I will send reinforcements your way," Ramirez added.

"Good." Stroud promptly cut the channel. He turned to Mayo. "Sergeant... daylight's burning. We need to get to the bridge—sooner rather than later, if you take my meaning."

"Yes, sir." The sergeant, with a sense of purpose, began swiftly moving down the corridor toward her team. Her steps were rapid, echoing slightly in the confines of the ship's interior.

"This is not good," Burns said, glancing down at the dead men. "Not good at all."

"I know," Stroud agreed, and with that, he started after Sergeant Mayo. "I don't like anything about it."

TWENTY-ONE

GARRETT

The vessel trembled violently beneath Garrett, her frame groaning and creaking as if in agony, a symphony of stress echoing through her hull. As he gripped the armrests on his chair, Garrett felt his scowl deepen, a reflection of the anguish he felt for his ship, almost as if she were an extension of himself. The dim lighting of the bridge flickered momentarily, casting eerie shadows across the array of consoles and screens, each displaying a maelstrom of data.

Shaw, his expression a mask of stoic professionalism, continued to monitor the situation, his fingers dancing across the haptic interfaces with practiced ease.

"Another breach," Shaw announced tersely. "An assault boat made it through the shields. The breach is not too far off, three decks down from the bridge."

"Inform the marines," Garrett said. "Have them task a reaction force to the location. I want the enemy contained posthaste."

"Aye, sir," came the crisp acknowledgment.

"Mister Keegan," Garrett said, "is there any way to boost

our shields further, perhaps rerouting additional power, maybe shifting the intermix ratios some?"

"Shields are already operating at one hundred twenty percent," Keegan said, a hint of concern creeping into his otherwise steady tone. "If we boost more power to the emitters, we run the risk of overloading them completely. They're already working beyond safe capacity levels."

A call request from Major Ramirez flashed urgently on one of the displays. Garrett's eyes flickered toward it, a momentary hesitation crossing his features. He chose to disregard it for the moment, his focus remaining on the immediate crisis at hand. The decision to delay was not taken lightly, but Garrett's mind was occupied with the dire state of his ship, the assault boats attempting to overcome their shields, and the enemy dreadnaught on the field a couple hundred thousand kilometers distant.

"Captain, I'd strongly advise against doing that," McKay cautioned, his face etched with concern. "Especially considering we've already changed the shield polarity twice now. The emitters are under tremendous strain and will at some point need to be shut down and recalibrated. We are looking at a real failure if we attempt to mess with them any further."

"So there is nothing more to be done, then," Garrett said, unhappiness clear in his tone. The words hung heavily in the air, a sobering acknowledgment of their predicament. "Other than weather the storm."

"Correct, sir," McKay said. "See the storm through, that is my recommendation."

"We've managed to keep most of the enemy assault boats from penetrating our shields," Shaw pointed out.

"True," Garrett conceded, "but a few are still finding a way through. There are clearly weak points that they are exploiting."

"That could just be luck," Shaw said. "Our PDS and attached squadrons are killing them wholesale, sir, and those that get by... well, most of their assault craft are essentially suiciding on our shields, and at this point, there aren't very many left."

"I don't believe in luck," Garrett said. "This will be something we will want to study at a later date, how they broke through, what they were aiming for."

"Agreed," Shaw said. "I believe we are past the worst of it, though."

"I concur," Garrett said.

"Sir," Tyabni began, his eyes locked onto the complex array of displays that showed the ever-shifting battlefield in the void of space, "the enemy dreadnaught has shifted her fire to a battlecruiser. They just loosed a volley of missiles. We are no longer their focus."

"That's because they want to take us as a prize," Garrett mused aloud, his gaze fixed on the HTD. The display's luminescent grids and icons illustrated the dire situation: a Confederation battlecruiser and battleship had maneuvered into engagement range and were now unleashing a barrage against the dreadnaught's formidable shields, aided by the station's guns in a relentless attempt to breach them. Garrett couldn't help but feel a grudging admiration for the resilience of the enemy's shields, how tough they were. With the beacon neutralized, taken out by his missiles, this dreadnaught stood as the last significant adversary in their immediate vicinity.

"How long till missile reload?" Garrett asked.

"Forty seconds, sir," Tyabni replied promptly, his fingers moving swiftly over his console as he monitored the status of their armaments. "I've had a number of faults on the reload system, more than I'd expect. Damage control is addressing them."

"This is their first real stress test," Garrett said. "Faults and failures are only to be expected."

"Sir," Shaw said, "Major Ramirez is calling. He says it's a priority and needs to speak with you."

Garrett, his mind a whirlwind of tactical calculations and command decisions, issued his response without hesitation. "Tell him we are about to engage the last enemy dreadnaught on the field and I will be with him shortly, once I have dealt with her."

"Aye, sir," Shaw acknowledged.

As Garrett returned attention to the HTD, a text message flashed across the screen, its red *PRIORITY ONE* tag impossible to ignore. The message was from the major. Garrett felt a serious stab of irritation. The man wasn't giving up. He thrust the irritation aside and swiftly tabbed the message open, ready to address whatever issue Major Ramirez deemed so urgent.

The message was startling in its brevity and the gravity of its content. It read simply, yet with profound implications: *THE ENEMY THAT BOARDED THE SHIP ARE HUMAN. THIS IS CONFIRMED.*

The revelation hit Garrett like a physical blow.

"Holy shit," he exhaled, the words barely a whisper. Garrett shook himself free from his shock and sent the message over to Shaw's console. "Commander, take a look at what I just sent you."

Shaw, upon receiving the message, looked over with a mixture of surprise and skepticism. "Really?" he asked, his voice tinged with incredulity as he pointed to one of his monitors where the message had appeared. "Is this true?"

"We must assume it is," Garrett stated firmly. "There will be time to find out more later."

"Sir," Tyabni announced, "volley up and ready."

Garrett, his gaze moving to the HTD, responded crisply. "Fire."

"Firing," Tyabni confirmed, his fingers deftly executing the command. "Missiles away."

Missile icons seemed to blossom from *Surprise* on the HTD, exploding outward in a wave of death and destruction toward the enemy dreadnaught. Garrett felt a tightening in his stomach. He was about to kill thousands of the enemy. Were there humans manning that dreadnaught or were they alien?

"One hundred twelve good launches," Tyabni reported. "Forty-two seconds till impact."

Garrett and the entire bridge crew held their collective breaths as they watched the missile trajectories race across the HTD. No one spoke for a long moment.

"The rest are the faults?" Shaw inquired, breaking the silence, his eyes scanning the data for a full understanding of their offensive capability.

"Yes, sir," Tyabni confirmed.

Garrett, meanwhile, rubbed his jaw, thinking on their next steps. The ship was moving away from Midway Station at a velocity of twenty gravities, which translated into forty-four kilometers per second. No other enemy combatants were within easy engagement range, leaving only the dreadnaught as their primary focus. In less than forty seconds, with good fortune, she would be eliminated, scratching out a serious threat.

"Helm, swing us about," Garrett ordered with authority. "Plot a course back to the station. Reduce speed to five gravities. I want us within shuttle range of Midway. Once we are, bring us to a full stop."

"Aye, sir," Foster responded, his hands moving deftly over the control panel. "Swinging about, reducing speed to five gravities. I will bring us to a full stop when we are fifty thousand kilometers from the station."

The ship responded to his inputs, her massive frame beginning to pivot gracefully in space as maneuvering thrusters fired and the gravity drive began to manipulate space-time, rapidly slowing them down.

"Shaw," Garrett said, "contact the CAG and prepare to

launch boats to recover our people who were on the *Celestial Fire*, along with any other escape pods that are on the field and in the immediate vicinity. Let's render what assistance we can, while we can."

"Yes, sir."

Garrett watched intently as the plot on the HTD updated in real time, showing their ship's gradual change in course. With the station's shields now raised, the ministerial operation had been effectively put on hold, perhaps even halted for good.

Despite the fighting going on, the space around them was still a chaotic picture of various spacecraft in movement, a mix of civilian vessels and warships. A good number had pushed back from the station just before the enemy had arrived.

Shaw lowered his voice so only the two of them could hear. "Why bring us back to the station? We have long-range boats with strong gravity drives. I'd have thought you would have wanted to make best possible speed toward Nikura."

"Not anymore," Garrett said, glancing over.

"Ten seconds till impact," Tyabni announced. "Enemy point defense is firing."

Garrett's gaze shifted back to the HTD, his expression a mask of calm detachment. The HTD displayed the relentless advance of their missile volley toward the enemy dreadnaught. He watched, unflinching, as several missile icons began to flicker and then vanish from the plot as they were knocked out by the enemy's PDS.

Then, the moment arrived. The shipkillers, true to their name, reached their target. One after another, they impacted the dreadnaught with devastating precision, their detonations brilliantly illustrated on the display. The dreadnaught's shields, which had been teetering on the brink of collapse, faltered, then fully failed under the powerful onslaught. In the next moment, the enemy ship was engulfed in a cataclysmic explosion, her existence snuffed out in a blinding flare of light and energy.

As the representation of the dreadnaught vanished from the HTD, a collective, almost imperceptible sigh made its way through the bridge. Garrett himself exhaled a breath, a subtle release of the tension that had gripped him throughout the entirety of the engagement.

"What do you mean, not anymore?" Shaw asked Garrett.

"What?" Garrett asked, confused by the question. "What are you talking about?"

"Aren't we supposed to make best possible speed for the Nikura jump point?"

"Think about it," Garrett said, suddenly understanding the question and looking over. "They infiltrated and took over our jump beacons. There's no going to Nikura now."

The widening of Shaw's eyes and his suddenly ashen complexion were a clear indicator of his comprehension of the gravity of what they were now facing.

Garrett had already cross-referenced the TFC and the HTD to verify what he'd suspected from the moment the first enemy dreadnaught had come through the beacon. Shaw was just now grasping that reality and the situation they faced.

Deep within the system, the enemy had taken control of numerous beacons. These now presented an insurmountable obstacle, at least in Garrett's estimation. The enemy was not merely holding these positions; they were actively using them as rally points, bringing in powerful combat units.

There was no way to destroy these enemy-controlled beacons. By the time *Surprise* got underway and left Midway Station, there would be a truly overwhelming force waiting for them somewhere along the way to Nikura. There was absolutely no doubt in Garrett's mind about that. His ship was a high-priority target. They were effectively cut off from Nikura, as if the enemy held the jump point itself, which they didn't.

"The Midway Central beacon was just taken down, sir," Cassidy reported, looking up from her station. "There are six enemy dreadnaughts, along with four carriers over there mixing it up with ours. It looks like one hell of a brawl, sir."

Garrett's gaze fell upon the HTD. With a few deft inputs, he zoomed out, broadening his perspective on the unfolding situation, specifically around where the Midway Central beacon had been. The conflict he observed was a significant distance away, over two million kilometers from their current location, far out of immediate threat range.

There were only two beacons that directly served Midway Station. With each of these beacons now destroyed, the enemy's ability to rapidly reinforce their forces near the station was severely hampered.

Garrett checked the plot. Any enemy reinforcements would have to jump to another beacon within their control and then make a prolonged journey toward Midway, a trip that would take at least seven hours at best speed. And—he spotted several enemy ships doing just that.

Garrett's attention shifted to the chaotic battle playing out on the HTD by Midway Central. It was a fierce and brutal engagement, far more intense than the skirmish they had just endured, for the enemy had more weight on the field.

The screen was ablaze with the movements of at least twenty Confederation warships who were actively engaging the six dreadnaughts and four carriers. The display showed a maelstrom of missiles and energy weapons, each streak of light representing a deadly exchange in the heated battle. As he watched, a Confederation battlecruiser was destroyed as a massed volley of missiles from three of the enemy dreads slammed into her and overwhelmed her shields.

"They are well out of our missile engagement envelope," Shaw noted. "Unless we move the ship within range."

"That will take too much time. They need help now," Garrett stated, his mind already racing through alternative strategies. After a moment's contemplation, he turned to his weapons officer. "Mister Tyabni, is the main battery charged?"

"Aye, sir, the gripper cannon is fully charged and ready," Tyabni reported.

"Mister McKay," Garrett said, "are there any issues with us using the main battery? Do you see any faults on the board?"

McKay shook his head. "No, sir. I do not. Everything looks green."

"Kindly pick out a target that will cause maximum damage to the enemy," Garrett ordered. "Lock the main battery on said target and prepare to fire upon my order."

"Aye, sir," Tyabni said with a powerful sense of eagerness that Garrett could feel himself.

"We don't have permission to do that, sir," Shaw cautioned.

"I think we are beyond permissions. The Fleet units here at Midway need a chance to organize before more of the enemy can burn to engagement range. Besides, our people are fighting and dying over there. I intend to help give them that chance."

A priority call chimed, and Garrett's attention immediately shifted to the incoming communication. Seeing that it was from Tam, the ship's chief engineer, he quickly accepted the call. The call from Major Ramirez was still waiting. The major would just have to cool his heels a little longer.

"Just the person I wanted to speak to," Garrett greeted as Tam's image appeared on the screen, the chief engineer's appearance telling a story of its own. The man's hair was disheveled, and his ship suit bore the evidence of a recent scuffle, torn on the right collar. A patch had been placed over the tear so that in the event of an unexpected decompression event, it could still function as intended. However, most striking was the bruise forming on his right cheek. "What happened to you?"

"We had enemy soldiers attempt to breach engineering," Tam explained sourly. "One of your marines took it into his head to drag me to safety. If he'd left me alone, I would have murdered them all."

Garrett's frown deepened as he processed the information. "Is it safe down there?"

Tam's reply was somewhat sardonic. "You tell me. I have marines everywhere. They are underfoot and getting in the way, but the fighting has stopped, at least here. I understand there are active firefights throughout the ship."

"We still have the enemy aboard," Garrett said. "Until the situation is contained, you're stuck with Stroud's marines. Is that why you are calling?"

Tam's response took a different turn, his tone accusatory. "No—you are planning on using my weapon." It was a statement rather than a question.

"I am," Garrett admitted. "There is a nasty engagement two million klicks from us. Our forces are having a tough go of it. I intend to help, and I thought the gripper cannon might be the best way to reach out and pay my regards to the enemy." He paused, becoming suddenly concerned, and glanced at McKay, who was bent over his station, working away. He turned his gaze back to Tam. "McKay said we were good to go. Is there a problem with the weapon, a fault of some kind that he didn't know about?"

"No," Tam admitted. "The cannon should work just fine. Unless it doesn't."

"What do you mean, unless it doesn't?" Garrett didn't like the sound of that.

"The cannon is untested technology," Tam said with a shrug. "You know that."

"Consider this a test then," Garrett said simply.

"What are you going to shoot at?" Tam asked.

"Weaps, have you selected a target for me yet?" Garrett asked.

"Aye, sir, a dreadnaught. She's rather close to two other ships, another dreadnaught, and one of the carriers."

"Tam, did you hear that?" Garrett asked.

"I did. Recommend you utilize forty percent power in generating the wormholes. That way we don't overload the system with our first shot."

Garrett paused, his mind delving into the intricate calculations and physics involved with the use of the weapon. This was not a decision to be made lightly. The main battery required careful consideration, especially when it came to power usage. He had studied its capabilities and limitations exhaustively, understanding both its immense potential and the risks involved.

"Will that be enough power?" Garrett mused aloud, voicing his concern. "We will be unzipping our fly if it doesn't work, showing the enemy our potential capability and giving them something to study."

"It'll work," Tam assured him with a confident nod. "The range is only two million kilometers, and by operating under reduced power, perhaps the enemy will assume our true range and capability is limited, that forty percent is the best we can do. Besides, the wormhole doesn't need to be that large, and as I said, the range is short. Use a fifty-millimeter round, not one of the large bastards. With luck they won't know what hit them and will be chasing their tails for years to come, trying to figure out what we did and how we did it."

"I like it." Garrett looked up. "Weaps, forty percent power on the gripper cannon, fifty-millimeter round, please. Make sure all space around the weapon on our end is clear. I don't want the distortion event interfered with."

"Forty percent power, one fifty-millimeter neutronium shell with a quantarite core coming up."

Garrett turned back to Tam. "Now for the real question. Is the gripper drive ready?"

"I figured you'd be asking that," Tam said.

"You've been following what's been going on?"

"After the enemy tried to force their way into engineering, I decided to lift my head up from the hole I live in and start paying attention." Tam scowled, and his tone filled with irritation. "You do know they are human? At least those that attacked engineering were human."

"I just learned that moments ago." Garrett rubbed his jaw. "And you know we must use the main drive—that is, if we are to save the ship?"

Tam gave a nod. "There are enemy all over the system, and they are already moving to block the way to the Nikura jump point. The gripper drive is ready. We just need a destination plotted. Will you be able to get us one?"

"I'll get us one, soon enough. I just need to help the fight by Midway Central first, then I will reach out to Command."

"Blow those bastards to hell for me," Tam said, suddenly cheerful. "Show them what we can do to them."

"I intend to." Garrett closed the connection. "Weaps, how are we coming on that targeting solution?"

"Ready to engage on your mark, sir. The dart is loaded and primed in the railgun," Tyabni said. "The space is open on our end. We are clear to engage."

Garrett looked over at Shaw as silence settled over the bridge. The commander gave him a firm nod. Garrett turned his attention to the HTD. "Mister Tyabni, fire the main gun."

"Firing."

A rapid spike in energy pulsed through the ship. This surge was more than just a reading on a display; it could be felt, causing the lights on the bridge to dim noticeably, casting the room into an eerie half-light. Outside the ship, there was a subtle warping of space-time from the immense forces at play.

Simultaneously, several alarms blared across the bridge, the ship's sophisticated sensor arrays and systems reacting to the extraordinary phenomenon unfolding just off the ship's hull. These alerts, however, were short-lived, falling abruptly silent as the initial shockwave of energy dissipated as quickly as it had appeared.

The entire event was transient, lasting only a fraction of a second, but in that brief window, the event horizon of a small wormhole materialized. It was a breathtaking display of technology and physics, bending the very fabric of space-time to create a direct path across the vastness of space.

The dart, a projectile of incredible destructive potential, was already in motion even before the wormhole fully formed. Accelerated by the ship's railgun to an astounding fifty-thousand gravities, it was propelled outward with unerring precision and speed.

Just as the wormhole opened, the dart entered and vanished. Roughly two million kilometers away, the corresponding end of the wormhole emerged into local space-time, allowing the dart to enter into the target area. The moment it exited, the wormhole collapsed behind it, erasing its existence as though it had never been.

The dart, coated in neutronium and carrying a payload of quantarite, an exotic and highly volatile substance, struck its intended target with unparalleled force, slamming into the enemy dreadnaught, its momentum and design allowing it to penetrate the ship's energy shields and defensive screens.

The impact of the weapon was immediate and catastrophic. In one moment, the enemy dreadnaught, a powerful vessel unleashing destruction upon the Confederation fleet, was a serious threat. In the next, from a range no other Confederation ship could touch, she was transformed into an expanding cloud of gas and debris, her existence obliterated in a massive explosion.

The shockwave was colossal, radiating outward with seemingly unstoppable force. The first victim of this expanding maelstrom was an enemy carrier caught directly in the blast radius. Her shields, designed to withstand conventional attacks, stood no chance against the onslaught of energy and excited matter washing over her. The carrier's demise was swift, her structure collapsing and detonating in a blinding burst of light.

Nearby, another enemy dreadnaught was engulfed by the wave of destruction. The ship's defenses, overwhelmed by the sheer intensity of the blast, buckled and failed, leaving her armored hull exposed and vulnerable. She was torn asunder, her integrity compromised by the relentless energy storm spreading outward.

Farther away, two additional enemy dreadnaughts bore the brunt of the explosion's outer edges. Their shields faltered and failed under the strain. One dreadnaught suffered a catastrophic loss of power, rendered inert, lifeless and adrift in the void of space, with secondary internal explosions rocking her hull and internal structure.

The other, though still operational, had taken significant damage. Garrett thought it a miracle she had managed to survive the blast, though her offensive capabilities were clearly significantly diminished, her weapon output reduced as she struggled to maintain her assault on the nearest Confederation ships, even as her drive began to fail.

In the wake of the astonishing display of raw power, a profound silence enveloped the bridge. The crew, each a witness to the unprecedented destruction wrought by their new weapon, were momentarily lost in a collective state of shock and awe. The enormity of what they had just achieved and done hung heavily in the air.

"I think we can chalk that up as a successful test," Shaw remarked. The comment, while light in tone, couldn't fully mask the underlying awareness of the weapon's terrifying power.

Garrett, still absorbing the magnitude of their action, considered Shaw's words. To him, it felt like the understatement of the century. By his estimation, the tide of the battle at the contested location had been dramatically turned in favor of the Confederation ships. The enemy, reeling from the sudden and devastating strike, was now at a significant disadvantage, and the Confederation warships were moving to take full advantage of that.

"Sir," Tyabni said, "permission to recharge the cannon."

"Granted."

"Recharge process beginning," Tyabni said, "six hours and counting."

"It's a good thing we didn't use a two-hundred-millimeter round," Shaw commented. "We might have taken out part of our own fleet and the station to boot."

"Yeah," Garrett said, "I think you are correct. We will have to—"

The relative calm on the bridge was shattered by a heavy, ominous thud from behind. Garrett, along with the rest of the crew, turned sharply toward the sound. The sight that met Garrett's eyes was not only foreboding, but deeply alarming. The hatch to the bridge was glowing an ominous red.

"Down," one of the marines yelled with urgency, throwing herself to the deck in a defensive posture. "Get down!"

Garrett, reacting instinctively to the marine's warning, literally leaped from his station, throwing himself to the deck. A second later, there was a tremendous explosion. The force of the blast sent a wave of intense heat sweeping across the bridge, followed by a rain of debris that peppered the area. Ears ringing, dazed, and momentarily disoriented, Garrett found himself on the deck.

As he tried to orient himself amidst the chaos and smoke, a series of heavy, muffled thuds pierced through the ringing in his ears. It was the unmistakable sound of weapons fire, a realiza-

tion that struck Garrett with chilling clarity. The enemy had
breached the bridge, the heart of the ship.

He suddenly wished he had taken that call with Major
Ramirez. But now was no time to second-guess his actions.
Without hesitation, Garrett reached for his sidearm, a P-95
pulse pistol equipped with armor-piercing and exploding
rounds. His movements were swift and practiced as he disengaged the safety and prepared to defend himself. Rising to his
feet, he turned toward the source of the intrusion.

The scene around him was one of destruction and smoke.
The hatch had been obliterated, blown inward, leaving a gaping
maw in its place. Debris from the blast was scattered clear
across the bridge. Amidst this turmoil, the grim reality of their
situation was starkly evident in the fate of the marine who had
given the warning. She lay near Garrett's station, a tragic first
casualty. The blast had partially torn her in two. A pool of blood
was expanding around her.

The other female marine, reacting with trained precision,
had already positioned herself on one knee, her pistol trained on
the thick smoke that obscured the enemy's approach. She fired
determinedly into the haze.

A series of brilliant muzzle flashes cut through the smoke, a
deadly reply and response to her fire. The marine's bravery was
met with a hail of bullets that rocked her backward, her body
jerking and twitching with the impact of the incoming rounds.
She fell backward and lay still.

Then, a figure emerged from the smoke, an enemy soldier
clad in black armor, his rifle trained on the downed marine.
Garrett, propelled by instinct, acted without a moment's hesitation. Target in sight, his hand steady, he aimed his pistol at the
armored figure. The round he fired, designed to penetrate even
the toughest armor, hit its mark with lethal efficiency. The
impact was immediate and forceful. The enemy soldier was

knocked violently back into the obscuring smoke from which he had emerged.

Almost simultaneously, another figure appeared from the smoke. But this time, the response came from Garrett's left. Someone else on the bridge had joined the fight, firing at the intruder. The enemy soldier stumbled forward under the onslaught of rounds, dropping to one knee under the weight of his injuries. More rounds hit him, and he toppled backward, neutralized.

It was Shaw.

A round device spun through the air and landed with a clatter a mere meter from Garrett. It bounced once with a heavy metallic ring before coming to a halt on the deck.

"Take cover!" Garrett bellowed, his voice cutting sharply through the chaos of the bridge. He threw himself behind his station, seeking whatever meager protection it might offer.

The grenade detonated a mere heartbeat later. The explosion was blinding, a flash of intense light that engulfed the bridge. The concussive force of the blast was tremendous, sending a shockwave rippling through the confined space. The deck, once stable underfoot, seemed to leap up violently, striking Garrett with a brutal force. With it, the world went white.

TWENTY-TWO

GARRETT

The disorienting aftermath of the explosion left Garrett grappling with his senses. As he shook his head vigorously, attempting to dispel the daze clouding his mind, the sharp, persistent ringing in his ears only intensified, an agonizing reminder of the blast's proximity. Struggling to his knees amidst the chaos, Garrett surveyed the catastrophic damage to his station. Once a hub of meticulously arranged controls and monitors, it was now a grotesque sculpture of destruction. Twisted metal jutted out at impossible angles, while a chaotic web of cables and composite materials lay strewn about.

Miraculously, Garrett found himself mostly unscathed amidst the devastation. He clutched his pistol with a grip born of desperation. The air was thick with smoke, clouding his vision and stinging his eyes, but it did little to dampen the urgency of the situation. The ship's alarms, usually sharp and commanding attention, now sounded muffled and distant through his ringing ears, as though echoing from the end of a long tunnel.

Peering cautiously around the remnants of his obliterated station, Garrett's eyes locked onto two ominous figures charging toward him. Clad in black armor that seemed to absorb the sparse light of the damaged bridge, they were unmistakably the enemy. Without hesitation, Garrett raised his pistol, its familiar weight a small comfort in his hand. He pulled the trigger. His shot found its mark, striking one of the assailants in the leg, sending him crashing to the ground.

The second figure, however, reacted with lightning-fast agility. Diving to the deck, he rolled and swiftly oriented his rifle toward Garrett, who ducked back under cover. A burst of gunfire erupted, a deadly rain of projectiles that hammered against the ruins of Garrett's station.

He recoiled instinctively, feeling the violent and heavy vibrations as the rounds pummeled the station's remnants, each impact a harbinger of potential death. Garrett's heart pounded in his chest, his breath quick and shallow. Hidden behind the scant protection, he braced for the next move in this deadly dance of survival.

The crack of pistol fire pierced the air from Garrett's right. Risking a quick glance around the remains of his station, he witnessed the aftermath of Tyabni's precise marksmanship. The enemy soldier now lay motionless on the ground. Garrett's gaze shifted just in time to see his weapons officer repositioning with a calculated calmness that belied the chaos around them. His aim settled on another enemy combatant who had just burst onto the bridge. Tyabni's pistol barked again, striking his mark in the leg.

As this opponent fell, he unleashed a retaliatory burst of gunfire. The rounds struck Tyabni with brutal force, the impact contorting his body in a grotesque dance before he collapsed, face-forward, onto the cold deck.

He did not get up. Nor did he stir.

Garrett, pulling himself back under the scant shelter of his decimated station, scanned the bridge. His eyes landed on Shaw, sprawled on his back with a hand clamped over his right shoulder. Thick, oily blood seeped through his fingers, painting a crimson stain on his ship suit that spread with alarming rapidity.

Shaw's eyes were wide with shock, filled with horror and disbelief. His gaze locked with Garrett's, a silent exchange that conveyed volumes. Garrett could see the glimmer of an unspoken plea in Shaw's eyes, which blinked rapidly, as if he were trying to dispel the nightmare he found himself in.

The relentless staccato of gunfire continued to resound. This new wave of firing, however, emanated from just outside the bridge, in the corridor. Garrett, summoning a cautious courage, on his stomach, edged around the twisted metal and shattered remains of his ruined station for a clearer view.

Peering into the corridor, he noticed the smoke that had once shrouded the area was now dissipating, revealing the full extent of the devastation. The hatch leading to the bridge, once a robust barrier, was now obliterated. It stood—or rather, failed to stand—as a grim reminder of the ferocity of the assault. Only the twisted remnants of its hinges clung stubbornly to the frame, speaking to the explosion's might that had blown it inward.

Beyond the ruins of the hatch, Garrett's attention was drawn to two enemy combatants. They were clad in the same ominous black armor as their fallen comrades, making them seem like spectral figures in the clearing haze. Positioned strategically behind alcoves along the corridor's sides, they seemed to have established a temporary stronghold. Remarkably, their focus was not on the bridge but directed farther back down the corridor, away from Garrett's position.

The enemies were engaged in a fierce exchange of fire with unseen adversaries deeper within the ship. Muzzle flashes lit up their hidden positions in the smoke, casting eerie shadows that danced along the damaged and pockmarked walls.

Garrett's legs trembled imperceptibly as he stood, a subtle but unmistakable sign of the adrenaline coursing through his

veins. His ears continued to ring, a persistent echo of the explosions and gunfire that had ravaged the bridge. Pushing past the
disorientation and the physical toll of the fight, he forced
himself to stand upright. His gaze fell upon the two wounded
enemies lying behind his station and before the entrance to the
bridge, their black armor scuffed and damaged.

Behind their faceplates, the features of his adversaries were
undeniably human. The realization did little to soften Garrett's
resolve. Spotting movement, he saw one of the enemy soldiers,
eyes locked on him with murderous intent, reaching slowly for
the pistol holstered at his hip. Without hesitation, Garrett raised
his weapon and fired a single decisive shot at the soldier's faceplate. The impact was immediate and lethal; the enemy's head
snapped back and to the side, a life extinguished in an instant.

The second enemy soldier, the one previously incapacitated
by a shot to the leg, was in a desperate struggle to reach his rifle,
which lay tantalizingly close. But before he could grasp it,
Cassidy appeared. She stood over the wounded soldier, her
pistol aimed unflinchingly down at him, authority emanating
from her despite the blood that trickled from a laceration on her
temple.

"Don't bloody move."

In response, the enemy soldier, recognizing the futility of
resistance, gave up the struggle, rolled onto his back, and raised
his hands in a gesture of capitulation.

"Don't shoot. I surrender."

Cassidy, momentarily taken aback, turned to Garrett. "He
speaks English, perfectly," she noted, her voice tinged with a
mix of surprise and wariness.

Garrett's focus was abruptly wrenched back to the corridor
as another burst of gunfire erupted, the sharp, rapid reports
slicing through the tense atmosphere. The two enemy boarders,
entrenched behind their makeshift cover in the alcoves, were
still fiercely engaged in combat. Though their adversaries

remained unseen from Garrett's vantage point, he surmised it was his marines engaging the enemy, a silent hope bolstering his resolve.

Acknowledging Cassidy's presence and her control over the surrendered soldier with a brief nod, Garrett issued a succinct command. "Keep him there."

He then moved with purpose toward the mangled remains of the bridge hatch, the sharp, metallic scent of recent destruction and burnt composites filling his nostrils. Positioning himself at the edge, he raised his pistol, his grip steady despite the fatigue and adrenaline coursing through him.

Peering down the corridor, he carefully aligned his sights on one of the enemy soldiers. His finger squeezed the trigger repeatedly, the pistol's recoil familiar in his hand. The rounds found their target, striking the soldier in the back. The enemy's body lurched forward under the impact, then slumped lifelessly to the deck.

The remaining enemy soldier, alerted by the gunfire from behind, spun around in a desperate attempt to locate the new threat. As he began to raise his rifle toward Garrett, a fusillade from down the corridor intervened. The rounds struck the soldier with lethal precision. He arched in pain, a cry escaping his lips before he collapsed in a heap, his rifle skittering away from nerveless fingers. A second burst of gunfire from the same direction ensured he would not get back up.

In the wake of the firefight, a profound silence descended upon the scene. Breathing heavily, Garrett slumped against the remnants of the hatch, his body bearing the weight of physical exhaustion, the mental toll of personal combat, and the realization he had survived.

"It's clear," Garrett's voice, strained but resolute, echoed down the corridor, cutting through the stillness. "The enemy are down."

"Who am I talking to?" The voice was familiar and tinged with wariness.

"Stroud?" Garrett called out, recognition dawning as he identified the voice. "Is that you, Colonel?"

"Captain," came the reply, a tone of respect evident even through the fatigue. Colonel Stroud, accompanied by several marines, emerged into Garrett's line of sight. They advanced cautiously down the corridor, their weapons trained on the fallen enemies, ready for any sign of a threat.

For the first time, Garrett's attention broadened to the full scope of the conflict in the corridor. Scattered across the floor lay more than a dozen enemy soldiers. The marines, disciplined and methodical, began checking the bodies, ensuring there were no survivors who might pose a risk. Two rushed past Garrett and up to the wounded man Cassidy was covering. They roughly turned him over and, producing zip ties, secured his hands behind his back.

"We have a prisoner, sir," one of the marines called back.

"Very good," Stroud replied.

Exhausted, Garrett stepped back, allowing Stroud and his team to fully move onto the bridge. The colonel's gaze swept over the scene, taking in the extent of the damage and destruction. His eyes then settled on Garrett, noting the pistol still held in his hand, the spent casings on the floor. A brief understanding glance passed between them before Stroud gestured toward the fallen enemies in the hallway.

"Your doing?" he asked, his voice a blend of inquiry and implicit approval.

"I wasn't about to let them take my ship," Garrett replied gruffly.

Sergeant Major Burns strode onto the bridge, his seasoned eyes quickly surveying the scene. "Corpsman!" Burns glanced around once more. "This is a shit show, a fucking shit show if I ever saw one. Corpsman! Get your ass up here on the double."

Almost immediately, the corpsman materialized, his medical kit clutched tightly in hand. "Sir?"

"See to the commander," Burns ordered, waving a hand at Shaw, his tone brooking no argument. The sergeant major then turned his attention to the nearest marines. "We're going to need a stretcher. You two, go find one and fetch it quick."

Two men rushed off as the corpsman hurried to Shaw's side and knelt beside the wounded man. Garrett, watching the scene unfold, felt an instinctual urge to assist. However, he quickly checked himself, recognizing that his presence there would not change Shaw's immediate outcome and would potentially interfere. His role as the captain demanded his attention elsewhere. Despite what had just occurred, there were decisions to be made, orders to give, a ship to manage.

Garrett's gaze swept across the bridge, noting the state of his crew. Cassidy stood out as an exception. She, Tyabni, and Shaw had actively engaged the enemy. The rest of the bridge crew, however, had taken shelter behind their stations, a majority seemingly frozen, their weapons undrawn and still holstered.

This observation lodged in Garrett's mind as a critical point for future action: the crew needed more training, specifically in small arms and reacting to threats. They might have had basic training, but the reality of combat had shown a glaring need for more intensive preparation.

"Back to your stations," Garrett snapped at them. "Helm, are we still moving toward the station?"

Foster's response, tinged with uncertainty, reflected the disarray that the surprise attack had inflicted on the bridge crew. "I—ah—don't know, sir," he admitted, rising tentatively from his cover.

"Check on it. Foster, Heller, get to your stations and confirm that," Garrett commanded. He noticed Heller, the other helm officer, still cowering behind the helm console, clearly paralyzed by fear or shock. Garrett hardened his tone. "Now, gentlemen, get a move on."

Heller's response was prompt, albeit tinged with a hint of trepidation and shame, his cheeks coloring. "Yes, sir," he acknowledged, standing up and moving to take his position at the helm station.

Foster, however, remained immobile, his attention fixated on his left arm. Garrett's eyes followed Foster's gaze, noting the bleeding wound on his bicep. Foster's actions were those of a man in shock, touching the wound with an almost childlike curiosity, as if he couldn't quite believe he had been injured. His voice, carrying disbelief and mounting panic, broke the tense silence. "I've been shot. Holy shit—I've been shot. They shot me!"

Garrett turned away and continued to focus on the task at hand, his concern for his crew balanced with the necessity of maintaining operational command. He addressed Heller as he moved toward the weapons station, stepping past Tyabni's lifeless body. "Heller? What's the ship doing?"

Heller, now seated at his station, responded with a growing level of composure that contrasted with the earlier trepidation and shock. "She's still moving for the station, sir. I have control," he reported, his voice steadier now that he was clearly back in his element. "I will stop us at fifty thousand kilometers, as previously directed."

"Very good," Garrett acknowledged with a brief nod, his voice measured. His gaze swept momentarily over Tyabni's lifeless form. Garrett felt a stab of sadness strike him. The man had been exceptionally good at his job and had died defending the ship. Without allowing himself to dwell on it further, he redirected his focus to the HTD at the tactical station, seeking a broader understanding of the battle's status.

The point defense guns were now silent, their purpose fulfilled. The display showed no enemy attack craft remaining in the immediate vicinity, a small victory in the grand scheme of the conflict. Only friendly squadrons of fighters and boats were in space around his ship, several dozen.

Garrett manipulated the controls on the HTD, zooming out to assess the broader situation. The tactical display revealed that no enemy ships were within two million klicks of their position. For the moment, at least, the immediate threat had subsided. The battle, however, continued to rage on the other side of the station. Yet, from what the HTD indicated, the Confederation forces had now gained a decisive advantage and were in the process of overpowering the last remaining enemy ships.

The ship's alarms continued their persistent blare, a lingering echo of the attack on the bridge. Keying in a command single-handed, Garrett silenced the alarms, bringing a momentary peace to the bridge. The cessation of the alarms felt like a deep exhale, a brief respite in the aftermath of the chaos that had engulfed them.

Holstering his pistol, Garrett took a moment to observe his crew. Despite the devastation that had swept across the bridge, his people were returning to their stations and getting back to work. Among them, a marine was attending to Foster, skillfully wrapping a bandage around his wounded arm.

The marine's words conveyed reassurance and professionalism: "We will get you right to medical, sir. It's a minor wound and they will fix you right up."

Stroud's approach drew Garrett's attention away from Foster and the marine attending to him. The colonel, flanked by Burns, regarded Garrett with an expression that was both inscrutable and intense. Their gazes, unflinching and serious, conveyed a depth of experience and understanding unique to those who had faced the crucible of battle.

"I was right about you," Stroud said.

"Right about what?" Garrett's voice betrayed a hint of weariness. The lingering effects of the battle, the incessant ringing in his ears, and the pervasive ache in his body were a continual reminder of the recent ordeal.

"You could've been a marine," Stroud stated plainly.

Garrett responded with a slow, contemplative nod, his mind briefly traversing back to the past, the incident off Antares Station. "I could have been," he admitted, accepting the label, not with pride, but as a fact shaped by necessity and survival.

Garrett met Burns's gaze, a mutual recognition and respect passing between them, before turning his attention back to Stroud. His focus shifted to the immediate needs of his ship.

"Colonel, I want this ship swept for the enemy. Root them out."

"We're already on it and working that problem, sir," Stroud said. "We have got all the boarders contained and should have them eliminated shortly."

"Not to worry, sir, we're gonna kill 'em all," Burns said.

Acknowledging this with a nod, Garrett allowed himself a brief pause, a fleeting moment to absorb the gravity of what had transpired. Yet, even in this respite, his mind was already turning to the next steps, the multitude of tasks and decisions that awaited him. There was no time to dwell on the past, loss, or the pain; the relentless march of duty called, and as the captain, he was not only required, but ready to answer.

Garrett's gaze scanned the bridge, quickly locating Keeli, who had managed to return to her station. "Keeli?"

"Captain?" Keeli responded, her voice steady but her face betraying the strain of recent events, an unnatural paleness having washed over her features.

"Put in a priority one call to Admiral Yenga," Garrett instructed. "I need to speak to him immediately. I will take it in my office."

"Aye, sir," Keeli replied, her fingers already moving deftly over her console to establish the high-priority connection.

Garrett's attention was momentarily diverted as he noticed

Shaw being carried from the bridge on a stretcher. The extent of his injuries was unclear, adding a silent weight to his already burdened thoughts. He hoped his friend would pull through.

"We will take care of him, sir," Burns assured him, his voice bearing the confidence and dependability that came with years of service. "He will be in medical and under the care of a doctor shortly."

Garrett gave a thankful nod. A stretcher had also been brought for the wounded prisoner. The corpsman was attending to him as well, while two armed marines watched, their weapons held ready. Eyeing the man in black armor, Garrett felt his heart harden.

"Admiral Yenga on the line, sir, in your office, as requested."

Nodding to Keeli, Garrett turned. "Lieutenant Heller, you have the bridge," he said, formally handing over command in his absence.

"I have the bridge, sir," Heller confirmed, his voice much steadier now.

Before departing, Garrett addressed one final concern to Stroud. "Can you get this mess cleaned up?" His gaze swept over the aftermath on the bridge. "Remove the bodies?"

"I will see it done, sir," Stroud responded.

With these orders given, Garrett made his way to his office, each step taking him away from the immediate aftermath of battle and toward the next phase of command. His mind was already shifting gears, preparing for the conversation with Yenga and the strategic decisions that lay ahead.

The hatch slid shut behind him with a definitive hiss. In the seclusion of his office, the sounds of activity were muted, allowing him a measure of solitude.

Admiral Yenga's image on the wall screen immediately captured his attention. Garrett exhaled deeply, letting some of the stress out, then stepped into view of the camera. Yenga's reaction was one of undisguised surprise and concern.

"You look like shit," the admiral remarked bluntly, his eyes narrowing as he took in Garrett's appearance. "Jim, you're bleeding."

Feeling a warm, wet sensation on his neck for the first time, he touched the area, his fingers coming away stained with blood. Probing gently, he found a minor laceration under his chin, stinging slightly upon touch. His inspection also revealed a gash on his forearm, bleeding, but seemingly not severe enough to demand immediate attention.

"We were boarded by the enemy, sir. They made it to the bridge," Garrett reported, his voice steady despite the physical reminders of the battle and the adrenaline still coursing through his veins. "They tried and failed to take my ship."

"I see," Admiral Yenga responded grimly, his expression shifting to one of understanding and acknowledgment of the gravity of the situation.

"The ship is secure," Garrett added, ensuring the admiral was aware that, despite the breach and the ensuing chaos, the situation was now under control. "Did you know the enemy are human?"

"I just found that out," Yenga said, looking disturbed. "It was news to me. We think some are human and the rest are alien—turncoats."

Garrett gave a tired nod.

"That was some show you put on." Yenga's words carried admiration and acknowledgment. "You proved you were the right person for the job, the one Fleet should have chosen from the beginning. Heck—Jim, you proved that all those years ago off Antares Station. Killing Marlowe was the correct call. If it hadn't been for Omaga, you would have had your own command by now."

"I know," Garrett said softly, then cleared his throat. He took a brief moment to glance down at his hands, collecting his thoughts and pushing the past away, shifting his thinking to the immediate future. He was acutely aware of the strategic implications of their situation. "There's no making the Nikura jump point, not now."

"No, there isn't," Yenga agreed, his expression turning grave. "You and anyone left at Midway are on their own."

"We have the gripper dive."

Yenga's nod was contemplative, yet he remained silent. Unlike their previous conversation a few hours before, the background behind the admiral was calm. There was no one demanding his attention, no shouting. Most of the orders that needed to be given likely already had. It was also clear he was still aboard a ship.

"I intend on using the drive to escape." Garrett's tone shifted, a surge of anger lacing his words. This was more than a tactical decision; it was a personal mission now. The fury within him, a response to the onslaught they had endured, sought an outlet. "I will not scuttle my ship. I want to take the fight to the enemy. There are warships here at Midway Station that are now cut off. Let me bring this ship to her full potential, operate her how she was meant to be used. Assign those ships to *Surprise*. We can form a scratch task force with which to strike back. We can take the fight to the enemy, hit them where they don't expect, make them feel the pain for a change."

Yenga took a contemplative intake of breath and gave a slow nod, indicating that he was seriously considering Garrett's proposal.

Garrett seized the moment to emphasize his point. "As you have noted, Admiral, this ship is a capable weapons platform. It is time to use her."

"Jim, let me give you a picture of what Fleet is currently doing here in the Midway Star System. Even though she is falling back toward the station, Admiral Isabel is in a bad position. She will soon be engaged with the enemy. I do not expect her to survive. She doesn't either and has ceded command of the system and charged me with overseeing the evacuation. I am currently on a stealthed frigate. We are falling back on the Nikura jump point with the intention to leave the system when the remains of the fleet are fully assembled—those units that are not cut off. Once we're through, we will mine the other side and prepare to resist the enemy's advance when they decide to come. At least we will be better prepared, but I do not expect we will stop them there."

Garrett absorbed this update. "All right, I had guessed much of that already. What about my ship?"

"You think you can pull this off?" Yenga asked plainly. "You believe your ship, which is still unfinished, can do the job for which she was intended?"

"I do."

Yenga looked at him for a long moment. He gave a slow nod. "Then I will assign you your task force from among those ships stuck at Midway. Orders will be coming shortly."

Garrett's heart rate accelerated, beginning to pound away in his chest.

"And what about an admiral to oversee this task force?" Garrett inquired, probing the chain of command.

"I don't have anyone suitable that I can get to you on short notice."

"What about on the station? Surely someone can be found there?"

"Anyone with senior rank left on Midway is a station-bound officer and is not suitable for command, not for what you will be doing. Besides, there are thousands of enemy soldiers overrunning the station. No, my friend, you are the most capable officer on hand for this mission. Effective immediately, you and your ship are detached to the Special Missions Group. You are now under the direct command of Admiral Gray. Additionally, I am field promoting you to commodore."

"Commodore? Special Missions Group?" Garrett echoed, surprise and disbelief in his voice.

"Commodore," Yenga affirmed firmly. "You are answerable to no one else but Admiral Gray, is that understood?"

"Yes, sir."

"Now"—Yenga let go a heavy breath—"I have a lot to do to make this happen, to get your task force organized, and not a lot of time to do it. By my estimate, you have six to seven hours before additional enemy fleet units reach Midway Station and potential engagement range. You will need to be away before then."

"What about the evacuees we have taken on?"

"I am afraid you are stuck with them for the time being," Yenga said. "There's nowhere for them to go, other than with you, and it not be a death sentence. Try to put those you can to good use."

"Yes, sir."

"Stand by for official orders." Yenga suddenly seemed amused. "Oh, and congratulations, Jim, on your second promotion of the day."

With those final instructions, along with an amused smirk, the screen went blank as Yenga ended the transmission, leaving Garrett alone with his thoughts.

He stared at the wall, absorbing the weight of his new title and the daunting task ahead. Slowly, he moved to his chair and sank into it, the events of the day, from the intimate start with Tina to the harrowing battle and now his unexpected promotion, all swirling in his mind.

"Commodore Garrett attached to the Special Missions Group," he reflected aloud. The day had unfolded in ways he couldn't have imagined. Garrett understood he was on the precipice of a new chapter, one that would shape not only his destiny, but also potentially the course of the conflict and his people's future.

EPILOGUE

GARRETT

"The *Achilles*, *Palestro*, and *Valkyrie* have successfully docked and mated, sir," Keegan announced. "All three ships are secure."

Garrett, seated at Shaw's station, shifted his gaze from the array of monitors displaying various ship metrics. At least two of his friends were safe and going with them. There was a measure of comfort in that for him. He did not know what had happened to the rest of his friends. There had been no time to check on them.

It had been six and a half hours since the fight on the bridge. The bridge, which had once been a scene of chaos, death, and destruction, had been hastily tidied. The dead and injured had been removed. However, traces of the conflict lingered. Blood-stains on the deck and the physical damage bore silent witness to the violence that had transpired.

Surprise had moved away from Midway Station at twenty gravities and then come to a complete stop, angling her bow to the preprogrammed course.

"Twelve ships, sir, with *Achilles* being the last," Keegan continued, his tone steady and professional, though with an underlying weariness. "All are securely mated to the hull."

Garrett acknowledged the update with a silent nod, his eyes lingering on the tactical display that illustrated the composition of their newly formed task force. The Mothership, a colossal and sophisticated command vessel, now carried a formidable array of warships: four fast battlecruisers, bristling with heavy armaments and reinforced armor, not to mention powerful shields; six destroyers, agile and lethal; and two frigates, versatile support vessels capable of a variety of roles in combat.

In addition to this impressive lineup, several squadrons of fighters from Midway Station had been tasked and integrated into their force structure. These swift and deadly craft, remnants of a larger contingent that had managed to escape the chaos, had been arriving for the last few hours. The last were currently touching down in the landing bays.

Among them were the surviving members of the Nighthawks and the Cobras, two squadrons that had been assigned to the ship shortly after her commissioning. They had been in transit across the system when they'd been reassigned and had arrived at a pivotal moment. Their skill and bravery had been instrumental in repelling the enemy's assault boats, but at great cost. Between the two squadrons, only six craft remained.

The rescue boats had also returned, picking up the crew and marines that had been left on the *Celestial Fire*, including any escape pods they could locate that had been in the vicinity.

As Garrett reflected on the day's events, a somber realization washed over him. The loss of life was staggering, and the day's toll was heavy on his mind. The thought of how many had fallen—and how many more would fall in the hours, days, months, and years to come—weighed heavily on him. The conflict they were engaged in was far-reaching and complex, with no immediate end in sight.

The reality was stark and unyielding: the killing was far from over. In fact, it had just begun. This war, like many before it, demanded sacrifices, and as the commander of this newly formed task force, Garrett understood that the path ahead would be fraught with challenges and further loss. Yet there was a determination in his gaze, a resolve in his heart to navigate the perils that stood in their path.

Garrett's focus shifted back to the HTD, where the realities of the battlefield were laid bare in glowing lines and icons. The display showed the enemy's spread across the system, their forces like a dark cloud encroaching on the scattered lights of the Confederation Fleet assets.

Admiral Isabel's plight was vividly depicted. Her fleet, engaged in a relentless, retreating battle, was clearly in dire straits. Despite her efforts to fall back toward the station for reinforcements, her situation appeared increasingly hopeless as she slugged it out with a numerically superior force that had overtaken her when she'd changed course. She was making the enemy pay dearly, but Garrett, analyzing the strategic overview, could not envision a scenario where she could successfully break through.

The strategic situation was grim. The enemy had managed to seize control of ten of the system's jump beacons. In a preemptive move to deny the enemy further advantages, Confederation forces had destroyed other beacons near the Nikura jump point.

A formidable enemy force had established itself between the station and this critical escape route, growing in strength and power with each passing hour as more and more enemy warships jumped to those captured beacons. Meanwhile, at Midway Station, more than three dozen Confederation warships, along with hundreds of civilian ships, were trapped. These vessels, now hastily assembled into a scratch task force, were preparing for a desperate attempt to break through the enemy lines and win free to Nikura. Garrett did not think they had a chance. But still, they were going to try.

The rest of the Confederation fleet, a group of over one hundred warships of all types, was retreating and falling back upon the Nikura jump point. Their objective was clear: to regroup and pass through, transitioning to the safety of the next system.

For Garrett and his crew, the bitter truth was evident. The battle for the Midway Star System was lost. The Confederation's loss was not just a tactical setback, but also a significant blow. Losing Midway was a strategic defeat, and a major one at that.

As Garrett watched the HTD, with the bulk of the fleet executing a withdrawal, his thoughts turned to the next phase of this interstellar chess game. He knew that the enemy's eventual advance into the Nikura System would encounter formidable resistance. The fleet, though retreating now, would regroup and prepare for the inevitable confrontation. It would be a fierce, bloody affair, and Yenga would ensure the Confederation's defenses were as lethal as they were unyielding. The enemy would have a tough go of it.

His attention then shifted to Midway Station, a key strategic asset now partially under enemy control. The HTD showed the station as a contested hotspot, a microcosm of the larger conflict. There, intense, brutal fighting was unfolding, a grim battle of attrition as the enemy forces advanced deck by deck, station component by station component.

The station's commander, an admiral, likely had his own set of orders. Garrett surmised that Midway Station would not fall into enemy hands.

Amidst these unfolding events, he was acutely aware of his own role in the grander scheme. His orders were clear: to strike back at the enemy, to take the fight to them, to be the first hammer to fall. Garrett was prepared to lead his task force in delivering a decisive blow for the Confederation.

Yet, before he could embark on this aggressive campaign,

there was another mission to attend to first, something critical and urgent. These orders, still sealed, held the key to his next move. This undisclosed objective added an element of mystery and urgency to the situation.

"Sir," Keeli said, "Admiral Yenga on the line for you."

"Put him through."

The admiral's face appeared on the screen. The admiral was still in transit to the Nikura jump point.

"Commodore," Yenga said by way of greeting. "I called to wish you good fortune."

"From captain to commodore in one day," Garrett commented, thinking on the irony of things. Just the day before he was a Job captain, a veritable untouchable among the hierarchy of Fleet Command, someone deemed unworthy.

"You have your ship and command. There is no one Gray or I trust more than you to do the job that's been assigned. As I said earlier, your actions over the last few hours have proven that out. Do you have any questions?"

"Once we're away, I am sure I will," Garrett admitted. "But by then it will be too late to ask, won't it?"

"I have no doubt, and yes it will," Yenga said. "Visiting Indigo—I mean 66-Lima—is important. You will find out soon enough when you open your orders."

"Yes, sir," Garrett said. He still had no idea where they were going, only that the destination had been preprogrammed into the navigation system and locked out. 66-Lima was simply a code name. Yenga's brief slip, the mention of "Indigo," lingered in Garrett's mind, suggesting a deeper significance or perhaps a covert aspect to their mission that was yet to be revealed. Or was it the system's true code name? He supposed he would find out soon enough.

"After you get to 66-Lima, your secondary orders kick in. Execute them at your discretion. Is that understood?"

"Yes, sir." Garrett still had no idea what those were either, other than to strike at the enemy.

"Under no circumstances are you to relinquish command of this mission or the ship to which you have been assigned to anyone, unless you receive a direct order, in writing, from the CNO or Admiral Gray. Is that understood?"

"It is crystal clear." Though Garrett could not see how that would happen. There was no one senior to him aboard any of the ships they were taking with them, at least that he knew of. Before pushing back from the station, they had taken on a lot of evacuees. That was one more headache to consider, for there were civilians among them.

"Oh," Yenga said, "I forgot to tell you, a shuttle was sent to your ship a few hours ago. On board are a team of special operators. Utilize them as needed. They are the best the Confederation has on hand. A Lieutenant Commander Senica was aboard as well. I have assigned her as your intelligence officer. She will brief you when you are ready. Lean on her, for she is quite capable."

Garrett gave a nod.

"With that, I will say goodbye."

"Good fortune, Admiral."

Yenga nodded and then the transmission terminated. Garrett sat there for a moment thinking. He looked up and, with his implants, opened a channel.

"CAG, bring the last of our birds aboard," Garrett said. "We are leaving Midway."

"Aye, sir. They will be aboard within the next two minutes."

Garrett cut the transmission. "Helm, are we aligned properly?"

"Yes, sir," Heller replied. "Though I have no idea where we are going."

"That is the general idea," Garrett said. "Is the gripper drive ready to be engaged?"

"Gripper drive is active," Heller reported. "Ready to go and make our first transit, one of three that are programmed into navigation."

Garrett pulled up a display of the diagnostics and readings on not only the reactors, but also the gripper drive. He spent a few moments looking them over. He was sure Tam was doing the same.

"McKay, do you concur that everything looks good?" Garrett asked.

"I do, sir. Commander Tam agrees as well. We are good to go."

"Sir," Keeli said. "CAG reports all birds aboard and secured."

"Keeli, set condition yellow for transit," Garrett ordered.

"Condition yellow," Keeli reported.

An alert was sounding throughout the ship.

Garrett felt regret that Shaw was not here to witness this moment. He deserved it but was currently in surgery, his second in the last five hours. Though his wound was serious and his condition listed as grave, the chief surgeon had assured Garrett that Shaw should make a full recovery.

"Lieutenant Heller," Garrett said, feeling a stab of real excitement, for they were going into the unknown. "Activate the gripper drive and prepare for wormhole transit."

"Aye, aye, sir. Gripper drive engaged. Wormhole forming."

As Garrett watched from his station, the drive ignited with a surge of power, spooling with intensity, a brilliant display of engineering prowess and controlled energy. The lights on the bridge flickered and alarms sounded.

The space before the ship, a vast canvas of stars and dark-ness, began to warp and distort, the very fabric of the cosmos bending under the influence of the drive's advanced technology. In front of the ship's bow, the event horizon of a wormhole materialized, a swirling vortex of light and energy that ripped a hole in the very reality of their space-time layer.

This spectacle was awe-inspiring and unnerving in equal measure. Wormhole travel, the stuff of theoretical physics and speculative fiction, was now a reality before Garrett's eyes. The formation of this wormhole, a gateway bridging vast distances in the cosmos, marked a pivotal moment in space travel, not to mention warfare. Until now, such feats had been confined to experimental trials, conducted on much smaller test ships over extremely short distances. The ship's gripper drive was far more powerful. Never before had something as large as *Surprise* attempted this daring leap through space-time.

Garrett, witnessing this historic moment, felt a rush of apprehension. The enormity of what they were about to undertake was not lost on him. He inhaled deeply, a reflexive response to the tension that gripped him and everyone else on the bridge. The breath he drew was sharp, filled with the cold, recycled air of the ship. He let it out slowly, attempting to steady his nerves.

Yet, amidst the apprehension, there was a sense of exhilaration, excitement. This was uncharted territory, a bold stride into the unknown. The crew of *Surprise*, under Garrett's command, were about to embark on a journey that would test the limits of their ship, their technology, and their own fortitude.

As the wormhole stabilized, creating a tunnel through the very fabric of space-time, *Surprise* was poised at the brink of this cosmic maw. The ship was ready to plunge into the wormhole, to traverse distances unfathomable by conventional means. Garrett was about to lead his ship and crew into the annals of history, through a path that twisted the very laws of physics into the vast, mysterious realm that lay beyond.

"Mister Heller, take us through."

A LETTER FROM MARC

Dear reader,

Writing *Off Midway Station* has been a labor of love and a joy. It is my sincere hope that you love it as I do.

If you did enjoy it, and want to keep up to date with all my latest releases, just sign up at the following link. Your email address will never be shared and you can unsubscribe at any time.

www.secondskybooks.com/marc-alan-edelheit

I also want to take a moment to thank you for reading and keeping me employed as a full-time writer. For those of you who reach out to me, I simply cannot express how humbling it is, as an author, to have my work so appreciated and loved.

From the bottom of my heart...*thank you!*

Reviews keep me motivated and help to drive sales. I make a point to read each and every one, so please continue to post them. You can reach out and connect with me on social media and my website.

Again, I hope you enjoy this book and would like to offer a sincere thank you for your purchase and support.

Best regards,

Marc Alan Edelheit

KEEP IN TOUCH WITH MARC

www.maenovels.com

facebook.com/MAENovels

x.com/MarcEdelheit

instagram.com/marcedelheitauthor

youtube.com/@marcalanedelheit9572

patreon.com/marcalanedelheit

ACKNOWLEDGMENTS

I wish to thank my agent, Andrea Hurst, for her invaluable support and assistance. I would also like to thank my beta readers, who suffered through several early drafts. My betas: Steve Koratsky, Marshall Clowers, Paul Klebaur, William Schnippert, David Cheever, Sheldon Levy, Walker Graham, Jimmy McAfee, Joel Rainey, James H. Bjorum, James Doak, Nathan Hildebrand, Tom Moore, Michael Brown, Dragos Emil Ramniceanu, Kieran Maisonet, Lance Dahl, Lee Adrian, Brian Thomas, Ed Speight, Dominick Maino. I would also like to take a moment to thank my loving wife, who sacrificed many an evening and weekend to allow me to work on my writing.

Editing Assistance by Hannah Streetman, Brandon Purcell, Audrey Mackaman, and Jack Renninson

Cover Art by Tom Edwards

Agented by Andrea Hurst & Associates

PUBLISHING TEAM

Turning a manuscript into a book requires the efforts of many people. The publishing team at Bookouture would like to acknowledge everyone who contributed to this publication.

Commercial
Lauren Morrissette
Hannah Richmond
Imogen Allport

Cover design
Tom Edwards Design

Data and analysis
Mark Alder
Mohamed Bussuri

Editorial
Jack Renninson
Melissa Tran

Proofreader
Angela Snowden

Made in the USA
Coppell, TX
02 October 2024

38013164R00246